This writer uses his vast life experiences to enhance his fiction.
In her book, *My Father The Prince of Montenegro*, Princess Milena Petrovic-Nejroŝ said:
'Joe O' Flaherty is one of the world's rare people if only in life we could meet them all!'

He lives a reclusive life in Ireland writing, and gardening with his wife of fifty years.

The Sand Hog

Joe O'Flaherty

The Sand Hog

Vanguard Press

VANGUARD PAPERBACK

© Copyright 2018
Joe O'Flaherty

The right of Joe O'Flaherty to be identified as author of
this work has been asserted by him in accordance with the
Copyright, Designs and Patents Act 1988.

A CIP catalogue record for this title is
available from the British Library.

ISBN 978 1 784652 94 4

Vanguard Press is an imprint of
Pegasus Elliot MacKenzie Publishers Ltd.

www.pegasuspublishers.com

First Published in 2018

Vanguard Press
Sheraton House Castle Park
Cambridge England

Printed & Bound in Great Britain

To my wife

Chapter One

Their situation was pretty desperate.

They sold everything before leaving Ireland to pay hospital expenses in Philadelphia. Now, they were almost broke. Attempting to rebuild their lives again they needed money. So, that meant looking for work in New York.

Arriving by train to Penn Station they took the exit to W. 34th St. It landed them in the middle of Manhattan. This whole trip was an intense experience, they had never been city people. It would take good fortune to make things right. Rita always said their luck would change one day. Joe was convinced that time had come. This firm resolve brought them to America.

The month of February before Valentine's Day was bleak. Wind whistling through the tall buildings sent a chill to the marrow of the bone. They headed up Eight Avenue, a slow passage. Sometimes standing to stare in wonder, as the city's captivating energy unfolded before them. Rita pushed the baby buggy; her long strides wove a path through the busy sidewalk.

While he moved doggedly, struggling to keep up with her. With mixed emotions about the Philadelphia visit, the memory of it still bothered him. The doctor told them the sad news. Prospects were bad for their only child. She was profoundly handicapped, that's the way she would always be. There would be no miracle cure. Any hope they harboured disappeared.

So, they left Philadelphia without the comfort of optimism that sustained them on their arrival. They hadn't the heart to discuss what the next move for their little girl might be.

This problem would remain in their heads for them to ponder. He took another rest break to enquire directions from a passing stranger. The chirpy little man with a leather hat pointed a gloved hand in a westerly direction. "This is Hell's Kitchen, get right over there, guys."

The best bet to find cheap accommodation was in 10th Avenue, he assured them.

Rita shivered. "It's the coldest Hell's Kitchen I've ever been in."

Joe had to get his family off the street for the night. That was a time consuming ordeal in itself. The big hotels flashed their brilliant presence all around them. But they would have to seek out more modest accommodation. They had been forewarned about the bitter cold weather New York held in store for them. So, they were suitably attired in long heavy winter coats over jeans. Rita's mother hand knitted wool sweaters especially for the trip.

Back home in Ireland, before they were married, when they snuggled together in the local cinema, the name Times Square, Broadway, seemed familiar. Bright city lights of New York brought back memories. It seemed, even then, a world imagined in their fantasies. Now they were here.

He turned towards her; the worry was still there in her eyes. She could feel him searching for it.

"We must keep going, Joe, Mary is getting cold."

The anxiety she felt about the whole arrangement just wouldn't go away. He convinced her in Philadelphia, there was nothing left for them in Ireland without sufficient funds to start up a small horse breeding enterprise. She agreed to try New York for a while, but that was subject to several conditions. He looked down at the child remembering wrecked dreams. The lump was there in his throat again when sadness came over him. Would it ever go away?

The sky darkened. Yellow street lights glowed through a thick freezing fog. Manhattan was turning over the night time mood. Sidewalks crammed with anxious people rushing for subway trains raised his sense of urgency. "We'll find a place soon, Rita, don't worry."

She gave him an encouraging smile moving on. He picked up the big suitcases again to follow her. Years playing football kept him fit. Before leaving Ireland Rita cut her hair so it would be easier to manage on their travels. The thick soled leather boots made her as tall as her husband. With a soft complexion, high cheek bones gave her eyes almond shapes. She rubbed cream from a small tin box into her lips periodically, without once missing her stride.

The money that remained after the Philadelphia trip wouldn't stretch far. New York wasn't budgeted for in the beginning. Joe felt under pressure to deliver on all the promises he made by finding a place to stay, then a job as soon as possible. So he wouldn't feel guilty dragging them to this city, he convinced himself it was the right thing to do. If only some of the stories could be believed. The American dream was just around the corner, waiting for them.

The small neon 'Hotel' sign appeared over the sidewalk, flickering like a Christmas light. He pointed it out to her excitedly. "Look over there, Rita, our own little place. Like a shining star inviting us to shelter."

He laughed. There was some relief too when she became joyful for want of comfort.

The old brown stone hotel was sandwiched; it appeared quaint, between tall office blocks. With eight bay windows overlooking the street, a hint of old world charm, weathered with time. It might have been a private dwelling in some previous life. A black cast iron fire escape on the front of it caught their eyes. Its broad steps once forged caringly in delicate floral design were splattered white with pigeon droppings. It was a first impression that didn't register well with Rita. But the door was wide open, so in they went.

A middle aged man wearing a baseball cap sat behind a glass hatch. He was absent minded picking at his long nose. Before they

11

had time to say anything he shouted at them. "Do you want a room for a long or short stay?"

"How much for one night, please." Joe asked.

"Thirty bucks." He spat it out with cold indifference, going back to the nose thing again, ignoring them. He didn't seem to care, staring at ice hockey on the television. Rita felt itchy looking down at the old tiled floor. Not having seen a mop for so long.

"The room might be nice though," Joe whispered.

She flashed the whites of her eyes towards the office. "I don't like it, it's dirty."

"But it's dark outside Rita, just for one night. We can find a better place tomorrow. Look how long it took us to get here. We haven't much choice or money either," he pleaded softly.

The man in the office sensed their dilemma, springing to his feet shaking his head from side to side. He screeched at them through the hatch. "What's the story eh, you guys, God damn foreigners for Christ's sakes. It's not the Waldorf Astoria you want is it."

Too intimidated to protest they paid up in advance. Then he informed them they had to share a bathroom on the first floor. Joe felt a relaxed soak in the tub would not be a priority. The janitor ushered them towards a room on the ground floor, right down the narrow hallway from his office. He gestured with his hand the benefit of the location. "Good for a baby buggy, look, no steps." Opening a door he attempted the tour guide routine. "See, a view of the street from the bay window there. It doesn't open anymore it's security."

"Where's the toilet?" Rita asked coldly.

He indicated through the wall. "Out there, in the hall."

Joe didn't have to wonder what she was thinking about, her jaw firmly set, standing there taking it all in. The pale blue room had stained net curtains on the window. A threadbare velvet drape hung loosely outside them. A dishevelled bed, an old wooden table covered in cigarette burns was all the furniture in the place. She switched the light on to avoid his attempt at soliciting a tip.

He acted as if he didn't expect one shrugging his shoulders, pulling the door after him, still muttering. "God damn foreigners."

Rita shivered. "What a horrible man." She folded her arms across her chest. "Oh my God, this must be what a prison cell feels like." She stared at the bed a look of disgust on her face. "There's no way I'm getting into that dirty thing, never, I'd rather die first."

Joe stood at the bay window staring in front of him. It was going to be a long night out there wandering the dimly lit streets of Hell's Kitchen. He was dreading the thoughts of it. But she had other ideas; it was time to get started.

"Help me get this place sorted before I go mad looking at it, will you Joe?"

She had to organize the sleeping arrangements in the bird shit hotel. That's what she called it. The doorman reminded her of a vulture. Accepting the predicament, she could handle it.

Striking busy mode, discussion was abandoned so she gave directions. The aviary had to have a new nest, she declared. Pleased at having his worst case scenario resolved, he opened the bags while she started to unpack, spreading the bath towels on the floor. Then she placed the child on top. "Stretching her legs will do a world of good," she said, in a calm matter of fact way.

The pain of Mary's handicap she endured with dignity, hiding her sorrow was the difficult part of it. She wouldn't want to burden anyone with that. But they talked things through.

The disappointment so great, there would be no more children. Joe could see she was exhausted, that gave him a bad feeling. In the past he sometimes escaped into oblivion, alcohol induced good times that left him gripped in insecure bad times. He watched her lift the little girl turning her over, pulling her legs out straight, she counted ten. The hospital programmed a daily exercise routine. He struggled to be part of it. Professors gave lectures on the fine functions of the human brain. But his interpretation had potential to disappoint. That brain cells rejuvenated by repetitive exercise routine was not an exact science. Success rested on the hopeful efforts of vulnerable parents.

The severity of Mary's condition was hidden from them, caringly smoothed over in the beginning. As she grew older, the problem became more apparent. But they latched on to some hope. It was all finally shattered on a cold windy day in Philadelphia. At least now, they felt everything possible had been done for her. That had to make the journey a worthwhile undertaking.

Rita's mattress creation used items soft in texture to make a big bed. She instructed him to try it out. He lay down to stretch his legs the full length of it. "It beats walking around in the cold all night long." He was sure about that.

She got Mary's feed ready taking the lid off the Tupperware dish. Spoon feeding mashed bananas with yoghurt was a slow process. The child was inclined to hold food in her mouth; it frequently caused her to choke. She spat out more than she swallowed. Rita kept her husband well away from the feeding task, saying men were too rough for such delicate matters. He was relieved. The difficulty of trying to cope with his daughter's handicap increased the burden on his wife's shoulders. She offered the food many times. In this way she got the only positive interaction from her daughter. She needed to feel something.

Rita called out a list for him to write down: "Toilet paper, rubber gloves, bucket, disinfectant, pick up some kind of take away food except chicken, a few bananas, two bottles of drinking water, you can find some yoghurt for Mary, pizza for me. Don't wander far to get it. I can't afford to lose you now."

While he was pulling on his coat she had a new concern. "You won't be going into a bar will you, couldn't handle the drink on top of all this."

"Of course not, what would I be doing that for, Rita; don't open the door to anyone."

"Don't worry about me, Joe, be careful. I love you."

"I love you too, I'll be okay."

It was well known that the best place to get help in New York was an Irish bar. Having spotted one earlier he remembered exactly where it was. He quickened his step going up the street.

The neon Irish Shamrock sign hung loosely in the front window. It was a small building on a corner. The name Celtic Bar was painted in bold green letters over the front. That made him nostalgic for his own country. He stepped into the familiar smell of beer. A mug full would go down well, it might ease his anxiety. Inside the window a tough looking bunch of men stood drinking at the bar. They were light-heartedly harassing the barmaid. She gave back as good as she got, much to their amusement.

He took a barstool at the exit flap near the end, an elderly couple sat in a booth beside the juke box. Drinking beer, listening to country music, they didn't seem to notice him.

"Where can I find a hardware shop?" Joe enquired from the barmaid.

"I haven't heard shop used around here since I was a kid. You're from outa town, just arrived in the ole US of A, eh, young fella, that it?"

He noticed her eyebrows arch, just like his grandmother's when he told lies as a kid. "I just got in from Philadelphia." He looked down the bar to see if anyone picked up on his mission.

"Don't worry about sand hog guy's, honey, they're full a shit, hear nothing, see nothing. I'm Rosie O Connor." She offered her hand out to him with a kind smile.

"My name's Joe Flanagan."

"You need a hardware store at nine p.m. at night, son, tell me about it."

She found that notion humorous apparently, the smile still on her lips. The new arrival comment put him on high alert, being labelled illegal, dumped out of the country was a concern. He hurried off to the toilet to gather his wits about him. The coffee irritated his kidneys, something beer never did.

A blast of cold air from the basement hit him at the black doors. One of them was locked; the other had Hogs written on it.

Ladies must have to share, so he snapped the bolt closed. Just in case.

When the barmaid's shift finished she had a gin up at the counter beside him. "You live in the neighbourhood?" she asked.

"Yes for a while."

"Where are you staying at?"

"There is a hotel near here."

"I see, what age are you?"

"I'm twenty-five."

"My son Bobby would be your age, if he was still alive." Joe waited to hear more about that. But she was more interested in him. "Where exactly is your hotel?"

"About ten minutes' walk, I'm not good with directions, we just arrived."

"We?"

"My wife, I have a daughter as well."

"What age is your daughter?"

"She's two."

"Ahaa isn't that nice."

She was studying him, he told his story she was a good listener. Maternal instincts switched to high alert hearing it. She enquired if his wife needed anything for the child. He took the shopping list from his pocket.

"Here, let me look at that." She read through it before calling out to the men at the end of the counter. "Hi you Onion Head, get your ass down here pronto."

A small man wearing thick glasses arrived on the scene in a hurry. She handed him the list.

"You can read I hope, go down see if these things in the storeroom. Put them in a refuse sack, okay."

The barmaid barked orders like a sergeant major, before turning her attention to the noisy group of men again. "Where's the boss today, guys?"

"Duggan's at a meeting, Rosie."

"Tash Doyle, come here a minute."

A broad shouldered man with a black moustache came waddling towards them. He cradled a jug of beer in his massive fist. She gave him a rapid account of Joe's mission in America. He listened intently. When she was finished he made no comment, just turned to re-join his friends. The barmaid seemed okay with that.

Her attention focused on the little guy again when he arrived back from the basement carrying a bag. "All the stuff's right here, get food from the Deli down the block," he suggested confidently.

She was quick to reprimand him. "Onion Head's not an ideas man, taking orders, what he got to do."

"Sure, Rosie, I've no problem with that," he replied cheerfully going back to his friends.

Joe produced some money to pay for the supplies but the barmaid wouldn't hear tell of it. She seemed to think money might be one of his biggest problems.

He hadn't convinced her about the location of his hotel, that bothered her.

"Got to get my coat, I'll walk with you on my way home; you're too much of a greenhorn, wandering around Hell's Kitchen in the dark. It's not safe. You have family waiting for you."

While they walked, she asked him why he drank so much coffee. He told her alcohol was a banned substance because his wife thought it didn't suit him, it changed his personality.

Having experienced booze related problems all her life, she knew about the trouble it caused. There wasn't much wondering to do about that.

She took him to a delicatessen, instructing him to select from the food on display. In the absence of pizza, pasta plates proved irresistible. Tuna with sweetcorn a little mozzarella cheese; there was fresh fruit salad with cream for Rita. He liked the look of a meatball dish with peppers for himself. The best thing of all was Mary's yogurt in banana flavours. Rosie insisted on carrying the

Deli food upright to keep it from going all over the place. He would never have thought about that.

When they got to the hotel, she couldn't hide the alarm in her voice. "Ye're staying here?"

"Rosie, would you like to meet my wife?"

"Yes, of course I would."

She was taken with the attractive young woman, as soon as she opened the door. But Rita got a bigger shock. A visitor imposed on her, she flushed with embarrassment explaining her predicament. "Joe, the room, it's an awful mess."

Rosie cut in to help her out. "Don't bother about it, honey, found him looking for a hardware store on the street. I could tell right away he was lost."

On entering the dismal room, her eyes were drawn to the make-believe bed on the floor. It was such a stark reminder of her plight all those years ago.

She put the Deli food on the table, before going into one of her over the top barmaid routines. The only way she could make light of a bad situation. "Ooh' my God what a cute family. Your husband picked up a few things; tomorrow you can do the store thing. There's one around the corner at the back of this place. He said you like pizza. Well I know the best pizza place in this city. Tell you what. Let him take care of babysitting duties, I'll give you a guided tour myself."

The bubbly fast talking lady soon put Rita at ease, she agreed, in spite of herself. "Oh thank you, I would like to know my way around."

After they engaged in small talk for a while Rosie left so they could have something to eat. Deep in thought she made her way to the front door. She might never have noticed him if he didn't shout at her.

"Shit if it ain't the old barmaid–give us a shot' an' a beer Rosie."

She hated the guy, always made him stand waiting for his drink when he called into the Celtic, hoping it would drive him off to stink out some other bar in the area.

She marched boldly over to the hatch to have her say. "I'll tell you what I'll give you, a kick in the ass you smelly scumbag. Now hear me good. Nothing bad happens to that young Irish couple. You know, with the kid landed in the shit-hole here. Understand me! Do you?"

"What you doing here, back on the game are you, dirty old broad." He took delight belittling her, something he might have wanted to do for a long time.

Rosie didn't register hurtful feelings anymore. As calm as you like, she gave him the bad news. Something he ought to know more about. "They're Boss Duggan's cousins from Ireland; you do a little business with him. He mightn't like it if some of his family members were badly treated. Especially by a person he could lay his hands on easy."

That bit of information she was pleased to see made him wince like a bullet in the gut.

Dropping her heavy mascara eyelid, a knowing wink, nodding her head, she took off out the door. This young family's predicament struck her heart like a cry of despair. Memories from her own life flashed before her. Desperate times she went through with a young child to take care of too. This Irish guy needed to get a job in a hurry, before he got himself into trouble.

He reminded her of her son. Strong, blue eyed fond of the dammed alcohol, emotionally fragile too. Bobby was gone now; he made one visit too many to the Celtic. He ended up paying the ultimate price for making that mistake. The reason why she took the job was to gather evidence on Duggan–the owner of the joint. It might take some time. Now she had another mission to keep her going–helping these kids whatever way she could. The sooner she got them out of there the better. The best way to start was calling in the assistance of Tash Doyle. He was the only one of the sand hog crew with any decency. She knew that.

Rosie was raised in the neighbourhood; it held no fears for her any more. This part of New York earned a bad reputation over the years. It was well founded. These kids wouldn't understand anything about that. They were desperate to believe that hotel was a place of comfort. Just like what it said on the sign over the door. But nothing was ever what it seemed to be in Hell's Kitchen. She had already decided to do what had to be done, in honour of her son's memory. It was deeply engrained in the Irish way to help one another. On her way back to the Celtic, she remembered the history of the area. Her grandparents' arrival in the city from the old country started off badly. But they toughed it out, their story of survival was passed down through the family.

A desperate race of ravaged people fleeing the blight of potato famine in Ireland landed in America. They were exhausted, hungry, in poor health. These Irish refugees settled in their thousands on the Island of Manhattan. Here a new survival challenge took shape around them. They called the ghetto Hell's Kitchen while they set about making it their own. Their first foothold in the new world promised food for their families. That was as much as they dared hope for. Indeed they were survivors coming from a dark place.

When the American civil war was over, some of the famous Irish brigade, the Fighting 69th, arrived back in New York. Many of them headed to this shanty town that sprawled along the banks of the Hudson River. The bravest of soldiers returned home to be with their kin.

A tortured, battered race of people for sure, but broken, not once. The savagery of the civil war they fought so valiantly made their will to survive stronger.

The Italian immigrants arrived; refugees from troubled parts in Europe swelled the numbers. The population of Hell's Kitchen grew to three hundred thousand in the late1800s. The area as it is today from W. 34th St. to W .59th St. across Eighth Avenue to the

Hudson River was their turf. Most of these immigrants found employment as dockers. Others toiled as railway workers or worked in slaughterhouses. Some took jobs as sand hogs when a tunnelling project started near the area. But there could never be enough employment for everybody.

Poverty imposed itself on people that had once escaped its fearful clutches. The return of struggle rekindled the fiery embers in desperate men. Irish gangsters in the early twentieth century took control of things when crime was accepted in Hell's Kitchen. It would become a way of life there for a very long time. In an atmosphere of murder, people of the area remained tight lipped. Intimidation was the rule of law. Police were not safe patrolling the district, crimes remained unsolved.

The gang system, eliminating informers, was a powerful deterrent–they literally owned the streets. They had a hand in all sorts of racketeering. From numbers rackets to loan sharking, prostitution to strip joints–anything that turned a few dollars.

In the 1960s history repeated itself. Once again Hell's Kitchen's sons returned from war. This time it was the killing fields of Vietnam. Just like their civil war forefathers some took up guns in civilian life. Now gangland murder moved on to a different level. They used butchers' knives to dismember victims. Late at night in back rooms of bars owned by gang bosses. Body bits were disposed down sewers or dumped in the river. They knew many of the people they killed–friends didn't count for much.

With the culture of tight lip firmly in place, they got away with it for almost two decades. This period (mid-1960s to 1980s) was the bloodiest in those riotous days. In Hell's Kitchen the number of disappeared varied, depending on who's looking or counting.

Chapter Two

The Celtic bar in Hell's Kitchen was buzzing. Rays of early morning sunlight filtered through the big window. Clouds of cigarette smoke rolled in its brightness, like a gathering fog over their heads. Sand hogs, tough construction workers, were on the drink again. It was like a religion to them–they couldn't stay away from it. Night time had passed them by without much fuss. Day time would hardly register at all. These guys worked hard, played hard too. Maybe it was a release from tension they had on the job.

They toiled way down under the ground. It was a hazardous occupation blasting through the deep rock foundation of New York City. As they bored this hidden world trouble was a constant companion. These were solitary men–so compatible with danger they might have been bred for it. There was hardly one among them that didn't relish the task.

The barmaid was busy tidying up for the day shift. Rosie O Connor cringed when the sand hogs got louder by the minute. Tash Doyle was busy stirring up shit, for his own amusement. "Rosie," he roared at her, as if she was miles away. "Onion Head just said you tried to get him to bed with you again last night."

He paused awhile, stroking beer out of his long black moustache. Using downward drags, applied with forefinger an' thumb. Time allowed for this perceived insult to register.

"Say's he told you up front. No fucking way," he guffawed.

Onion Head propped up at the counter beside him was having a great time. All the free beer he could drink enjoying the witty Doyle. But the fun had just taken a little walk. Onion Head would never want to upset Rosie. His very existence depended on her goodwill.

"Aw, Rosie, honey, I never said that."

She cut him dead. "Don't honey me you horrible runt of a man."

She straightened up, dusting down her apron, unconsciously adjusting her blond wig. It was a visible hint of her annoyance. She wore a black baggy pant suit, a red silk scarf tied loosely around her neck. A white apron deliberately tight, to give her waist shape. The black canvas shoes were ordinary looking by comparison. Rosie was adamant, she didn't mind doing sexy. Not as long as it wasn't dangerous. Breaking a hip on the slippery floor was her worst nightmare.

"Tash just made it all up, Rosie," Onion Head pleaded.

Slicing up lemons she waved the big knife in his direction, with a warning. "You know what, if I get those damn pants off, you're bed time future will be non-existent, so will your little shrimp of a dick." She spat out the last word like it was poison.

"Jesus, Onion Head, that's heavy shit, man, the whole place knows about your small dick now," Doyle laughed heartily.

It was the dumb expression on the little man's face that made him laugh so much. His massive shoulders shook, his big brown eyes twinkled with delight. This fearsome looking hulk of a man was a teddy bear. "I don't know how she can say stuff like that to me. She shouldn't talk like that," Onion Head lamented shaking his head in disbelief.

Rosie knew the plot well, how to play it was her greatest talent. She knew for sure Onion Head wouldn't have made that remark; she couldn't care less if he had. Working the Celtic it might be one of the kindest things said to her. It looked like the start of another long day. She'd be better off taking hold of the bait. Pretend offense. Let them enjoy her annoyance. There were a few dollars tips to be had doing that. To have them laughing at her was a better option than fighting with each other. When these sand hogs were partying like this, she was on her guard. Their foreman Vietnam Duggan owned the Celtic. That helped to keep her alert. There had been some misfortune in her life; she blamed him for an awful lot of it. She had a bartending job on Ninth Avenue one time; she barred Duggan from going in there.

Now she worked for him, shared her apartment with his father Thomas. She knew that didn't count for much with his mobster son. With a cigarette dangling from the corner of her mouth she turned her attention to the only man she liked in the bar. He leaned over the wooden counter top now, in a sort of trance. Amusing himself with the coin game again, another distraction she had to put up with. He was spinning the damn quarter with manic repetition. She hated that.

"Hey, Tash, look at me, look when I talk, damn it."

"What's up, Rosie?" Not once lifting his head from the game he played.

"See here, Tash, see here." He looked up at her through red rimmed eyes. She pointed a painted fingernail to an old Irish shillelagh. A plastic truncheon left hanging behind the bar for years. Some St Patrick's Day relic, covered in thorny plastic bumps. The sight of it, discoloured with nicotine an' dust.

Rosie took it down between her legs to shake at Doyle. "Look at this dirty thing, reminds me of Thomas. Look at him," she jeered, pointing at the poor pock faced Onion Head.

"Can you imagine what his little dick looks like eh?"

She roared a long bawdy laugh. It was highly infectious for her drunken customers. They joined in her laughter. Loudest of all was the resilient drifter Onion Head. His survival instinct taught him a way with these tough sand hogs. It was a neat trick to be inoffensive, nodding at whoever paid for the beer in front of him. His slight frame perched on a high stool left his feet dangling off the floor, while he smiled warmly. No one knew his real name or cared to ask. He arrived the previous year from Boston.

When the money ran out, he hung around the Celtic, helping to clean up the place. Sometimes running errands for a few drinks he was guaranteed a dry place to sleep, on a makeshift bed of old coats beside the heating boiler in the basement. The sand hogs adopted him, christened him Onion Head. His rounded head looked like an onion they said, with a tuft of hair stuck up in the middle of it. But he couldn't care less what they called him. Just as long as the drink kept coming across, he had all the time in the world to lap it up. No matter who paid for it? He was living the life of a free man at last.

Another thing, he didn't have to be proud any more.

Everyone had a good laugh at Rosie's reference to Thomas. The sand hog boss John Duggan didn't think it was funny. He took the whole performance as an insult to his father, Thomas. Realizing what she said, the barmaid couldn't bear to look over at him. She could feel his eyes never left her. A polished performer enjoying her own shocking behaviour, she got carried away with graphics of the act. She was well aware that the owner was always dangerous. No matter what Duggan was posing as. She had good reason to remember that too.

Rosie persuaded Doyle to get a job for the stray Irish immigrant. He must do it for the sake of his young family, she insisted. She knew how to tap into the big rogue's kindness. Of course she had great faith in him to keep her name out of it.

The Irish guy was enthusiastic about the likely prospect of work, but Rita would be full of questions, she'd expect proper answers. He was trying to find out more information about the job from his new boss, so he could tell her all about it.

He could barely contain his excitement. "Will I be okay working as a sand hog? I have no experience, mister Duggan?"

"I'll make a fuk'n sand hog outa you or you'll die trying. Blasting rock, get that shit wrong your head's gone flying through the air." He displayed one of his cruel sneers into the young hopeful's face.

The prospect of that sickening event must feel pleasurable to this gorilla.

"But everyone will know I'm a greenhorn, mister Duggan."

That set the boss off on another rant. "Everyone is me, Flanagan, no matter who you meet. Now you don't have to be a donkey from the other side to learn that. Do Yaw!" he roared, gathering himself up to his full height, a couple of inches shorter than his new employee.

Maybe that's what was bothering him. Something about him made Joe feel uneasy. The way he talked to him. As if he existed on some lower form of life. Getting a job was everything, so he didn't care what he called him.

He listened to the boss talking down to him. "I'm your boss now. I say what's happening; I'll show you the ropes. Nothing simpler than that is there. I'll make sure you don't forget the fuk'n ropes either. Another thing, you're staying in a shit hole."

"It's a hotel mister Duggan."

That statement tickled the boss, he laughed until his red face almost exploded. Then he lost his sense of humour, to carry on with the bad mouth stuff again. "Hotel my ass, you've landed your family in the worst whorehouse in this city. I'll have a word with the janitor, see if he can make things better for you. I can do kindness too, sure. You'll have a proper permit for tunnel work. Get you past paperwork inspection first. Don't worry about paying for it just yet. Give me a few hundred dollars later, when you're fixed up more. We can talk about money, when you have money to talk about. How's that, Flanagan? That okay with you?"

"Okay, mister Duggan."

"Yeah, just drop the mister will you. I'd rather be called an asshole than that shit."

"I'll call you Duggan then."

"Call me what you like, long as it's fuk'n respectful. Meet us outside the Celtic here tomorrow morning, seven a.m. You'll walk with us to the job. If you're late you'll miss us, now fuk off with yourself. I've a pain in my head looking at you already."

Joe would never forget that first day down under ground. The drop into the darkness hundreds of feet to the pit bottom petrified him. Then he had the gruelling prospect of the decompression chamber to face. It was said that some miners unable to withstand the build-up of pressure, suffered burst eardrums. Five tortured minutes sitting with his head exploding. All that time he waited anxiously for something bad to happen. His ears filled, like take off in an airplane, only ten times more. He curled up waiting for the worst to take him.

"Are you all right, boy?" He looked up at the concerned lock keeper standing over him.

"He's okay, Bruno, sit down; he had too much whiskey last night."

Duggan's gruff reprimand startled the old man. He moved quickly back to his station.

"New recruits from the old country, I don't know. They're not as tough as the old stock, eh," Doyle remarked, with a smirk.

A small train called a loco ferried them into the tunnel face. The cramped area was barely able to accommodate five men. The height, five feet six inches made it impossible to stand upright. Working in a crouched position took a bit of getting used to.

The hard hats supplied by the company were too cumbersome; some men didn't bother wearing them. They moved about instinctively. While they always managed it without cracking their heads, Joe was learning it was painful. It soon became obvious that he wasn't up to it, making all the wrong moves. He had a bad technique for shoveling earth. But they said nothing. The barmaid told them the new guy was Duggan's relation, over from Ireland. He might be under his wing. They'd wait to see how things worked out.

"Get that fuk'n muck shoveled into the skip, Flanagan. Be quick about it!" Duggan roared above the noise. It was early indication that the new sand hog would have to prove himself. Shape up, or ship out, was the miner's way of describing that situation.

Back in the hotel room with her husband safely out of the way. Rita tackled the main problem. Pulling on rubber gloves she turned the bed over against a wall. Then she covered the unpleasant sight of it with a bath towel, putting the two suitcases on top. It would serve better purpose as a luggage rack. She fetched a bucket of water from the bathroom upstairs. With a spare hand towel, lots of elbow action she scoured the walls. The ceiling in the room was high. The top of the walls remained outside her reach. She thought about standing on the small table, but it wouldn't support her weight. Nevertheless, she was pleased with the result of her effort. Then she got down on her knees to wash the floor. A move to better accommodation might take some time.

She was struggling to dump the itchy feeling she got looking at the grimy state of her new abode. It was impossible to abandon the way she was brought up. Her mother taught her to be house proud from an early age. The clean-up left a pungent disinfectant taste in the room. But it was more palatable than the sticky smell of stale cigarette smoke. The whiff of someone else's body odour mixed with dirt. She covered the table with red paper napkins from the Deli, to hide the cigarette burns. Now that the room was clean, that's the way it had to stay. In the midst of all this progress she missed the company of music, the absence of which created a hollow sound.

She made so many trips upstairs for water, the bathroom couldn't be ignored any more. As a problem place, it must remain off limits. The sight of discarded needles lying around freaked her. While she was at it, the toilet over the hall got a clean as well. Her husband put a lock on the door to keep it private. So far, they got away with it.

As days dragged by with monotonous certainty, time lost its meaning. There was nothing better for Rita to do except read a book. Even that was starting to bore her, troubled by an active mind. It was getting difficult to tell what day of the week it was. She thought about keeping track on a sheet of paper. Then she decided against doing anything like that. Such behaviour might convince her she was in an institution. The place might look the part, feel like a prison. That was as far as it was going to get, no matter what.

She refused to subject herself to confinement.

When her husband announced pay day, as he was leaving, she knew it had to be Friday. Traditionally a day she associated with shopping in Ireland. So after pondering her position she decided to take some positive action. The house bound feeling that crushed her free spirit was banished. Female fortitude answered a primitive call, shopping, that's it!

Shopping. She said it a few times till it felt like a key to freedom. The sound of its name raised her spirits. She started doing a few things to prepare for the trip. Looking down at a map of Manhattan spread on the floor. She set about figuring the best way to reach Fifth Avenue. Buses or trains were not an option. A city transport adventure could wait until she had more confidence. The walk would make her familiar with her whereabouts. It might help her sleep better at night too. Her husband wouldn't want her wandering far from home with Mary. He'd like to be with them, so they could explore the streets together.

She couldn't wait that long. He was at work; the sense of adventure urging her on couldn't be contained. Besides, once she made her mind up, there wasn't a hope of changing it. She didn't have any money to spend but that didn't matter. If it was only 'a window shopping trip' so what! That would do for a start to get her out of the awful room. It was still shopping on Fifth Avenue. A world famous destination, she could hardly wait. Would it be better to go up 10th Ave. to W. 59th St. then across a few blocks to Eighth Avenue? At that point go around Central Park into Fifth Avenue. Yes, that was it. Or maybe through Times Square would be quicker. After talking to herself she changed her mind. She settled on the trip around the park. There was something nice about walking through trees. The other place had a bad reputation, something awful could happen. She might be attacked. It looked about twenty blocks she surmised. With the whole day at her disposal, what else was there to do?

Just when she had her mind made up there was a knock on the door. She heard a woman's voice. "I don't want to startle you, Rita, it's me, Rosie."

She talked her out of the planned marathon attempt. It might be better put off for a while, at least until she was able to use city transport. But there was a flea market near where she lived. It was a great place to visit, full of bric-a-brac paintings all kinds of clothes. Only fifteen minutes' walk away too. Not as fancy as Fifth Avenue, but it was worth a visit just the same. It might be an opportunity to get some fresh air into the little girl's lungs. Rita would enjoy the exercise for sure.

While they strolled down Ninth Avenue Rosie did most of the talking. She explained her roommate Thomas worked as a doorman, while she did odd shifts in a bar. Her apartment was empty most of the time during the day. She wanted to give Rita a key to her home. The pleasure of having a hot shower would always be available, if she wanted to have one. Giving Mary a bath was something else that might appeal to her.

Rita was profoundly grateful for the kindness of her new friend. It would be wonderful escaping to some nice place. The opportunity of having a shower was the best present of all. The thoughts of leaving the hotel to visit a comfortable apartment made her happy. But she smelled the forbidden drink, hoped it wasn't that influence doing the talking. She was already familiar with that unreliable source of communication. It had done for her many times in the past.

They enjoyed rambling around the flea market for an hour or so. Then Rosie announced she was tired. It would take a large glass of gin to pick her up again, she complained. Her home was located nearby, in a modern building on 37th St. When they arrived at this destination, they took an elevator to the fifth floor. It was Rita's first experience of a proper home in America. She thought the living room was the essence of luxury. Rosie plopped into a big comfortable chair with a tall glass rattling ice in her hand.

She started giving instructions in a smoke rasped voice. "Make coffee, honey. All you need's right there, keep looking, honey."

Rita didn't mind being bossed around. She sounded like her mother. In the comfort of such a homely place, it was reassuring. With a big mug of coffee in her hand she turned to her child. Opening a carton of yogurt she fed Mary slowly. Rosie looked on while downing another stiff drink, the effect of which fuelled an eagerness to talk. Rita became absorbed in her story.

Hell's Kitchen was a different place back then. Opportunities for young women were limited. Domestic help was as much as anyone could hope for. Earning a living doing servile work for rich folk wasn't on. Too proud for her own good, her mother used to say. She preferred wandering the streets, doing things with the wrong crowd. Just like everybody else.

Her teenage sweetheart, Dan Ryan, was a gang member. When she got pregnant he left her to fend for herself. She desperately needed money to provide for her child. Caught up in the grip of alcohol dependency things changed. Unpleasant circumstances forced drastic measures upon her. It was a case of 'anything goes if money shows' she explained. When things went wrong, jail was there waiting for her. Her son was put up for adoption, she was told a rich family living on the west coast really took to him. She never heard anything more about him after that. Thinking about it now she was glad he got a better chance in life. She could never have given him that. At least the boy was probably still alive. He might be happily married to a lovely girl, with a few kids. Possibly might even be a doctor or something fine like that. A sense of pride came over her when she stopped talking for a while to enjoy the thoughts of it.

About a month after she was released from prison, she was unfortunate to get pregnant again. This time she resolved to change her ways when she took up a regular job bar tending.

Holding on to her son Bobby, she raised him up to be a fine young man.

He started hanging around with the wrong company. He developed bad habits. There were drugs involved. When he became addicted, it appeared that things couldn't get any worse. But they did when he paid the ultimate price for making that mistake.

"I'm all alone in the world now, honey, with nobody." Her speech slurred the forlorn sadness of a habitual drunk. Such a sad decline from a physician in the family moments earlier upset her listener.

Rita tried consoling her.

"Oh no, Rosie, you have someone to share your life. I see men's things here, you're never alone. Now you have me to turn to as well."

"Yes thank you, you're very kind. There is a friend sharing my apartment, he helps out with the rent. Thomas prefers the company of male friends dear. We seldom meet up. He helped me a lot when I was released from prison years ago. I cannot forget his kindness then. When I could offer him a comfortable home with no restrictions imposed on him, he moved in right away. I'm glad of the company sometimes to be honest."

Rita wanted to know if she had any family to contact. Rosie said no at first. When a gulp of gin helped her reconsider, she reluctantly admitted to an older sister. Then she let her listener know exactly what she thought about her. She was a religious nun that spent all her life in a convent. Down on her knees, same as any ole whore selling herself, praying to God. Could she not understand her plight, if she was such a good Christian? Snobby stuck up bitch; that gave her nothing but trouble all her life. She totally disowned her when she got pregnant. Her only a simple girl at the time that believed in love. To this day she wouldn't acknowledge her. Not even if she met her face to face on the street.

Only once, did she lose her composure, then she cried pitifully about her son, Bobby, such a gentle creature, tall, fair haired, soft pale skin like a girl. She knew it was gang related issues that cost him his life. Her boyfriend Dan Ryan found out that much for her. Bobby's body was denied the dignity of a decent burial. It was her heartbreak in life that she didn't have a place to visit. Where she could spend time talking to her son, telling him all her troubles. She would never get over it. No matter how long she lived.

Although her tongue was loose with so many gins, Rosie was still the crafty bartender, knowing exactly what not to say. While at the same time indulging her great pleasure; the well-rehearsed art of storytelling. She was careful enough not to mention any names of present gangsters. She had learned an important lesson over the years in Hell's Kitchen. One she'd never forget. 'Keeping your mouth shut ensured the benefit of old age'.

A friend of her boyfriend was shot dead on the sidewalk once. He was leaving the bar on Ninth Avenue she worked at the time. She had just served him his last drink – a whiskey sour. The memory of this incident remained a sobering thought. It was a good feeling though, setting the troubles of a lifetime free. There was the obvious comfort too, in knowing a complete stranger shared them. The young Irish girl was such a good listener that Rosie felt enormous pleasure sharing her company. She didn't want to scare her. The bad side of Hell's Kitchen's character would surely frighten the girl. There was no way she wanted to do that.

Unfortunately, her husband was hanging out with the worst of these gangsters. But he wouldn't know anything about that, yet.

When Rita drank as many coffees as Rosie polished off gins it was time to go. She'd walk off some caffeine adrenalin on route.

In order to postpone her arrival at the place she now called home, enquired directions from her host. How she might take Mary the long way round maybe see some ladies' boutiques on the way. Window shopping was as good as it was going to get.

She soon developed a feel for city life. Every day she walked the streets her confidence grew. Time passed by slowly, coming to terms with living in a brothel didn't help. It was about going on with more of the same. Since the conversation with Rosie her attitude softened. She found herself getting more curious about the working girls. Her friend's desperate story was a tale of woe that could happen to anyone. How a change in circumstance sometimes caused misfortune in life. It must have been that way for them too, she reasoned. These poor girls would have similar tales to tell, it was easy to imagine how their decline came about. That was enough to make her forget her own dire situation for a while. It started her thinking how she could help. Maybe if she talked to them like fellow human beings. That would be a good way to go. So, anytime she met them she said Hello. None of them bothered answering her though, but Rita dutifully excused this apparent lack of civility. She could easily understand their embarrassment. That another woman should know about their way of life. No one could be faulted for what life dumped on them to earn a living. She was convinced about that.

She continued saying Hi, to see if it made any difference.

Chapter Three

Two weeks into their New York sojourn when the foul nature of hotel life made itself known. They had just begun accepting the working girl's noisy conflicts. When on those rare occasions hostilities stopped for a time, Joe made reference to the fragile peace of tribal warfare. It didn't last long.

On this particular night, the harsh reality struck when a blood curling scream in the early hours woke them. They shot upright in bed at the sound of it. Someone made a mad dash down the hallway, they could hear pitiful moans.

"Rita, what's that?" He jumped up. She opened the door to peer into the hall.

"Careful, let me go first."

She was out there ahead of him. A young blonde girl lay on the floor, her head propped awkwardly against a wall. The yellow dress was stained bright red near her left shoulder. Her body trembled.

"Oh my God." She went down on one knee, to hold the girl.

"No, we can't touch her, Rita, leave her alone."

She pulled her hand back quickly. Then they heard police sirens outside.

The familiar voice of the janitor boomed in from the lobby. "She might be dead, officer."

They slid silently back into the room. Closing the door, they leaned against it, listening to the words filtering through.

"Easy, easy, you're going to be all right, ma'am. You're going to be just fine."

They could hear someone trying every door on the corridor. "Come on it's the police. We want to check out the room or we bust it in."

The janitor's voice again, more excited this time. "Easy guys, no need to wreck the place, I got a key, see."

"Any witnesses?"

"No, Sergeant."

"What about this door right here."

"Irish couple with a kid live there."

"Irish, are they in there right now?"

"I guess so, Sergeant, didn't see them leave."

"Open up, police, open the door now, it's the police."

Joe opened the door slowly. He saw a shiny badge in front of his nose. The tall red haired police officer was casually dressed.

"Hi, I'm Detective Brady are you guys Irish?"

"Yes, we are."

When he dropped his head like a condemned criminal, the detective grinned. "Don't look so worried, it's not that bad is it. I just need to ask you a few questions about this trouble in the hall. Do you mind, I can step inside for a minute."

He took account of what they heard, all they witnessed. When that formality was over he folded his report book. The conversation lightened up a bit then turned to more personal matters, showing a great understanding of where this young Irish family were coming from. He listened intently to their story nodding his head, occasionally looking over at the child. Trying to reassure them he talked for a while; giving some sound advice. Before leaving he suggested a change of address might be a good move. They liked the detective; he was a kind man that just happened to be one of their own.

After the knife attack ladies of the night couldn't shake the cold feeling of fear. Their vulnerable lifestyle had been so violently exposed. They sought comfort in each other becoming more sociably inclined.

Two of them started talking with Rita on the street one day. She was eager to chat, listening patiently to personal grievances. Gaining insight into what life was like for them. Once, they were young girls with exciting plans. They had dreams for a happy married life. That was before they arrived searching for opportunity only to lose their way in the city of dreams. It didn't take long for hope to abandon them.

The girl in the yellow dress was somebody's daughter from Ohio. Alone on a cold hotel corridor in New York she ran out of time when the end came calling early. Rita knew that could be anybody's story. Their situation was worse than hers. She couldn't help but feel sorry for them. Good tidings spread about the kind Irish girl, with the sick child. At last she had something to occupy her mind. She couldn't wait to tell her husband all about it.

Joe hadn't collected any wages for his first week's work. It was saved, like money in the bank Doyle explained. He would have it paid to him when his employment ended. Then he loaned him two hundred dollars, to keep him going. The gang would have to get a round of drinks though, a treat from his first pay packet. This was tradition, it might have been said to discourage him from breaking with it. They didn't have to worry. He was pleased with his progress, anxious to keep them friendly towards him. Everyone called him Flanagan now; Christian names didn't register with anyone on this job.

He was delighted when he received the first money earned in America. Buying drinks was the least of his concerns. Maybe he owed it to them for putting up with him. He felt some apprehension when he began to understand their mentality. They were tough characters. Could he ever be like them, it hardly mattered now. Two weeks sand hogging he was part of them. He trooped off down the street heading for the nearest bar, proud to be seen in their wild looking company. It seemed everybody on the street was looking at them.

They ambled along the sidewalk, dirty green trousers tucked in steel toed rubber boots. Their bare muscular arms displayed with a swaggering gait. The chill in the air hadn't reached them yet. They didn't give a shit anyway. In such a place where everything seemed to fit, New York couldn't smother their presence. Hookers smiled when people sidestepped. This kind of treatment was usually for them.

A black girl with a blonde wig made a move. "Want to get laid, boys?"

"We gets fuked down the hole all the time, bitch," Duggan grunted back at her, nastiness all over his remark. He might as well have been talking to himself. She was smiling at his friend now.

Doyle had a much better idea for her, giving off his coaxer grin. "See you down the bar, honey, we'll talk there." He was serious.

The hooker wasn't going for it though; time spent learning tricks of the street, too cautious to be dangled. Doyle didn't miss the big smile anyway. He liked them all.

The street wise predator could feel it. "Thanks, babe," she called after him.

At the next corner taunting street kids jeered at them. "Sand hogs, sand hogs, stay down the sewers, smelly hogs."

Duggan roared abuse back at them, something uncomplimentary about their mothers. They ran off, but still jeered from a safer distance.

The bartenders weren't too busy in the Last Chance bar. It was a rickety old neighbourhood joint, well-worn juice heads revelled in the company of likeminded souls. Even the bartenders were of a rough nature here.

They were pleased to see the sand hogs arrive in, greeting them cheerfully. The tunnel job up the street was a kind of windfall for them. They'd get a ten dollar tip for each pay cheque cashed. Flanagan gave Doyle his two hundred back. Then he lined up a round of drinks for the crew. He was the good guy with them at last.

Everything was in order when he did what was expected of him. But he had to hang around for a while enjoying their company. Especially at the weekend, hanging out with the gang was the expected thing to do. He didn't want them to think he was some sort of loser, to be seen rushing off home like a woozy to the wife.

"Are you asleep again, Flanagan?"

"Just looking, that's all."

"Looking me ass."

Duggan was impatient, shouting above the din. "What's your drink?"

"A coffee's okay again, same as last time."

"Coffee, what are you saying, dude? Have a whiskey. You're a sand hog, not a fuk'n pussy," Duggan sneered at him throwing back a whiskey in one gulp. Then he wiped his hand, the glass still in it across his mouth glaring at him. As if he was dirt.

"Really, coffee's fine for me, what I want, Duggan, okay."

Boss Duggan wasn't going to break him. He was determined about that. Hadn't he tried hard enough for two whole weeks already? Now the hard graft was over, he was still shouting in his face, making a show of him in a bar full of tough guys.

"Right maybe glass 'a milk suits ya better, really me ass, yer a bitch, are ya." Duggan spat the words out before turning to talk with the barman.

"Don't let Duggan bother you, man." Doyle moved closer to stand beside him.

"Tash, I'm pissing him off." Turning to look at the grinning miner, he desperately wanted someone to talk with. "Tash, last year America was a place far away from me, having a simple life in Ireland, then all that changed in New York, working a job I don't know. The crew can't be blamed for wanting me somewhere else. There's nothing I can do about that it's just the way it is. I'm going to make it doing this sand hog work, no matter what I have to put up with. I won't be breaking you can be sure about that. I'm determined I tell you."

Doyle just smiled, dishing out his greatest compliment yet. "You're okay, Flanagan."

Hanging with a hard drinking mob is difficult at any time. But staying sober in their company requires effort. Being accepted as a coffee drinking weirdo was even more challenging.

As soon as he paid for their drinks, they forgot about him, revelling in the charged atmosphere of each other's company, arguing about problems they faced down below, while at the same time planning the destruction of fuckers they didn't like. That kind of crossover conversations drinking men blow themselves up with. It could turn threatening.

When they were so distracted he slipped quietly away, hurried back to the unlikely sanctuary of the hog hut. A good shower would get the romantic thing kicking off. Rita was particular about smells, prone to homing in on the whiff of a bad one. He wanted to go home to be with her, pursue some of those loving intentions he thought about. A bunch of flowers from the woman at the street corner might set the tone for pleasurable weekend activities.

The toughest two weeks of his life was behind him. He could handle working a shovel, when there was a job to do. This tunnel digging was torturous back breaking work without any let up to it. He had to make himself fit the role whether he was able for it or not. His hands were blistered. The fingers cramped tight sorting a few coins for the flowers. But there was a sense of relief winning the battle as if he came of age. He couldn't wait to see Rita's face. The look on it, when he handed her over his wages. Such an amount of money there was a wonderful feeling of success about it. The constant worry was easing. A bit of a break to soothe aching bones was all he needed now. Maybe a chance to finally explore Central Park, they talked about it often enough.

Away from the sand hog crew at last Joe had time alone. There were things to think about. He considered the benefits of a comfortable apartment, to escape from the noisy hotel. Far away from the sound of screeching fighting bitches, the cursing drugged up pimps. Some place where safety welcomed them into the arms of a good night's sleep.

The janitor told him he was keeping a look out for an apartment like that, near a park somewhere. That would be perfect if he delivered on the promise. It would be great to leave the confines of this cold unfriendly concrete jungle every so often. Wouldn't it be pleasant exercise, 'rambling along nature's way' as Rita declared in her poetic voice? She that was brought up in the country missed the consoling company of trees. Life's experiences could hardly have prepared her for all this. The way she adapted to the struggle of meagre existence, creating a home in a room full of nothing. She made such little fuss about it too; maybe her approach to life was the right one. He was only beginning to think like that when the guilt of bringing her down so low finally kicked in. If he had any respect for her at all, he'd have to match her efforts. She deserved that much for sticking by him.

His plans for building a house in Ireland were always on his mind. It didn't matter what he had to endure as long as he ended up with that. He could see the whole thing happening now. This first amount of money confirmed it was possible. He'd dealt with a few situations in his life already, learning some hard lessons along the way. New York felt like more of the same, the location was different, but he'd been there before. Maybe this is how it was all supposed to happen. He'd finally get breeding the horses he dreamed about. Thoughts of getting it all together made the hassle bearable. He remembered some of the things his father used to say. One of them was, 'anything you get for nothing, doesn't last very long'. He could never figure how his father worked that one out. He couldn't remember getting much for nothing either, except all the kicks up the ass he was subject to. They lasted long enough.

Chapter Four

The hotel was quiet; the janitor had time to brood. He was sitting in his office, turning a few annoying things over in his head. It was time to be cautious. Not only had the tramp barmaid called him to order, the bloody cop stuck his nose into the mix as well. That know all detective sergeant laid it on heavy. He whispered it to him when he was leaving. A bit of venom in the way he said it too. "Don't let anything happen to the Irish kids. I'll hold you responsible for that. Do we understand each other?"

Then there was that prospect of the psycho Vietnam Duggan involvement. He was related to the Irish family according to reports; he had to take him into consideration too. That was giving him the creeps since he heard it.

Didn't want any trouble with these people, if he had to kiss ass that's what he'd do. Get them out of the place or he'd never have a minute's peace. A friend of his had a client that wanted to sublet her apartment. Hopefully they would move into it right away. There would be a few bucks in it for him. So everyone was happier doing a little business. Some good would come from the hassle of it. The sooner it was history the better for him, he figured.

Joe sat cross legged on the floor looking at his wife counting. Most of the wages were in small bills, it took time to get through it. He'd planned it like that. So she could count all the money she had. It had been a terrible struggle for her.

"The janitor says he found a nice place for us, Rita."

"One of the girls said he just wants our money, Joe."

"Rita, come down here in front of the fire with me, remember old times."

"Speak for yourself; I'm still doing young times." She giggled burying her nose in his chest.

"How long have you been talking to these women, Rita?"

"I sometimes stop to talk with them coming from the Deli. They all know me now, Mary too. I know a few of them by name, Debbie, I like her the best. She wants to stop being a prostitute. Wish I could help her get away from it." She was pleased he wanted to hear about her new social work activity.

"Don't get too buddy with the whores. They're dangerous bitches."

She recoiled at his harsh attitude. "Joe, that's unfair. They are somebody's daughters, sisters; some of them were wives once too. I might have to start doing it myself, to get rid of the boredom. We could do with the money."

The thought of that proposition made him grimace. She was looking for that reaction. She had to giggle, when she was right.

"Are you jealous?" she whispered mischievously.

"How come?" he muttered.

"That's not the right answer, how come?" she repeated. You know it means nothing, I know it too. Are you jealous yes or no?"

"No of course not, what have I got to be jealous about."

"You've got me to be jealous of."

"Why, what are you going to do to make me jealous?"

"Nothing much, for the moment anyway."

"So what are we talking about it for then."

"It's just jealousy, it shouldn't be there. You don't want me talking to them. You think they're not good enough for me. Come on out with it, say it."

"Are you not going to eat that salad Rita, can I have it?"

"Yes, but stick to the point, Joe. If you don't cooperate with the inquiry I'll tell you anyway."

"It's an enquiry now is it? What turned the discussion into an enquiry?"

"You're trying to put me off. I'm not for off, except off my chest. I have to talk to you. You are jealous of them near me. That I could possibly be like them sickens you. By being friendly with them would be enough. Guilty by association isn't that it. Just like a man to cloak his hang ups about women, at women's expense too. Mr Man makes them pay on the double. But think about this, Joe. Only for men using them they would find other ways to live. You're in a foul mood since I started talking to them. Trying to pretend it's not happening at all. There is no reason for calling them bitches. Men are the most spiteful bitches of all."

He put his arm around her stroking her hair. "I'm just worried one of them will stick a knife in you, Rita. I don't know about jealous," he whispered. "I am, if it means I want you for myself. I can't get enough of you. These women think differently than you. They have different values. Most are drug addicts; their sole purpose in life is getting money for the next fix–all that's important to them. If they can use you in any way to that end, they will do it. When you're dealing with them, keep that in mind. That's all I ask of you. They're doing a dangerous job here. That makes it risky for us. A lot of weirdos coming to visit them, as we already know. We must not get too friendly, drawn into something we wouldn't want any part of."

She buried her head in his chest again with a sigh. "I feel so sorry for them, Joe, I really do. They have to take terrible beatings. It's not fair they should have to put up with so much. Sometimes, I feel lucky by comparison."

He realized the conversation wasn't likely to favour his opinion. It was better letting it drop. That great feeling of having dollars in their pockets created options. For the first time since they arrived in New York he could take her out for a meal. Arguing downtrodden women's cause came naturally to her. He took the easy way out changing the subject. "Com'on, I'm still hungry let's take Mary out for a walk. We can go for something later. Celebrate the first pay packet coming in, Rita. What do you say about that?"

The hotel janitor had changed his personality overnight it seemed. He surprised Rita with his consideration. It started off by opening the door for her when he saw her in the lobby. One day, in a fit of boredom, she brought her new mop bucket down. She spent some considerable time giving it a good going over.

To her surprise the floor tiles she presumed to be green, turned a warm creamy colour. It was such a revelation when the sticky dirt was removed.

She couldn't help wondering. If the water was boiling, would the tiles turn white?

He praised her effort of course pledging hot water from his apartment when she wanted it. She might take him up on that offer, she explained. She'd give it a more thorough clean next time around. He told her his name was Dulche.

But when she repeated mister Dulche he quickly became his arrogant old self again. "Don't put mister before it, the name stands there on its own right. Like Geronimo, he gushed, "My action man name doesn't need mister."

Oh My God. She couldn't think why she'd made such a stupid mistake. She became more convinced men would never understand the subtlety of women's intent. Mister would never again pass her lips, if she needed to address this idiot again, first impressions were best. She was sure about that now.

Mario Catapani the sand hog general foreman was a legend. With a reputation working down the hole that lived on. His escapades were told from the tunnels of New York to the snow-capped terrain of Alaska. The word was tough but fair. In the sand hog world getting old didn't take toughness away. Respect made sure everything stayed exactly the same. Just like it always was. Mario wasn't going to be ruffled by a fat cat office shark. The fact he stank out his hut with cheap cigar smoke, only irritated him more.

He looked across his desk at the asshole. The guy hadn't stopped talking crap since the beginning. He was still at it.

"See it like this, Mario, no deadline reached. no bonus for the company, no joy for you."

Jim Sullivan put the cigar down in a saucer, to wipe the sweat off his forehead. "Have you an air conditioner or what."

Mario smiled. The fat suit couldn't handle the heat.

He threw logs in the stove earlier, with him in mind. He made sure to close the windows tight as well. The company engineers had screwed up big time. They underestimated the type of ground the tunnel was going through. They priced the job too low. Their assessment was based on incorrect information. Some of the going was soft in texture, hard to stabilize, prone to cave in. But the bosses weren't having any of it. They expected him to put pressure on the workforce.

He rose from his chair indicating the meeting was over. Sullivan picked up on it heading for the door. He knew better than to offer him a handshake. A vice wouldn't do as much damage.

"Take it easy."

The general foreman said nothing.

In fifteen months he would be retiring to his father's village in Italy. The thoughts of watching days drift by fishing kept him going. He could tell the company go to hell.

But his son Luigi was hoping to fill his position someday. Now that kind of situation made all the difference. He had never seen sand hogs hate each other as much as this job. Must be all the alcohol, he mused. He spat out his tobacco chew when he thought about it. Watching a stain of brown spittle spread on the dry floor. He smiled when the idea occurred to him. 'Booze, now that might solve the problem.'

Mario understood sand hog mentality, a culture all their own, rivalry that filled the pages of folklore. Men that could handle any situation with a fierce competitiveness fueling aggression that made them work like demons.

Four hours in any day was the maximum time allowed by law for men working in compressed air. During that shift each gang was expected to extend the tunnel by nine feet. It was a time cut to the finest for completing this amount of work.

The job in Manhattan continued around the clock. It was all the same underground.

He arranged for a meeting to be held in the hog hut. On his arrival he was greeted respectfully from all sides.

"How are you doing, Mario?"

The older more familiar men privileged to address him thus.

Others remained silent, gazed at him as if he was divine.

He beckoned his son Luigi to his side. "I have a proposition for these guys."

Luigi banged a rubber torch light against a locker door. "Shut up, men, The Messiah wants to talk with you all."

The corny reverence, a liberty restricted to family was greeted by laughter with a few cheers. Another bang on the locker brought a hush over them.

"I want to tell you some information, men. Tomorrow is the start of a new week. I would like to offer on behalf of the company a little incentive. They want to reward the best outfit on this job. The gang that drives past the required three rings every shift, that's the measured nine foot, will have the extra ground calculated at the end of the week. Those men will receive a six pack of beer per man with a quart of whiskey between them."

He paused while they cheered.

"So, the pit boss here, Luigi, can supervise all measurements. This will happen at the end of every shift. A referee will go down to sort out differences. I'm appointing myself referee."

He surveyed the room deliberately.

"Don't drag me down the hole with nonsense arguments. I spent long enough down there. It will go on a weekly chart in my office. I can monitor progress. I was privileged to work with the best sand hogs in America. It will be interesting to compare them to you guys. You can drink the spoils in the hog hut on Fridays only, good luck, may the best outfit win."

The keeper controlled air lock pressure before admitting miners to the compressed air tunnel. A small trolley train called a loco carried everything into the face. On the return trip, it hooked up dumpsters of earth for disposal.

At the start of every shift railway sleepers were removed from the pit face. Two men crouched in front with heavy air spades hacking at the packed earth bringing it down, while the other two men used short shovels to pitch this earth into a dumpster behind them. When filled it was pushed to a layby that accommodated six dumpsters at a time.

Six full ones cleared enough room for building a complete circle of steel. There was a four-hour shift to dig out eighteen dumpsters of earth to assemble three rings of steel. That action achieved a nine foot drive. The men were mean all right, the pace was a race.

They had a chant to keep them pumped up for the job, like marines they roared it. "I'm a miner, I'm a mucker, I'm a mean mother fucker."

Maybe it helped dull the pain, it kept aggression primed. The fact they were among the highest paid construction workers in America helped. Any large rock formation was blasted another hazard to deal with. The steel arrived in two semi circles. One was placed on the bottom, the other on top. The four inch steel was tapered at the ends like a guillotine, to fit evenly. Then the joints were sealed with a specially treated rope. The whole structure bolted together by another air machine called a mule. It was unthinkable that any crew could fail three rings on a shift. Reputations were treasured down below.

The hog hut was basic in every way. A small kitchen inside the door had a hatch for dishing out mugs of coffee. Wooden tables lined the sides connected by bench seats. In the centre twenty-four lockers stacked back to back. A tiled shower area took up most of the end space. It was big enough for a dozen men.

The walls were colourfully adorned in loving care with pictures of nude women. Some of the men scrawled obscene inscriptions on their favourites. Crude details of how they'd pleasure the lovely creature. The juke box blared continuously with a mind of its own. It played tunes for free operating to the touch of a selection button if anyone bothered their ass using it? Caretakers sometimes changed the feel of these hog huts. The man in charge of the Manhattan site was called Limpy. He was a sour individual of blocky statute, in his late fifties with grey dead eyes. Some of the men could hardly tolerate the look of him. His attitude didn't help either, a bitter old bastard they called him.

They made their own coffee to avoid any contact with him.

The hut had its fair share of characters. Some were likable, others not very. Story tellers among them too, men who liked to brag about sex with women. Those that wouldn't believe them no matter what they said. Boastful talk about brawls they fought in faraway Alaska. Tough jobs they worked. In times putting pipe lines down the freezing snow. How they kept themselves warm humping native women, whose company they shared for the cold lonely evenings, with nothing else left to do in the land of the midnight sun.

It was a tale told by Limpy that Flanagan liked to hear most of all. He witnessed the abuse Duggan hurled at the caretaker. Feeling sorry for the old man, he talked to him. He became captivated with his story. Long after his workmates went to the bar he waited for the caretaker to sit down for a chat.

"I almost lost my foot to the son of a bitch of an alligator. We got too close to Chinatown always a few hanging round there, see."

He was a leading miner, his gang carried out maintenance work. Some brick had collapsed on the floor causing a blockage. The gang worked away, while he armed with a small pick axe, looked for other problems. He was checking the brick structure encasing the tunnel. The area he covered was different every day; then he'd compile a report from his findings.

"A waste of time those damn inspections," he declared. "City authorities never acted until a cave in, for good reason." Limpy's face contorted, his empty eyes riveted far away. "Why?" Flanagan was eager to hear the scary part again.

"They're scared; the place is full of blind slimy albino bastards. Creeping around in the sewer down below, that's why."

"If they're blind how could they see to attack anyone?"

"Sound, they use echo location like bats; live on rats."

"But how do alligators get into the sewers?"

"In that rich world out there those with nothing better to do with money buy baby alligators as pets; keep them in glass tanks like fish."

He observed his listener before continuing. "When they get too big they just flush them down the toilet, see. Sometimes they drop them into sewers on the street. Have you been down Chinatown way?"

"No."

"Lots of bloody offal in that area, attracts big fat rats. Waiting silently in ambush white alligators, whatever moves they get it. Humans move don't they?"

He waited long enough to let his listener dwell on that. Then he continued. "I walked through sewers looking for damage to the ceiling. Never knew what hit me, damn nearly took my foot in one bite. Now look, I'm called Limpy. Not much sympathy for me these days. I blame that bastard company man Sullivan for it all. There's good men left down there, forgotten. I know that too."

His listener didn't like the sound of it. "Men just don't go missing."

"You think not you're new to this city. No alligators eating people in Ireland, eh? Look in any of the city newspapers, over time. See what you come up with. How many men have lost their lives in tunnels? Urban legends my ass, them alligators are real. You'll see, still there to this day. Management ignores the claims to avoid publicity."

He leaned closer. "I'll tell you kids will start lifting sewer covers on the streets. They're at it already. They will be taken when they go down."

"Can they not be shot?"

"Shot, alligators get no sun down there. Bastards light in colour, camouflaged. You know about them when it's too late. There's ten thousand miles of sewers under New York City. That's an awful lot of ground for the slimy reptiles to hide."

He went into another mad rant about the city council again. That awful disgrace of not having the alligators exterminated. Sounding wistful, hoping for the end of them, rid of the bastards plaguing his sanity. Like some modern day Captain Ahab who admired yet feared his Moby Dick. Limpy's hatred was thorough. Every ill wind that blew came from the sewers of Manhattan. Imminent disaster would come down with a vengeance someday soon.

"A curse is upon the lot of them, it's coming from men crying out to be found."

He gave a crackling laugh without any sound of delight.

"A few more sand hogs missing won't matter. The money men will not miss them, soon it will happen again. It might be you next time, young Flanagan. Go back to Ireland where you'll be safe. A whole life's ahead of you, maybe, if you're still able to walk."

He was off pushing his broom again. The sight of his dead foot gave some form of credence to the mad caretaker's story. It was a frightening thought for his young listener.

The sand hog gangs usually stayed together for the duration of a job. It suited their way of life to keep things going like that. They built up confidence in each other's way of working. They could move around in gangs from one job to the next, or sometimes from one State to another. It mattered not where the tunnel work took them. The gangs now placed in strong competition were a mixed bunch of characters that were well known to each other.

The six gangs consisted of:

Leading miner Luigi 'Fishy' Catapani, all Italian American called The Mafia.

Leading miner Doug 'The Blast' Johnson all black men called The Brothers Gang.

Leading miner Lee 'Wispy' Steel all men from the Deep South, The Hill Billy's.

Leading miner Charlie Sweeney from Donegal in Ireland called The Donkeys.

Leading miner Danny 'Rocky' Moran, from Hell's Kitchen, called The Westies.

Leading miner John 'Vietnam' Duggan, Irish American, called Duggan's Gang.

Mario's reward scheme was underway, which of these gangs was going to earn the bragging rights. All of them figured they could win any time, confident of getting a positive result when they wanted to. But competition would create pressure when desperate men came into grips with some of their own. Anything was liable to happen then.

Chapter Five

Detective Sergeant Ben Brady requested a few days off work. It was his son's birthday; he looked forward to spending time with his family. He roared along west side highway heading in the direction of home. The hooker attacked in the hotel died in hospital. That incident was now a homicide investigation. The janitor's account of events on the night bothered the cop. Vague on detail for someone so close to the scene, he claimed he was in his apartment when the girl was attacked. When he went down the hall he found her on the floor. He said she was bleeding, lying there unconscious. Then he went back to his office to call 911.

But the Irish couple heard someone running when the girl screamed. Would that have been the killer or the janitor? The girl was conscious when the cops arrived, too shocked to talk. In his opinion, the killer would have to be an Olympic sprinter to get out the door. If the janitor didn't see something, that was suspicious. He told the cops that most of the hotel rooms were wide open. Maybe the guy ran upstairs, escaped through a window down to the street, he suggested. How did he know the attacker was a guy the cop asked him?

The janitor had no answer for that.

When the officers checked the rooms they were surprised. Not one of the windows in the hotel could even be forced open. The team were now investigating all the women using the place. To see if any of them had a motive for wanting her dead. It would take time to round them all up. They usually scattered when trouble arrived. Police inquiries turned up a few related facts about the hotel. The company that leased the property was registered to a Mrs Marie Duggan. Detective Brady was well aware of her son's alleged criminal connections. Police files contained references to his Celtic bar as a possible cover for illegal activity.

Any association with this criminal outfit was one good reason why the Irish couple should vacate the hotel. The detective's wife was informed of their story, she enquired about them all the time. She asked her husband to look out for them. That was something he was naturally inclined to do. She'd be looking for an update when he got home. On a sudden impulse, he wheeled off the highway cutting across 11th Ave. to turn south at 10 th Ave. John Jay College of Criminal Justice was on the right.

The autopsy report confirmed the prostitute didn't have sex just before her death. Still, it couldn't be ruled out that a client was responsible. He felt that the doorman knew more than he was inclined to admit. A little pressure now might reap some benefit later.

Brady just finished questioning him when the Irish lady arrived in with a few shopping bags hooked on the baby buggy.

"Detective Brady, it's nice to see you again."

In spite of her cheerful greeting, she appeared flustered. He stooped down to stroke the child's arm. "I have a two year old daughter, as well," he said, turning to look up at her. "I can fully understand how it is for you. The circumstance you're in. It must be a difficult struggle."

He noticed her lip tremble. Standing upright he barked out specific instructions, for the shifty looking janitor to notice.

"I'm giving this lady my number, she needs to call she uses the phone in your office, okay."

"Okay Sergeant, sure no problem, got no problem with that, sir."

The detective scribbled on his pad before handing it to her. "I was a new arrival from Ireland once; I know what it feels like," he whispered.

"Thank you, Detective Brady, you are very kind." She waved after him walking out the door, with tears welling in her eyes.

Later on, in the afternoon, the janitor made it his business to meet up with her husband. He stopped to talk with him on his way in from work. There is a vacant apartment on W.48th St. he told him. The lady owner was transferred to Washington DC. She liked the idea of a family staying in her home for a year. A security deposit was required which Joe could afford. It would be returned when the lease expired, if everything was as they got it. They could move in next day. There was a special agreement on the rent for suitable clientele.

"I got t' have the deposit money up front though."

"Don't worry about it, Dulche, I'll be back with the cash for you, right away!"

Life in the hotel room had been wearing him down long enough. Suffocated in the tunnel, stifled at home, he longed for the smell of open spaces again, like an ache in his heart.

Sand hog's work was taking its toll on him; he needed a good night's sleep in a comfortable bed. Rita said he was selfish; she could do with some sleep too. A pleasure she hadn't experienced since they set foot in America.

Having a place to move into at last was exciting. He ran up the hall to give her the good news. When she opened the door he knew something was wrong. Her red rimmed eyes, the fearful looking face said it all. His heart pounded as he reached out to her. She ducked underneath turning back into the room, ignoring him. He'd never seen her behave this way before.

"What's wrong, Rita, everything's all right now? We're moving to a new place."

"I've lost the money, Joe, it's all gone." She cupped her face in her hands to sob.

"Oh shit no. Was it in your purse, it has to be here somewhere. I'll look for it meself?"

She shook her head looking down at her shoes. "Don't bother, Joe. Two of the girls started talking to me out on the street. One of them must have taken the purse from my bag, when I was so distracted! I was good to them, listening to their problems. They repaid me by stealing my money. I shouldn't have told them we had enough saved to get out of here."

He jumped up from the floor, this time her sobbing irritated him. "The whores, I told you they were dangerous, Rita. You did the Mother Teresa shit. They were setting you up all the time, till you had a few dollars. We'll never get out of this place now."

"Please, Joe, don't shout at me, please. I can't take it any more, I'm telling you."

He blamed her for everything. Even warned her about them, told her they were no good. She refused to listen. Now it cost them.

"We're stuck in this whorehouse forever. You let them bring us down to their level."

He roared at her, sitting down on the bed white faced, to think about it. If he could get her to tell him what they looked like, he'd go after them, get the money back. He asked her to describe them, but she wouldn't. That angered him more.

"We can't tell the cops either, can we? We're not supposed to be working in this country."

He continued on with this rant, upsetting her more. Winding himself up, till he knew he deserved a drink. Whiskey would make him think better. Get to hell out of the room; it was closing in around him. He headed for the door without looking back at her, calling over his shoulder, "I'm going down to the Deli to get us something to eat."

Another pitiful cry followed him into the corridor.

"See if I gave a shit about her," he swore.

The depressing room overwhelmed her spirit again. With the will to struggle leaving her she cried bitterly. The tears had been welling for a long time. She slumped down on the ground letting them flow.

He pounded the floor with hurried steps on his way to the front door. The janitor's inquiring gaze was met with a hostile look. "This shit hotel," Flanagan swore at him.

He turned for the forbidden sanctuary of the Celtic bar.

"Hi, Flanagan, take it easy, the wife dump you out or what," the bartender exclaimed, surprised by the state of him.

"Give me a whiskey, I want a beer chaser too, Murtha," he said staring at his reflection in the bar mirror, before gulping it down.

He wanted to do that for a long time. Next time he wouldn't need an excuse.

Then he slid the shot glass across the bar to him, like he saw seasoned drinkers doing. "Put another one in that, Murtha."

He dumped it back with the same purposeful intent then boldly approached his boss for a chat. The new recruit was already displaying a rise in confidence.

"Let's have this talk in fuk'n private, my office." Duggan was inclined to take him serious.

When the sand hogs looked at each other, someone muttered, "What the fuck's up?"

Tash Doyle shook his head. A grim expression clamped the moustache tight. Still, he managed to voice his opinion. "Something tells me we're going to meet the other Flanagan soon." There was a hint of regret in the way he said that.

Back in the hotel, Rita struggled to choke back tears. She remembered her father telling her that crying was just the same as giving up. He would never want her to do that. She was so far from home now. The memory of learning how to cope renewed her strength a little.

Well she knew her husband was gone off on the booze. She had been there before. There was no amount of money worth the torment of watching a loved one disabled by alcohol. He would do her head in when he came back from the bar. That could be anytime. The sight of her powerful man staggering around helpless like a new born foal was heartbreaking for her. She knew she couldn't summon the strength to help him. Her child, the appalling circumstance had taken every ounce she had left, trapped again.

She'd wait; wait until the worst happened, whatever that turned out to be. It would take all her resources to cope when he eventually decided to return home. The one reassuring factor he never displayed any violence towards her. That wouldn't be tolerated under any circumstances. His mental disorientation created enough trouble for her on its own.

Before her marriage she worked as a school teacher. She liked children, looked forward to having her own one day. When things went wrong she put her trust in God. Believing he dispensed life's troubled burden on those best able to carry it. These strong principles had always been part of her family's way of life.

On so many occasions in the past few years those capabilities were sorely stretched. Rita dutifully kept taking it, even though it was wearing her down. It was something to do with strength of will, passed down through her mother's family. Anything that attacked her was met by powerful resilience. Her sense of loyalty to whatever cause she committed to was her most admirable quality. It's just the way she was.

Loud banging on the apartment door jolted her sleep. "Rita, open the door, will you."

"Oh my God, please give me strength,"

He threw some food on the table putting his arms around her. "I'm sorry, Rita."

She smelled alcohol of his breath pushing away from him. "Was the Deli busy, Joe? You were a long time away? Maybe you met someone you knew in there."

"The Deli was jammed all right, I had a long wait."

She watched him take salads from a bag, handing her a pizza.

"When was the last time we talked?" she asked.

"We're always talking, Rita."

"Are we listening to each other when we're talking? That's what I want to know."

"What's that supposed to mean?"

"From Philadelphia we came here because we were broke. We wanted to recover some of our savings. We agreed booze was a no go right. I smell alcohol on you now."

"Rita, I had one beer."

"Please, for God's sake, don't start drinking again. With everything else going on. It would surely kill me, so let that be the end of it. You know what it does to me seeing you like that."

The alcohol debate would have to wait until she felt stronger. His behaviour appeared rational enough. That was more than she dared hope for. With an uneasy atmosphere prevailing, they tucked into food. The close confines made silence unbearable, he was first to crack.

"I'm sorry for blaming you, Rita, I was upset. I had to try fixing things for us."

"It's okay, just don't always blame me. Try some other way of dumping your frustration, Joe. I've had enough of it."

"We're moving into our new apartment tomorrow, Rita."

"Tell me about it, I could do with a bit of a lift."

He told her about his visit to the Celtic bar. She frowned at the mention of the place listening for the sound of the good part. He explained he went there to borrow money from his boss.

"Don't you owe him a fortune already? How will you pay all this money back to him?"

"I'm about to explain that. He has another job lined up for me."

"Will you be able for more work? I think you're doing enough already."

"No listen, nothing like tunnel work, more of an office kind of job! He mentioned collecting accounts. Money owed, a few hours in the evening. There would be good commission paid on what I collect."

It appeared John Duggan had many other business interests. Joe seemed so pleased. She didn't want to spoil it for him. That could wait until she found out what the work entailed. If it was a job that took him around bars in the evening. Now, that should be reason for alarm. The way things stood right now, he wasn't drunk, they were moving into a new place. It wasn't progress by any means just a slight improvement on her worst expectations.

"It's a kind a white collar job, babe," he was saying. "Don't even have to get my hands dirty either."

Did she hear him calling her babe? That's a new one. "Please don't use that babe stuff, Joe, it's not you."

He laughed at her.

She dived with her hands on his shoulders. He fell backwards on the made up bed, cracking up laughing. Trying to be funny wasn't exactly what Rita had in mind. She sat cross legged over his chest, pinning him down. Her adrenalin pumped energy gave her tomboy power when she started wrestling with him. Convinced he couldn't match her strength laughing so much. She tried to subdue him.

Struggling to twist his arm behind his back, her effort took him into the giggles.

'The nerve of him laughing at me, I'll show him.' She seized the moment to tickle his armpits. It was something he could never take.

"Babe my ass," she said, "Give me a yield, or I twist your wrist, break it if I have to."

The sight of her jaw set made it so serious. The bitchy determination made him helpless. Laughing so much till he almost wet his jeans.

"I submit, I submit damn you, please get off me," he cried, banging his hand on the floor like a wrestler.

"Promise anything for me," she demanded.

"Anything, anything, I promise, Rita, he roared."

"Good, that's you knocked down a peg sand hog my bum."

The two of them fell around the bed when she said it like that.

"Posh Rita was back too soon," he complained.

She relaxed her effort then. The battle won, the laughter made things feel better. With quiet satisfaction softening her face she smiled at him. Their gaze lingered, mellowing the mood for love. Her fingers stroked his face, he sensually caressed her thighs. For a fumbled excited reaction! Quickly rid of interfering clothing, fondling hands explored intimate places. Swelled pink nipples turned up to heave.

"Kiss me, ooooh, yes, my darling."

Moving, turning, rising rhythm, moist sensual sounds vibrate off the cold linoleum floor.

"I love you, Rita."

"I love you too, Joe."

"We will always be together, won't we?"

"Yes, Rita, forever."

"I hope so."

Consoling words, far removed from the stark reality of where they lived. Intimacy nurturing bond made them feel like one again. In the reality of life's struggle they forgot for a while.

The loving way it used to be.

Chapter Six

Rita was delighted when they moved into a new abode on W. 48th 'St. She could never have imagined such good fortune. The living standard she was subjected to in the hotel had lowered her expectations. As a result she was pleasantly surprised. The new place was called a railroad apartment because of its long narrow layout. It was an old building.

The inconvenience of not having an elevator didn't bother her that much. Carrying the baby buggy up three flights of stairs, no problem either, it was exercise. She needed some of that.

This new location brought her nearer to Rosie O Connor. She couldn't wait to have her over for dinner. Let her see how an Irish girl could cook. The place had all modern conveniences. She had already mastered the stove. The next trick would be baking bread, if she could locate the flour she needed.

Her husband was delighted with the cooking; things were improving on the home front. They were getting a settled feeling about the place. It could be called home.

The kitchen was separated from the living area by an arch. The window overlooked a walled in flower garden, at the back. The borders were already sprouting crocuses; an array of different colour, spring was here. It delighted Rita, her garden, even though she could only see it in the distance. It always brought a smile to her face. The front bedroom window looked over the street. The real luxury of the place was a bath; selections of perfumed bath salts were top of her shopping list. With a few scented candles the apartment was fragrant. Cooking was her greatest pleasure; so, she was in her element.

The living room's bright pink walls were covered in photographs of people partying? Rita got great insight to the lady owner's cheerful character just looking at the pictures. The room was laid out to maximize comfort. A red tweed couch set in a semi-circle, with a coffee table in front of it. Reading lamps, paintings, blue cushions. It occupied Rita's mind to dream of the way she was. After a while it got rid of the bad memories of hotel existence. She knew this lady must be a beautiful person; she wanted to take good care of her home. There wasn't any need to worry about that.

Down on the street her husband was returning from work. He stood to admire the big tree opposite their building. A horse chestnut they could see it from the bedroom. The buds were beginning to sprout. Soon the whole lot of it would be covered with flowers. He ran to his apartment building leaping the steps up to the front door. The night's sleep was sounder; the work was getting him fit, life was good. A neighbour told Rita those steps were called 'the stoop'.

In true New York tradition they could sit there to relax when the weather got warmer. To pretend the tree across the road was in their front garden. We can spend a whole month watching squirrels mating on its branches, he told her. Not the kind of information she was interested in hearing. But he knew that. Rita was easy bait for a negative reaction to perverse notions. She always made her case with ruthless determination. He hooked her in all the time for the fun of it. Only to wish he didn't sometimes. She'd defend her stance steadfastly. That was the good part.

"I'm busy cooking something nice for you," she informed him kindly when he came in, sharpening her voice then giving instructions. "You will shower before dinner because you're not getting into my white sheets tonight. Stinking like that, no way. You're not putting a smell around my dinner table either."

Rita was her bossy house proud self again. Not much point telling her about showering in the hog hut. She had already voiced her opinion on that place. Just the name alone was enough for her.

She could imagine the smell of pigs in it. Now that was good enough reason to have another shower, better again if it was the second one that day. It was great to see her getting into the run of things. A pain in the ass hearing it, there was no getting away from it.

"Okay, maybe the two of us could fit into the shower."

"I'm ignoring that remark, too busy for fun, try not making the usual mess. There's nobody paid to tidy up after you, most importantly, clean the shower."

She scolded, as if he was ten. He had to take his orders like a good boy. Things were improving; she had him under control.

"Right, missus, will do, missus."

She hated missus, seen it as a put down, but she wasn't inclined to go for the bait. Much too intent on cooking, listening to her favourite song on the radio. She sang along with it. If it drowned him out that was too bad.

He thought about other things he could say, to hook her in for a bit of devilment.

"Broads are all the same randy hot one minute, ice cold the next," he sang out when the song finished, making for the bathroom.

She went after him all right, a menacing look on her face. "I heard that, I'm not a broad, awful tag for a woman worse than missus if that's possible. Broads are the unfortunate women you with the rest of your crony's lust after. The pity I have for those poor girls having to listen to that stupid nonsense all the time. Just give your mouth a clean out while you're in there."

"Yes, missus."

"I'm nobody's missus, told you that a hundred times." She turned on her heel wriggling her ass back at him. "Bet you never saw anything as nice as that on the street. You randy old hog you."

These antics made them laugh, silly behaviour, play acting they called it.

He rubbed soap through his hands in a frothy lather. Things were shaping up nicely after all the hassle. Maybe that bit of luck had finally arrived. It would take two month's work in Ireland to equal a week's wage here. He could now realize a house built for Rita. The tunnel work could pay for it in a short space of time.

They might be going home in less than a year. That was reason to remain focused. He knew you could stay too long in New York, if you were light headed. It was easy getting carried away with the run of it. Just to think of Onion Head's meagre existence in the Celtic.

How could anyone want to live like that? Not that it bothered the drifter from Boston; he appeared immune from it. He didn't seem to mind being the butt of every joke, victim of the barmaid's wrath, treated with contempt. It wasn't fair the way life turned so bad for people.

That happened when you finish up being nobody. Everyone can do what they like to you then. But in spite of it all he had the character left to smile his way through it.

What was he doing beforehand, that made this current situation a better place to be? It must have been hell. Without a home, just a dirty place in the basement, a bed of old coats to sleep on, a rat for a buddy. It couldn't get much worse than that. Onion Head didn't seem to need anything else, content with his lot. How did he manage to lose so much pride? Was there a way back for him, did he want it. Or would he die living like that? It could turn any direction.

Joe lay in the bath after his shower. The scheming never left his head. Horse breeding with Rita, her business knowledge would be valuable. The going was tough but the prize was worth fighting for. Happiness was her goal in life, she always said. It sounded so simple he didn't know what it felt like. She promised to bring him there if he listened to her. He was no good at listening, never having formed a habit of it. No good at school either, couldn't be bothered listening, far too occupied with his thoughts, a mind that never stopped enquiring.

He found it more interesting than what was forced on him. But there was always something stopping him getting there; that elusive place to find what he needed. Would he know it when he found it; he hoped he would, else there was no end to it. It was a concept he couldn't figure out yet. It might be a help if he knew more about it. Maybe that's what he needed, worldly experience. More knowledge about life would enable him to make better decisions. That was simply it. They couldn't all be such crazy options. Some of the bad ones he'd been subject to were hastily made. The heart ruled the head. If he only knew what the right ones were, he'd know a lot. It was always the same; questions piling up, testing his spirit. There'd be no better place to learn some answers than America?

The small apartment they shared in Ireland was confined. He wanted to build a house of their own, stables near the back, so he could hear his horses whining. They had a name picked out for the house already 'Bo Ness'. That was the name of the small village in Scotland where Rita's grandmother originated from. It sounded like a nice place, a visit there sometime was part of the plan. Something left to do when everything else was nearly done. The house would be built in natural stone with enough space around it for a garden. Joe joked that it would be a stable yard with flowers in it, not a flower garden with a few sheds for horses. They talked about it designing every detail; Rita came up with new places for flowers every time. He accused her of being a bee in a previous life. She didn't rule it out in fact she rather liked the idea. Bees were such an important element in nature's plan she claimed.

He began to think about his old job. Having to give it up when he was doing so well was a source of annoyance for him. Secure income was difficult to obtain in Ireland.

Chapter Seven

His job entailed travelling around the country as a commercial sales representative, wearing a suit to work every day, like a banker. A big American refrigeration company moved into Ireland to service the retail grocery trade. The consumer revolution was spreading fast throughout the country. Small grocery outlets would soon be a thing of the past.

Every little town wanted a new supermarket. His company could provide refrigeration equipment to cater for all expansion requirements. The shopkeepers vied for advantage over the opposition. Demand for refrigerated display units, cold rooms, was big business. He'd been lucky to get one of four jobs available in Ireland; a position with good prospects for a young man thinking of getting married. His footballing exploits gave him a profile in the area he worked. A county player representing the company was good for business. Everybody wanted to talk to a footballer. The wages were good; a company car with all expenses paid, commission cheques gave him more security. He was his own man working the area where he played football. Would his previous work colleagues or customers believe what he was up to now? Sand hogging was a big departure from the white collar status of company representative. How many of them would think he was capable of doing it?

Like most young men he spent his leisure time seeking out female company. This couple he knew invited him to a house party one night. He jumped into the back of the car with them.

It sounded like a tame event but he'd persuade them to leave if it was boring. As things turned out it became a life changing experience. It was the first time he ever saw his future wife. He made his way to where the attractive girl stood talking to an older woman.

Dressed like a bit of class she must be on vacation in the locality, he reasoned. Most likely home for the holiday period these attractive girls sometimes showed up for a party; in the middle of nowhere. He heard her asking if anyone wanted to try some chicken. He waited for his chance to get talking with her. The way she looked would keep his mind occupied for a while. A blue polo neck sweater clung to the outline of her shapely curves. Tight jeans, with black boots on the longest legs he'd ever seen. That look finished it off for him; he panicked making an awkward attempt, with a lame approach.

"Do you work here?" he spluttered out when she passed by him feeling like an idiot the minute he said it.

But she had a question for him. That was more to the point. "Why do you ask?" she enquired with a relaxed smile.

He couldn't answer that simple question. The brain cells rattled empty. All he could do was gaze into her eyes, big pools of wonder. Her confident presence overwhelmed him.

He wasn't familiar with the powerful attraction symptom yet. This lost in the middle of nowhere feeling was a first experience. He managed a more precise request next time.

Can I have some food, please?"

"Of course, I will help you." She took a plate off the table, moving to a pan of cocktail sausages. "Would you like some of these for starters, chicken here too, if you'd prefer."

She was still smiling. Was she laughing at him for asking the stupid question, he wondered.

"Yes sausages, chicken would be nice."

"I'll get more chicken from the kitchen."

He watched her coming back carrying a tray. "I'm Joe Flanagan," he announced full of confidence.

When she put the tray down on the table, he hoped his footballing reputation registered with her. In this area it sometimes did. He knew that playing for a successful team gave him an advantage with the ladies. It had worked so often in the past. This time it didn't seem to click. She was oblivious to football, not referring to it. He would have to think of something else. But she was doing the talking.

"How do you do my name is Rita, helping out my friend for the evening. Ruth the daughter of the house here is my best friend in boarding school."

She spoke with a soft cultured accent it sounded English. On holiday in the area he presumed. That explained everything; these girls were usually worth the chase.

He wanted to make amends for his earlier blunder. So he took into the story to rescue all stories, a more thought out version of that first attempt.

"When I said 'do you work here' I meant 'do you live here'."

"Oh, I wasn't sure what you said, I was listening to music."

He thought about that one for a second. The sound of music was the most noticeable absentee in the 'party' atmosphere.

"I don't hear any music."

"My little radio, in the kitchen, I can hear it, let me show you."

It was a sedate affair, older people gathered in familiar groups eating, drinking. The talk was all about Christmas; it would be upon them before they knew it. They were drinking hot punch; all of them had the same rosy cheeks as if they were getting a Christmas look about them. This time of year when lots of pretty girls came home on holidays, adding a little spice to the festive season, with some mystery too, for these social occasions.

She returned from the kitchen with a small radio in a black leather case. "See here it is, I've used it all through school, my constant companion."

"Can I have a look?" He turned it around in his hand feeling the softness of the leather. "It's got a lot of handling. When were you at boarding school?"

"I'm finishing this year. I will miss it." She spoke with regret. That surprised him.

"You must enjoy boarding school, I didn't like the place."

"I enjoy it, except the abuse I get on the hockey field. My height is a disadvantage. I'm like a beanpole," she laughed.

"Abuse?"

"Yes, I get a good bashing with sticks to the legs. I'm a house leader at school. Some girls take the chance to cut me down to size. I can give it back as well," she assured him.

He noticed her jaw set then into what he presumed was 'this fierce hockey field look'. A pre-warning she was capable of handling any matter that needed sorting. This inner strength made him smile. Her easy going manner, the natural warmth drew him in.

Love at first sight is a powerful order. That feeling of difference stayed forever with him. This connection remained through everything happening to them from that moment on.

It was a meaningful night; he had a notion to tell her everything. This was not the usual procedure as far as he was concerned. Only the foolhardy spill all in the beginning; he soon discovered it wasn't an emotion she succumbed to as easily. She maintained a perfectly reserved distance. Approachable at the same time, so conversation flowed. It was hot in the house but he couldn't take off his jacket with the tattoo on his arm, remembering to keep it well covered. He didn't want her looking at it, wondering what she'd think of it. He wished it wasn't there any more. Maybe the mark of dubious character would drive her away.

In the crazy world of not knowing what to do, he rolled up his sleeve so she could see it for herself. He didn't know why he was doing it. But it felt like the best thing to do.

He couldn't hide anything from her; some other kind of thinking came over him. She didn't seem to be the least bit put off by the sight of the tattoo; instead, she talked about learning from mistakes. There was nobody that hadn't made them. As to the benefits of lessons learned, she laughingly suggested, it might be a good enough reason for making them.

Her honesty refreshing, her critique easy on the ear, he enjoyed talking with her. There wasn't an ounce of pretentiousness about her. He realised she was special, a touch of class, this rare specimen you hear about, but seldom encounter. Any time she went away to serve food he remained rooted to the spot, waiting patiently for her return.

The dating protocol was based on rural values. It was important for young men to have good prospects. They knew all about playing the dating game. They usually sought to embellish their chances through fiction. It wasn't such a bad thing; girls were accomplished in the art of make belief as well. All sorts of stories were concocted to attract an interest. Truth might out eventually if the attraction blossomed. The cause always seemed to condone the means, giving slim chance more hope. Capturing a girl's interest was an acquired art; the craft came later under the stars. A passionate evening the ultimate goal, one that didn't make any allowance for falling in love. That misfortune couldn't possibly happen to men; women were the only ones subject to that most undesirable fate.

As the night progressed he became enamoured by her. Fondness gave telling lies a miss. There was more freedom not having to remember them. The easy way they connected on that first meeting set a relaxed mood between them. As things progressed respect created a bond that would stand the test of time.

When his friends announced they were leaving the party he'd be left stranded. That was okay, he let them head off without him so he could talk some more. They chatted about horses too. He was thrilled to learn of her interest in breeding. Surprised by the experience she acquired listening to her father. If she didn't know something she'd confess to a lack of knowledge on the subject. She could have bluffed him if she liked. He wasn't as well versed. He couldn't imagine what it was like to be so naturally honest. She made it seem so easy.

They discussed films, found common interests in music. When he invited her to see a movie showing locally she agreed. The Bridge on the River Kwai, with Alec Guinness, was the one everybody was talking about.

When people started leaving the party the night came to a premature end. Rita excused herself to help her friend tidy the house. A kissing attempt didn't present itself; there would be another time, when the desire was mutually felt.

He parted company with her, going out into the night with a carefree feeling in his head. It was one of the few times he'd left a party without drinking a lot. That was when something better took its place. A pity he didn't apply the successful remedy permanently.

Life's secrets don't come easy for the young at heart. The adventurous nature of free spirits puts a different slant on many things. He had a fifteen mile walk ahead of him; it would take some time to get home. That didn't bother him at all. He opened his hand near a window to look at the piece of paper she gave him. Her telephone number was written in a stylish scrawl. He took great care how he placed it in his inside pocket.

The journey was bound to feel shorter thinking about her. When he set off down the road his head was filled with the nicest thoughts, enough there to last for a hundred miles. He'd met the girl he was going to marry, without doubt he loved her. The feeling took him over; all he could think about was meeting her again. He could listen to her reassuring voice forever.

Chapter Eight

Monday morning the sand hogs were wrecked after indulging another ravaging weekend. Hangovers have the same feeling no matter where you go. As Vietnam Duggan's gang made their way into work, grumpiness cut short the usual mindless banter between them.

Flanagan was chatty enough though, he hadn't felt so good for a long time. With the home situation in such a healthy condition there was time to think about other things bothering him? "What do you guys think about Limpy's alligator story?" He asked the question of nobody in particular.

"He's full a shit." Mitchell picked up on it quick enough.

"So what happened to his leg Red?" Flanagan persisted.

Duggan had something to say about that, he cut in to explain it. "He walked through the tunnel, up to his knees in shit; I'll tell you what happened to him, jams his foot in a hole; fuk'er thinks an alligator's got him. He hacks with a pick at the thing that's biting his leg. Getting no insurance money was the killer part of it I'd say. That drove him mad altogether."

"Hacked his own leg, yeah man, he was our boss dem days," Butcher added some mystery to the story saying that. He was a stocky beast of a man with black shaggy hair, wild eyes, a dumb expression with no intelligence to change it.

"Shut up, butcher, you know nothing about it, right." Boss Duggan's reprimand, closed him down.

"The foot shattered when the alligator had it," Red Mitchell said, drawling it out. He was never as weird as when he tried to be normal.

Joe Flanagan had developed a morbid fascination for the freaked out caretaker's story. The thought of their secret slimy presence spooked him a lot more than he'd like to admit. Both his legs were necessary for putting his financial worries behind him. How could you start up a horse business without legs? He was glad he'd never be working anywhere near alligators. They were giving him nightmares thinking about them.

A spill of torrential rain left the muddy ground slippery near the door. "Limpy, clean the muck up, you with that alligator shit freaking my men out."

Duggan bullied the old caretaker as soon as he rounded the corner, working himself up into boss man mode before the shift started. This week he was determined to lead the wall chart, his outfit needed some respect. He was pissed off, the hillbilly gang winning the tunnel drive done his head in more. It was hard to put up with their attitude strutting around the hog hut as if they were hot shit.

He had a bad thing for men from the Deep South–it wasn't about to go away. Something he harped on about, venting his scorn. At every opportunity he let them have it. 'Them no good hillbilly bastards could have got me killed in Vietnam,' was one of his favourite comments when they were in earshot. That made it impossible for the hillbillies to tolerate him.

Lupe the oddball miner from Tennessee spotted them coming in. Looking over at his cronies he winked raising his voice. So the taunt could be heard around the hog hut. "Hell, man, taking that crazy Vietnam Duggan out, is a mighty good day."

Duggan heard the snub all right, but took his anger out on his regular target Limpy. "Hey cripple don't touch my coffee."

The caretaker put his head down, shuffled awkwardly away.

"You want coffee, Flanagan, that's your poison right?" He shoved a hot brew into his hand.

Duggan's gang used the lockers at the jukebox end of the hut. Doyle was sprawled on the bench in his work gear, listening to his song again. He eyed the boss warily. "Chill out, Duggan, we're going to kick ass.''

"You'd better not limp round the hog hut Friday night. When I'm full a free whiskey. I'll take the other leg off you with a bite, alligators me ass." Duggan roared at the caretaker when he was leaving.

The old guy kept his head down cleaning mud away from in front of the hog hut door.

Shapers were sand hogs holding registered work papers that didn't have a full time job. They provided casual cover for men failing to show up for work. This practice called shaping the job had its own rule of conduct. When a boss took a shaper down to work he knew the story. If the shaper got work for three consecutive days, the job was his. If the boss wanted to hold the job for his regular man he'd use a different shaper each day. There was another rule that made some of the men wary of them. A shaper could claim any sand hog's job that didn't possess a proper work permit. Singing dumb around shaper's was the thing to do.

Flanagan didn't bother going into the Celtic any more after work. He hurried home instead to his new found family life. Rita got him more involved, helping out with their little girl's needs. His laboured attempts at nappy changing amused her. She soon dropped the idea.

He helped out with the daily exercise routine. That was enough for the time being but she resolved to keep him at it. There were excuses offered but she persisted.

Sober time made him appreciate more the pleasure of her company. He kept remembering how lucky he was to have her. Enjoying a few cans of beer at home watching TV was Rita's reluctant compromise, so she could keep an eye on him.

The Sunday lunch tasted like home too. Roast beef, potatoes with mixed vegetables. A long-time family favourite served up with gut busting desserts. She was full of praise for a wonderful

Polish butcher she discovered on the corner of 52nd street. All the trouble he took cutting the beef rolling it the way she liked prior to cooking it.

They got into walking excursions at weekends, a different direction each time, to get to know the area better. Things were looking up for them at last.

The American Museum of Natural History was first up for discovery. They carried the baby carriage up a hundred steps. Well that's how many it felt like when they reached the top.

It was such a wonderful experience in there, beyond anything they could have imagined, full of learning too. Plenty of realism gave them a fascinating insight of the past. They spent all day ogling the exhibits till evening time came. It was only the start of their adventures, strolling through Central Park was a great escape for them. Wide open spaces, horse drawn carriages. A rural environment for people to roam, a charming old stone bridge curved over water, shaded by trees. Like a picture postcard scene from any place except New York. Now what more could anyone ask for, in the centre of the city there was a picture of home, Gapstow Bridge. This dream place resembled the way it was before everything went astray.

An old man told them why he brought his monkey to the bridge every day. He wanted the little guy to see the trees, where he came from.

They felt sorry for the monkey so close to freedom, yet trapped on a chain, so far away. They could identify with his plight. They seemed happy in each other's company though, just like themselves. They took Mary around the park identifying picnic spots for the summer months.

Their favourite hangout was a quiet spot near the lake's edge watching ducks. Discovering the wonderful spectacle of carriage horses pacing around the green oasis, they made a pact to try it out one day. The Wollman Rink, the Carousel, seemed like wonders of the world, they felt like kids again. Central Park let them forget their troubles for a while. For a few hours every week it brought them away from where they were, closer to where they longed to be.

Rita knew Fifth Avenue wasn't far away, just over there behind the trees, near the Plaza.

A grand old hotel, if all accounts were true. They should have taken up residence on their arrival, instead of having to settle for the dubious comforts of the bird shit hotel. They joked. Now the bad memory of that place seemed far behind them. Fifth Avenue would be there next time round. When they had a few dollars to spend, Rita could tell stories about shopping in New York. They were settling down at last, a routine was taking shape, their lives were becoming manageable. The city was beginning to feel like a nice place to live in.

In spite of themselves they were enjoying it.

Chapter Nine

John Duggan devoured a breakfast of scrambled eggs with bacon. He didn't acknowledge his mother pouring him another cup of coffee.

Marie Duggan was always glad to recall her happiness when John returned from Vietnam. Sometimes she got dismayed at the noise he made with his street women.

On those occasions he entertained them in the apartment on W.48 th St. She'd take her rosary beads from under her pillow, pray God would understand what the war had done to her only child. It was never during prayer she remembered her husband Thomas. The night he left for work, never to return. When she later found out whom he was living with, the pain was unbearable. Sometimes she walked to the Celtic to stare in through the window at the painted barmaid Rosie–the shameless hussy that took her man. She hated her so much she'd like to kill her. She wasn't going to lose her son no matter what happened. God would be preparing a special place for her beside him in heaven. For all the trouble she endured in her life.

"Are you working today?" she ventured to ask him.

"Nope, have a meeting." He spoke hesitantly from the side of his mouth.

She turned to face him, raising her voice. "You still employ that hussy, Rose, in the Celtic, her that cast a spell on your father?''

He looked up with a blank expression snarling through his teeth. "You go down there looking in at her through the window. Don't ya, yer old scarf tied around your head so nobody can see you. Everyone knows it's you, can't you see them laughing at you?" He spewed out his irreverent slang like he talked to his workmen in the tunnel.

Marie Duggan would seek comfort in the good book. Crossing the room, she took it from a shelf. She carefully selected her passage before she began to read.

"It is said, if a man goes from his wife to become another woman's, he may return to his wife again – having played the harlot with many lovers - greatly polluted thou will become ravaged – said the Lord."

She looked at him coldly before closing the book, turning to put away the breakfast things.

When John Duggan volunteered for Vietnam he qualified for Special Forces. There he rose to the rank of sergeant, planting mines behind enemy lines. During one of these missions he was caught with a booby trap. His school pal Doyle carried him back to the safety of base camp, bravely fighting rear guard action with Viet Cong all the way. They were soul brothers since childhood. The injuries Duggan received on that occasion could be blamed for his impotence. But the mental scars went deeper still.

The money he earned as a sand hog foreman wasn't enough to support his lifestyle. But there were other ways to get his hands on extra cash. He had an angle on a few of them. Business interests would keep him close to Hell's Kitchen. His house in Jersey was a welcome refuge when he needed out of the city. There were times when he had to escape the religious bullshit. He had a private life too.

The Good Book reading was her way of getting messages across to him. She hoped it would make him alter his ways. Why did his old man leave him stuck with her? He blamed his mother for putting Thomas out to mass on Sundays, a place he never wanted to go. He would visit the Celtic instead, chat for an hour with the barmaid. Rosie O Connor accepted him for what he was, so he moved in with her. If his mother had done that, there wouldn't be a problem. He didn't like her prowling the street at night stalking the barmaid. He knew that she was the talk of the neighbourhood; it was making him look bad. He was losing some of the hard earned respect, convinced people had for him. That wasn't good for business.

Back at the Manhattan site, boss Duggan hadn't turned up for work. Red Mitchell was making the most of the nonappearance–assuming the leading miner's role in his absence. With a self-important swagger, he recruited the service of a shaper. The gang was still at the bottom of the chart in the general foreman's hut. Mitchell wanted to change all that.

He was confident that he could make a name for himself. With Duggan's absence an opportunity presented itself. Down in the tunnel he roared orders just to hear the sound of his voice. He mimicked his boss shouting at Flanagan to work the air spade faster. "Put a bit a power ina da fuken ting."

Standing at the face beside him Doyle gave the other spade hell. In the midst of this thundering noise the earth tumbled down burying the shaper up to his waist–welcome to the real gang sucker.

'We work like son's a bitch's on this job. See if you can take it. Shape up or ship out'.

A time worn ritual, designed to test the new guys metal, he would be gone next day.

As soon as the shaper struggled with a heavy boulder it gave the boss another reason to shout. He remembered what to say. It was roared at him often enough. " Com'on put a bit a power inta da fuken ting."

With Butcher's help they got the rock into a skip. Then they set about clearing enough space for a ring of steel. Butcher lifted the top plate of steel on his shoulders. They would have done this job thousands of times before. But the pressure brought to bear by the new foreman changed the outcome. This time protruding earth knocked the steel forward, it came down severing half the shaper's finger. The petrifying scream filled the confined space when he stared at his mangled hand.

"Tie his hand with a rope; stop the blood, butcher." Red Mitchell's shout was more timid this time, half his confidence gone.

The rope they used for sealing joints was lying in a bucket of smelly creosote. Butcher cut a length of it, attempting to console the shaper. "You gon'ta be okay, man, except he laughed when he said it.

Butcher's rasped voice alone would startle most people.

When he tightened the rope around the man's wrist the scream could be heard down the tunnel. The creosote burned into the wound like a kettle of boiling water.

"That'll sterilize it," said the Medic with an insane looking grin.

Enough there to make anyone wish they were dead.

The temporary boss was in radio contact with the lock keeper. "Get a dam loco in here quick. I need another guy down here right away, Bruno."

He cut the radio dead, sounding off with a snarl. Then instead of giving the victim any pity he blamed him for everything. The future leading miner job had slipped away, he knew that. So he got stuck into the shaper to rid his frustration. It was his fault.

"Hey, ya should have shaped some other gang ya clumsy fucker ya. We have to waste more time looking for yer fuck'n finger now." He glared at the ill-fated shaper, shivering in shock.

The next shift down would be the hillbilly gang. Duggan's outfit were doomed with ridicule sure to follow this accident.

The hillbilly guys would tell the story the way they wanted it heard. Not only did one of them lose a finger the tunnel drive wasn't complete. The hillbilly outfit were only too pleased to finish the last ring. Their boss Wispy Steel ordered Lupe to be respectful about it. "Be cool Lupe, let it lie, Vietnam Duggan's ass will burn on its own."

Next day Duggan had a lot to answer for. He tried to explain that correct protocol took place. Every rule covering the absence of a leading miner catered for. His gang were properly briefed on all important regulations. Sullivan the company trouble shooter wasn't accepting that. He told Duggan that a dick head like Mitchell shouldn't be in charge of anything. Doyle was the only one qualified for that job.

Maybe he should take his gang outa sight till it blew over.

"Go work maintenance for a while."

Duggan knew what he was saying. Red Mitchell had let him down. He'd never forget it.

After the accident, the hog hut buzzed with speculation. The story of a complete novice in charge was everybody's word on it. Sullivan recommended that Duggan's gang be taken off the job for a while. There wasn't much Duggan could say about that. The way he was fixed.

The hillbilly gang were seen as great guys. They made up the ground lost by Duggan's gang as well as fulfilling their own shift. It made heroes out of them. They liked that, it justified them busting their balls doing it. It meant everything to them that Duggan's outfit was in the shit. Now that they had bragging rights forever, they could set them off just by sneering at them. Pure hatred simmered more than ever. Rivalry took a step higher than competition level. Rage turned ugly in the heads of bitter men. Madness has a way of going around crazy.

It makes some effort for a while, leaves naked intent simmering, for as long as it takes. Then it does what has to be done.

Flanagan sincerely hoped this extra work he was doing would break up the aggro he felt in the hog hut. When Doyle brought him on his rounds to show him the night job routine, he looked forward to the change. It would be a nice sideliner for him, a white collar job like he said. But before that first night was over he was under no illusion what the deal was. He soon picked up on the resentment by some operative runners they called on.

There was a suggestion of violence that made him very nervous. Doyle introduced him to the customers as the new guy. Some of them didn't seem to appreciate the visit; they made it known to Doyle. But they handed over cash anyway, just to get rid of him. To help lighten up the otherwise tense evening, Doyle told him stories of his love life, between calls. But his stories never mentioned names it was all about descriptions. He explained how he usually finished up with the woman he chased, a high success rate, he boasted.

Some of it had to be exaggerated Flanagan surmised. He seemed such an unlikely playboy. Listening to his stories was a way of getting to know him. Even if the tales were told to impress, it was another side of Doyle's character, a much lighter one. The shady business of a numbers game was Duggan's best money maker. It kept his name alive on the street, a gangster to be feared. The mere sign of faint hearted effort would be seen as weakness.

In this law weakness presented opportunity for a predator to take over. Duggan, the master of takeovers, would be watching for that. It wouldn't happen to him. If you're taken once you can be taken any time, the way he saw it. He had availed of faint hearted participation by opponents in the past. He could smell its unwilling presence now. Others in the racket had operatives working runners from cars, bars or street corners. The poor areas bet small, but there was plenty of money for gambling. No tax on it sweetened it even more. There was credit available too, not to be had in legitimate gambling. Aqueduct Racetrack was the most popular bet in New York. The last three digits of the day's total bet, was the winning number on the street? Everybody knew about it. If the track's total take was $15,158,253 the winning number would be 253.

Doyle called around collecting money from operatives. They in turn collected from runners carrying money with betting slips. The cut got smaller down the line, starting with Duggan at 25% Doyle's at 10% so on. It was worth the risk for gang leaders, providing cash to finance other operations. The illegal incomes were laundered through owning legitimate bars or hotels for prostitutes to ply their trade. Sometimes it happened that operatives couldn't pay Doyle. Having spent the money was usually the problem, but no excuses were accepted. Shorting the HQ fund was discouraged. Discipline was always violently administered. They knew that coming up short was risky business. Runners were beaten or sometimes killed.

If Doyle was ever challenged, his reputation alone sorted it. All he had to do was pull on the tight black leather gloves, a clear message. It didn't have to go any further than that. A sensible decision was reached without any action ninety percent of the time.

Flanagan knew it could turn violent any time. It was dangerous; he was expected to do it. That was something he wasn't prepared for. He owed John Duggan for his financial help. But he wasn't going to break the law for any reason. It wasn't in him. How close to breaking the law was it going to get. He wouldn't be getting involved in any criminality. That line he was not prepared to cross. The intimidating nature of the whole thing was too much for him. It was a business they were prepared to maim or murder for.

He was back into drinking booze, the living nightmare end of the stick again. They kept telling him to keep his mouth shut, difficult for a paranoid drinking man not knowing what to say or who he shouldn't say it too. He didn't want his wife figuring it out either. She was already talking about leaving New York. That didn't suit his plans; it would take longer to make a go of it without her support. That's why they were there in the first place. He must stay safe for a lot of reasons. It he got caught immigration would have him deported.

He made up a better story, lied about the job. A debt collecting agency might sound good. When she saw the boozed state of him coming home, she was in no doubt. No matter how he protested, she knew what his nights were all about. She wasn't stupid. Couldn't she smell it? He was becoming deceitful about everything. With things going so well, she forgot to keep her eye on him. Quietly like it happens, the worry crept back in again. She wondered what was going on. Her experiences told her when things seemed perfect. A change in direction was the most likely turn of event. Now she was heading back into the suspicion quarter again. Everything comes under scrutiny in that situation.

She hated the annoyance of dreading something. The thoughts of coping with it haunting her, while he pretended sleep without discussing it. They had been there before.

He kept the alcohol level topped up all the time, drinking vodka so she wouldn't get the scent of it. By times he didn't care, dumping a few whiskeys on top. He told irrational stories with a change in his voice, talking like in the movies. She reached the point where she wasn't able to recognize his behaviour any more. It was breaking her heart to have those strange feelings for the man she loved. When she thought about it, booze was the worst thing to come between them since they got married. In any partnership, if you don't trust who you're hanging with any more, you haven't got a hope. Chances are you could end up hanging on your own.

Tash Doyle approached the building that Flanagan never wanted to see the inside of again. The bird shit hotel loomed in front of him like a den of iniquity. Doyle couldn't give two damns about shit like that, more intent on talking the new guy through the routine.

"Not your concern how they feel about you, just remember the names. Don't forget the faces either. If they don't have the money ready that's not your problem. You're just the new collection guy. They know there will be someone along later to sort out any problem you encounter. They know all that. I'm talking about shit you can't handle. The real heavy stuff, Flanagan, this guy in here is an asshole, hasn't long left on the team. Know what I mean."

Dulche the janitor just ignored the Irish guy, as if he never knew him. He was more interested in telling Doyle the bad news. "The cops are still snooping around since the broad was stiffed on my watch."

"I don't know what yer talking about." Doyle was in no mood to listen. He stuffed the envelope in his pocket. The guy wouldn't let it go.

"Look, her drug habit got heavy on dollars, nice kid too."

"We gotta go."

Dulche got cocky when Doyle started to leave. "I'll have to talk to the cops, if any more shit happens."

"Enjoy your vacation," Tash called back to him.

The janitor was full of fight. "Vacation my ass, I know too much," he screeched.

"The guys that look after our business interests aren't nice to be with," Doyle told him walking to the door, with Flanagan on his heels. When he heard all that he wondered if Doyle knew he lived in the place when the girl was murdered. Or maybe he didn't care about that either. He didn't know what the story was all about, but it wasn't good. He'd forgotten it when he hit the street with so much to think about.

But these guys weren't concerned about anything, as long as nobody interfered in their business. He wouldn't be worrying Rita with all this bad stuff. He was more concerned about telling Duggan that he couldn't do it for any reason. There was the fear of a backlash with his day job, getting dumped of the sand hog gang. It wasn't like he was an essential part of that operation either. The undocumented thing was a constant reminder of his vulnerable position. He was always aware of it. It was a topic spoken about in hushed tones by illegal immigrants throughout the city. These were decent people, that didn't like breaking the law.

But they were desperate people too. Eager to work, pay taxes, contribute to this great country they lived in. The desire to have a job was a powerful survival factor. It didn't notice barriers.

Fears of getting deported from America gave him constant worry. The shame of being sent back home, barred from re-entry was everybody's dread. What could he do now, the answer was straight forward. Don't break the law for any reason; abandon the numbers racked side-line immediately. It was that clear cut. One night on the job told him all he needed to know. But how was he going to get out of it. The pressure was too much for him, he was getting more unsettled. Rita was watching everything closely. He could see that.

Chapter Ten

Fridays were depressing days for losers in the sand hog unofficial tunnel race. It couldn't come quick enough for winners though; the hog hut was getting a taste of what the best sounded like. The hillbilly outfit had won it again humiliating Duggan's gang in the process.

Sure, they were a crazy bunch, but boy could they work. To make the win a more memorable occasion they brought their banjos in to the job. No point being the best gang, if ye can't rub it in with some ole banjo picking music.

As soon as Duggan's gang surfaced from another tough shift they walked straight into hillbilly celebrations. This triumphant banjo music was driving Duggan crazy. "Scumbags, Tash, for bringing that shit noise in here."

The big man with rhythm in his soul was enjoying the sounds of it." What's up, banjo music's good-relax, man, get into it."

"Into it me fuk, I'd like to break the thing over his head."

"Two banjos going down there which one is annoying you?"

"Don't you be an asshole too, Tash. I thought you'd be the last one to turn on me. Is there anything sacred in life any more?"

Duggan had been complaining about his gang doing badly in the competition. He had his excuses; he blamed the ground, the heavy going with all the rock in it. He knew some of the other gangs weren't bothering their asses with the competition. They saw through the scam.

Why should they break their balls working harder for booze when some of them didn't even drink the stuff? So all they had to do was beat the hillbilly. But the rock was stopping them.

Doyle pointed out to him the same rock slowed the winners down too. The ground was just as bad for them. Duggan had nowhere to go. His desire to be the best was driving him mad. It was difficult for him to accept the hilbilly gang's superiority. He hated them with a vengeance, particularly the loud mouth Lupe. There was some history there with him.

Sullivan the company man called around to the Manhattan job regularly. He often tried slipping some whiskey in the caretaker's coffee. The company man was interested in having a snitch in the hut. He knew how valuable it would be to have someone eavesdropping on the workforce. But the caretaker wasn't interested, he had a long memory. He'd done Limpy wrong in the past. Sullivan spotted him listening to conversations several times. It was a hog hut rule not to let the caretaker hear anything they didn't want repeated. It would go straight to the ears of the general foreman.

The shift rotation brought gangs into contact periodically. Open rivalry reached intense level with the tunnel competition. As Mario knew alcohol could blow the lot up. The slightest incident could spark it off. He took a gamble hyping up the rivalry. He was depending on the company to buy in, if things ran smooth. He had his son on the job working with the men. That was an ear on the ground he could rely on. As soon as this contract reached its intended target he'd call a halt to the competition.

Tunnel men were prone to a gut felt dislike for each other. That played into the hands of dissent. Petty jealousies moulded opinions that carried prejudices for men aggressively primed anyway. To sort out their differences, sand hogs wouldn't hesitate to use violence as the only alternative. It could be said they wouldn't let a whiff of agro get past them.

John Duggan's hatred of Lupe cut deep into his psyche. Because he was doing so well in the tunnel race, it ate away at him.

"Outa the way, Limpy, you crippled son of a bitch." He took his anger as usual out on the caretaker.

Lupe, his tattooed fingers plucking banjo strings spotted him coming down the hut. Singing words of his own to suit the mood of the moment. "Duggan's gang can't win shit a looooooser for shoooo." He bawled it loud enough to be heard across the river in Jersey.

"Ignore him he's drunk," Doyle warned.

"If he's looking for trouble I'm ready."

He didn't stop, kept moving on for a shower. Doyle played a few songs on the jukebox to chill things out.

The second banjo player shouted, "Dem trash just turn jukebox up, drown us out, we winners an all. Can't beat us down the hole, can't drown us in the hog hut."

"We smother them assholes anytime or my name ain't Lupe man."

"He don't like you none, Lupe, that Vietnam son of a bitch, c'mon boys let's kick ass."

While Duggan was having a shower, Doyle was trying to dump the bad vibes. "This shit will blow over in a few minutes you'll see," he was telling anyone interested in listening.

But he was wrong this time. It all kicked off with a bellow of rage from Duggan, charging from the shower. With his fists swinging, Lupe was expecting him. This time, there was nothing but aggression between them, the sickening sound of fist on bone. It had everybody in the hog hut rooted there on the spot. Sullivan the man with a gun for protection went pale. Nobody tried breaking it up.

The mesmerizing sight of men fist fighting is a compelling factor for males primarily. It's a reminder of challenge for supremacy in the herd. Who'd fall down in a heap first was the bloodthirsty requirement. Maybe spiteful madness spurred it on. But it was the bitter taste of resentful feelings that made it last. The likes of it was never far away from men like this. It must find some release no matter about the excuse. As sometimes happens in moments of danger action took on detail in slow motion. Every thud could drop one of them on the floor, but raw hate kept it going. Brute ignorance made it stand up for longer.

The whole fracas lasted until some of the men moved to intervene. Doyle tried to calm Duggan. His party lifestyle didn't keep him fit enough for battles like this. A fallen chief can have the effect of deciding hostilities. But there was no winner here.

Lupe bloodied, roared a few threats at his tormentor. "This not over yet, I could've killed the bastard."

Duggan gasping for breath shouted. "I'll take your fuk'n arm off, hang it in your locker."

Doyle worked the referee role, between them. "Leave it men, there's no need for it, leave it be."

Words were all that would happen now. A silence hung.

Every person in the hog hut felt the weight of its presence. In the kitchen where Limpy hid from the melee, he knew this wasn't good. Any time Vietnam Duggan threatened like that, a whole lot of bad shit happened.

When Limpy was a tunnel boss he discovered a big secret. It was so bad that even to this day, it could get him killed. There were scores to settle, all the ranting about alligators couldn't hide it either. Any kind of story would do, except the real one. He would see the end of this man one day, all he had to do was wait, that's what he was good at. Waiting!

Duggan threatened him every day of his life humiliating him with abuse. Would he ever get what he deserved, see who was crippled then.

Lupe should be good enough to do a job on him, if he was brave enough to try it. Sullivan, the company mouthpiece, wanted Duggan in the east river. Limpy heard the talk; he knew who was doing the talking. The caretaker had it all figured out in his own crazy way.

He mumbled the words softly to himself; 'It's time to feed the blind fish again'. Then he whistled an old tune sweeping dust over blood on the floor.

The hard bristled brush made more dust rise than it gathered. He wouldn't worry too much about that either. Smiling at the sound of madness in his head, 'what did the preacher say dust thou art dust thou shall return. He knew that's the way it was going to be. Didn't he see it all for himself one time?

The Celtic was quiet; Murtha the bartender sat looking out the window. He spotted the barmaid coming up the street. "Here's your old honey, Onion Head."

The little man slid off the high stool in some sort of a hurry. He accidentally bumped her going out the door. Rosie steadied herself against the wall, screaming after him. "Son of a bitch, midget," she muttered obscenities, seating herself grumpily at the bar. "Damn nearly knocked me over."

The barman put a large gin on the counter in front of her. "Did Onion Head make another pass at you, Rosie?"

She ignored him. Rummaging in her bag she put a twenty dollar bill on the bar.

"Hey, Rosie, don't, no need for that put it back in your bag."

"He's a dirty guy, goddamn drifter. Dropped his pants one day, showed it to me."

The barman laughed.

When Rosie got bored drinking alone at home, she took her exercise walking to the Celtic. She often explained this unfortunate affliction to ladies she knew.

It may have been a strategy to keep them away from the place. Just in case she diminished in their opinion for working there. She dutifully informed them that ladies never frequented the Celtic bar. Unless they got drunk somewhere else–were unfortunate enough to regain their senses in there. There wasn't even a ladies' toilet in the joint. She'd heard rumours over the years. Times people never came back to their senses at all.

But she never talked about the night her son left the apartment, to meet up with John Duggan. That was the last time he was ever seen. Rosie had her own ideas about what happened it was the reason she took the job at the Celtic. She remembered seeing the ring on Bobby's finger when he waved goodbye to her that last night. The blue stone in the centre of it matched his eyes. She was never going to see it again.

Looking in the mirror behind the bar she straightened her blonde wig. Then she adjusted the long gold earrings carefully. In a schizophrenic attack she ransacked her handbag for her lipstick. She applied the red substance generously, paying particular attention to the detail of her top lip, exaggerating the curious dimple giving it a heart shape. She liked Murtha, fancied him as a matter of fact. But you couldn't get a word or a drink out of him when he studied form for his horses.

With considerable effort she approached the door to leave. "Hope your horse breaks a damn leg, you Irish Mick. You remind me of my old man, no talk, no action"

"Bye, Rosie, take it easy."

She was almost lifted off her feet by the sand hog crew coming in.

"It's that great lady, Rosie O Connor."

"Come on have a drink with us, Rosie, don't leave now co's we're here." Tash Doyle had his arms around her attempting to kiss her.

"Will you stop bothering me, Doyle?" She was less than convincing in her protests.

"Sorry, Rosie, didn't mean to turn you on. Join us for a drink before you leave. We heard you're getting married to your roommate one of these days. Will we be invited to the wedding?"

"That bastard Thomas tried to screw me." Taking her place again, sitting up on the barstool.

"Ah no, Rosie, what'd he do to you?" The phony Doyle sounded so concerned for her.

Gin helped speak her mind; she was pleased to have an audience. "Well I'll tell you if you must know. One morning I was in my kitchen making coffee. I didn't have anything on, you understand. Yes, I was completely nude. I was just standing there naked when he rubbed it against me."

"Jeeze that's a bit much, I mean, did he have a hard on, Rosie?"

"You want too many details Doyle, you should know ladies never tell it all."

Before this exchange could progress any further Onion Head arrived back in the bar. Rosie had the perfect foil for her contemptible opinions. "Look at him, Murtha, gives him corn beef, the cabbage will make him grow."

The barman put his hand across the bar to give the little man a pat on the head.

"I'll have a beer, Murtha."

"Sure, but don't get drunk on me now."

When Onion Head got drunk he went down to talk with his best friend Archie the rat. That left the bartender with no run around.

"Where's Flanagan?" Murtha enquired putting the drinks up on the counter.

"Gone home to his missus, she rubs baby cream into his hands in the evenings," Tash Doyle explained, laughing. The barman didn't want the sand hogs straying off down the block. He knew when these guys were on the town money was for spending. Every round of drinks was a dollar tip for him.

Doyle removed his jacket to hang it beside the jukebox. He played his favourite tune, a mining song he lived into, he bellowed the words almost drowning the jukebox out.

Rosie gazed at him as if he was Frank Sinatra. She tugged on Doyle's sleeve when he stopped singing. "You have a wonderful voice, Tash, you're putting me to sleep," laying her head down on the bar for a snooze.

In the midst of all this distraction no one noticed the boss man Duggan coming into the place. He was bored for entertainment, so he lay into Onion Head for a bit of his own kind of sport. "Bring up Archie to the bar for a minute. I'll buy you a large whiskey, if you do it."

Onion Head heard what the boss said. He disappeared in a hurry down the steps to the basement. Then Duggan moved quietly to a barstool beside Rosie.

"Did you bring Archie with you?" Duggan asked, when the little man returned?

*"S*ure did, can I have the big whiskey now, Boss."

"I want you to do something for me first." He whispered it to him.

Onion Head sat on the stool beside the barmaid taking Archie from his pocket. He put him on the counter next to Rosie's face. Archie poked his inquisitive nose out to investigate the lipstick then all hell broke loose.

Opening her eyes, she saw the rat. A shrill screech sounded through the smoke filled bar. From the pool table the hogs wheeled. Just in time to see her falling back off the stool. Her blonde wig hit Duggan.

Onion Head grabbed the rat before running. He stroked him, talking softly to relax him. "Nice Archie, my friend Archie."

To see John Duggan laughing was a rare sight. The men helped Rosie up off the floor.

It didn't take long for her to recover. She bleary eyed scanned the bar for her drink. "Give me back my gin." She touched her head when the vanity returned. "Oh my God, where is my hair piece, get it for me please, Tash."

Doyle looked around the floor but couldn't see it anywhere.

When he got the bad smell he spotted something, he couldn't believe it. "Oh shit! No, Duggan, don't do that."

Duggan was torching Rosie's wig with his cigarette lighter. "You're a sick mother fucker, that's what you are."

Doyle poured the contents of his beer glass on the wig to douse the flame. Then attempting to dry it he rubbed it furiously on his trousers. It didn't look too good after that treatment. Because he was a real gentleman he put it carefully on her head. That final caring gesture got the best laugh of all.

"I saw a dammed rat on the bar, Tash," she was telling him.

"Are you sure, Rosie, maybe too much to drink? We didn't see any rats, did we, guys."

Duggan got Onion Head to put the shillelagh between his legs to wave it in Rosie's direction. She could see what he was doing.

"Is that dirty son of a bitch waving his thing at me?" She climbed down off the barstool, then, staggered into the toilet mumbling.

Onion Head slid up to Doyle. "She didn't like that, Tash."

"You shouldn't have done it Onion Head, scare an old lady. Leave it back behind the bar."

"Boss Duggan told me to do it."

"Don't give a shit; you should've more respect for Rosie."

It was the last thing he heard before he got hit with a sweeping brush. Rosie picked it up in the toilet with the full intention of nailing him. Delivered with all the power she could muster, enough to reduce him to a heap on the floor.

There was a loud guffaw from Duggan; it must seem like a Broadway show. He was quick to move over to offer the lady his valued opinion.

"I thought you'd hit him earlier, when he brought the dirty rat up from the basement! I tried to stop him but he wasn't having any of it. That rat could have taken the face off you with a bite, very dangerous, Rosie."

"Where in the basement does he keep the rat?"

"Downstairs in his bedroom, the rat has a family."

"Why did he bring the rat up here tonight?"

"To frighten you with it I suppose," he sneered.

"Did anyone put that idea into his stupid head?"

"Who d'you think would do a fuk'n thing like that."

"It had to be someone just as stupid as himself. That's what I think."

She looked around at Onion Head recovering, she screamed at him. "Your days are numbered you scumbag, get out."

He got shakily to his feet. Duggan winked, shook his head at him, behind her back. Onion Head could see the boss was on his side.

"Rosie, he just took a knock on the head," Doyle pleaded. "We got to keep him here for observation purposes."

He winked at Rosie who wasn't sure what that was about. But she trusted him.

He might be warning her that the creep could press charges. Getting rid of the vile creature could wait a while longer, as long as it didn't cost her anything. That was a consideration Doyle came up with to protect her interests. She helped herself to another large gin from behind the bar. Making sure boss Duggan saw her pay for it.

It was over an hour later when the Celtic closed its door. Like most neighbourhood joints it kept its own hours. Finishing time was usually up to the bartender, when the mood struck him.

Less than a city block away from the Celtic a tormented soul prepared for revenge. It was something that had to be done. There was snoring coming from the other bedroom when she pulled the apartment door silently behind her, looking stooped with the overcoat dragging the ground.

The dim lit corridor cast her blurred shadow on the yellow walls. At the street corner below, she stood to secure her headscarf, fixing the knot under her chin to pull down over her face.

When she arrived down at the Celtic she peered in the window. The Red Miller sign lit the wall, barely a glimmer in the place. Just enough light to spot someone asleep in the booth. She felt the rush of panic. Taking a big brass key from her pocket she opened the door. Tightening the gloves she saw the glasses on the floor, she stood on them. The light under the toilet door was on; she curled her lips making her way towards it.

The barmaid was slumped on the toilet bowl snoring. With her head lying sideways against the wall, drunkenness had taken away any pride she had in herself. The blonde beer soaked wig was splattered comically on her head.

But fun was the last thing this early morning caller had in mind.

It was six-thirty on the bar clock when the bartender unlocked the front door. He shook his head looking around the place. The cleaning lady hadn't shown again. There was nothing strange about that. If he owned the joint he wouldn't clean it either. Now he had to tackle it, he methodically arranged barstools first. He collected glasses, emptied ashtrays.

Onion Head was stretched in the booth snoring like a pig. His glasses were in bits on the floor. Murtha went to get the brush in the toilet. That's when he got the fright of his life. Rosie O Connor was sprawled on the wet floor; the green shillelagh was sticking out of her mouth. He could see she was dead. He rushed to call the boss at home.

John Duggan shouted at him down the telephone. "What the fuk you call me for, Murtha, eh. I don't want to know about it, call 911." He hung up on him.

The police figured they had an easy task; there was no back entrance into the Celtic bar.

The front door was locked; you didn't have to be a genius to know what the story was here. There was a readymade culprit sitting there waiting for them. He wasn't too helpful with information either, just saying his name was Onion Head. He lived downstairs in the basement; he kept repeating he saw an old lady in the bar. The cops weren't too happy with such little information. Who was he? Had he a record. They needed a background check.

"You were so drunk you didn't know what was going on. But you killed her, right?"

He told them all about the barmaid attacking him. He insisted he would never harm Rosie.

The cops pieced together the story as if they saw it happening. He scared the shit out of the old dear with a rat? Earlier! She hit him with a brush, knocking him unconscious on the floor. That's why he murdered her. Onion Head said his place to stay depended on the barmaid. He had nowhere else to go; he didn't want to go back to Boston. He couldn't harm her.

"Right," said the cop. "So you're from Boston. Now we're reading your rights. Taking you downtown, maybe you'll remember more about it there."

Onion Head couldn't understand why they wouldn't believe him. He thought he saw an old woman in the bar one time before going back to sleep again. He knew nothing more.

He was arrested on suspicion of murder. Cuffed, taken away. There was nobody left to feed Archie. That's what bothered him most.

'Poor Archie, no one cares for him any more," he lamented, when they were putting him in the police car.

Chapter Eleven

The grey Plymouth slowed to a crawl turning in off 10th Ave.

A young woman stared out at the Celtic bar; the driver was telling her all about it.

"That's the joint right there, Ann. We know that some people come to a vindictive end termination in that place. It was a butcher's store years ago. Now it's a bar, we assume some kind of mob headquarters. We've got nothing solid; they keep it real tight. The barmaid was murdered in there a week ago."

Detective Sergeant Ben Brady scanned the street as he talked. "It looks like they're busy tonight, let's go." It was not the first time he teamed up with Ann Spellman. He had a lot of respect for her. She worked undercover; the seasoned cop knew she was good at it too. If anyone could get near them, it would be her. Taking calculated risks in the line of duty didn't worry her. That bothered him.

"No past convictions, Ben?"

"They're clean except after hours drinking. We're holding a drifter called Onion Head, running a check on him in Boston, his prints were on the murder weapon. That outfit are connected to another joint near here. A Hotel whorehouse, guess I'd better show it to you. We have an open case on a working girl killed there recently."

The car surged forward.

"People in this neighbourhood are too scared to talk, Ann. We'll keep digging. One slip or loose lip is all it takes. For starters, we need you in among them."

"That's right, Ben, in amongst them, that's where I wanna be," she drawled, a slow grin breaking across her tight angular face.

This young woman followed a proud family tradition. Her father was a police sergeant. He worked the famous Precinct known as Fort Apache, in the South Bronx. She was thrilled to finish up there from police academy. It felt like joining the family business. Working the fringe of danger appealed to the young police officer. She relished exposing criminality taking pride in the fact nothing got in the way of success.

She was barely a year out of police academy when this flare for daring almost cost her life. Ben Brady was her partner on mobile patrol when they pulled over a driver. Hyped up on drugs he shot her as she approached his car. It was a serious shoulder injury that almost finished her career. She was a long time in hospital, months of physiotherapy before she could use her arm properly again.

The doctor advised time off from the job to shake the trauma. It gave her an opportunity to pursue her hobby of amateur dramatics. Immersing herself in character she found her alter ego called Betty Ann. It was such a wonderful discovery. There were things Ann Spellman the Irish catholic cop from Queens wouldn't do, which Betty Ann the undercover cop took in her stride. She treated life less serious. Making the story up as she went along was how she explained the difference between them.

They were a great team, one girl up for it, the other one wouldn't touch it. The good cop, the bad cop all rolled into one. The whole contradiction made perfect sense to Detective Spellman. On official police duty the world of undercover vice girl was where Betty Ann operated. Behaving like a prostitute, but living like a virgin was a conflict of interest for the attractive young cop. She claimed this emotional imbalance caused a whirlwind romance with a police colleague. They fell in love on a drinking session then married on the loneliness of a hangover. It turned out to be a huge mistake. Her new husband agreed. They called it a lesson learned.

Police work as a prostitute was predictable after a while. She applied for a transfer from vice to homicide. An interest in murder procedures developed. An elite undercover squad formed, she was rewarded for her experience. When a plant was called for, Betty Ann was dispatched on undercover duty again. The actor inside had more room to manoeuvre.

She moved into her new abode in Hell's Kitchen. A studio walk up on west 50th street, it was sparse. Not much in the place except a bed, a couch, a table. She picked up posters of Ford's latest models in a car dealership, covered the walls with them in an attempt to brighten it up. The small bedroom beside the bathroom had a full-length mirror. She busied herself putting the finishing touches on a new appearance examining the result in the mirror. No matter what, she'd look the part, turning to check her ass out; she pursed her lips in a pleasing smack. The tough part came with the facial make up, she rarely used it. So, she took into applying it rather generously. Then, it was only a five minutes' walk to the Celtic bar. She could hardly wait to get in there. Pounding pavements, making contact, would yield information. Looking like a harmless drop out young woman with nowhere to go. She might hear something, nobody would be suspecting her.

She knew the routine well, learned the hard way, working undercover. The job of being someone else, but never forgetting who she was came automatically. Now Betty Ann was ready for a spot-on stage again.

"Hello, what's up?" said Tash Doyle, when he spotted her. Reaching across the pool table, her jeans stretched tight, this was not a regular ass in his local bar.

"Is there something wrong with that broad?" he asked Murtha, the barman.

They were all waiting to see if Doyle had the balls to hit on her. He looped his leg over a barstool asking for a beer. There was lots of time to study his prey. No point rushing it, none of them would take her; it wasn't often he had such an easy run at it. She was good to look at too, dressed like that. A nice rounded ass made Doyle's nose work like a gun dog on top of his game. He relished the scent of it; to make things more enticing it was going nowhere.

"She might be a fuk'n cop," John Duggan boomed, loud enough for her to hear it.

She picked up her beer then to sit up at the counter. "Hi, you guys?" She held out her glass to them.

"Who the fuk are you?" Duggan demanded.

"I'm a cop."

Shrugging her shoulders indifferently, a daft look on her face, she eyeballed herself in the mirror fixing her hair. The beer glass tilted precariously in her hand.

"Careful with the beer, missy, don't mess up the floor. You're a cop are you, I see, where you working at?" A sneer twisted his face glaring at her.

"Well, nowhere right now, they kicked me out. I'm looking for a job around the neighbourhood. Not having much luck with that, they don't like cops."

Duggan started to laugh at her. He could see she was a nut job. The kind that was easily handled. Duggan liked them like that. She was attractive too; might spice up the Celtic a bit, having her around. If she was no good he'd let her go.

"Ain't that something, I can help you out here, missy. The guys like the look of you I can see that, ever done any bartending?"

"Sure have, mister, in Detroit; I'm good at it."

"Okay, we'll try you out for a while, take it from there." He walked over to put his hand on her arm. With parental understanding he assured her, "I believe everything you said."

He winked back at his cronies. "Murtha, give the cop here a beer on me will ya. Looks like we got ourselves a brand-new barmaid. Ain't that something?"

Rosie O Connor's murder depressed Rita Flanagan. She was like an American mother to her, with such colourful history; it kept her mind off all the other hassle sometimes.

Talking to her helped her understand life in the big city, a world she could never have imagined. Now it was her absence that Rita found so hard to bear. How could she possibly exist in this place without someone to take her mind off her troubles? When she confided her concern about her husband's drinking, Rosie promised to keep an eye on him, keep her informed. Between the two of them, they kept track of his whereabouts. Now since she was so cruelly removed from her life, she felt more vulnerable than ever.

She could never settle in a place like this. How she longed to be at home in Ireland, she missed her mother so much. The pain in her chest was heartfelt. Her child required constant attention. That made it hard for her to do anything else. The helplessness was the worst part; it would always be an empty space Mary lived in. She would never go to school or make a life for herself. No friends to enjoy girl talk or go dancing. Her life over, before it began. Rosie was the only one she met in New York that sounded remotely like a normal person. Maybe they both would be better off dead like her. Robbed of her comforting, staring in at the stove, it seemed like the only thing to do. 'Turn on the gas stove, go to sleep with Mary, never be unhappy again.' It sounded like the best thing to do.

But her family would be heartbroken, how could she do it to them. They showed her how to cope, gave her strength when she needed it most. Told her what she must do to get over the bad times. Always talk to family they said. Take care of yourself, things change, tomorrow might be a better day. Put trust in the power of God, pray for his help when you need it, he'll take care of you. Her husband was never going to drag her down lower than she wanted to go. Nobody would be allowed do that to her. Her father wouldn't like it. The family would blame themselves for driving her away. Maybe they were right when they objected to her marrying him. But that's what she did; now the rest was up to her. She must save herself care for her child. Changing her mind about doing harm switched off the demons.

She went into the bathroom to wash her face. Then she emptied her make up bag out on the floor. There wasn't much in it. Painting on a false face might help. The old one lived in for longer than she could remember. It had a nowhere to go look etched into it, police sirens screaming in her ears was all she could hear any more.

She tried to remember the good times. Those light hearted occasions when her mother instructed her how to make fluffy white soda bread for her sisters, scones, apple tart for the whole family, it was such a wonderful time, long ago. Telling stories that made them laugh so much, passing winter nights drinking cups of tea round the fire's comforting warmth. She needed to heal the hurt, be strong again to leave behind this city she could never understand, everyone in such a hurry, she with nowhere to go. New York was holding her in such an unfriendly grip, it made her heart ache.

When family feuds started her mother always took Rita's side. It was so good it had to change. The conflict arose between them one day amid the joy of her romance. Her mother finally broached the subject that had been bothering her for long enough. In the family tradition, saying it the way it was, she let her daughter hear it.

"Rita, are you aware that this boyfriend of yours, has the fame of notoriety."

She went rigid when she heard it. That even her mother could say anything bad about the man she loved. So, without any considered kindness then she let her reply go, the way it was meant to sound. "It's none of your business, Mother."

Rita with that blank look on her face, staring back at her, the jaw set defiantly. It was a moment in time. She had never spoken to her mother in such a way before then. It was the beginning of difference between kindred spirits. People like that, can keep it going for a long time. Nobody, it seemed wanted her to marry him. This constant attack from all quarters, the pressure of having to defend her man-made Rita stronger.

Twenty-one was old enough to know enough she imagined. The whole drawn out saga caused friction that never went away. Rita was not one for making excuses when it went wrong. A bit of effort would fix things at some later date when everything settled. It had to be like that. She must believe it, or else she would have nothing to hold on to at all.

After the police forensic job was complete Rosie O Connor's body was sent to the city morgue. There were no family members to shed tears over the corpse. Her one remaining relative was not interested in forgiveness. She disproved of her younger sister's colourful lifestyle, ignoring her for nearly thirty years. Marie the nun was consumed by shame when Rosie abandoned the Catholic faith, selling her body to pleasure men.

Some religious people it appears have a given right of moral authority to behave like that, even though it's against Christian doctrine to be unforgiving. Human nature always finds justification for prejudiced beliefs. Hypocrisy doesn't care about hurting anyone's feelings.

Someone else was trying to cope with her memory while playing the hypocrite as well. It called on him to visit her one last time in spite of the stress it caused him.

Dan Ryan struggled through the morgue lobby; his sore leg was acting up again. He grumbled out loud about how he shouldn't be there at all. It was such an effort. His only true intent was to establish for sure she was dead. He was obliged to pay these last respects to his son's mother. Someone convinced him it had to be done. He wasn't likely to break with tradition by getting over sentimental about her tragic death. Saying that he loved her wasn't going to spoil the party either. When he first met Rosie robbery was called work, everyone wanted a bit of that. Ryan was a young gang member in Hell's Kitchen then. He knew how it played out, watched it down through the years. Became part of it just like everyone else he knew, the rules were simple. The code of silence was money made, fear kept it in place.

He understood the ruthlessness of Vietnam Duggan's criminal activity. He knew what became of his son, where they disposed of his body. Rosie disrespected him too many times, so she would never know about it. That would have been dangerous for both of them.

She could have looked all over the Celtic, there was nothing to find. It kept her from tormenting him; maybe her curiosity got her killed. He eyed the body lying there on the cold slab. Trying not to remember any good times they shared. Yet, struggling to forgive her he vowed to make things right for their son. It was all he had left to do. That bit of venom he'd spew out in her direction. That was as reverend he'd get, the promise to settle it for Bobby.

Before leaving he rambled off his version of prayer, in a garbled slur. It was hardly a pardon but if she could hear it she'd understand. "So long, Belle of Hell's Kitchen, always breaking my balls give the devil the respect you never gave me."

While at that same time some distance from the morgue Rosie O Connor's last partner was doing it differently. Thomas wanted to spend time in the Celtic bar. A place Rosie had specifically forbidden him to frequent.

The bartender Murtha found it difficult to contain himself. This guy's flowery accent was pissing him off. But, he was Boss Duggan's father; there was a lot of shit he had to accept. So, he tried speaking respectfully. "I hope they fry that bastard, Onion Head, in the electric chair, sir." He leaned forward rubbing his damp cloth over the bar counter in front of him.

The comment sang dumb for his inebriated customer. "What might that be about, dear boy?" He asked him.

"The drifter that murdered Rosie, he's called Onion Head, sir."

Thomas preferred to remember her in a more positive way.

"Oh yes indeed, a popular lady my dear friend Rose. My son John was very fond of her too. When he called to tell me the sad news, he cried bitterly. He was so upset about the awful tragedy. They didn't always see eye to eye mind you. It was all on account of his mother you know. He's very close to her. Neither of them forgave Rose. Because they think that she persuaded me to leave home, that's not true at all. I can assure you about that."

The bartender didn't want to hear all this shit. It sounded like something he shouldn't know about. A shrewd judge of mood swings, he'd met them all. This guy assuring him about anything was bad.

He'd something on his mind, when he leaned closer to whisper a question. "Is the cleaner lady coming in here today?"

Murtha frantically wiped the bar, this dude was killing him. Why didn't he take off to a gay joint or something like that? The questions were not welcome either. "No, sir, boss told her not to come in for a week. I made the call myself, sir," he replied, before moving off towards the end of the counter, as far away as he could get. Murtha knew a lot of things. Bartenders hear everything; say nothing when it suits them.

Thomas bore no physical resemblance to his hulk of a son, who, he claimed took after the mother's side of the family. That was how he explained the obvious physical difference between them. Thomas worked a doorman's job in a Park Avenue building. He was supplied with a stylish green uniform that he kept well pressed, the brass buttons polished up like a general in the US army. He was a dapper kind of man that loved himself. Under normal circumstances he avoided the Celtic. But these were not ordinary times.

Like everyone else under the influence of booze. Standards became automatically lowered. His son John would like him to move back home. He urged him to get over whatever dispute he had with his mother. But Thomas wouldn't even consider doing that. The times spent in a family without any emotional bond were lonely days for him. He had stacked up too many years squandered already. That left a lot of anger drifting between them. It wasn't going to disappear overnight. The vicious banter he sometimes engaged with Rosie was never heartfelt. They fought sometimes, but remained connected in a union that didn't require the trimmings of love. Now he really missed her. Their secrets died with her, they'd never be revealed to anyone.

He was subjected to his wife's religious beliefs at home. When he no longer wanted prayer in his life, she refused to accept his wishes. They both agreed to abide by certain rules before getting married. Just to have it all forgotten after the event.

His wife found her peace communicating with God. In the family home that belief lay down rules. Standards based on her interpretation of Christian values. He no longer wanted any part of that. Such an intrusion created distance between them. This intensity she brought on him so demanding, long before it became intolerable. Thomas carried out his duty diligently, keeping true to his promise of providing for their son. Honour bound, he accepted the lifestyle subjected upon him. Until Rose finally rescued him by giving him a nice place to stay. Anything she laid on him more pleasurable by comparison. To the hell he endured long enough.

When the noisy sand hog crew arrived into the Celtic, he was pleased to see his son. He called out, inviting him to have a drink. The rugged mining boss had other ideas, giving instructions to the barman. "Cut him off, Murtha, he's had enough, call a cab too. My mother won't like all this shit."

Duggan ordered his father out to the sidewalk, then he jumped into the cab after him. He demanded to know if he was going home to his wife that always cooked his favourite steak. Onions, mashed potatoes with trifle afterwards too. Just the way he liked it.

But Thomas was not that far gone. He responded bitterly, for such a genteel man. The alcohol soured his thinking when he let fly. "I would rather starve out the rest of my life alone, than hunger for the love your mother never gave me."

He turned around in the seat to face his son. "Do you understand where I'm coming from, John? Tell me that, please."

"I don't care where you're coming from, Thomas. All I know is you left me alone to listen to religious bullshit. Day in day out it never stops. You don't seem to care either."

The driver stopped his taxi on Park Avenue. He wasn't getting any help from his passengers. He interrupted their heated exchange in the back of his cab.

"Come on, guys, that's enough take it somewhere else."

The miner got out, helped his old man with some rough assistance. When the driver dropped the window to collect his fare, it was the last act he remembered doing. John Duggan's fist hit him a vicious blow to the side of his head. He slumped in his taxi as if he was having a nap. Calmly the aggressive tunnel boss took his dad off up the street, without as much as a backward glance. That pent up fury would always find an outlet, no matter who was on the receiving end of it. Somebody had to get it then. The driver was just unlucky.

"John, listen to me, the driver didn't deserve that."

"Fuk him, he was talking when he should've been listening."

The cruel intimidating sneer was there, a sobering effect on his father. He'd been doing all the talking; he knew there was nobody off limits, from the wrath of his son's uncontrollable temper. Violence was always his way when it came to sorting problems.

Thomas had known about that for a long time.

Chapter Twelve

Detective Ann Spellman sat in the East side diner. She was relaxing, drinking a big glass of orange juice. Too much coffee fluttered her heart, she told Ben Brady.

"You're killing me telling me this shit, Ann, you told them you're a cop." He stared hard at her. "Are you serious or busting my balls."

"No, Ben, it went down just fine, trust me, they think I'm eccentric."

"Oh yeah, I wonder how they got that idea."

She laughed at him.

The sergeant could see himself telling his boss who had him on a short lease already that Detective Spellman disappeared without trace. The chief was sceptical about allowing her into that Celtic place from the beginning.

"I know shit about this mission remember that, Sergeant, in case it doesn't work out. The roaches under the floor know each other in that joint."

The chief already held him responsible for failure. If successful, then it would be a different matter. Brass was always there, standing by for the credits. Detective Brady was well aware of the risk involved. Ann took a bullet with his name on it once, now she was putting her life on the line again. The difference this time around it was him that proposed her for the job. If anything happened to her, he'd feel fully responsible. Someone else should have taken this assignment. It was too personal, but he should have thought of that sooner.

"Ann, you need to run some of this shit past me. I don't want you taking unnecessary risks."

"No, Ben, you left it up to me to get in amongst them, now it's up to me. I heard them talking about me. Said I was a nut job. They're convinced I'm an idiot. It's going to work out, Ben, trust me, I'm into it now. Where's your balls, Sergeant?"

"On the line, Ann, first hint of trouble you're out of there, tell me you got that."

"Yes, sir, I got that loud an' clear, sir."

She saluted him, in that crazy way she thought was funny. How he wished she'd take the assignment thing more seriously. But then, if she acted normally, she couldn't swing it.

The murder of the barmaid spooked the detective. He was having second thoughts about the Hell's Kitchen mission. That wasn't something Ann wanted to hear. She let him know it.

"I've only been in the bar a few times. I'm just getting to know these guys."

"If they find you out, you're dead, Ann."

"Lighten up, Ben, all undercover work carries risk, part of the job. Now are we going to move on from talking about not doing it to more positive thinking? Huh, what do you say, Ben Brady, let's shake on it, let's go get them."

As they shook hands she posed the question. "Why was the barmaid's body just left there, they could have dumped it, right."

"It's strange, Ann, why would they do it in their own backyard. Why whack an old barmaid? What could she have known? It looks more like that drifter, a revenge attack for the way she treated him."

The sergeant stirred his coffee cup, looking across the table at her. "It cannot be mob related. No there is something odd about the whole thing. Even the fact that this outfit would allow a murder on their property is strange. It's not in their interest to have police all over the place."

He referred to the Irish shillelagh as the possible murder weapon. He wondered about the significance of it. Could there be some sort of ritual motive in that she asked.

"She was strangled before that Irish souvenir thing was stuck in her mouth. The Irish shillelagh is just a crude stick, once used for grudge fighting in Ireland. Is someone saying she was killed on account of a grudge? No, that can't be, but maybe it is. You'd better start looking up Irish grudges, now that's some minefield to consider."

It was difficult to equate this act with that timid individual called Onion Head. But his prints were all over the murder weapon, right now he had questions to answer. He didn't seem to have any interest in answering them. He kept repeating that there was an old lady in the bar. Sometime in the middle of the night, it was all a blur he said. He knew nothing more about it.

"It doesn't make any sense; maybe he's trying to hide from us. We are doing a background check on him in Massachusetts. We'll figure him out soon enough."

There were a few more important things Brady needed to get across to her, if only to satisfy himself that he had covered everything. To remind her once again how dangerous a situation she was in. It might help him sleep better at night too.

"Most of the Duggan gang was brought in for questioning. They know nothing of course, nor did we expect them to say anything of significance. They're hardened criminals; know how to conduct themselves under interrogation. They don't let much slip. There was one thing we discovered though. The barmaid's wig wasn't recovered from the scene. Her lipstick was missing too; her big gold earrings not in her ears. That was strange, considering her handbag; money, were left there untouched."

"The killer must have taken them."

"Well they didn't walk out through the locked door, Ann. If we get the blonde wig, the earrings, we got the murderer. The drifter didn't have them, we searched the whole property. We even got into that locked room, the office with the black door. Duggan likes keeping his business private, nothing wrong with that."

"Wouldn't it be more like a woman to take woman's gear?" She suggested in anticipation.

"Where's the sense in that, you're implying the drifter did see an old lady in the bar. Can you find out if there are many old ladies going in there?"

"There's an old cleaning lady that starts very early in the morning," she said, in a matter of fact way, sipping her orange juice looking at him.

"Nobody reported that fact, you know anything about her?"

"I only saw her once. Dresses like something from the old days all in black. An Amish sort of person that never talks to anyone, strange woman, I believe."

Then she told Brady about the old couple that sat listening to country music on the juke box all the time. The woman said she went to school with the cleaner. She knew her all her life. But it was strange the cleaning lady never once acknowledged her?

"When she left the bar, the jukebox woman tried telling me about her."

"She's John Duggan's mother," she began in a whisper, but her husband shut her up as soon as she started. Right there in front of me. Told her it was none of her business. I just thought it weird, why so much secrecy about the boss's mother cleaning the place. Big deal, in Hell's Kitchen everyone's scared about knowing anything. That's the way it seems to me, Ben, if the guy in custody saw an old lady, maybe it was the cleaner woman, that early in the morning. But why didn't she discover the body, report it to someone."

"We thought he was giving us a story, to convince us he was drunk. If she's got a key, we should have known about it, everyone with a key has questions to answer, Ann."

She explained how she was trying to make friends with the old couple. Particularly the woman, she might be more inclined to talk. They lived in the neighbourhood all their lives; they must know what's going on round the place. But the husband was blocking everything.

"I'm working on getting them to trust me. I also want to find out more about them. See who they are connected too. Everyone

114

around Hell's Kitchen seems to be related, Ben. I can't ask too many questions it will take more time snooping around."

The sergeant reached down under the table to get his folder while he talked. "These sand hogs work regular jobs, live double lives. It's hard to keep track of them. They might seem to be ordinary working guys; but they are into other things as well. Most of them have criminal records since they were kids. I want you to stay focused know who you're dealing with. The more you know the safer you'll be."

He took a picture from the briefcase, placed it on the table in front of her. "This is Duggan the bar owner you know that. Tunnel boss, Vietnam, call him what you like. He runs many rackets, loan sharking, prostitution, murder for hire. Just to name a few. He's chief suspect in the barmaid's son's disappearance. Somehow, I know, involved in that hotel murder."

"I've seen all the pictures already, Serge."

"Good," he said. "Now let's see if you remember much about them, tell me about this guy."

She gave him a salute. "Yes, sir, he's Tash Doyle," fluttering her eyes, "the friendliest of them all."

"Stick to police work, Detective, we're merely the observers. Take this guy here for instance, his name is Mac Williams. He once worked in a slaughterhouse, that's where his nickname, Butcher, comes from. He's known to be damn handy with a knife. It wouldn't worry him if it's still alive when he skins it either."

"Ben, you're making my skin creep."

"Good here's the ferocious thug known as Red Mitchell. He enforces the gang's hostility, does all the thinking for the illiterate butcher Mac Williams. Tells him who to skin."

He noticed she was concentrating a bit more.

The detective produced the last picture from his file. This time he handed it across the table to her. A photograph she hadn't seen before, so she stared hard at it. The older man in the photo had unkempt grey hair, his bulging dead looking eyes made her shiver.

"This guy's name's Dan Ryan, the barmaid's long-time boyfriend. He would be capable of murdering her, have no doubt about it. He might have wanted to do so over the years. I have interviewed him on a few occasions for different reasons. He's a complicated bitter man.

The only reason he's not a possible suspect is because he would have done it out on the street. He can't walk too well, wouldn't be sneaking into bars late at night where John Duggan might see him. Anyway, I don't think Ryan murdered her. His only motive was hate, that's being around for a long time. Maybe hate was the real motive for this murder. Whoever carried it out? Do you have any questions now, Detective Spellman?"

He looked across the table at her again, shaking his head. She didn't give a damn, he knew that, impossible to scare her. The line of duty dictated the pace of events for her that's all that mattered. The risks didn't really deter her, that's how she worked, the real deal. There was no point trying to change her style now. That might be a shame.

"Hey, you want to eat or what, are you cooking at home, taking care of yourself."

"Hell's Kitchen's where I live if you want to call by for a meal sometime."

"If I was not a happily married man I'd take that as an offer?"

"No, Sergeant, don't do cops or buddies any more. Been bitten already, not into bosses either. More particularly married bosses, so you're out on all counts."

She twigged his nose with her finger in a childlike reprimand. Pretending to be disappointed, but she knew he wasn't. She was always glad to have him there in the background. When things got tough, she could depend on him, hope there was enough time for him to arrive with back up. Detective Spellman liked meeting up with Sergeant Brady. She would never underestimate his valued opinions.

Their banter was normal for colleagues on the force, underneath all that, she had a lot of respect for him. It was all

116

about connecting the loose ends. Hard work can solve most crime eventually; there would always be the ones that got away. A bit of luck sometimes changed everything in bringing the perpetrators to justice. They hoped for as much as they could get.

Chapter Thirteen

For three long boozed up days, nights full of squabbling, the rugged rascals ran.

Duggan's gang plagued the bars in midtown Manhattan. Winning the tunnel competition was driving them mad. They even ventured the doors of a gay bar, Doyle's idea to see if Red Mitchell would succumb to its atmosphere.

Like most other places they visited, their stay was brief, usually responding favourably to requests from bar staff, 'go try another place'.

Known everywhere as ball breakers, nobody wanted to see them coming.

The thing they had in common was a passion for gambling, a love of drink, with special intent on brawling. If someone as much as looked at them hostilities broke out. In spite of Duggan's optimism, 'every two bars that didn't serve them, there were 'ten that would' it was a problem finding them. If only they knew which bar the hillbilly gang holed up in. That would be some sort of special treat for freaked out bar staff.

They slept little, whenever exhaustion overtook them. Leaning over bar counters or crashed out in booths. Not losing power of the limbs was what the marathon entailed. Slow beer drinking to maintain the high. Occasionally a few shots of whiskey to keep madness lit. That extra ingredient fuelled desire to keep going, pumped up for some far out zone that understood madness. Sinking shot glasses full of whiskey into big mugs of beer, glass an all. This mixture, boilermakers, would keep rational thinking at bay. For as long as it lasted. It was a lesson for Flanagan, how to pace a serious drinking session. An education he could have done without.

"When you're this long on the booze, Flanagan, there's something you should know. You gott'a walk as if you have a foot on each track in the tunnel," Duggan informed him, staring hard with that spaced out look of his, frothy slobber congealed around the side of his mouth. Like vomit on a sidewalk Monday morning.

"Why is that then?" He shouted from the side of his mouth, trying not to look at the state of him.

"You know wide apart so as not to fuk'n stagger," the boss explained.

He was already mimicking the slow deliberate sidewinder walk. The ambling bear like gait presented him with a different message. As if it was the natural behavioural character action of a seasoned sand hog, a role Flanagan at last felt qualified to assume. Having spent so much time stooped below, moving around up top was unsteadying.

He'd been doing the walk for a few days, that's why he hadn't fallen over. Having completed the full circle, running out of friendly places to go, they were back in the Celtic again. Acting more subdued in spirit, fatigued physically from their antics in the bombed out zone. That space, where drinkers get the impression of doing all they want to do, but can't remember a thing about it. Their new host, Murtha, wished they'd stayed there, when they were so terrifying. What could he do but put up with them. He couldn't refuse to serve the owner with his bunch of ball breakers. Much as he'd like to.

"I'm going to work tomorrow," Red Mitchell not happy with his thoughts spouted out. It might have been an attempt to crack the awkward silence.

"You couldn't work up a hard on, Mitchell." Boss Duggan picked on him straight away. The tunnel accident disaster was still a painful memory. He'd have to deal with the fallout for a long time to come.

Any thoughts like that quickly registered annoyance with the boss. "Why is Betty Ann not working? She puts a bit of glamour in the place," Doyle said, steering Duggan from confrontation.

"Why don't we all go down to the tit bar?"

"Holy shit, Red, now you're talking."

Doyle could see it happening already.

"What's a tit bar like?"

"It's like a whorehouse, Flanagan," said Mitchell, pleased to be so informing.

Doyle laughed, hoping to draw him on a bit. "Easy now, Red, we'll go to the topless place first. See if we can raise expectations in there. We'll have to watch Mitchell he's hot to trot for sure."

Doyle got a kick out of the red haired man that knew nothing. He figured Mitchell's limited experience of the fair sex was about as useful as his tunnel knowledge. Helpful as tits on a bull he used to mutter when he looked at him. Flanagan wanted to get there to have a look at New York's raunchy side for himself. Going home to his wife never entered his head. It didn't dawn on him that she'd be worried. Into the heavy drift of alcohol consumption, he was in a different world. With the power of booze reason had long since vanished. He might be grateful for its absence.

Somebody called two cabs; Doyle gave the drivers instructions to travel in convoy. So nobody got lost.

Flanagan spotted Doyle sitting up in front. Like some sort of man about town. Wearing the recent purchase a wide tweed cap, that gave him such a distinguished look. He told him he was like some posh farmer back in the old country. With lots of money in the bank, land all around his house, a load of kids to keep his moustache trimmed.

Doyle tipped the rear-view mirror away with his hand, much to the driver's annoyance. He fixed it for himself. The thought of them puking all over his cab was his big concern. The smell of booze made him think about it. From his many years driving drunks, it usually finished up on his floor. If he got them there in a hurry, they wouldn't have time to throw up on him. So he drove like hell towards his destination.

They sat in silence as the yellow cab sped through Manhattan. Flanagan watched New York flashing by, the neon lights blinking in through the window at him. The gloss of tinsel town vanished. The streets got darker. Solitary figures shuffled through the shadows becoming shadows themselves, in this bleak kind of other world. The grim look of it sobered him.

"Where are we now?"

Nobody answered him.

"Hey, driver, what's this place called."

"It's the Bowery, man!" The cab driver shook his head. With a cynical laugh he looked in the mirror at the guy slouched on the back seat. He didn't look like a ball breaker, more an asshole maybe. But there could be a tip coming, he must remember kindness was business.

Slow, like a preacher he said his bit. "Those poor souls out there look like human beings, not so. They lost for good, yes sir, poor sons a bitches!"

He sounded so sad it looked like even cab drivers could have feelings.

At the next traffic lights the windscreen got splashed with water. A bearded dishevelled figure holding a dirty rag was intent on cleaning the window. That's when he took off into more familiar cab driver territory. Dropping the window he gave him the special cabbie blessing. Formed over the course of time by cabbies that seen it all happening before.

"Git ta fuck away from my cab, dirty scumbag, go get a job," he ranted, ducking the contents of the bucket when the man splashed it at him. "What's going down in this city, man, homeless motherfucker," he complained, rubbing the water off his clothes, powering off. Good vibes disappear when bad vibes remember.

It wasn't long till he pulled over in a brighter part of town. The name Dolls Home lit up in big pink neon letters over the entrance.

Three burly doormen gave the sand hogs a good look over, before letting them in.

The beat was fast, pulsating, ready to go music. Flanagan's mouth hung gaping at the horde of topless beauties. Up there, they danced on a high ramp. That stretched from one end of a mirrored bar room to the other. They paraded seductively, cavorted teasingly peering into the snake pit of leering men. Where, out of reach dumb rabble roused each other up for a hint of promise ¬ anything, to imagine sex.

"What do you want now, Flanagan, bitch or beer?" The laughing Doyle pleased with the reaction wanted to show how much he knew about it. He danced around, pure product of the sleazy way that gets you noticed. The rest of the gang were restless, unconnected with the power of the place. Doyle moved closer to the ramp, eyeing a tall attractive blonde. She gazed down under hooded eyelids, pouting at him, swivelling her hips, struggling to control such fiery passion. Was this a wonderful promise of things to come, was she going to strip the lot off.

Flanagan waited for it to happen. The booze took him on many journeys in the past; this might be one of the best. Such a place wouldn't allow him to remember his responsibilities wherever they were.

"She's thinking money the bitch, that's all. How much she's going to take off the ass holes tonight, getting no dollars from me," his boss bellowed into his face.

"Duggan, I don't want to talk, I just want to watch."

He moved away from him, closer to Doyle the man of the moment. He had shaken off the tired fit, now he was tuned into an impressive recovery routine. His hands above his head clicking his fingers swaying his hips he grinned up at her as if he was hers. Not unlike a Spanish gypsy, synchronising her subtle moves, making her laugh.

She raised her arms higher to encourage him. Every movement copied by the man in the cap, dancing together, having fun. The blonde was answering the call. There was a happening going down between them. It appeared.

"Will ye look at Doyle my hero?" Red Mitchell was drunk enough to be envious. It got worse when he got competitive. He moved in beside Doyle. In a vain attempt to compete he tried improving the show. His dance routine was not as polished as that of his friend. With convulsive jerks, frantically pumping his knees, flapping his arms like a cornered chicken. It looked so strange, as if he was shaking off the pain of a boulder falling on his toes in the tunnel. Not something you'd ever pay in to see.

On the ramp the blonde turned her attention to a new arrival. The tall man stood near her, his black Stetson too much for her to ignore. She snatched it off his head to manipulate her well-developed bosom into its crown, arching her back, stopping it slipping from its cosy perch. She wriggled it for her appreciative audience to applaud. The owner didn't want all the attention, or like what was happening to his hat. He growled at her demanding it back. When she ignored him, he sprang up on the ramp to grab it off her chest.

"Tash, look at your man will you." Flanagan pulled on Doyle's arm excitedly. "He took the hat off her tits, Tash, I saw him."

The guy wasn't hanging around, running for the door before doormen put him through it.

Doyle seized the chance; with the guile of a true predator he approached the ramp. Removing his cap he presented it to the blonde dancer, with a bow. This gesture was well received; her ego had suffered a slight setback. It was only temporary.

She responded well to the confidence boost, brightening instantly. Smiling she walked up the ramp spinning it around her forefinger. At the same time talking down to the reptiles hissing at her from the pit below. For a few seconds soliciting dollars vanished, warmth came to the fore. Gazing coyly at her rescuer, the smile was real, Doyle could see that. The grinning hero waited for her dance routine, he wasn't going to be disappointed.

She buried her face in the crown of Doyle's tweed cap. Looking down at him she called out for everyone to hear. "I can smell kindness from this cap. Here's something any woman would know. Tonight I've been honoured by a real man. Not the asshole that just left."

Blowing a kiss in his direction, she started to dance. Doyle returned to the bar beaming with delight. Duggan looked at him distastefully as if he had just diminished as a man before his eyes. But Tash rejected all negativity showering praise on their surroundings.

"I'll tell ye, guys, this is the place to be. There is nothing like a room full of topless women to bring the lust for life back into any good man."

He remained immune to the silent contempt of his boss. Instead he set about giving the party atmosphere another shift, calling over a beautiful young waitress serving drinks.

He tried rallying the gang from alcohol induced blues.

"Hey, guys, over here, let's see what this pretty lady has to offer."

"She's a gook." That was Duggan's opinion of the young beauty.

"Come on over, Duggan, nobody's listening to you, we hear enough shit from you down the hole. I want to buy the guy's tequila from this lovely kitten here. A little bit off Mexico goes a long way?"

The rogue laughed heartily at himself, as only such characters can do.

"That's the last you'll see of your cap, Tash."

"Who cares, Duggan, when was the last time a lovely lady put her tits in your cap, eh?"

He winked up at the blonde dancer on the ramp wearing it proudly. Doyle wouldn't mind if she kept it for herself. He was delighted to play his part in restoring some dignity to his artistic angel of mercy, as he called her.

Wouldn't the world be an awful dull place without the sight of them?

"You're an asshole, Tash, that cap cost you thirty bucks. Are you letting her have it for nothing?"

"Leave it, Duggan; I don't give a shit about the cap. She'll give it back if she wants."

Duggan couldn't believe that Doyle was so stupid. To think a woman in a club could be a decent person? He laughed at the crazy way Doyle's thinking worked.

"He thinks the bitch is going to give him back his cap," he roared into Red Mitchell's ear.

"She could do," Mitchell said, too drunk to concentrate on saying the right thing.

"Now I'm going to open a book on the return of the cap." He rummaged in his pockets taking out a fifty-dollar bill.

"Hi, Tash, over here, Flanagan, Butcher, you guys, let's see who has the balls to cover this fifty how about that. I say the whore does a runner with Doyle's cap."

"Duggan, there's fifty on top of it, I'm taking it all myself." Doyle planked out fifty on the bar to Duggan's absolute delight.

"You've gone soft in the head, Tash, bitches do that to you. Now it's going to cost your fuk'n ass."

Duggan scoped up the money but Doyle held on to his arm. "Let Flanagan hold the bet, that way I'm sure I'll get it," he rasped, with a steely look, the chill factor. Even Duggan wasn't going up against that.

The two guys took off looking for better company to spend time with. This party might burn out if some excitement didn't keep it lit. Duggan was like a bucket of piss on top of everything. He'd quench the flames of hell with his attitude. Everyone knew that.

The Mexican senorita was all smiles. A petite beauty with long black curly hair tied behind her head. A scarlet ribbon held it together, big gold earrings looped to her shoulders.

Flanagan told Doyle she was like something you'd hang on a Xmas tree. The bikini she wore didn't take much material to make; it was scarlet to match her lipstick.

"Scarlet the sunshine colour in Mexico, I know that cause I was there," Doyle was telling Flanagan.

"You guys like tequila?" she asked, her Mexican accent flavouring the words. "Right lets have five shots."

She turned to Doyle still smiling, after pouring tequila into glasses on the tray. Her long scarlet finger nails tapped the bar counter, expectantly.

Doyle paid up for the lot saying, "I'm getting this money back from the boss guys."

She gave him a cute mascara eye flutter with a smile. "Catch you later, amigo, adios." Off she went purring down the bar, to hook someone else up.

"I never had a drink of tequila, Tash, have you?"

"Sure have, Flanagan, remember getting bombed one time on the shit…"

His speech trailed off when the cap was placed on his head.

The dancer leaned her perfumed smell close to kiss him on the cheek. She had a soft drawling voice. "Thank you for your cap, my friend."

He smiled back at her, that special Doyle way. "It's a real pleasure, lady." The words polished too.

Flanagan spotted it happening. A flickering eye contact melting time, the vibe good in the Dolls Home, one doll was hanging round for a while longer. The energy around her soothing the moment, the enticing smile was there, this time it was real.

Watching them chatting, she was attracted to the moustache, he thought. He wished he had a moustache as well. Then he'd have to work on the smile that was pushing it. Some things were all style, that ingredient was a natural call; it couldn't be acquired any other way.

Doyle was the only one he knew with that charming way of displaying teeth. In Flanagan's foggy opinion, the rogue was beginning to take on the appearance of a Mexican gentleman. Did Doyle have a natural ability to transform, or was it planned purposefully. Like a predator blending with whatever happened around him, to take advantage of his unsuspecting prey. In any case the guy was as good as it got.

But it didn't matter when she liked him. "I want to buy you a drink," he heard the dancer say.

"Sure, that would be nice, if you can join me a pleasure." Doyle was as cool as you like.

"Yes, I'm finished for the night; I must put some clothes on first. I will be back soon, okay."

She squeezed his hand for a little promise maybe. Flanagan was beginning to believe all Doyle's stories now, so impressed with the slick moves. He was convinced the whole hat move was strategy, from the very beginning. Nothing could be as polished as that.

"Tash, it was the look that clinched it, I saw it all."

Doyle wasn't getting too excited about anything.

"She's a west coast girl, here in New York."

"Oh, how do you know that?"

"I know by her accent."

"Right, she might be just the one for you, Tash, you never know."

Doyle looked at him sharply. "What she wants from me, Flanagan, is not romance. She might have seen enough of that already, I'd say." He had a swig from his beer. "No, I'm going to jump her bones, shove her all the way back to California. The only romance you're likely to get in this place is the romance that you pay for? Don't think anything different, Flanagan? Seen you check out that Mexican chick pouring tequila. Smile all over your face like an idiot. Bet you were thinking nice romantic things about her, eh. So you're just like me. You'd jump on her bones in a heartbeat."

Flanagan hesitated. "No, I was just thinking she looked like a doll that's all."

"Doll my ass, you're weirder than Duggan. Likes to play with dolls do ya, eh that it."

Flanagan wanted to change the subject. "Ah that's it, Tash, Duggan lost the bet, didn't he." He took the money from his pocket. "Here's your prize money, congratulations."

While down at the other end of the bar, the rest of the gang were alert to the proceedings.

"She just left Tash back his cap, Duggan."

"Yeah, I saw it. There's a right smell of it now. She probably pissed in the fuk'n ting."

The blonde dancer returned to the bar in a different mood. She was more striking with her clothes on, designer denim jeans under a long black flared velvet jacket. With her hair weaved in a classic plait behind her head, standing there a cameo broach enriching her lapel. Like a Jayne Eyre creation, a big wide grin across her tanned face.

"I'm back, Jessica is my name."

She held her hand out gracefully. Like a business lady representing her company. Then she wrapped her arm around Doyle less formally. "Why don't we leave? I don't like hanging around here wearing clothes. It's not comfortable like that." She laughed.

"You could bring her home to your mother," Flanagan whispered, Doyle just smiled that old confident smile.

"I'll be mounting them Rockies on route to California." He shrugged his shoulders looking back at him. Some trips just had to be made.

Seeing them leave the club made Joe think. It was something he had avoided doing for a few days. He began to feel guilty; it was time to go home. A withdrawal from booze was the worst kind of remorse. The gang winning the tunnel drive had set him off. They hit the booze immediately after; he couldn't but join in with them. It even convinced him it was the right thing to do. But with all the excuses lined up, it would still be no good. Rita wouldn't buy into it; he could hardly blame her for that. At that moment he regretted doing it.

The excitement just walked out the door with fun loving Tash Doyle. Now he found himself in the company of drunken men. There wasn't as much as a smile between them. To catch up, he took more tequila from the Mexican girl. It helped fix the guilt, so he had another one. Just to be damn sure it stayed like that.

She showed him how to drink it, licking salt from her hand. She squeezed the bitter taste of lemon down his throat. He didn't care much for ceremony, the quickest way of dumping it on the troubled spot would do. Guilty feelings were hardest of all to get rid of.

Vietnam Duggan was beginning to get weirder by the minute. He seemed to be in touch with something haunting him from his past. His face contorted in a display of rage. "Gook," he hissed.

Swearing it over Flanagan's shoulder, the lovely Mexican girl was his petrified fixation. He seemed to have developed a special dislike for her.

She picked up on it moving to the end of the bar to get away from him. But he slouched over the counter aiming his fingers at her, making those noises with his mouth, like bullets speeding in her direction.

"Duggan, stop that you're scaring the shit out of her."

"She's a gook, Flanagan; I can smell one a mile off."

"A what!"

Duggan's eyes fixed in a distant empty stare. That look reminded him of Limpy's far out trance telling the alligator story in the hog hut.

He looked around for Mitchell. "Red, I think it's time for us to get out a here."

Two doormen pushed past in a hurry.

"A gook man, I'm going to shoot the fuk'n gook."

The miner's rant was getting louder, looking like someone who wasn't all there. The heavies closed in around him manhandling him towards the door. In this struggle Duggan connected with one of them, a punch on the jaw, it took off from there.

Mitchell his red haired flailing presence got stuck in then, swinging punches in all directions, connecting with a few of them. Butcher was on to it in a flash. He was much sharper when it came to violence. He nailed the second doorman. Seemingly induced drunks came alive to action, fighting brought on a fast recovery. The doormen soon discovered what it was like; getting ass kicked the sand hog way. They came under pressure when one of them took a weapon from his pocket. He hit Butcher on the head from behind. The miner crumbled in a heap on the floor, turning to do Mitchell, the doorman waved the blackjack again.

But Flanagan had seen enough, he made contact with the doorman's jaw. It was a sickening blow that stretched him out on the floor. The manager had called the cops; they rushed in to sort things out. It didn't take them long to get everyone under control. There were enough of them in it.

"Come on, buddy, you're coming with us."

Six cops rounded them up they didn't take any shit doing it either. For the sand hogs, celebrations finished up in traditional style. It wouldn't be a real-booze up if it didn't.

They were handcuffed, read their rights then escorted to a paddy wagon parked on the street.

Flanagan realized how lucky Doyle was, spending the night with Jessica. He had a woman at home too but the difference was he was headed for lock up. He didn't have the brains to stay with her, now it was too late. There was a more sobering reality to mull over. The undocumented sand hog was on his way to jail, that was as bad as it could possibly get. The Dolls Home proved to be the bar too far.

Chapter Fourteen

Rita stared at the phone number for a long time.

She was thinking about calling Detective Brady. Scared it was the wrong thing to do. Could it be happening so soon again? Or would there ever be an end to it. Such a short time since her husband was on the last booze up. Now he hadn't made an appearance for days. Maybe he was dead, how would she ever know. She lost ten pounds weight since she arrived in America. Her hair was falling out; the bald patches were getting harder to hide. She was the colour of death. In a flurry she took out the suitcase to pack a few clothes. Then she changed her mind, putting it back in the bottom of the wardrobe again. The self-confidence gained from bluffing the bad times was gone. The positive stories she told herself didn't work anymore. There was something in the pit of her stomach; it must be hunger, a reminder that Mary had to eat as well. She prepared herself for a trip to the Deli.

Rita knew the time had come to get her child away from this place. Maybe she might cope better if things were different. If she had a job, go to work every day like a normal person. Have a life outside of this constant struggle. Where worrying about her erring husband's ways had become the sole purpose of her existence.

Time spent caring for her handicapped child, wasn't so much of a concern for her. Everything had been going great for a while it shouldn't end like this. For a time it seemed things were beginning to improve. The comfort of the new apartment was like coming alive again.

But just when she started believing in it, he began drinking again. It wasn't as if he was violent towards her. That was something she wouldn't tolerate. She would have left him by now.

To explain the problem alcohol didn't suit him. It changed his temperament, was the kindest way she could say it. He wasn't able to call a halt to the party feeling, when he drank; something else took hold of him. Without a clock in his system that registered full, the compass in his brain directing him home didn't work. Someone she loved, such a strong man. To imagine his helplessness frightened her. So strange she couldn't understand it. Or tolerate it. More than anything else the fight was gone out of her, she was insecure? That feeling would break her. It was giving her the urge to run.

She put the phone down when Detective Brady answered her call. Lost her nerve, got scared of something she imagined. Becoming hyper in the next instant, she started rummaging furiously under the carpet in the bedroom. The bundle of hundred dollar bills was well hidden. There was the feeling of guilt taking the money. But it had to be done. Now she had to write the letter to him. There was no use carrying on with the pretense. He didn't need her any more. She lay in a heap on the floor sobbing pitifully. Her confidence had never deserted her like this before. Once she was left to contend with it all alone, it was never going to be any other way. The worst thing was it had almost worked. The scourge of the demon alcohol, made sure it didn't.

That afternoon Rita called into the airline office to book a flight to Ireland.

When everything else failed she must be strong. No judgement could fault her for doing what she could to look after her daughter. All she hoped was that she wouldn't regret any of it. It was the only way; it just had to be done. The situation was agreed in the beginning when he undertook to abide by certain rules in Philadelphia. The drink issue was well covered then; all those promises were broken in New York.

She left the letter for him to find when she was gone. Then she had to endure the longest wait of her life. She packed her bag before sitting down.

Four days had passed since she last saw him.

The way you're brought up moulds character. Rita knew from an early age how to stand up to her responsibility. The lesson learned 'it's your business take charge of it'. Fighting for the man she fell in love with was part of that same conviction. However, she expected him to do his part too. That wasn't the case. Joe was not the same guy she finished up with in New York. Drink changed him a lot. He was a much stronger man in the beginning of their relationship, before booze took him over. The first time she saw its deadly effect was in Ireland soon after they got married. He'd been drinking whiskey so he was sleeping off a hangover. The sound of his screams brought her running to the bedroom. He was sweating profusely half sitting up with his eyes wild in his head.

He pleaded with her to take the snakes off him. In his mind, they were crawling towards his head to devour him. She took them off him slowly, one snake at a time, to make the horror go away. That was her first introduction to the effects of his alcohol induced hallucinations. From that moment on the memory scared her every time he took to the drink.

How he had a mind capable of handling this horror she didn't know. Or if it was something that happened to everyone, she was a non-drinker that couldn't tell. But it had been a struggle for both of them. The battle of New York was the last stand. The war was finally over she was sad about that in spite of everything. But it would drag on longer for him.

When her husband arrived back to the apartment Rita had fallen asleep on the couch. He was more subdued than she might have expected. Not surprisingly, he had a worn out look about him. He was bound to be a bit shaky in himself, she decided. That might suit her parting scene better. She was only slightly interested in his story.

He was eager to tell her all about it.

"I was hauled in by the cops from work a few days ago. There was no way I could get word to you, Rita. They're still investigating Rosie the barmaid's murder. So, they dragged me in with the rest of the crew. It was all a big mistake, you see. When they realised that I wasn't in the bar the night she got killed. I was released from custody straight away. The rest of the guys are still there. It's wrongful arrest, they put me in the can by mistake. I wasn't witness to any murder, as you know."

She flinched, listening to him, talking with an American twang. He didn't have it a few weeks earlier. Why was he changing so much from the man she used to know? Speaking like a gangster sometimes, acting like an idiot most times. She didn't know him any more, talking about murder as if it was normal. The influence of his new workmates no doubt, doing collection runs for gangster's money. She found out about that by accident. That's why she lost all the weight, the worry of it, she couldn't hold anything down. Rosie let the information slip when she was drunk. Rita figured it all out for herself.

It was all so far away from where they both came from, much too frightening to live with. She couldn't wait around any more either. It was like being trapped all over again.

Now she was sure the right decision was to leave New York.

"Joe, I have decided to take Mary back home to Ireland. We're leaving tomorrow, everything is ready." She was relieved to get it out so quick.

He just looked at her, his face getting pale. In spite of this the first thought was for him. "You can't just leave me here on my own Rita."

"Why not, you left us here on our own."

"Oh, I see that's what it's all about, is it."

"Look, Joe, I don't want to fight with you when I'm leaving. It will do neither of us any good. We had just better talk about things before I go. That way we will both know where we stand. Do you agree to do that?"

He didn't have to think about it for long. She had her mind made up. It hardly mattered now, so he nodded his head. "Okay tell me."

"I'm not doing a post mortem, no point, we both know the story. I want you to help me make my mind up about the future. Do you still love me Joe?"

"I do, you don't have to ask…" She interrupted him.

"That's all I wanted to know. I still love you, but I can't cope with your carry on. Not the way things are in this situation. Not when I have to take care of Mary. Her future wellbeing just has to be my first concern. Things are coming between us that need talking about. When I go back to Ireland, you sort yourself out. You must make up your mind what you want to do. I am not going to stay with you when you're drinking. Nor do I want to be here any more. Not like this. I'm trapped in a box in the sky with a sick child. I worry all day about you. If you get this drinking thing eliminated from our lives, you know where I'll be. You can come to get me then, if you love me as much as you say you do."

"Is that it?"

"Yes, that's it, drop the booze or I'm out of the picture, permanently!"

"I see."

"Good, now do you want to come out to the airport with us? Or, do you have someplace else to go."

"The airport, of course I will."

"Right I have nothing to give you to eat. You're on your own now."

"Don't worry I'll go down to the diner, pick up something for…"

"No." She shouted it out. The fright she got when he suggested that, almost losing her composure. She struggled to maintain it. She had to be indifferent to preserve her strength. If he left the apartment that would be the last she'd see of him. She wanted him at the airport to say goodbye to his family. Like the way it should be.

A few hours later they were hanging around the departure hall in JFK Airport. Rita was searching for hopeful signs. True to expectations it was a different atmosphere. For all the wrong reasons, she could see he had his drinking buddy Doyle waiting in the wings.

He couldn't even wait till she was gone. A reality check all right, all the tears he shed, the promises he made couldn't take the hurt away from it. Not caring has a distinct way of showing its true face. It doesn't take any consideration. Up to the final moment of departure the bad feeling hung like a dark cloud over them. They were overcome by it.

Rita was okay with that, she couldn't wait to get away from him, no longer interested in what he had to say. She knew promises made through drink weren't the same as real promises. Praying hadn't worked either. She could try hoping again, it was easier to do when she was leaving. Getting out of the city was the good part; she would get her life sorted at home. Or else she'd be no good to anyone.

She knew that Joe had good qualities, understood the great pain his daughter's handicap caused him. He was still the guy she fell in love with, in spite of everything. When she no longer felt that way about him the situation would change. If only she could have done something positive about it before she left. But there was nothing more she could do about that now.

A confident young woman robbed of her voice, the one place she'd never want to end up.

She could hear them saying 'We told you so'. The sound of it was ringing in her ears already. There was nothing left of the man she had respected so much. It had all been taken away by drink, now she was taken by it too. The saddest part was he didn't seem to realise it. How was it possible, this emptiness lurked where their passionate love used to be? She could never have imagined it happening to them a few years earlier. Then everything, including the hassles seemed to bring them closer together. Especially the struggle they had to get married, that made them stronger. When they made plans for their future lives together.

It never sounded like this.

She'd keep her dignity as best she could, not allowing her emotions get the better of her. It wouldn't serve any purpose to shed tears of hopelessness now. They were all left behind in the Manhattan apartment, where nobody would ever see them. Now wasn't that a big price to pay for the sheer madness of drinking booze?

A drug that took sense of reason on a trip it should never go on. Maybe the dream of happiness was gone forever? She didn't want to think about that any more.

When they boarded Aer Lingus flight EI104 to Dublin the flight attendant greeted them warmly. Her Irish accent so comforting, that Rita was finally overcome. Hearing the voice of home for the first time in so many months was more than she could bear.

The flood of emotion she'd struggled to contain finally found its own release. While she fastened her daughter into the seat her eyes welled. The tears flowed freely when she sat down next to her. She covered her face with her hands to sob whispered words of relief.

"Thank God, it's over I've been so alone."

When the kind attendant noticed her distress, she went to her assistance immediately. "Does flying make you uncomfortable, madam?" She enquired.

When she became aware the young mother was exhausted from a prolonged stay in New York, as well as having to endure the trauma of getting hospital treatment for her handicapped child, she understood everything. Then, the green airline cavalry came to the rescue. This initial heart rendering contact between them would ensure a carefree trip to Dublin. She brought Rita a cup of tea soon after take-off that was much appreciated.

She was pleased that her daughter was sleeping soundly next to her. The snooze she so desperately needed would take longer to arrive. A troublesome thought was taking shape inside her head. As if she hadn't enough concern already.

For a long time, she wondered if her husband's excessive drinking was a sickness. It was all she could think of to explain the insanity away. His behaviour at the airport seemed so bizarre. It would be easier coming to terms with the problem if he was addicted. She would need to learn more about it. Anything would be more acceptable than this immature conduct, losing the plot when it came to accepting responsibility.

Maybe she wanted to accept it like that, just to have an excuse for him. Claw back some self-respect at the same time. It wasn't a nice feeling, left abandoned for the cursed drink. If there was another woman in the picture, she could identify that problem.

But he was too dependent on booze to bother with anything else.

If this personality disorder turned out to be a sickness, had she deserted him when he needed her most? She hadn't thought about it like that before, wouldn't be leaving now if she had. Sometimes ignorance provides good reason for dismissing annoying things. It wouldn't stop her from doing what had to be done.

Trying to make sense of everything, where did it all go wrong? She could never come up with an answer to that question? There were so many obstacles put in their way from the minute they started dating. It took them a while to notice the problem in the beginning. Young love has a way of shielding itself. Some kind of frivolity prevails keeping it cocooned, helping it flourish.

Now as Rita was heading back to Ireland alone, it appeared that bond was finally broken. Disposed of in a concrete jungle; shattered with dismal agonizing pain. The cruellest way for their love story to end filled her with regret. With many of the passengers wrapped in the comfort of sleep, Rita talked to God. She prayed for a loved one she was forced to abandon in New

York. Hoped he'd find some way of dealing with the alcohol ruining his life.

People have different ways of coping with sorrow while some people can't deal with it at all. Her husband's way of managing his personal demons was finding a refuge in drink; it became medicine to remedy hurt, a tonic for bad feelings. The cure became the disease that might kill him. There was nothing she could do about it now. That was difficult for her to admit, the helplessness wouldn't go away.

It would keep her awake for the whole flight to Dublin.

Back in Manhattan the taxi driver dropped the two guys off in familiar territory.

Flanagan picked up a bottle of whiskey from the liquor store heading home. He wanted to be alone. Doyle went straight into the Celtic; they couldn't wait to get away from each other. It was all bickering since the disastrous farewell spectacle at JFK airport.

Doyle was furious that he was persuaded to attend such a private family occasion. He blamed Flanagan for this apparent lack of sensitivity. He was irritated too, by Rita's obvious annoyance at him being there. But he understood her point of view.

"When a woman says goodbye, she doesn't want an audience. She didn't buy your story, Flanagan, about being lonely on the trip back into Manhattan either. If you weren't lonely at the airport when she was leaving, it's unlikely you'd spring a leak going home in the cab to start missing her then."

But he didn't see anything wrong with having a friend consoling him when his wife was taking off. Rita made up her own mind about it, the whole show was discredited. She didn't believe in the sentiment when booze was the only thing on the agenda. The guys were left in no doubt what caused the hostile atmosphere at the airport. No matter what kind of a slant they put on it.

The apartment felt empty without her, the fact she wouldn't be coming back any more was a bitter reality. He resented Mary taking up so much of their time together. When he thought more about it, pangs of guilt depressed him. Not much point blaming a child for something she knew nothing about. He opened the whiskey bottle, poured himself a glass. That driving episode in Ireland years earlier came back to haunt him when he was low. He'd put it through his head so many times since his daughter was born? Guilt was the silent assassin awaiting the opportunity to strike. When vulnerable got remorseful there was nobody to blame but himself. He'd been doing that since the birth of his little girl. It was just 'bad luck' they said.

Rita was seven months pregnant when his football team won the final. It was custom to travel country roads calling on bars, showing off the trophy. She wasn't up to enjoying the celebrations. To his annoyance, she insisted on waiting in the car. It only made him drive faster while she held her stomach. He could never have imagined any possible repercussions. Young, invincible; alcohol gives recklessness a free hand. It doesn't know anything about dealing with consequences.

The doctor insisted the child wasn't damaged in the womb during bumpy driving episodes. Maybe he was only trying to console him. But he blamed himself; those times he drove over rough country roads when Rita was pregnant caused it? No matter what medical professionals said to the contrary. That conclusion plagued his thinking.

They were married for almost two years before the baby was born. The pregnancy was two weeks overdue, the delivery complicated. The umbilical cord squeezed tight, the child had difficulty breathing. A lack of oxygen resulted in brain damage. The hospital was unable to explain exactly what happened. Instead the medical profession dived for cover.

Not performing a caesarean section was dispelled as unwarranted. But more informed opinion stated that was proper procedure for such a complication. In any event, the hospital report concluded, 'it was bad luck'. They even put it in writing.

That excuse was intended to sound normal, but it wasn't normal, neither was the child as a result. It never became the subject of legal action, just remained another number with the tag of 'bad luck' attached to it. Like all the unfortunate parents hospitals failed. Those badly let down unhealed sufferers. He was one of them. Rita could cope with it better she was made of tougher stuff. Women might have a more robust constitution for dealing with disaster than men? They probably have more need for it too.

Sometimes the story doesn't register properly with the guys.

This hospital explanation makes no reference to human error, no culpability for failing to prevent the occurrence. It would appear that 'bad luck' may not be a mitigating factor if due diligence prevailed. Therefore the situation would not keep recurring. There is management culpability in hospitals where lack of due care prevails. The newspapers say it happens all the time. In the aftermath of the child's birth Rita was adamant. 'Nobody is going to make money from our trouble, Joe'. This is God's will, she stated.

Good people pray to God for guidance, whiskey can provide refuge for others. But comfort sourced from a bottle only lasts as long as the whiskey. This little girl is just a vegetable, was what the doctor said. Moving away from it was an ongoing struggle. Rita knew her husband was having great difficulty with that. He was set in his ways, a man with merit as well as contradictions. A sensitive man would find difficulty overcoming such disappointment. She accepted how his daughter's handicap affected him.

His tendency to revisit the past he couldn't get rid of. When they talked on those long winter nights, holding each other close. She tried consoling him. Hoping things would change when acceptance eased the pain. Now he'd have to get there on his own. She wanted desperately to believe he'd survive the trip. Take his responsibilities head on; become more determined to make it work.

But there was a wild streak in him too that was hard to curtail. That element of reckless freedom of manner nobody wanted to understand. She took it on board from the start. She knew all about it. All the time the guilt ate away at him, pulling him back to the quick fix alcohol dispensed. Waiting there was the self-destruct phase again. It was never far away when guilt reached out for it. Would he stand there to let it destroy him eventually?
It looked as if he might.

Or could he find enough in him for coming to grips with himself. With whiskey doing the thinking the devil did the talking. Every time he looked at the child he blamed himself for her condition. To ease the pain he tried not looking at her at all. After a while he wanted to forget about her altogether. Even that didn't work so he'd have to live with it instead.

Lightly on the spirit ache of hurt lies where the affliction becomes tortured soul.

Christian belief teaches that prayer resolves things in God's time. He was never able to rationalise a belief like that. The bad things that happened all around him couldn't be God's caring work. Why create a world full of suffering, for everyone to become afflicted. Why not remedy things when the power is there to succeed. Wouldn't that be something God could easily do? There is only sadness attached to despair. Is all religious belief not subject to some form of hypocrisy; if malice, violent discrimination combines to preach the message? Then let each of them stand up to be counted.

Religion would not solve his problems. He would react to his situation instinctively. That was his way. Then he could see what was happening in front of him, when he was capable of seeing it. Rita was gone back to Ireland without him. That justified him getting lost without her. He could let anything happen now.

No matter how it turned out he didn't care any more.

Chapter Fifteen

Mario Catapani got up to pour himself a mug of coffee.

Steam wafted a strong smell, wrinkling the nose of Jim Sullivan. He was intent on giving Mario a more positive slant on the Duggan gang disaster. That's if the Italian guy would listen to him.

More importantly believe him.

"Duggan twisted his knee he didn't show for work; he lied. How could he be held responsible for a tunnel accident in his absence?"

Sullivan got a feeling the general foreman wasn't hearing him. The thought struck him that maybe he couldn't care less about Duggan. Other than he wanted him working somewhere else. He could understand that, but he had to be cautious, consider everything. Maybe he was worried about his retirement package.

"We must be careful, Mario. It's in no one's interest to have the job closed down. We have to try working together to fix these issues. How long do we know each other? A hell of a long time, we've sorted many problems down the years. We mustn't lose the plot at this stage of our lives."

The general foreman knew Sullivan had a different view of things. He sailed close to the storm a lot of times, but he had to admit he got it right often enough. So he deserved to be heard, Mario was desperate to listen.

"How do you see things, Sullivan?"

"The miner, Mitchell, was in charge we must make a positive report. Mario, shit happens. Everything will be in order for insurance purposes or otherwise. Can you leave it to me, I will keep you informed."

"Okay."

Sullivan took that as fair comment. Riding his luck he put his hand out. The general foreman took it. His faith sealed with the shake of a hand, Sullivan was eager to leave, there were other things to think about. He made his way to the jeep. Putting on a competition for booze wouldn't go down well. Everyone knew that. Mario knew it too, so he was cornered.

Any solution keeping that information from surfacing was the proper way to proceed. The sharks in head office wouldn't be impressed, if the insurance company found out about booze for moves. Sullivan was in a tricky situation. But that's what he was good at, chancing his wit against the odds.

It had started to rain heavily again. He cursed the bad luck of getting his clothes wet for the second time that day. He needed a shower, some fresh clothes. It was Friday he was knocking off early.

"To hell with it, why do I always leave my coat in the damn jeep?" he moaned.

Jim Sullivan drove out the main exit. He'd think it all through when he got home to Staten Island. A comfortable chair, a glass of whiskey, did it for him.

Back in the office Mario was deep in thought. He was sure of only one thing. This was the last job he would ever do. A disruptive nuisance could give him a few more grey hairs to take into his retirement. That pain in the ass was making trouble on his job.

Jim Sullivan had arranged to meet up with John Duggan. The location was the 'Volcano' a hide-away on 23rd St. off First Avenue. He was getting impatient, the bar was full of scumbags the miner was late. The weird looking bartender was about his own age. Except he wore earrings, nail varnish with his hair tied in a ponytail. Too much for an old guy, Sullivan reckoned. He liked women, but not the two sitting up at the bar. They had Adam's apples, stubble, for Christ's sake. He hoped they'd think he was a cop. Imagine Duggan wanting to meet up in a place like this. Was he trying to freak him out, or something? He succeeded, the son of a bitch. Was it a coincidence that a hospital caring for the criminally insane was only a few blocks away?

The company man was convinced that Duggan played the mad thing up a bit. All to good avail, if people weren't afraid of him. Would they have got away with it for so long? But it was getting dangerous. Vietnam Duggan was hard to predict. Never know when he would blow the whole thing. Sullivan had to accept the partnership had run its course. But he couldn't let the mining boss suspect anything was amiss. Meeting up with him would keep him sweet. That's if he ever arrived. He pulled the grey mackintosh coat across his chest. He tightened the belt. The concealed gun felt good against his side, made him feel secure.

He ran his fingers through the mat of curly grey hair with a sigh of frustration.

"How are you doing Sullivan?"

He was standing behind him.

"Hi, John, you're having a drink." Duggan pointed a thick grubby finger at Sullivan's whiskey glass.

"One a them, with a mug a beer chaser."

Bartender! Sullivan ordered drinks, his curiosity getting the better of him.

"Didn't see you come in, John."

"I've been here a long time, talking with a bunch a people back there. Watching you, Sullivan, you're sure one hell of a nervous fuker."

He felt an annoying sting when spoken to like that.

"I hope you didn't worry about keeping me waiting, John," he said hopefully.

But Sullivan wasn't there to cultivate Duggan as a social companion. It was all about business. He picked up a job for his daughter, a secretary in the company's head office. Processing permits for miners was one of her tasks. She didn't know that

146

some information supplied by her father was false. That he had his own little side line going on for years.

It was a simple operation. John Duggan got 20% of the proceeds accumulated by Sullivan from the unofficial workers that utilized these special permits. There was 5% deducted for an emergency fund from miners' wages each week. When the job was laid off they could claim some funds back.

Miners on unofficial permits were not entitled to this payout. Under normal circumstances it was difficult to get proper permits for underground work without going through official channels.

There were licences required for using explosives, rigorous tests for working in compressed air conditions. Duggan despised the fact that Sullivan got a larger share of the action. He seized every opportunity to vent his scorn.

Talking disrespectfully to the company man was one way he displayed this frustration.

The sand hogs laboured in two types of working conditions. Subway tunnels for the expanding underground rail system. These were big construction jobs. Twenty men at any one time required to work jumbo machines as they blasted their way through the rock bed under the streets. Then there were small pipe jobs carrying sewage around Manhattan's ever increasing population. On these jobs the work space was more restricted. A maximum of five men were required to work a shift. Sullivan had a concern that too many of these unofficial permits were being allocated to small water tunnel projects.

"It would be much safer, John. To have our special permits issued in subway jobs."

"Why is that then?"

"Bigger jobs, easier to hide a rookie with a special permit."

"I've more of an outlet in water tunnels, the job I'm in."

"Yes, I know, but this last incident we had to deal with highlighted a few weak spots."

"A what?"

"Places where our little arrangement could become exposed. We might get caught then what. When miners work close together they have lots a time to talk. They might get around to comparing notes. Know what I'm saying, John. Try to restrict our permits to big jobs only. Where there is a lot of noise, guys can't hear to compare shit then. John let me tell you something. I don't want to show my authority, but you have to know. This aggressive behaviour with the hillbilly gang must stop. It could cause too much aggravation on the job. It leaves our arrangement vulnerable."

"No shit, Sullivan, gonna do something about it are ya?"

"Don't mess with me, Duggan. I always carry a gun."

"Vietnam's full a dead guys pointing guns at me. Now fuk off before I take yours shove it up your asshole too. Don't ever forget how much money I'm making you, Sullivan. Think how quick that could change. Remember that, we understand each other."

With those words the fraudulent business partners parted company.

Sullivan's face was white with rage walking along 23rd St. mumbling.

"This bastard will get me sent up the river. I need to close it down." He swore, making a vicious kick at a cigarette packet on the street.

The hog hut the following Monday was a depressing place to be.

It was also Sullivan's day for an official visit to the Manhattan site. Men could talk about grievances, if he was in the mood for listening. Today though, Sullivan had other things on his mind. Hearing complaints was not a priority.

He was more intent on passing time easy getting to know people personally. He was thinking about taking a few hands of poker, he watched the hillbilly gang play. There was an opportunity of getting acquainted with Lupe. He sat down at the

148

card table beside him. "Ya'll play a neat game, buddy." Sullivan spoke the compliment like one of them.

Lupe hadn't won a hand all day, losing his few dollars he was pissed off. This was a hot shot from the company talking to him. Lupe couldn't figure it out. Why was the guy talking with a southern accent? He wasn't about to mess up though. Conscious of the way things were with his working papers, an' all. "I ain't doing shit at poker, dude, ya'll see it."

Sullivan ignored Lupe's wry comment. He came across as a psychopath. This maniac with hate tattooed on his fingers could be the guy he was looking for. He might plant a few seeds in his stupid head. He might even enjoy doing it too. If the way he looked was anything to go by. He offered his hand then grimaced when the roughneck applied undue pressure on his fingers. Lupe took note of this discomfort. Soft hands northern boy, soft as shit fella.

It pleased him to think about the company man like that. He lost the run of himself. "I'm crazy ole Lupe from the mountain," he said with an evil looking grin displaying brown stumps of broken teeth. That comment hit Wispy Steel's ragged crew of wild men. Their throats rasped raw with moonshine hollered raucous laughter when Lupe said that. Sullivan was quick to join in too. It was a cameo role from the man handler. That's why he was the trouble shooter.

The hillbillys liked Sullivan's laugh. The red face of him the mad looking head on him. He looked like one of the guys from back home in hill country.

He was all right, no harm treating him good, he might provide down the line. He was supposed to be a big whiskey drinker. That was good. They had a drop of the hard stuff in the locker. Damn, wasn't moonshine best whiskey? Wispy Steel fetched the bottle of hooch to the table. Illegal my ass, he muttered, sitting down, knowing alcohol could only be drank Fridays in the hut. The company man knew the rules too. If he wanted a little booze, everything was okay.

Sullivan was up for it. "Pleasure to have a drink with ya'll."

Raising the mug to toast them he got his first taste of the foul stuff. It was hard to stomach, but still he chatted friendly to the hillbilly boss. "Guess ya'll have no problems with the job, winning an all that."

Lupe was quick to latch on to it. He had something more to say. "Just one hell of a problem, dude, Vietnam Duggan son of a bitch the problem."

Not a comment his boss Wispy Steel would be in favour of airing. He cut in to silence his troublesome lieutenant. "Mr Sullivan doesn't want to hear that shit, Lupe, he card game man."

Sullivan continued on with the good stuff. "I should be congratulating ya'll. Your success in the tunnel drive. The general foreman is very pleased with ya'll."

Wispy Steel grimaced. A northerner trying to talk southern didn't sound right. But he had just praised his gang, best let him talk the way he liked. When the job ended gangs would get laid off. He wanted his outfit to be last going down the road. That man from the company was best placed to make it happen.

"We're just mighty proud to work for Mr Catapani, Mr Sullivan, sir."

Sullivan rattled on the moonshine was helping him. Maybe it was doing all the talking. "There's always a job for you guys with Catapani. I will be there to make sure you're looked after. Just come talk with me. If I can fix it for ya'll, call it done."

Wispy Steel, a predator by instinct was quick to confirm the spoken word. "We see eye to eye, Mr Sullivan, sir. Eye to eye, take ya'll on kindness, sir."

He reached out to force the reluctant hand of the company man; it wasn't Sullivan's intention to pledge anything serious. It was only remarks that didn't mean shit. The booze was making him say it. The double dealer in him tried edging for a little space.

"I haven't as much clout as I used to, with young guys getting promotion in the company. All the old guys like me retired now. Them you can trust to get the job done, gone, everything's changed."

He winked at Wispy Steel, that wink was intended to say it all!

The tunnelling company was a tight place any more, the good stuff that used to happen, past. New men running the company saw everything different. Wispy Steel looked back at him nodding in agreement. He could see the difference in things too. But he hung in there just the same. Where he was coming from you never let the fish wriggle off the hook. That's how you lost it.

"We trust ya'll, Mr Sullivan sir, like ya'll say, get the job done."

Sullivan gave up on them, not to bother digging up more annoyance for himself. "Cut the deck, get the cards turning," he said. "Let's play poker, boys."

The rest of the men had enough poker; they headed for the hog hut door. Now Sullivan had Lupe all to himself. It was the chance he'd been waiting for. They whispered in low tones for a while, moonshine made it easier to talk about things.

Sullivan had the address of the Celtic bar ready for him on the back of an envelope. He watched Lupe stashing it in his plastic wallet. Then he winked at the hillbilly. As if bonding some agreement between them. Lupe finished off the rest of the moonshine with a gulp.

"Might call for a beer in there before I get home, Mr Sullivan, just might do."

The company trouble shooter heard all that. Declining the offer of more hooch, he had one last message for him before taking off. "Vietnam Duggan don't like you none be careful in there."

"I got me a gun stashed in my locker, sir."

That was the best part of the conversation, hearing that information. Without another word he walked off, as if he never knew him. He left behind a dangerous maniac that hated Duggan.

Now he knew where to find him, if he wanted to. He went out the door leaving the intoxicated miner sitting alone.

Limpy the old caretaker maintained his silent presence. He slouched back in the shadow of the locker staring after him. When Sullivan was gone Limpy's lips twisted in a vicious scowl. "Goddam company man's a killer."

There was a story going around the hog hut. Lupe's absence from the hillbilly outfit gave Duggan's gang an edge to win the tunnel drive. That rumour might have been started by the hillbilly. Anyway, that's what happened when their enemies finally overcame them.

There would never be a chance of it happening again. They took an oath on that one.

The Duggan crew would never have beaten them if their wayward cousin was working that week. Rumour that a Puerto Rican woman had besotted the mad miner was all the talk. No one believed any woman wanted to spend time with him. But his buddies claimed he was so well endowed that the sheep in Tennessee stalked him. They swore he moved in to her apartment at her expressed desire. The sex would keep him there till she tired of him. She must be some beauty bothering her ass with the guy. That was the view on rational thinking concerning the topic.

In his absence, Duggan got the success he craved by winning the tunnel drive. It was all a big mistake, like it should never have gone down in the first place. The hillbilly raged about it. No way would it ever happen again.

The men from the Deep South were pissed off no doubt about that. It added another chip to the block already on their shoulders. But now Lupe had gone missing again. This time Wispy Steel voiced less complimentary on his sexual prowess more inclined to heap scorn on his henchman. He stated Lupe was paying for all the sex he got. Anyone could do that if they had no loyalty to their workmates. Hearing their boss turn against Lupe dampened the gang's respect for him. With the services of a good shaper they could still take on anyone in the tunnel work. When Lupe returned they planned on giving him a hot reception, just to get the message across to him. You let us down when we needed you most. As far as Duggan's gang were concerned, it didn't matter who was missing. It was time to win the drive again. They were good enough to do it. Let the hillbilly complain all they liked. Nothing could take it away from them; they did a number on the red necks already. They planned on doing it again. In the process shove the hillbilly noses in it; with or without the low life Lupe.

Who gives a shit?

Detective Ann Spellman applied her make up heavily. She was moving over to alter ego. Studying her well-toned body in the mirror she smiled cupping her hands under her breasts. She liked the look of them, bigger would be too much to carry around.

Whirling on her toes to check her ass out she was pleased with that too. She was finally ready for Betty Ann's performance. The dancer was becoming more in demand. It was time to hot up the show make it more energetic. It was always her intention to please. That would increase her fans in the Celtic. Then she'd be asked to work weekends.

This was her third week in the place. It was a rough hangout. There were only a few women using it, none of them were young. That was good. It might be embarrassing to perform in front of them. Since she started work in the bar nothing of a suspicious nature happened. She rummaged looking to find a special outfit. If they liked what she was doing they might ask her to work late at night when the door was closed. That's when the bar was strictly for them. If only she could be there on those occasions, when according to rumour, things happened. Her self-appointed bodyguard Doyle would look out for her in case things got out of hand.

She liked the respectful attention he gave her. She'd have to be careful though, didn't want him getting romantic ideas, displaying any kind of possessive behaviour. The way he looked at her, those big brown eyes of his. Moving things around for her when she passed by, like she was a lady. Of course she was delighted with all the attention. He was such a rough looking man with big hands. Yet he was kind. It pleased her more than she was prepared to admit. She would never confide it to anyone, enjoying the thoughts of it on her own.

Now it was time to get on down there to kick ass. Let Betty Ann loose to raise hell in the joint. She liked to dance, but it was hot work. She didn't care about that, when the clothes got lighter, her popularity grew. It was becoming a topic of conversation in her absence. That one day she'd take her whole kit off. Tash Doyle had his personal opinion, he was adamant about it. He defended her virtue like a man possessed.

"No way, no way I can tell you, it'll never happen!"

"Why not, she's only a whore," growled Red Mitchell disappointed his lewd suggestion was so badly received.

"She's a lady," Doyle insisted.

"Tash likes the bitch, careful I tell you!" Butcher tried shutting him up.

They giggled like idiots much to the annoyance of Doyle.

They were right to be ogling her though. He couldn't blame them for that. He was pussy struck in that direction himself. Maybe it was time for him to do something about it.

The memory of looking at her didn't last long enough, bed time always arrived full of regrets. But he wasn't about to blow the lot by being hasty. In spite of all his efforts she wasn't giving him that spark, letting him know it was okay to come across. He needed to feel that, getting shot down with some lame attempt was bad for the ego. There could be no comeback if that happened. He'd play the game, look for interest showing up. It was bound to happen if he made the right moves, better to leave the timing with her. Women were more inclined to dance if they turned on the

154

music. That's what he discovered over the years working his ass off looking for it. Sometimes when it was hard to get, it wasn't worth the trouble. Doyle was one man always ready to be surprised. It was this flair for difference that made him a legend.

Betty Ann was exhausted when she finished her stint. She planned on hurrying home for a shower. Earlier, before her dance routine began she sat for a chat with the Dillons. Their only child was killed in Vietnam; they had sort of adopted her.

Mr Dillon didn't seem to care about anything except his wife's gossiping. He'd like her to shut up about Hell's Kitchen's history. It was nobody's business. Their neighbourhood was full of secrets, he said, looking straight at his wife. But when the grumpy husband headed for the bathroom, the wife became more relaxed.

She said John Duggan had no idea Rosie the barmaid was his aunt, or that his father was a gay priest. How all that came about was maybe the biggest surprise of all. It would have to wait for some other time. Mr Dillon was back glaring at her again. Betty Ann's mouth was left hanging after hearing all that.

Her eccentric behavior allowed her to fit in. Mrs Dillon cared for her like a daughter; the sand hogs enjoyed her. They didn't want her moving to a place they might be barred from entering. There were a few of those scattered around the neighbourhood. They probably wouldn't get served in the Celtic either, if their boss didn't own it; but this new barmaid was worth looking after.

She fulfilled a role that Rosie O Connor vacated. But the fun was different with this one. She was younger, enjoyed gyrating to tunes on the jukebox. That bit of action did it for them. It saved them going off looking for fun somewhere else, to get hauled in by the cops.

John Duggan could see dollar signs, a younger readymade tart to enhance the bar intake. That was something he was always looking out for. This bitch just wandered in off the street. Not wanting her drifting on to take up in another bar down the block he decided to make her a permanent fixture. She had potential for other things too. The sand hogs liked the idea. She introduced changes that appealed to them. Eye candy in their local place, it could get more risqué, you never know. Waiting for it to happen was almost as exciting as being there when it arrived. A little extra money helped with the rent she told them. She performed erotic dances for dollars in tune with the jukebox. The dance rules were firmly established in the beginning. Removing clothes was not part of her show. Touching her in any way would not be tolerated either. If any of these rules were broken, that would end the performance, for good. Jesus, they couldn't take a chance on that.

Duggan's gang were been scrutinized by the cops again. The Dolls Home bust up was one reason for hauling them in. Detective Brady wanted another chance to question them. Turning the heat up on the boozy bad boys wouldn't hurt; he knew it was unlikely to reap much benefit either. But removing them off the job might put pressure on them. The hillbilly gang roared obscenities in their ears when they were being led away.

Duggan growled back defiantly. These guys were pros when dealing with the police. A lesson learned all their lives. They knew how things worked. Lawyers present before doing any talking. Then back to the Celtic to laugh their asses off about it.

One man on the site got special satisfaction seeing that.

Limpy leaned forward to peer after them from his kitchen. He liked the young Irish kid that reminded him of his own boy. He was annoyed that Duggan led the guy astray. The rest of the crew could burn in hell. The sooner it happened, the better. Would anything end the torment Duggan caused him? He whistled the tune Garryowen. Haunting sounds of the 7 th cavalry's marching anthem, before they were slaughtered at Little Bighorn. The feeling was imminent disaster. The most unpopular gang on the job were being escorted downtown again. It was great to witness it happening, gave his bad leg a break. The memory of getting that leg injury came back to him in a flash, those bastards laughed when he couldn't do anything about it. Everything that goes around comes around, he heard that so many times. One day it would all come right. There would be payback time then.

Mario Catapani observed the police all over his site; Sullivan was there too, witnessing it from his hut. It might enhance the general foreman's opportunity to get rid of them.

They watched the Paddy Wagon going out the gate.

"This is a sad day for me, Sullivan, police all over my job."

"I understand your concern, Mario, but it's nothing to do with work. Some barmaid got murdered. They've been taken in for questioning, that's all."

"Murdered – you say it so casually; these murderers are on our watch. What I hear their aggression with the hillbilly is out of hand. It's likely to blow up into something more serious, I've been told. You're aware of course, that some violence has already gone down between them."

"What have you got in mind, Mario?"

"At our last meeting you said no, to transferring Duggan's gang to maintenance work."

"No gang wants to go down to work live sewers, Mario."

"Nevertheless, one gang must do the job. That's the way it has to be. You're the boss, Sullivan, so see it gets done right away. The company won't be paying any extra bonus."

"I see, I have nothing to bargain with, Mario."

Why do you need to bargain with Duggan? Just tell him get to hell down there, end of story?

"I need a while to figure this one out."

"You have another week, that's it, want a scotch?"

"No, no I got another site to visit."

"Okay, Sullivan, mind how you go."

"Take it easy yourself, Mario."

Sullivan had a bad feeling in the pit of his stomach. Mario had a lean on him; no doubt about it couldn't be bothered trying to hide it either. That was a bad sign.

On the drive home to Staten Island Sullivan thought about the situation. They wanted Duggan's gang off the job, out of sight, far from trouble.

Introducing a competition for booze was a bad idea. Somebody forgot to think of the consequences. A confrontation with the hillbilly outfit would look bad on Mario's record. He was expected to fix it, by making sure it didn't happen. Or maybe his crooked business dealings were common knowledge. Now that was something he didn't want brought under scrutiny. He suspected a long time ago that Duggan could bring him down. Now he knew he was right about that. What could he do to save his ass? Sullivan had worked out the plan very carefully in the beginning. He had his illicit income stashed for his retirement. How long would it remain safe, if an investigation got under way? Even Al Capone with all his connections couldn't beat them, locked up for tax evasion.

He had to think hard about that possibility too. The last thing he wanted was his daughter's job on the line. She would never stay with the company if he was disgraced. She knew nothing about the scam, always trusted her father's good judgement. He loved her more than life itself; he would do anything to protect her honour. It was getting tricky all right. Scandal relating to him would affect his entire family, a shame on all of them. A tight knit community, he was active in his church, in charge of Sunday collection. A fall from grace would be devastating. The only person that connected him directly to this racket was John Duggan. Sullivan knew the hillbilly Lupe wanted Duggan dead. That plan would solve many problems, if it worked.

Chapter Sixteen

The humidity was making Joe Flanagan drowsy. Booze sweating through his skin drenched the shirt on his back.

Two weeks since Rita left, he felt bad without her. Thoughts of the cold damp tunnel, so often his place of torment, felt like refuge. His appearance changed since he stopped taking care of himself. Shaving was gone out the window, he was growing a beard.

A rumour going around that Duggan's gang was being sent down to do maintenance work had him freaked. That prospect made him sweat as much as the humidity.

There were scary things going round in his head about white alligators that terrified him.

He was withdrawn most of the time. Although he could still make it into work when the hangover wished he didn't. A shift was only four hours; he needed the full salary. He was struggling; the will to go on wasn't there any more. Loneliness for Rita was slowly killing him. He didn't give a shit what happened to him.

The Dolls Home incident cost him five hundred dollars. There was the chance of a lawsuit; the doorman's jaw was broken. The Mexican waitress testified she saw everything. The judge wasn't impressed. He was fortunate the illegal immigrant status didn't surface. No previous convictions got him off with a fine. The legal fees cost more money so the boss came to the rescue again, paying another five hundred dollars for the lawyer. Duggan admired his performance in the club battle. The way he stepped in to lay such a big punch on the doorman. 'He didn't look as if he had it in him', he claimed; a sort of compliment Duggan style. They might have come under pressure except for that one, he reckoned. He was a great advocate of the killer instinct, convinced that the Irish guy had it. He could see them hanging out taking care of business together. The Flanagan guy had a lot of potential now that he owned him.

As a result he was getting deeper in debt, falling behind with the rent. Rita wasn't there to sort him out any more. All he had was the letter she left him; he cried drunken tears reading it every night. He was scared to miss work knowing shapers would be lining up for his job. People on the train were giving him fleeting paranoid looks. Most of the commuters didn't mind the sticky heat. It was each other that caused them so much concern. A bearded weirdo in dirty work gear staring at them with a vacant expression only added to their woes.

Were they all judging him? He wanted to ask them why they were looking at him. But he couldn't. He was afraid of them.

Limpy liked the idea of Duggan's crew moving on. They were going down where alligators roam. The caretaker was gloating about it. "You're going down to Chinatown, Flanagan, that's the last we'll see of you. Everything I said you'll see, they'll kill you all. Go back to Ireland; you'll be eaten alive down there." He laughed his mad laugh to frighten the shit out of him. Limpy was enjoying it. Was he on his way to the alligator's lair? He was wasn't he?

That question would be answered soon enough. Flanagan was dreading it. The accident in the tunnel was old news. No one was fired as a result, there was loads of other stuff happening. The miner that lost his finger wasn't wearing his company issued gloves. The insurance didn't have to pay up. No gloves no cover. Everyone moved on with the job. Except for Duggan, he remembered bad stuff for longer than anyone else. He never missed an opportunity to bring it up either.

It was the start of a new week. The boss was trying to pump the gang up. He preached the good message loud in the hog hut. He saw himself as a motivational speaker not a shit scaring lunatic.

Tash Doyle was still meeting up with Jessica the topless dancer. He missed a few days' work, much to Duggan's annoyance.

The all-conquering hero was under pressure. The men claimed that the sexual demands of the blonde stripper took its toll on the old war horse. He couldn't hack it any more they said. As a direct result he was unable to complete a full week's work. He had finally met his match. Doyle would never discuss his private life with anyone. They could only use their imagination.

That might be difficult for those that couldn't get laid at all. The way he seen it. Tash explained it like that to them. It was a shut your mouth up sort of thing to say.

He was quick off the mark when it came to hitting the spot. Doyle was capable of handling any kind of attack. No matter how it came at him. A deliberate lack of loyalty to his workmates gave Duggan a bad feeling about him. He admired Tash like the brother he never had. But putting pussy before winning was not appreciated. He'd have a private word with him at some later stage. Just to get the real story across to him.

Lupe poked his mad head around the locker at the wrong time. He looked the part of a forgotten soldier, wearing this long confederate army trench coat down to his boots. His tobacco stained teeth stripped in a hateful growl. He heard Duggan's rallying pep talk.

"Ya'll gonna see some alligator shit, Vietnam, ya'll dead."

Then he moved out from behind the locker, holding a brush under his arm, like a machine gun, spraying the place with bullets. The look on his menacing face said, he meant every bit of it. It was one of Duggan's favourite things to do. When his worst flashbacks brought him back to Vietnam he did it all the time. That sort of crazy action leaves people in fear of you.

It took the strength of two men to hold Duggan back from Lupe. The hillbilly wasn't about running, he was a psycho too.

"Let him go, I kick his ass, boy." Lupe screeched.

As his workmates hauled him back down the floor, Duggan white with rage swore after him. "It's not over yet, in bred mother fucker, I'm gonna get you good."

Drinking was a full time occupation for Joe Flanagan now. The four hour shift in the tunnel was getting difficult to complete every day. The length of time working was never long enough to sober up, before he was back on the drink again.

The body adapts in some ways but the mind struggles keeping it going like that. He found it easier to just crash down in a booth in the Celtic when the shift times rotated, going to work at four a.m. When he got into the habit of that, he couldn't be bothered going back to the loneliness of the apartment any more. The rut was getting deeper. He was running up a big bar tab too. It felt like he was getting all the booze for free. There should be a law against drunks getting bar credit. He had acquired this aggressive attitude since Rita left him, quick to react to any provocation, the fuse was short. If anyone defied him, he was ready to fight. The smart ones left him alone, there was enough trouble brewing between miners already. Men who made their living working in this responsible job didn't appreciate the intimidating side show in the workplace. They were wary of trouble flaring up underground, causing accidents that could kill or maim any one of them. The whole scene was scaring Flanagan. The tense atmosphere was affecting his head. Problems were combining to justify his drinking. But he didn't need any excuse.

Sergeant Brady picked up on something that detective Spellman said. There was a cleaning lady with a key to the bar; she was John Duggan's mother. The cop discovered the Celtic bar, the whorehouse hotel, were owned by the same person. Both were registered in the name Mrs Marie Duggan. Why wasn't that a surprise? That old girl had two joints, already two people were murdered in them. About time to have a talk with the owner, see what she had to say about that? His team had some information on her, the phone number as well.

She would be expecting him. He rang the doorbell of the old building. The buzzer admitted him when he identified himself. He headed down the hall towards the door of her apartment. The yellow concrete walls cooled down the corridor. A great escape from the humidity outside. The red-haired police officer was feeling the heat.

She welcomed him with polite reservation. He knew about her, a private woman with a deep faith. A religious person wouldn't lie, he was raised to believe.

He could see she was a formidable woman. Yet, she displayed courtesy, sitting him down at the end of the kitchen table. In a quiet matronly voice insisted, there would be no discussion, until coffee was served. The sergeant was glad to sit quietly in her presence. It gave him time to study her. The clothes she wore made her strangeness more apparent. The old style garments in keeping with the Amish tradition was not a common sight in this city. She moved around in a flowing black cotton dress to her ankles. A black bonnet trimmed with white lace on her head. It was tied in a black velvet bow under her chin. She appeared straight off a horse drawn carriage in Pennsylvania.

Mrs Duggan was eager to explain to him that she knew nothing about any business dealings. She was just a simple housewife that dutifully signed paperwork for her son, without question, when he presented it to her. Trusting that he knew what he was doing. He was running his bar as best he could. She often went down there to tidy the place; men were not good at cleaning. They didn't seem to notice dust or dirt; she knew nothing about any hotel though. Maybe the detective was mistaken. John was such a hard worker, she said. He had a job with a city contractor on top of everything else.

Sergeant Brady knew about other incidents in the past. He had dealings with her son. She was bound to know about them, religious or not. He explained his visit was about the barmaid's murder. The crime took place on her property. Did she know the barmaid personally?

Yes, she knew all about the deceased. Rosie O Connor was her younger sister. They grew up together in Hell's Kitchen. They hadn't talked to each other for over thirty years. Their father was a constant drunk, very cruel to the young girls. Their mother put him out on the street when she could no longer tolerate or thrust him around the family home. She entered a convent on her sixteenth birthday. In the beginning it was just to escape from home.

With the community she prayed for the love of God. Her faith strengthened with the power of belief. Her sister Rose took a different path through life. It was not one that she approved off. Rose brought shame on herself, disgrace on her family.

When she got up to refill the sergeant's coffee cup she seemed to lose some of her composure. The quiet spoken woman appeared to make contact with something distressing from her past life. That memory changed her demeanour. When she raised her voice the cop pulled back in surprise. "She became an evil woman of the night sergeant, sold her body to pleasure men. She had her first son taken into care, when she went to prison for prostitution.

She raised her next boy so bad, he got murdered selling drugs. So it's said. These things don't happen to good people. When God is not invited in, the Devil has his way."

She blessed her face with the sign of the cross when she had all that said.

The cop knew about Rosie O Connor's past from looking at her record.

The drifter in custody for her murder said he saw an old lady in the bar on the night in question. Right now here was an old lady with a key to the place, she might have probable cause. It was obvious that she had scant regard for the deceased.

"You were a nun with a catholic order, Mrs Duggan."

"Yes, Sergeant, for fifteen years."

"I apologise for intruding in your private life. I would like to talk with you about that time."

"You want to know about convent life perhaps, Sergeant?"

"Starting with why you left the good sisters ma'am."

She got up to refill the coffee pot again, not to rush her reply.

"You want to know about my romance with Father Thomas. Is that what you want to hear, Sergeant? I'm sure you know all about it. There was gossip. But then there always is. When falling in love is under threat. It's been like that since the beginning of time, but I didn't mind. Father Thomas was the Chaplin to our order. Over the years, we had many consultations. Our discussions involved personal problems as well as spiritual inclinations. He was a true man of God at that time I would say. When he chose the Devil's company he lost the faith."

"Was your husband a lover of your sister Rosie ma'am?"

The answer was swift. "You might be better off asking him that question. I can't answer it."

Brady had enough experience to know that the music was over. She was turning sour, there would be another time. He had some information to check out; she would be asked to sing again. Better if things were left to cool down for a while. Or maybe it was the right time to hit her when she was angry. He went for it.

"You have resentment towards your deceased sister?"

"I had disgust for her, Sergeant. She was never a lady."

"You were sad she was murdered, ma'am."

"It was the will of the Devil, Sergeant. He'll be the last one to bed her, to each his own."

The cop got a bit thrown by that one. It was the nearest they came to talking sex. The ex-nun brought it up, wasn't that unreal, he didn't know what to say. Then it came to him. "Why did you hate your sister so much?"

"She let the family down with her ways, Sergeant. She let me down by her deeds. Rosie was my only kin. I despised her for what she was. I have ignored the woman. Now that she is dead, it's finally over. I have peace. I've already tried to tell you that, Sergeant."

Like a priest absolving her confession. She let Ben Brady hear it all. He just sat there thinking his mother was right. Sister Marie Duggan was a good catholic, no matter how things seemed to be. In spite of the fact she got turned on in the middle of the nun job. It wasn't the first time that happened. Prayer locked horns with passion before.

He met up with his partner in a dingy diner on Ninth Avenue. Ten blocks from where she lived. The coffee here was the best; they had a lot to talk about.

Detective Spellman thought of something important. "Why would a nun leave the convent to marry a gay priest?"

"I didn't say Thomas was gay," Brady reminded her.

"No, the woman in the bar told me, bitching about Mrs Duggan leaving the bar so dirty. She should stay at home with the gay priest, he dumped her to live with her sister, she said. Getting her to spill it in little bits, when her husband goes to the toilet, only chance I get."

"Well what has this to do with the barmaid's murder?"

"You brought Mrs Duggan up, Ben."

"Yes, I guess I did. Having spent time talking to her I feel that we need to know more about her. Gay priest you say. It came across like a love story when she told me about it. She didn't tell me that part. Maybe she was embarrassed by it. What unlikely course of events are we dealing with here, Ann?"

"The drifter's story, an old lady in the bar, the middle of the night, that's unlikely, right, Ben?."

166

The cop thought about that possibility for a while before talking about something else. "Duggan has a gay priest for a father, a preaching manic nun for a mother. Young brat Duggan must have been a demon, delivered unto them for a living hell. He had all the flawed attributes to test them. The gay priest having sex with the nun, he has to be bi-sexual. So, he must have been in some sort of sexual liaison with Rosie, right."

"I would say the missionary position it mightn't feel right any other way, Ben."

"The voice of experience knows all positions, essential information Detective Spellman."

They had a good laugh at that.

"Ann, the DA's office is considering charging the drifter Onion Head. They have him on the scene; he had a fight with her. His fingerprints are on the possible murder weapon. The assistant DA believes they have enough. He may have seen something that night, but passed out drunk, did he see, or dream. Yet, he never changes his story from the start.

"After my meeting with Mrs Duggan she could be what he saw. There are several possibilities that might have occurred. She could have opened the door for the killer. She probably knows Dan Ryan, Rosie's old boyfriend who might have had an axe to grind. We need to put him on our chat list. Then there is John Duggan who didn't know Rosie was his aunt. Why didn't he know? Why was it kept secret from him for so long? I think there's something else we're missing. We need to know more before we can reach any conclusion. That's for sure."

"Rosie shacked up with his father Ben. Maybe that pissed the son John off."

"Maybe, but he could have her killed on the street. Why take a chance doing her in on the job. John Duggan didn't want any notice from the police. I don't believe he is that stupid. It doesn't make sense. There must be another explanation. We have to check them all out. We are still waiting to get Onion Head's criminal record from the Boston police department. If he has a record, that might change my opinion of him. Right now I think he's innocent, in spite of all that's going against him, a timid man, with a rat for a friend."

"How's Donna doing, Ben, do you still take the kids on those hunting trips? Boy you're a risk taker, some grizzly will run off with that lovely wife of yours. I'll tell you, don't think you can come looking for me. No, sir, rather take my chances with the old bear instead."

"Hey come on, I'm not that bad am I?"

"Of course not, Ben. Just teasing. You're so sensitive. What about that Irish guy Flanagan. Tell me, where he fits into all this. I can't figure him out."

"He's clean, Ann; I kinda like the guy, I know where he's coming from, he's just trying to make a buck to return home to Ireland with his family. The guy's illegal here in the USA, I reckon he's still a bit green, just impressed with the hard core guys, trying to be like them, I think. They wouldn't trust him, no way. Hey, you want something to eat?"

"Yeah, I'd like some fries," patting her stomach, "You think I'm getting fat?"

"No, you're real skinny, that's the right answer, I know it, I'm learning at home."

Chapter Seventeen

When Rita left New York the problem multiplied. With no woman there to curtail it, alcohol took her husband out of control. It was the way he wanted to be, did everything to encourage it. Drinking was a way of life everything else had to fit in. As the booze twisted his thinking, he blamed Rita for everything. 'The wife packed up her bags, left me here all alone.'

That was the story he repeated, to anyone interested in listening. In the Celtic this version of events got no hearing. It had happened to most of them too. But loneliness would never get a chance to make them regret it.

Booze drowned those feelings, left them with a bad understanding of women. They were all whores' bitches; anything they had worth having could be bought. Paying for it got rid of any guilt. That suited them better. Joe was one of them now, with no woman holding him back.

Some men feel threatened when women try organizing them. From the dark conflicts of maternal wasteland, lingering doubts come back to haunt them. Women spot the demons all right. But instead of running, have this inclination to fix it. They're trapped in maternal instinct too. When it all goes wrong they get blamed for causing it.

It was hard for him to spend time where Rita used to be. The loneliness so unbearable, weekends he drank all the time, feeling sorry for himself. The whiskey took him over; he was in the grip of disturbing hallucinations. Unable to hold on to reality for long he drifted into periods of illusion. This was his reality for as long as it lasted.

The experience took the power of deep intensity exaggerating its frightening content. It played games with his fragile mind when he failed to cope with the fear of it. Hostile images arrived with a startling presence. His most consistent persecutor was a tall stranger, with a purple turban, a dark beard masking his ghoulish features. He glared around the door at him. Sometimes he opened it, to reveal his entire presence in the room before him.

A dark western suit denied his true identity.

He pointed to the window with a disarming gesture indicating to go see for himself. In the beginning the smiling expression tempted him to do the stranger's bidding.

His fear intensified seeing a chilling threat revealed in his eyes. He was trying to get him to jump out the window. That was his sole intent.

"No I won't," he screamed at him, trembling uncontrollably.

Suddenly as he arrived he disappeared, leaving him fearful. He was convinced he lurked outside in the hallway waiting to finish him. Afraid to rediscover him he cowered in the farthest corner of the room, gulping from the whiskey bottle. Taking sups of torment to make reality better. That only fuelled the horror.

Hostile images returned. The alcohol sweating made his skin reek. The smell reminded him of a fatal accident he came upon in his youth.

That reminder of past anxiety made him more scared. He cried out for Rita to help him, flailing his arms in a vain attempt to protect himself. Then recovering long enough to wonder if he was imagining it, it took hold of him again for doubting it.

He screamed, wailed like a man possessed. "Make him go away, Rita, he wants to kill me," he sobbed, scurrying around the floor looking for the letter again, wanting her to be with him in the room. She'd know how to handle the stranger. Rita could fix anything. He stared down at her handwriting, felt safe with her words. He could even hear her saying them.

My Dear Joe,

I am leaving this letter for you as it is with deep regret that I have decided to return home to Ireland. The trauma that I have endured has finally got too much for me and I am unable to manage living in New York any longer. We have had some happy times here when you were sober and we could live as a couple and enjoy our life together, but things have been getting worse and drink has taken my place in this marriage and I am unable to cope. I have felt so very alone in the apartment not knowing when you would return and having nobody to help me with Mary. She is our daughter and I know it is very difficult for you to accept her handicap. Each day I have to contend with Mary and while I managed for a time I am both mentally and physically exhausted and I feel so sad and useless. I have nobody to talk with and Mary needs a more secure environment with more love and my individual attention. The final straw came when she had an epileptic seizure and I knocked for help on the apartment next door, the lady closed the door in my face. If I was in Ireland that would not happen and I would be able to get help. I need family and friends to help me and talk to me and keep me going; someone to share my concern. I love you, Joe, and always will. You have always been kind and caring but unfortunately drink has taken all that away. The change in your personality is frightening and I really think that you don't know what you are doing or saying. With drink you become arrogant, argumentative and very nasty.

I always seem to get the blame and am accused of doing something to drive you to drink. I know, Joe, this is only an excuse but I haven't got the energy any more and feel unable to deal with your drink problem. I am returning to Ireland under a great cloud of sadness. I am so worried that something bad will happen to you and your health is at risk right now. I hope you will be able to get help and when you do I'm only a phone call away and I hope at some stage when you get sober you will return to Ireland and we can somehow put all this behind us for good. Please, Joe, don't throw everything away,

I cannot bear to think of you, such a sensitive man, finishing up alone with a bottle of whiskey for company and you are so much better than this. We were almost so happy at some stage so why let the demon drink take everything away from us. Please try and look after yourself, Joe.

Love Rita. xxx

In the hog hut the unlikely alliance of Sullivan played out with Lupe. Discrete negatives about Duggan kept the mad miner wound up. Hazy evenings rolled back on his porch in Tennessee nurtured a compulsive habit, sharpening his knife.

He was sitting at a table greasing the sandstone with spittle. Working patiently turning the blade over, cutting his thumb testing the razor edge made Sullivan winch when blood trickled down on the wooden floor. He'd been watching him for a while; time he said something.

"Duggan says there's no rabbits to skin in New York."

Lupe grinned at him when he heard that. Tobacco slobbers trickling down his unshaven chin. "I take his head off clean, with ole Jim Bowie here."

When Lupe slid the knife close to his throat the company man swallowed. "No rabbits in that bar he owns either, I bet."

"You know ole Lupe going there when times right."

"Every Friday night he drinks late, walks home alone."

Sullivan signalled Lupe to follow him.

Limpy listening behind a locker got irritated when they went to the washroom. He hadn't heard enough yet. Lupe wanted to kill Duggan he was sure about that. Getting that job done was a difficult matter. Duggan's training. His experience in Special Forces was primed instinct. The hillbilly wouldn't know what hit him.

No matter how much he wished for the end of Duggan it was unlikely to happen that way. He didn't have much respect for Sullivan either, screwing him up bad after his accident.

He was on his hit list too.

Duggan's gang was finally sent to work contract maintenance. With all the hassle going down on the main job it was a welcome transfer in the end. At least they could remain removed from tensions associated with the tunnel competition. Out of sight out of mind sort of a scenario. But it provided some breathing space for everyone concerned. That was one of the aims of this undertaking; the other involved much needed repairs.

First, they set up stall on the street by erecting a coloured canvass circle around the manhole cover, passing down all their equipment. It was a slow descent through the cramped darkness on small iron steps. The sewer tunnels were constructed in curved brick, the old way of doing things. The workmanship of those long deceased men was of high calibre. Standing up well to the demands of time, but they were not intended to last forever. Though the city monitored their condition regularly, the cement pointing between the brick's finally eroded. That caused the structure to loosen; replacing it was a slow tedious job. The maintenance program was about finding brick's that needed replacing. Occasionally some of them fell on the ground causing a blockage. Duggan's gang had been working on this job for a few days, making good a recent cave in. The first part of the job was stopping the flow with sandbags some distance upstream from the problem site. The gang then removed all the collapsed debris.

The entire area was hosed down with strong detergent. This got rid of all greasy loose matter, so the cement could set. Duggan sent Flanagan to monitor sandbags up from where they worked. It was not something he liked doing, too much time to think on his own. Problems annoyed his troubled head. Some of his greatest fears would come back to haunt him.

He was looking up at the row of iron steps leading down from the street. They were just wide enough to take the size of a man's shoulders.

It would be difficult getting back up there in a hurry. Being savaged by alligators on the job was his biggest worry. In the close dim lit place the sweat poured out of him thinking about them. Duggan's last words were still ringing in his ears. He seemed to know something.

'I won't be checking on you any more, Flanagan, keep your eyes on them sandbags. If they start moving, call us, so we can get outa the fuk'n way."

"Move where, Duggan, where can that wall move to."

He'd pointed to a trickle of water dribbling over the middle bags.

"Ya see there. When it gets higher the pressure can push it on top of ya. It could come rushing down the tunnel like a dam bursting. Drown the fuk'n lot of us so keep your eyes on it. Don't let them alligators near us. They might eat us all."

Duggan left him to re-join the gang downstream. When he was walking away he dragged his leg after him, like Limpy. It was something that only a sicko like Duggan could laugh about. The sewers were a sludge hole full of dangerous reptiles Flanagan imagined. The gang seemed to be acting weird; Duggan wouldn't shut up about it, giving everyone the shivers. Everything indicated the slimy creatures were under the grey sludge just waiting to ambush someone. Doyle knew it too, telling Flanagan before the shift started. He said it in a concerned way because he meant it. 'Phone me if you're in trouble.' In trouble with what, he never said what kind of trouble.

As the trickle of water increased, it appeared to be putting pressure on the bags. Flanagan needed to talk with someone about that. He scrambled for the phone for Doyle's reassurance.

The line was dead. He got more anxious about alligators.

It was part of urban legend in New York City; there were many sightings of alligators in the city sewers confirmed down the years.

174

Some well documented news items as a result. Alligator stories repeated by the mad caretaker felt more real now. This freaked out guy watching the sandbags couldn't handle the pressure of it any more. It got into his head.

At about the same time, sickening events were taking place on the main Manhattan site.

Limpy made a complaint to the general foreman about a foul smell coming from Lupe's locker. Mario accompanied him back to the hog hut to get a whiff of the problem for himself.

When the locker was forced open he was sick to the pit of his stomach looking at its contents. The human arm hanging in the locker was decaying. There were maggots crawling all over it.

The smell was bad all right. His greatest fear realized, this incident would close the job down for sure. That's all that mattered to him. He swore in foul Italian lingo, before hastily addressing the men.

"Leave everything as it is get out of the hut immediately. I'll call the cops."

He instructed his son to take names. Let everyone wait around outside; the police will talk to you guys later."

He called Sullivan when he returned to his office, spat out the bad news to him.

"Somebody killed you say."

Sullivan sounded cheerful; Mario resented that, everyone else up to their balls in trouble.

"This Lupe miner, it's possible murder; get over here right away, Sullivan, the police might want to talk with you." He hung up on him.

The company trouble shooter at the other end felt a smug feeling coming over him. If it's Duggan great news, or Lupe, better still, Duggan would be prime suspect.

Detective Brady entered the general foreman's hut without bothering with formalities. The cops were in charge of the site now. It was a crime scene.

"Oh, sir, we believe the tattoos on the fingers identifies the origin of the arm. This Lupe guy got any enemies you know of?"

"I wouldn't know the answer to that question, Sergeant. Maybe some of the men could help you. My direct contact with the workforce is limited. It never gets on a personal level. The company representative, Sullivan, is the main point of contact for all miners. You could have a word with him, when he arrives."

The Sergeant made his way over to the hog hut then. Limpy was standing outside it. When the cop recognized him, he got the surprise of his life. "What do you know; it's Dan Ryan on his feet. Hey, you never told me you could walk."

"You never asked me that question, Sergeant."

"What's your job?"

"I'm caretaker here."

"Right, you know this Lupe guy?"

"Yeah, I know all the other men working here. The same way I know you, Sergeant, from a healthy distance."

"We'd like you to explain that a bit more, Mr Ryan."

Just then Sullivan rolled up on to the site. He wasn't allowed past the crime tape so he walked over to Mario's office. The general foreman was in a foul mood, looking ten years older, since twenty-four hours earlier. "What's going on, Mario?"

"It appears that there is a dead miner somewhere, Sullivan. You want to join the search for the body. Maybe company policy prevents you from looking for dead bodies, eh. Especially bodies with no official miner permits in our records shouldn't even be on the job."

Sullivan felt the panic. "Sure if I can help out in any way, but a missing body. Come on, Mario, shit happens, women, drink, everything goes."

With his palms up disarmingly, the look that Mario hated.

"Who's missing, Mario?"

"Lupe, the hillbilly guy, they're looking for his body. The killer's still at large."

Sullivan started worrying when he heard the news. He hadn't figured on that ending becoming a reality. He was getting concerned for his own future. He told the general foreman he wanted to talk with the men. Making that empty excuse he hurried from the site office. He remembered Lupe threatening, 'When the time was right, he'd get him; How wrong that foolish statement turned out to be.

It was possible that Duggan tortured Lupe as he killed him. Maybe he found out it was Sullivan that wanted him dead, before pulling his arm out of the socket, him probably still alive at the time. What could he do now, remain calm, if that was possible. Wait to see how things developed. If the shit started flying there was only one thing left for him to do. Sullivan knew he had the balls to carry it out. It might have to be done to save his family reputation. That's the way Sullivan's mind worked. It was all about pride in family. This outward appearance of domestic bliss conveyed to all interested parties everything was fine in the Sullivan household. That image, the charm of upstanding citizens was what it was all about. Nothing else really mattered.

What you see you don't get.

Chapter Eighteen

The tunnel detail was a living hell for Flanagan. Isolated on sandbag spotting, the gang weary of his company, his thinking confused, fear of alligators intensifying, he fought the terrifying voices in his head. 'Left there, so they could eat him, Duggan was trying to get rid of him for money he owed.' Or things he knew. Now he was sure of it. He trembled, staring at the wall of sandbags bulging before him.

His eyes widened in horror when it spewed a splash of grey sludge in front of him. He screamed when the alligator's jaws opened, the terrifying echo carried throughout the damp eerie hole. He scrambled through the tunnel, jumping to save his legs from been bitten off him. Stumbling, searching for eyes glowing in the darkness, fearing the sight of them. He made it to where the rest of the gang worked.

"Hey, Flanagan, what's up." Doyle didn't laugh this time.

"He's after me, the alligator's after me."

They shone their lights up the tunnel; the sandbags were out of range.

"Mitchell, have a look, will you."

"Will I fuck? Look yourself, Duggan." He even had the balls to stare his boss down saying it.

Fear alters course of respect when doubt challenges presence of mind.

Red Mitchell just discovered something he was more scared of than his boss. Taking a look at Flanagan changed everything, the price of loyalty tumbled; the difference of opinion was obvious. Arming themselves with picks they headed cautiously up the sewer. Butcher stayed behind to keep his eye on Flanagan. Doyle gave him strict orders what to do. "Take care of him till we get back make sure nothing happens to him."

Meanwhile back on the main site the crime scene was swarming with police.

 In the general foreman's office Mario cursed the bad luck of this job. He didn't want to listen to any more self-serving bullshit. Sullivan had arrived back; he was giving him the creeps talking. This guy had been getting away with too much for a long time.

"What can I say, Mario. Arm ripped off, real mafia stuff, don't mean to be personal."

Sullivan shook his head for his bigmouth. He'd heard all about the Italian connections.

Especially those warm relations with his Sicilian cousins. Everybody knew about it, but few of them made the mistake of saying it. He wasn't thinking right, just proved how hassled he was. He couldn't get it out of his head that Lupe talked before he was murdered. If Duggan knew he wanted him out of the way. Would the maniac be coming after him next? What could he do to protect himself, he had a gun but so did Lupe, look where he finished up.

All this police attention was freaking him out. His confident demeanour disappeared. "Open the door Sullivan, there is a police officer trying to get in."

"I got it."

"Excuse me, sir. I would like to have a word with Mr Catapani."

"Of course, come in."

"We want to speak with John Duggan. Where is he, right now?"

The general foreman made an issue of consulting his work roster. "He's working on another site. He should be here within the hour."

"Okay, sir," the cop nodded when Sullivan let him out.

"It didn't take the police long to figure things, Mario."

"I guess not, you'd better go over, see what's happening?"

Sullivan was pleased to get away from him. He hoped they nailed that Duggan bastard, in a hurry. He could be next. When he saw the sergeant, he headed straight over to him. "Detective, could I talk with you?"

"Yes, sir, want to talk right here?"

"This Duggan guy, Sergeant, is dangerous. People scared to say it."

"Oh yeah? Why is that?"

"Everyone knows he did it. He said he was going to do it, just like it happened too. He's far too dangerous to leave out on the prowl."

"Talking about crime is not the same as committing crime. There has to be sufficient proof, sir."

Sullivan was irritated by the cop's attitude.

"I want to ask you a few questions, sir," the cop said taking out his notebook.

"Sure."

"What's your employment title?"

"I'm the company representative."

"You have direct contact with the men, that right?"

"I suppose so."

"Did you know the victim?"

"No, not personally of course I know them all. But I don't know them well. My work involves more of the employment details."

"Take care of employment records, details like that, right."

Sullivan heard that one.

"Make sure everything is okay with them," the cop suggested.

"I guess so," said Sullivan.

"Thank you, sir!"

Sullivan wondered who was disclosing stories about work permits to the police. It had to be Mario trying to get him involved as some sort of a shady character.

The thing that concerned Sergeant Brady was why Sullivan denied knowing the victim Lupe? Because the caretaker Limpy Ryan had already made specific mention of their close friendship, he said they were always playing poker. Sullivan had just told him a lie for some reason. Ryan also said they spent lots of time talking together, in the men's room. Was he hinting at a possible gay encounter? Is that what the caretaker was insinuating. He doubted that, but there had to be something going on between them, if Ryan was telling the truth.

He was determined to find out more about it. Limpy was a good nickname for Ryan, it suited his unstable behaviour. He was shaky in every department as far as the cop was concerned. His previous experiences of him made him suspicious. Singing to the cops about someone generally indicates a cover up somewhere.

He would have to cough up more details on his eavesdropping next time he talked with him. That wouldn't be too far away. Ryan was a very slippery customer. Brady knew he'd have to keep both eyes on him since there were other possibilities to consider.

The action under the streets of Chinatown was still playing out. Duggan's gang had just seen Flanagan freaked out. They went cautiously through the sewer to where he worked. The pile of sandbags was still intact when they arrived, so the alligator story was bullshit.

Everything was as expected. They were convinced of his hallucinating; the crew blamed it on his heavy drinking. There was little sympathy with that condition. He was wasting too much valuable time. On their way back to where butcher waited, Doyle preached tolerance. He explained to Duggan how it was. Flanagan was freaked out all right. But he was one of them that should count for something. Duggan was less inclined to be forgiving.

"He needs to get his shit together; I'll straighten his ass out. He has us all looking bad creeping around the tunnel, like a bunch of fuk'n dicks."

Much later when Duggan's gang arrived to the hog hut, the place was cordoned off. Limpy peered out the window watching them pulling up outside. Flanagan was subdued in spirit; Doyle had been talking the good talk to him hoping for something to register.

"I see you dumping shots of whiskey into your beer. It's a bad habit to get into. Boilermakers will kill your brain eventually. It's bound to drive you mad in the head, I can tell you that. I once saw gorillas looking in the window at me. After drinking that shit. Except my apartment was on the fourteenth floor, I was only on it for a week at the time."

He was so serious that Flanagan laughed in spite of everything. Doyle could take on the appearance of a gorilla with his mud soaked hair dangling over his face.

"Maybe they thought you were family, Tash."

He'd just said that, when the cops approached the gang. Sergeant Brady arrested John Duggan on the spot, took him separately, while the rest of them were rounded up.

A few officers cuffed them. It was an all too familiar sight, Duggan's gang getting trooped off in the paddy wagon again. They ignored Flanagan for some reason, leaving him standing there as they loaded his workmates. Not one of the cops even acknowledged him.

The next day when Flanagan arrived into work he got a cruel reception. Without a gang of his own he tried shaping the other crews for a shift. No one would oblige him. He was very bad news. Treated with scorn by everyone he met. The victim of every bad joke, called Alligator Man, a failed sand hog. He must be a rat if the cops let him go, they muttered. Why wasn't he brought downtown to be interrogated, with his buddies? Doyle's intimidating presence had taken care of him so far, now that protection was missing. He was on his own. They let him know it. The respect he worked so hard for in the beginning was gone. The story of Lupe's arm ripped out from the socket had everybody spooked. The tale doing the rounds was growing out of shape. Everyone was speculating about something. He was glad they had other things to occupy them, it gave him a break.

Duggan was held in custody, the rest of the men were released. Doyle was put in charge of the crew by the general foreman. The gang were still toiling away on maintenance work.

Things were a bit different now. Flanagan was no longer allowed to be alone. The new boss was keeping a better eye on him.

Doyle's gang worked away under the streets of Chinatown. They never mentioned alligators to him any more. The atmosphere improved, Tash was a good boss. Flanagan was still drinking; the tormented soul got no peace. He slept in the bar all the time now, staying away from the apartment. Nobody could be bothered with him for being such a pain in the ass. His appearance was desperate looking, with a black unkempt beard. He showered in the hog hut using Doyle's fragrant shampoos. It didn't matter how rough you looked, if you kept yourself clean. He got his food from the deli, if he needed to eat. That wasn't often.

One morning, Doyle left the Celtic with Flanagan in tow for breakfast in a diner on the corner of 42 nd St. They got stuck into big steaks with fried eggs, pancakes as well. The place was buzzing, coffees to go, flying out the door. Secretaries, drunks, whores, doormen, pimps, labourers, cops, suits with briefcases. They were all in there, mixing it up on their way somewhere else. Some of them didn't like being together at all.

New York's variety of people weren't fond of seeing much of each other.

"How are you now, Flanagan? You okay after that big feed, more coffee?"

"Tash, what do you think about Duggan isn't he unreal?"

"Duggan is his own worst enemy. In Vietnam I had my leg busted. He could have left me there, but he didn't. Then a month later we got in another sticky situation. He was badly injured. After that things got all screwed up in his head!"

"He's crazy isn't he?"

"That's something to do with it, I guess."

Doyle stirred the coffee, eyeing him.

"I feel responsible for him sometimes. That's only the start of it. But I wish it was all of it, fancy a trip downtown for a look, Flanagan?"

"You know me, anything is better than going home, Doyle."

Flanagan tried to keep his eyes open with a little chatter in the cab. "Are you still seeing Jessica?"

When Doyle didn't answer he looked round to see if he was dozing, he wasn't. Flanagan had long established that they were all weird. He had to accept he was weird too. He took a look at his face in the mirror. There it was that same weirdness looking right back at him?

Doyle asked the driver to pull in off First Avenue; they came to a halt outside a joint called the Volcano. It would be hard to miss the name painted like flames of fire across the front. Flanagan stood looking at it when they got out. The inscription printed in big black letters underneath said, *When Volcano erupts anything can happen.*

"Good, another tit bar."

They had a few whiskey shots with beers, the perfect launch to another day.

"What do you think of it here, Flanagan?" Doyle asked with a smirk on his face.

Then it seemed every weirdo in the city charged in the door. Like as if it was planned. The Volcano kicked in all right, filling up with people in all sorts of leather studded outfits, party dresses, clowns, painted faces, mixing weird with wonderful, like the remnants of some Mardi Gras parade, where guys looked like

184

girls, girls looked like guys, all revelling in each other's company, daring for something different, touching in on another part of themselves.

"Tash, what are we doing in here."

"You asked me in the diner about Duggan. This is where he spends a lot of his time. Right here with these weirdos. Shit, thought this would be the last place he'd go."

Doyle pointed his finger, "See that door down the end there. That's where Duggan really likes to party."

Flanagan strained his eyes. "Is it a disco area?"

"I was only in here once before with Duggan," Doyle was saying."He asked me to be his invited guest at some sort of coming out deal. I wasn't listening to it. He was calling it his inauguration. I think he must have meant initiation, when he was accepted as a fully-fledged member of the far out brigade here. He had to live his fantasies out in the open for everyone to see. He was cleansed, accepted on that occasion, it wasn't pretty. I wished he didn't involve me at the time but I was his only chance. Too big of a fuck up to land on anyone else, I guess. That was the rules if he wanted to be like them, he had to present a straight person that accepted him as he was. They humiliated him into it. He had to be degraded first it seems before they allowed him to be reborn again, freed. Never will I forget the scene."

"Why?"

"He was dressed like his mother." Doyle stopped talking, waiting for the question.

"He was what, tell me."

"His mother, he wanted to be his mother."

"Oh fuck me, I shouldn't be here, I know it now. How could he be his own mother, or anyone else's mother?"

"That's what this club is all about, Flanagan; you can be who you like in here. He becomes his mother, in front of one of his straight friends, that's me. That's why he invited me down here. I thought he was going to be a president or something. The way he said he was going to be honoured. I came along to see what kind of a nut outfit would be honouring him. He was crying first, then, he was laughing when he felt so free. The strangest thing, it scared the shit outa me."

Flanagan was already calling back at him over his shoulder. "Com' on I'm out of here now."

Doyle wanted to sit down for more drinks.

"Don't even think about it, Tash. I'm leaving."

Tash Doyle had off loaded his burden but it didn't feel good. Now he had someone else wondering about Duggan's sanity. He wasn't going to think about it any more. Joe Flanagan wanted to move away from it too. At least he wouldn't be asking any more questions about Duggan. That conversation was over. But Doyle wanted to do some more explaining.

He couldn't shut up about it in the cab. "It was supposed to be an honour for me, can you believe that. You know something; you know what the worst part was Flanagan."

"What could be worse than this, Tash?"

"He was dressed up like his mother when everyone applauded. He cried like a little boy, I remembered it from when we were young. It was exactly the same. Maybe that's why I was invited, I'd seen it before. Wig, dress, apron the lot, like he won a prize or something. Like those crowd around the bar earlier. I used to visit his apartment when I was a kid; his mother was weird even then. That's the way she dressed him up. He'd get paranoid attacks about it when he got older. He didn't know what he was, a boy or a girl. We can't tell anyone about this shit, Flanagan. It's our bond of secrecy; we keep it safe between us."

"Why did I have to hear everything?"

"You asked, Flanagan, I must protect him though, my duty."

Doyle offered him his hand in the back of the cab. He shook it. What they shared he wished he didn't know about. It was such a load a shit to dump on everything else bothering him. Was he going mad, how else could you explain it?

186

They agreed to sleep for a few hours then meet up later for more drink.

The cab dropped him off at his apartment building. He was still full of the bad Volcano vibes when he seen a few cardboard boxes at the front door. He fumbled for the key, cursing when a box tipped its contents. Then he stared at it for a while, was it some of his stuff.

The Irish passport on the steps was the best clue.

This situation was known as eviction in Ireland. He had come all the way to America to get dumped out of his home. The notice on the apartment door confirmed the agent changed all the locks. The thing about it was, he was glad. He didn't like the place any more. Drunks don't do a good job on rental payments, illegal aliens are reluctant to complain to the police. His deposit was gone he didn't care. He was glad he didn't have anything to carry with him. It was easier that way. Homeless, broke, what happens now. He had only himself to blame.

After making a hopeless kick at the pile of belongings, he picked up the passport. It would remind him who he was even if no one else wanted to know. He stuck it in his pocket taking off down the street. What else was there to do for an asshole no one wanted to work with?

This was the way it was finally meant to be. Alligator man, a danger in the tunnel. No thrust, no respect, no hope. There was a sense of freedom about it. He remembered what the cab driver said going to the Dolls Home club. 'See the bowery there, every poor soul shuffling round out there is hiding or lost.'

He'd hide where they couldn't get to him any more. Down the Bowery, with nowhere else left to go.

He'd been in a similar situation already, a long time ago, that first time when he finally broke free of them. He remembered how it helped him then, in the end; when he got used to it.

Chapter 19

A few days after volcano erupted Tash Doyle spotted her strolling down the street. She looked as if she had all the time in the world while he was rushing to their meeting place.

He was determined not to screw up by being late. He expected that she might be doing the same thing. But he was wrong about that. She was taking her time.

"That's girls for you"

He muttered, a pleasing smile spreading across his face telling the driver to pull over, opening the door to shout at her.

"Hi, want a cab."

"Sure do."

It was her night off; she was looking forward to meeting up with him again.

"What's up, don't you thrust cab drivers."

"I'm getting exercise Doyle."

"I thought you got enough of that in the Celtic."

She sat in the back beside him.

He didn't approve of her dance routine she could only imagine what that was about.

It was none of his business what she did with her life.

Men were having no part in her decision making ever again.

That was a promise she made, when she escaped from the last mess she got into.

She remembered her mother saying some women were attracted to men that were no good for them. Learning little from previous bad experiences was the curse of a woman's life.

But she thought it might benefit her investigations to date one of the bad guys. He could say something stupid that made perfect sense to a cop. Who's going to know about that? It's not as if she was going to tell Sergeant Brady what she did in the line of duty. Not when she was so looking forward to it. That might spoil the whole thing.

The cab pulled into the side, letting them out in front of the Old Haunt Bar. It was far enough away from the Celtic to get spotted. Out of sight, where sand hogs wouldn't go.

The bar was geared mostly for business types.

"Thanks, my shoes were starting to hurt. I didn't realize it was such a long walk."

She informed him.

"Heels like that." He said.

With that satisfied looking grin on his face, she totally ignored. Some guys see everything as a positive when they're on the hunt. Doyle was more interested ogling her shapely legs, stepping out on the sidewalk. Their previous date started off well, but a premature bedroom move ended the evening. It could be why he met up with her again. Men have notches on bedposts in their head a foolish sense of failure if it doesn't happen. The passionate embrace, the feel of her tongue in his mouth, still a lingering sensation.

He got the soft sweet scent of perfume opening the bar door for her. It was nice.

He was determined to make all the right moves this time round. Could be she was deliberately making things difficult for him, giving an impression she wasn't just anybody's.

He knew the story all right, been there before. Same as it ever was.

His effort would be well rewarded, Doyle knew that too. When they played hard to get, it was often worth having. Like a little bit of something not readily available, pampered, warm for the right guy. He had serious thoughts about this piece of ass. Nothing would throw him.

"I thought you'd chicken out."

She said to him.

He flashed the pearly grin.

"There was no chance of that happening."

"Oh, that's good."

She said, a bit flustered when she realized she meant it.

"You look great Betty Ann."

She'd put a lot of thought into what she wore, not wanting to look like a pole dancer was her primary concern. It was a more conservative outfit; plain black dress with matching handbag the black shoes had a buckle on each of them. A touch of class she thought, different.

Definitely not a 'fuck me now outfit' by any means. So far away from his familiar image of her, see how he handled a bit of style. When she noticed his hooded eyes brooding on her cleavage, she adjusted the neckline naturally, letting him see her doing that.

Maybe he might appreciate her modesty.

No point having him ogling down her front while she was trying to take control of things. Yet, she retained the composure to return his compliment.

"You clean up good yourself Doyle."

Smiling warmly, appreciating his effort to impress her. She had asked him specifically not to wear jeans. It was being respectful to make a good impression on a date.

She told him about her early upbringing in riches. A young society girl, the private school her father insisted she attend. Well educated in case she ever took to running the family business. But she was heading for stardom deciding to be an actor instead. On she went telling him stories, jabbering away ten to the dozen. Doyle listened, he wondered too. But he stayed quiet. Saying nothing, nothing till he knew. What the right thing was to do.

She couldn't imagine herself talking like this to Ann Spellman's prospective suitors. Not that they were plentiful on the ground, she was very hard to please. Betty Ann could have a different line on things. She reckoned that Doyle wouldn't be too concerned about what impression he made on a woman. As long as he got what he was after. That's why she could play him any way she liked; this wasn't going anywhere, until it suited her. If he made the right moves on this particular night, it could make all the difference. He must be interested in the whole package. Not just the sex, their primary objective. It was hard for them to hide it.

Allowing her the courtesy of choosing a table was another good move. She was pleased he was thinking the proper way of going about it. That would not be his usual consideration she was sure about that. He gestured towards the tables. She was careful to choose a quiet area, away from the window. New York was still a small place. Meeting someone she knew was a remote possibility. It was one she was always aware of in her line of work.

She didn't want to be recognized.

Doyle figured the dress sense to be a statement, a sign of intent; women didn't make that kind of effort unless they were interested in getting laid. That's the way these things appeared to him. While she hoped he'd remember the important part of the evening's arrangement.

The drawn out romantic dinner, dancing the night away, she had it all planned.

"Let's have a drink here first then we go over the east side for food."

"Where are we going?"

"It's a surprise Doyle."

"You look different when you're in the Celtic."

"Gee thanks, you're so observant."

"Am I,"

He smiled.

"You Am,"

She smiled back at him.

"Oh let's not talk about work anymore Doyle. Let's have a mystery evening instead."

"Mystery sure, I can do a little mystery."

The smile broadened.

"What kind of mystery you got in mind Betty Ann."

She considered for a while.

"Pretend we're two complete strangers again. We just hooked up."

"Betty Ann we know each other too well for that shit we talk every day for Christ's sake."

"That's it, that's it right there; we don't know who we are. I don't want to talk like that when we're out on a date. We want to be complete strangers. With no interest in each other's work for the whole evening. Right Doyle, you up for that challenge."

"But strangers want to find out more about each other real fast don't they."

She smiled at the simplicity of men.

"Yes of course, but wouldn't it be wonderful to be strangers for longer.

More magical I think to discover each other slowly, like an orchid."

"What's an orchard got to do with it?"

"No Doyle orchid, a delicate flower that chooses when to reveal its own loveliness, a bit like I am as a matter of fact, that's why I make such comparison."

"No shit, you're too much. Hey, for a little mystery I'm ready to play."

"See, I knew you'd have an adventurous streak in you, somewhere."

"You plan to do all this."

"Yes Doyle everything is planned."

She laughed.

"See how much fun it is."

"Why, what's it all about."

"Ah ha, no way, that parts a mystery."

"Come on spell it out to me, tell me where I'm going".

"Right let me see, I don't tell you anything because of the mystery thing. We deal with matters relating to the present this evening; we have just met up with each other.

Our very first date, you're besotted with me of course. We can't talk about the past or the future, haven't you heard Doyle that yesterday is history, tomorrow a mystery today present."

"Okay sounds good to me. Let's make our present the best."

He held his glass out to her; "Let's drink to that."

He knew that getting her into bed could be tough going. Last time she turned nasty on him when he thought he was there. He discovered she couldn't be rushed. She probably figured that he would tell the rest of the crew all the intimate details. Have them sniggering about her in the bar, he could hardly blame her for that.

As for the future part of it, he wanted to give her all the present she could take.

He'd even gift wrap it for her too. If that's the way she liked it.

She thought he looked like a movie star, his pink shirt was a remarkable choice, letting her see his feminine side. She had never seen him wearing a suit before now. It was a light brown colour good with the shirt, a tie would have been perfect, but that was too much to expect.

She noticed he had shampooed his hair, trimmed his moustache, it looked well. The flutter she got making eye contact, set the tone for the cab ride downtown. The driver got his instructions; take in Central Park, Doyle's idea for a romantic interlude.

They giggled, whispering, kissing sometimes. The warmth of her breath excited him.

All the way to the restaurant with plenty of time to become better acquainted.

Whitehall St beside the Staten Island ferry terminal was where it was at.

The cab pulled over to the side, letting them out there. The Cuban restaurants wooden facade was well weathered. It had been water sprayed for a long time. It gave the restaurant a most inviting look. The name Old Havana was painted in big lettering over the door. A feeling you saw it somewhere before struck you. The charm of the place reached out to you, helping you to remember it. Even in your worst moment in time you'd go back there.

A copper faced old man in a straw hat sat rolling cigars with his fingers in a cubby hole inside the door. It felt a privilege to discover him. He rolled up two for Betty Ann. She held them in her hand making for the dance floor. Then she started into a few eye catching salsa moves. Doyle put the cigars in his top pocket joining the action. Straight up his street.

He could Salsa as good as the best of them. It was all about the swivelling feeling he put into it. The seduction was in the moves. Doyle was artist in residence.

The intention to beguile deliberate.

The mating season could be brought forward with a few nifty shapes. He was sure of that. The magical mover was up for it every step of the way.

"Think you're there already."

She whispered in his ear when they came closer.

"I haven't stopped thinking about getting in there since I met up with you."

"Bad boy Doyle, I was talking about Cuba. The atmosphere here's like Cuba."

"I hope I'm going there with you."

"Are you not going to be waiting when I arrive? You're not very romantic are you?

I'm starting to get a bit disappointed. That's not progress Doyle, not good at all."

Doyle kept his mouth shut when he heard that. He'd do a few more poetic shifts instead.

Women were lethal when they started that playing hard to get shit. Sometimes the few drinks brought the madness out of them, when their guard dropped, the wrong word, game over.

He was smart enough to play it anyway she wanted. But he'd watch her like a hawk as well.

It was think about it time again. He grinned at her through the neatly trimmed moustache his head tilted, a sort of Che Guevara look about him. No matter what kind of shit she came up with, he'd stay on track all right. Like a professional soldier, a knight of the garter. He'd keep it up all night long too, if she liked it like that. There was something special about this one. But he didn't want to admit that. The truth was he wanted her more than ever now. He was even pissed off with himself for thinking it. He hadn't a clue about Cuban coffee, thought you could only get it there. Until she informed him the best brew in New York was right back in her apartment. Doyle was too much of a gentleman to contest that claim.

The cab journey back to her place was a more passionate affair.

Caressing each other whispering things they'd like to do. Even the cab driver got turned on listening to it. Prolonging pleasure thrilled the moment, but patience could run out of time.

Sometimes giggling fits if Doyle's moustache tickled her. The windows steamed up.

When Doyle discovered her intimate secret he mumbled appraisal of this most sought after of all conditions known to man.

He couldn't believe his good fortune.

"You're not wearing any knickers."

He was sort of accusing her.

"No Doyle, I've been expecting you all evening. You weren't clever enough to notice."

The old driver smiled in the mirror when he saw him going down. He took his foot of the gas to prolong the sightseeing. A service provided many times before to help his fellow man.

He tried the back seat a few times himself in the past. Something to tell his wife when the shift's over, the young ones were still at it, just like it was in their day. Some good things never change. Leave them alone, they'll be old soon enough. Such wonderful happenings might never come to an end for some passengers. But it did, in time to let the fantasy begin.

Betty Ann had tried fixing a few things in the apartment it didn't change the cheap feel of it. She didn't bother making excuses either, that might be bad for her image. It was clean that was enough? Importantly, Doyle was looking for more action. Now it was time to prolong the show. She watched him dump his jacket carelessly on the couch, so she folded her coat neatly, looking over at him. He got the message, fixing his own.

If he could be trained, anything was possible.

"A mug of coffees okay for you now, Doyle."

She put some thought into the visit, changing her bedclothes earlier in the day.

With a few feminine touches too, the scent of lavender. She had selected the track into the mystic that grew towards a climax. She loved catching the rising fall of it. Pressing the tape machine on, she could feel the heat of his eyes, watching her.

"Am I doing okay?"

"What's up?"

Doyle was tuned into scarcity of sound, the bullshit was over.

"You want a little whiskey in it," she asked.

"I don't do the whiskey thing. Not, before I do the pussy thing."

"Oh, I'm glad you remembered to tell me that. You're so romantic."

She handed him the mug on her way to the bathroom.

"Get real Doyle; this is not a pussy bar."

This is a cathedral of worship. I hope you remember that too."

Doyle lounged on the old couch sipping coffee, waiting. He had one of those would it ever arrive looks on his face. She strolled back into the room naked, letting the air blow through it.

Betty Ann wasn't one of the shy types for long, acting was expressive. She wasn't self-conscious either. It was all good. Dimming the light, she smiled, unbuttoning his pink shirt, whispering the words softly to him. It was all part of the present game.

"It took time to get the present. Now we have time to enjoy it. Don't open it too soon.

Cats like playing with things first. You want me to purr, don't you Doyle?"

"Yeah baby purring all night long, I'll do the worship thing on your cathedral."

"Oh you're so original Doyle, do you ever stop." She giggled.

"Not till I'm exhausted."

He wheezed.

Chapter Twenty

Jenny Lei Wovoka stepped out on the pavement from a rattling old service lift. Her hair fell in long black plaits each side of her bronzed features. Wearing a long coat, a wide brimmed hat with the crown banded in silver medallions. She carried a knife, a flashlight in her pocket, a bottle of cheap whiskey in the bag over her shoulder. It was just past midnight, the old buildings stood quiet. There was a full moon overlooking the whole proceedings.

Empty cardboard boxes scattered along Howard Street for collection in the early morning light. Not a sound to be heard, the kind of night she might get lucky. Sometimes searching this dangerous world could be risky, even for her. She headed across Lafayette past Canal Street to Bayard then Mulberry, where the lights of Chinatown illuminated the sky. Her destination Columbus Park loomed ahead of her, its intimidating presence shrouded in darkness. She moved with the prowling purpose of a panther. A path worn on the grass led her towards huddled figures stretched out for the night. Sleep was temporary release for these troubled souls, if they got any. She shone a light in the face of one disgruntled wino; he threw a bottle at her. His aim was way off. A gang of youths ran past, making little sound on the green turf. Quiet enough, for words to drift.

"Hey, Brazil, check out de Indian bitch."

"She's bad. Stick' a blade in your ass, Tiny."

She knew them to see.

A bunch of dangerous predators stalking the area for what they could get. They knew not to give her any trouble. Showing them her knife once, she wasn't going to be robbed or raped without drawing blood. The streets taught them how to mind themselves, they left her alone. She quickened her step. There were other places to check out before returning home. It would be worth the effort when she found him. She had been successful in the past, but they were gone now. Her talent kept demanding a new audience to appreciate her performance. Or else she'd never realize her dream.

By the time she arrived back in Howard Street the young thugs had set some boxes alight. The fire burned brightly. Jenny Lei piled more on top standing back to look into it.

Her native spirit became trapped in the warm glow of flames. She fantasized about her captivated audience watching her on Broadway. She composed herself clearing her throat.

Project the sound, Miss Watson, her drama teacher used to say. Let your voice rebound off the wall at the back of the theatre, return again, but quietly. She knew that she had all the attributes to be a good actor, it's just nobody else could see it yet. The success she craved wasn't far away. Practice would get her ready for that big audition. She could be called up for it at any time. The only sound in the dead of night was coming from the fire.

When she stretched out her arms a lamentable wail shattered the silence of her surroundings. "Double, Double toil an' trouble fire burn caldron bubble."

When she heard the sound of slow hand clapping, the laughter, she froze. She scanned the windows above her head; there was no one to be seen. It was coming from under a pile of boxes against a wall. She could see a man looking out at her. Her performance was not intended to be amusing. It was a serious production, that applause ill-timed, bad mannered. His laughter the worst insult of all.

"Son of a bitch," she hissed.

Storming over she pushed the boxes hard, collapsing the lot on top of him.

"God damn bum, you know jack shit about Shakespeare?"

Off she went down the street with his laughter still ringing in her ears.

Joe Flanagan had drifted into the street looking for a safe place to lie down for the night. It was good seeing the cardboard boxes, sorting them out didn't take long. The first night on the street was a learning experience, too near a bar, someone pissed on him. The second night's accommodation was more carefully selected. He bedded down outside a church. But police in a patrol car shouted at him to move on from there.

It didn't do anything to reinforce his belief in God. He learned to be more cautious making his way around smaller streets, where there were few police patrols. His new status of homeless illegal immigrant increased the anxiety. He begged for a few coins with a cup he picked off the garbage. Whatever money he got went on the cheapest wine he could buy. It didn't matter what name it traded under. If it made you drunk it worked. This was a whole new world of survival, the street rules were basic, be on the lookout all the time. When that resolve faltered, trouble started. He watched the girl storm off down the street after shouting at him. Her performance over the fire was funny. But she'd left her bag lying on the ground. He picked it up to go after her.

The lift wasn't coming down fast enough for her, she reacted instinctively. The sting of pain across the back of his hand stopped him there on the spot. With blood pouring from it, he dropped the bag to the sound of breaking glass. A bum running after you with your bag might be stupid, especially with whiskey inside it. But he couldn't be dangerous.

Putting the knife away she spoke quietly. "Let me fix it for you, I thought you were going to attack me. I have more whiskey upstairs; you can have some to drink if you want."

She indicated to the open lift. They sized each other up, but it didn't matter he'd heard the magic word whiskey. He stepped in. Picking her dripping bag up off the ground she followed him. The lift creaked its way to the first floor; neither of them spoke, standing in opposite corners, weighing each other up. He figured she could have stuck the knife in him if she wanted to. He took the chance; it was a better option than where he was at.

When she poured whiskey on the cut, blood reddened the washbasin. The sting of alcohol on the open wound made him grimace. But seeing good booze spilled down the sink was the worst pain of all. How badly he wanted a drink of that.

"Ag-haa shit that's sore."

"For infection, take some to fix inside."

He had a few swigs from the bottle. It was good, looking around him taking in the surroundings while she cut a white cotton shirt in strips. Using that knife again, the sight of which had a sobering effect on him. But sober was the last place he wanted to stay.

He had the way to drunkenness in the palm of his hand. With the presence of some kind of company a warm place with the bar open again. Right now who gave a shit what happened next? She seemed okay, taking care of his hand as if she was sorry. But he'd be watching her.

The plan was still the same, get as much booze as possible down his neck before he left.

The big open loft had a high ceiling with timber beams, like a barn. Cordoned off with couches, one wall was mirrored, in front of it a hitch rail fastened to the floor. He couldn't figure what that rail was used for, never having seen anything like it before.

A stairs at the back draped with colourful blankets. Two big windows covered in cobwebs looked down over Howard Street. Joe wasn't inclined to be positive, but it felt homely.

"Would you like coffee?"

"Yes, I'd like whiskey in it, for the pain."

"I was scared you were going to hurt me. Where are you from you're accent's strange?"

"Ireland, names Joe."

"You want a bottle to pour yourself, Joey?"

She produced another bottle of hooch from a cupboard, it looked cheap. The price of the poison never mattered; it did the same thing, maybe quicker.

He poured a good amount into his cup, she held out her mug. "I'll have some too."

"Is that rail at the mirror for tying up horses?" he asked for something to say. He was curious about it.

"It's a ballet barre for my dance exercises."

She kicked off the boots, doing a few curvy moves, one hand resting on the barre. Seemed like she knew what she was doing, it looked good anyway. How would he know?

"I can't do it, my jeans are too tight," she announced sitting down again.

"I was raised in a place called Wynckoop, that's northern Canada. Are you married?" she asked him quietly.

"Did you not see her sleeping in the cardboard room when you demolished it?" he replied in a similar easy tone of voice.

Banging her hand down on the table, so hard it made him jump. "Don't be a wise ass with me. Are you married or not."

He wanted to say No but blurted out Yes instead. As if there was something wrong with that!

"Men get the shits when asked that question," she hissed at him. "They start hiding already, no one cares if they're married or not, too dishonest to say yes, scared to say no. Men are all the same guilty lying mother fuckers!"

She didn't remain a nice person for long. But he had whiskey talking for him now.

Things always changed when that happened. Confidence poured out of him. "I don't want to know about your hang-ups; I dumped mine on the street."

Without another word, she ran up the stairs draped with blankets, disappearing into the room.

He reached out for the whiskey bottle whispering a few confidential words to it. "This is a crazy bitch whiskey, boy, I'll finish you off, then get my ass out a here in a hurry."

He adjusted his position on the couch to face the stairs. In case she crept up behind him with the knife. A quick exit after emptying the bottle was the plan. There was no need rushing things. It wasn't as if he had an appointment or anything urgent like that.

When she came back down her appearance had changed. With the plaits woven around her head this time. She floated through the room her arms stretched to take-off somewhere else. In dancer's clothes, black tights, red leotard, red ballet shoes. This was a complete departure from the knife wielding Indian woman that slashed him on the hand. Not more than an hour earlier. Then he heard soft music when she took into this dreamy dance routine. Raising her arms she twirled, delicately balanced, long fingers searching the air, so precise. Her demeanour changed completely, he soon became captivated by the sight of her. With such graceful elegance unfolding her mystery, he watched spellbound. A live ballet show was something he'd never seen before. For the first time since he met her, he relaxed.

Different person than this poetic creature had slashed his hand. It just had to be that way.

Everybody has some kind of trigger to reveal another self, his was drink. Dance was this Indian spirit's way of displaying hers. She was totally lost in it. He watched her quietly till it ended; she hurried off for a shower then. Living on the street it was almost a week since he'd had a wash. When she returned he asked if he could use the shower. Sure, she said as if she cared. He had been scanning the room. Now he knew where the booze was stashed.

He planned a raid when he was leaving. If only to cover the cost of damage to his hand, but getting that alcohol was top priority. He wasn't leaving the place without it.

When he finished in the bathroom, she was cooking, it smelled good. But food was something he learned to go without. Except for the café, when the hunger wouldn't go away he'd go down to Spring Street. A guy he met showed him how it was done. Telling him to hang around the big restaurant window there, they'd give him something just to get rid of him. So their customers wouldn't get upset looking at him.

The sight of him might put them off their food. Standing there, scratching his ass deep with his fingers, so they could see it. It was bad for business; romantic couples sat looking out the window. He'd stare in at them with a big dirty grin on his face, or slobber if he wasn't well, until he was coaxed to move on. That was the good part, the management must act diplomatically. Not to hurt his feelings. He wasn't breaking the law. It's seldom the tramp on the street can exercise any rights. There was some tasty food to be got for a convincing performance. He was a good actor too when the occasion demanded a desperate move.

Jenny Lei cooked pork with sweetcorn, there was fried rice too. Because she didn't feel like having any, it was all for him. He gulped it down hungrily, until the dry rice stuck in his throat making him cough. It filled him up quick enough though. His stomach learned not to expect much food the craving for it was almost gone.

But it was a different proposition with alcohol. He just had to have it all the time, if he didn't have it he'd start to panic. That panic would intensify until he got it. That was the kind of merciless grip he was under.

After dinner she introduced the Indian peace pipe. He had never seen one all painted that way, except in the movies. It seemed like a ceremony, chopping the tobacco so fine, carefully filling the pipe, pressing it down with her forefinger. The head of it, so small it couldn't last long when she sucked on it like that. There was one thing he liked instantly, the smell of it. Like incense at devotions in church when he was a young boy growing up. After he had a few sucks of it he could hear the church choir singing, all over again.

He remembered those old movies, Chief Sitting Bull smoking the peace pipe, always with someone in a sign of friendship.

Maybe she was telling him she was sorry she knifed him. Now they could burn all the bad vibes between them over a smoke from the pipe. A witch doctor might appear at any minute, dance around the coffee table to put a good spell on him. Maybe she might act the part herself, she could do everything else.

He'd never developed a smoking habit. His father made sure of that. It wasn't for a footballer to smoke he insisted. But homeless in New York, well, rules were first to shift. Good intention took off when attitude adjusted different situation. She put more tobacco in the pipe before passing it on, as if he was expecting it. He wasn't about to break with tradition. The first suck of the pipe nearly choked him when it hit the lungs. He might have puked but held on to it letting it settle. Tash Doyle had been encouraging him to try the odd cigar. So his lungs didn't react too badly with this first inhale of smoke. It would get better after a while, she assured him.

"Do you want to dance?"

"No I can't do it."

"I can teach you."

"Don't want to."

"Let me blow pipe smoke in your mouth, you'll like it."

"Okay."

When she blew smoke into his mouth he got new feelings for her. There was a reeling in his head to confuse everything. He started laughing thinking so many things. All of them nice reasons, funny for laughing. The dance idea didn't seem silly any more. If he could please her she had lots more whiskey. The peace pipe was great.

He called it Apache; she thought it was a good name for the pipe. He was happy to stand up at the barre with a grin on his face like an idiot.

He tried presenting himself properly for the dance lesson routine. "Not the usual bar I stand at," he joked.

But it didn't sound funny; she was in a more serious mood.

"Now copy all the moves I do, Joey."

"Hey I'm not a parrot; I'm not doing those fairy hand moves," he complained.

"Not the injured hand the other one will balance you."

"I feel like a fool."

"Try to remember, bend your knees like this."

The trousers split when he widened his knees; he had to hold on to the barre laughing so much. Like a teacher she reprimanded him, folding her arms.

"What's the matter with you?"

"I've burst my jeans. No underwear, have to stop now," he explained with a daft smirk on his face.

"Oh, just take them off altogether."

She was serious.

So he stripped off, stood naked in front of her.

"You're taking your clothes off too."

He thought to encourage her.

"Definitely not, how dare you. I'm a Prima Ballerina."

"Oh I see."

He picked his jeans up off the floor. "I've had enough of it Jenny Lei."

"Give them to me, I'll fix them, shower."

"I just had one."

"Have another one, after dance exercise. You're sweaty."

"No I'm not."

"Yes you are, shower I said, now."

She must be handled with care, it was her place she had the knife. He wasn't going to say anything to antagonise her. The throbbing in his hand was a constant reminder for him.

While he was having his shower he convinced himself of her fine attributes. Toyed with the idea she might not be crazy after all, maybe a little wild, sexy looking when he thought about it. There were a lot of reasons to think kindly towards her. It made more sense.

"Do you want to stay here?" she asked.

Throwing caution out the big windows he answered immediately. "Yes, I do."

It sounded like a marriage ceremony; he laughed at that idea. The erection in his jeans arrived unexpectedly it was gone for a long time. But now it was getting more tuned into things. It might be thinking there was something interesting coming up.

"We'll work out an arrangement," she was saying.

"An arrangement, I haven't any money."

"I know, but there are other ways, things you can do for me. I work late hours, we'll see what happens."

"What do you work at?"

"I'm a dancer."

"I should have guessed."

"How is your hand?"

"I need more alcohol for pain."

She talked about herself for a long time. As long as whiskey flowed, he'd listen to her stories, about drama school, acting ambitions, the disadvantages of being a woman. How cruel it was for them in a man's world. There were barriers put up against talented women like her everywhere. She didn't have a chance if she wasn't prepared to be exploited for the satisfaction of men. Something she'd never do no matter how bad things turned for her. That was the only reason she wasn't a big Broadway star, she complained.

Everyone was different he tried telling her. Confident secure women got on with it. They didn't bitch about it either. It's the same shit for everybody, he wasn't aware men had a monopoly on winning. In his position he could present an argument for failure.

She couldn't be bothered discussing that. Her own annoyances were primed for airing.

Every job she applied for there was a guy in charge that wanted the woman first. Then see what happens. Most women give it up, on the couch.

"When the bitch parts with it, she gets kicked out on her ass anyway. Men should have to pay for pleasure they take from women. Every goddamn time," she shouted.

The chat was getting her riled up again. Free whiskey was great but thoughts of getting knifed were sobering. He tried changing the subject.

"Do you have many people in your family?"

"My mother died. My father hangs round Columbus Park. I go down there sometimes looking for him. I have no one else in this world that I know of."

"You're looking for your father?"

"Yes, in this jungle it's difficult to find him but I know he's around that area somewhere. I might never find him. I'm so scared something bad will happen to him, it worries me so much. Will you help me find my dad, Joey, please?"

He was sorry for thinking she was all bad. He should know everyone has a story.

It's usually a lot different from the obvious one. Didn't he know more about that than anyone else? He wouldn't be telling her anything about his past history though. Something was telling him it wouldn't be the best thing to do. Thinking she was about to cry he put his arms around her, to comfort her. He felt her plight when she turned to look at him. The tears left moist streaks down her shiny face. Kissing her salty cheek lightly he promised to help her.

It could have been Apache doing the talking.

"I'll help you, don't cry, Jenny Lei."

She kissed him; her tongue darting around his mouth in a pretentious frenzy, without even a hint of passion in it. But this promise of sexual fulfilment dispelled the evil serpent of doubt. She took his hand leading him upstairs to her bed. Her nudity was easy on the eye, a muscle toned dancer's body, with the agility of a snake. Pretensions went out the window when an erection became a corkscrew for opening bottles of booze. The morning sun beamed through the windows for the start of another day. It didn't matter anyway; there was an artist playing games on Howard St. What else was there to do except join in with her?

When a bum's best expectations came alive again, rearing like a stallion, in a circus full of clowns 'Indian woman' was ringmaster extraordinaire. There was nothing about acts she didn't know, adjusting her position to accommodate them all.

He wouldn't be missing out on any of the performance either. This was someone as unpredictable as himself with the impulse for doing things the other way round. If he didn't look her in the eyes he could handle the fear. She'd hardly want to kill him now when they were such adventurous lovers together. Maybe all she cared about was using up enough cock before he collapsed with exhaustion. The whole show could be summed up as simple as that.

When he awoke he got a smell of cooking coming up from the kitchen. It got him out of bed in a hurry. All that energy spent preforming left a longing for food in its wake. She was wearing a red bandanna around her forehead with a yellow feather in it, standing naked at the cooker. He wasn't wearing clothes either, a fortunate choice for breakfast it appeared.

"Fried pork slices with scrambled eggs. I had some when you were sleeping," she sang out as if she was preparing a special breakfast for her main man taking a lot of care cooking it too. He couldn't help thinking he was lucky she knifed him. Reality was lost from the very beginning. Small enough price to pay for all he was getting. What a state to be in.

A big chest freezer covered with a blanket doubled as a table. When they sat down at it she started telling him to beware of street people. Weirdos of life that don't fit in she called them. Told him what he should be on the lookout for. A street code for losers she called it. The bad ones didn't stand out until they hit on you. She talked as if she didn't care that he was one of them. But as long as whiskey lasted she could say what she liked. The thirst so strong;

it prevented the obvious registering with him. He was too blind to see that she might be one of the most dangerous street people of them all. But in the law of survival who sees danger looking for a chance; the ones that never take it, or ever get it.

Even this bizarre situation could present some kind of opportunity. If only for a comfortable place to stay with entertainment as good as it gets. It was time to put his feet up for a while.

This drop out was best left foraging away trying to stay ahead. Keeping his wits about him was all he had to do. When she called him bum he didn't care, that's what he was. You pick things up as you go along if you're any way smart at all. He was a bit like Onion Head now, finding comfort in his place at the bottom end of things. Anyone could see his failings.

Over a few whiskey's Jenny Lei laid out her plans for the coming day insisting he accompany her to a laundromat nearby. She was attending a party for a friend that evening. If he washed his clothes he could come along as her escort. It was important that nobody thought he was just a bum. There were some principles she couldn't dump. Having a bum for a boyfriend was definitely not her style.

Her forefathers were once proud Indian chiefs, she boasted.

He sat still in the laundromat wearing her overcoat, watching his clothes spinning around in front of him. His attention was drawn to another wino doing the same thing. But he was apparently enjoying the experience, laughing so much; at the good of it all whatever it was that was funny. Must be his special entertainment show it appeared.

"He thinks the machines are TV programmes. He's like you, Joey, only longer at it, he has a wet brain now. Don't worry I won't let you get that bad, I'd get rid of you first,"

Jenny Lei whispered in his ear. Her strange laugh didn't take away from the threat of it.

No, that sounded more like 'put you out of your misery.'

He could smell the foreboding edge to it, a kiss with a whiff of bad breath on it.

As soon as they arrived back to Howard St. she started getting ready. It was going to take her a long time she warned, 'making a special effort for her special boyfriend Jack Ulke.'

When she went upstairs he took straight into the whiskey. He heard the bit about her boyfriend, but 'so what' he was only 'escorting' her. There was no problem to deal with yet. She was a forceful person he'd be afraid to say he wouldn't go with her.

He was trapped, but he liked that, it meant he had nowhere else to go. The freedom of choice was no longer available to him. So he didn't have to bother his head about it. These were the same conditions he accepted when he went for broke down the Bowery. In some strange way this scant regard for his own safety was keeping him alive. It primed him for a sudden move to the next detail on his way. Having nothing to carry or care about made it easy to shift. There was something else bothering him though, when he thought about it. During their sexual antics he asked her about the key on a silver chain around her neck. Why she never took it off. Was it for the safe where her money was stashed? It was meant to be a joke; he couldn't care less where she kept her money. It hit a raw nerve somehow.

Her reaction to this harmless question was hostile. Saying it was none of his business where she kept her money, following up with another threat. 'It could be the key to your grave'. Sounded like she was side tracking him. Not the kind of information you'd want to hear, when you're involved in such an adventurous happening. Maybe she carried the knife to protect her money. That she kept the key to it around her neck was the safest place for it.

He apologised for his remark. There was never any intent to find her money. He wasn't a thief, hadn't he given her the bag on the street, when she forgot to pick it up. So it was left like that. But she was slow to let go of things brooding about them. He couldn't figure her out. He was wary of her all the time except for when she danced. She seemed to get in contact with a gentler spirit then. That performance revealed the hidden wonder of her feminine side, I suppose. But that nice character didn't show up often enough. This coarse intimidating nature she regularly portrayed was her dominant persona. This trip to her boyfriend's bar had something unusual about it that he missed somewhere along the way. Why did she want an escort to visit her boyfriend that was strange? He hoped he wasn't along to make him jealous. There was something odd about the whole set up but he couldn't see it. He was too scared to confront her about anything. It was that simple.

"Joey."

He looked up to see her standing at the bottom of the stairs. Her appearance quite stunning, she knew that too; tilting her head to captivate. Satisfied he was hooked she made a slow deliberate walk towards him. An Indian princess; she had on a yellow appliqued leather dress flared below her knees. The suede moccasins on her feet were the same colour.

A silver necklace, delicately engraved matched the wide silver bangles on her arm. Her plaited hair held fast with similar decorative silver clips.

A thick red belt trimmed with blue stones, worn tight around her slim figure. She had that band around her forehead again with a red feather sticking up from it this time. She'd already told him red was for war. What did the yellow one she wore at breakfast signify? It had to be peace. He couldn't stop himself staring at her, not for the first time since they met up. If he didn't know her he'd think she was beautiful. But just as he was about to compliment her, she ruined it all again. One flick of the wrists turned the perfect picture into a blue movie.

The demon bitch arrived more daring than ever. When she hoisted the dress up to her waist beauty presented another source for inspection. The absence of underwear she took pride in. A fetish he greatly favoured himself.

On this occasion the large expanse of black hair had been remodelled; so artistically adorned with coloured beads into a heart shape. He'd never even imagined a pussy could be decorated like that. It was on some higher accomplishment he'd never heard of. A sight to behold no matter what purpose it served. He knew this Jack guy was all the focus now. He was the man. "See, Joey, all groomed, perfumed for the birthday boy's special treat. Now you know why you're escorting me, so his jewel arrived intact." She laughed. "Let him see what he's missing."

It was all well intended, the pressure was off him.

They walked the few blocks to a place called Little Beavers off Canal Street. There were only a few people having drinks at the bar when they arrived. While another small group chatted around a table at the end, in what appeared to be a private affair.

Immediately it was obvious that Jenny Lei was not a welcome customer in this bar.

Far away from the heart felt reception she craved. When she moved down the bar to mingle with the private party the barman spoke urgently into Joe's ear. "You'd better get that crazy bitch outa here."

"She's your girlfriend, got all dressed up for the party."

But the bartender didn't want to see it like that. "Look, wise ass, she's a whore, that's my wife down there take her outa here before all hell breaks loose. Tell her there's a guy at the bar will pay her fifty for it."

"For what?" Joe asked him.

"For a fuck, what else has she got to sell?"

"I can't say that, she's a dancer."

"She's a whore, get it wise guy, are you saying no?"

"Right I'm saying no, I won't say that to her."

Jenny Lei arrived back at that precise moment to order drinks. "Are you guys talking about me eh?" without realizing how on the mark she was saying that.

The barman had a wry smile. "There's a John wants a quickie for fifty."

"Screw you, Jack, I'm a ballet dancer now."

She glared black eyed madness down the bar at the guy who wanted to pay fifty for a fuck. Then she marched right up to him dumping his cocktail on his head shouting stuff that shouldn't be heard. He headed for the door in some hurry for a man of his advanced years.

Then with everyone in the bar looking on she gave her yellow dress a high lift, letting the barman see what the colourful delight of a pampered pussy looked like.

"You put that creep on me, Jack, giving him some of yours, tired of this already, your old lady giving you the poor stuff again, last time we humped you said she couldn't screw for shit."

Now everyone in the place knew the real story.

She was ushered out the door by a few eager customers. Joe followed her on his own steam. The party was over before it begun, but he was a much wiser man after that revealing performance. Dancer me ass as they say.

There wasn't a cab in sight. Who would pick this fare up if there was? She had her dress under her armpits wriggling her bare ass back at the window, in case they missed it already. If you wanted to advertise your insanity this was the way to go about it. She was a long way from the peace of the reservation.

They headed off in the general direction of Howard Street. When they were walking for a short while she grabbed his arm tightly. It brought him to his senses in a hurry. He'd been running the night's events in a panic sequence through his head. It wasn't adding up too good.

"Careful, Joey, they've spotted us. Go along with what I do."

The figures slouched on the stoop watched them from the shadows. Any one walking around here at night was just asking to be mugged. If they ran they would be caught. The glow coming from a light over the door put a spotlight on the performer. It was all she needed to set her off. Lifting her dress high she grabbed

Joe's hand to dance with her. This action caught their immediate interest. They laughed clapping their hands when she exposed the bare-buttocks again making grunting humping noises at it. Something they hadn't witnessed before. Only someone not right in the head would behave that way.

So they left them alone.

Jenny Lei explained it better. "If you're that crazy no one wants to mess with you. It might be like a voodoo or something. It's the law of the jungle, Joey."

When they arrived in Howard Street they started into the booze again.

The night out was first up for discussion.

"That was risky, Jenny Lei, showing your ass to those guys. How did you think of doing that? It could have got the two of us killed."

"I'll tell you about it, Joey, people on the street will stay away from crazy, that's what we are. Crazy unknown people are dangerous, unpredictable best left alone. I like to play crazy all the time but sometimes I'm not crazy."

"When are you not crazy?"

"Joey, I ain't crazy when I think about what my father did to me, he raped me at fourteen then sold me every day to his buddies for booze until I ran away at sixteen. Crazy stops when rage takes over. One day I will kill him for what he did to me." She wept bitterly.

That finally, was a rare display of vulnerable from a woman with multiple contradictions. Or a classic performance from the woman that wanted to act. Either way Joe knew he couldn't rally around her cause any more. She was getting under his skin too much. He didn't want to see her as a victim or allow himself to console her. He didn't want to touch her in case she drew him into another frightening sexual performance. He couldn't hang around her any longer. Their boozing session dried up soon after that, without anything left to say to each other.

He pretended interest when she suggested sex. But the barman in Little Beavers had put that action out of his head for good. He lay asleep on the couch until she went to bed. But he kept one eye open for her going up the stairs.

He listened to her rants shouting about burning him out in his house of boxes if he left her. The threatening feeling was constant from her now.

When horny wore off, control took hold; she had started laying down rules to him. It was all too much after such a night in her company. She could change her attitude when she felt like it; the bad attitude was threatening him again. It helped change his mind.

Making a getaway to sleep in a box on the street might be the safest thing to do. It was part of the instinct to keep him safe, it cut in when he felt threatened. He never doubted it. When he heard her snoring he slipped off the couch. At the drinks cupboard he reached in for a bottle of whiskey, quietly pulling the door closed behind him.

That 'Grave' reference finished it for him, once was enough to hear it.

There was something about the way she said it that didn't feel funny. It brought the chills back into his head when he thought she meant it. The mad bitch of the street was back into normal mode again. That's what freaked him out; he decided to split on account of it. She had threatened to burn his house of boxes if he crossed her in any way. He wouldn't want to be asleep underneath when that happened. He was sure she was capable of committing any foul deed she wanted to. He couldn't sleep in the same place with a person like that. Didn't matter how desperate he was. He'd never be able to watch her all the time.

When he woke up with a massive headache, he blamed the pipe for it. Time to head in a different direction to the usual route he took, in case she'd find him on one of those excursions she told him about, looking for her father. Great distance between them was the way to go. He set off walking towards the east side of Manhattan.

As far away from her as he could possibly get.

He heard the strains of music coming from somewhere near. The alluring sound he didn't think twice about going after it.

He headed in that direction to get closer; it was like a spell drawing him in. This young guy had a ghetto blaster on a stoop listening to the sounds. He had all the appearance of someone tuned into the spell.

"This was where it was at," he kept saying.

Joe asked him. "The music, who is it?"

"Zachary Cool Breeze, he's from New Orleans."

He liked the sound of this name; it kept the good feeling in his head. He moved slowly away from him repeating it in case he forgot it.

"Zachary Cool Breeze, Zachary Cool Breeze," over again, until after a while he knew it was his name.

He couldn't remember the name he started out with sometimes. It kept coming back to him before it took off again. Happier with this likeable one he found in its place.

Zachary Cool Breeze would suit better. It sounded more like him.

Chapter Twenty-one

Sergeant Ben Brady sipped coffee in the east side diner looking around him.

Detective Spellman hadn't showed up, he was getting fidgety. He took a few report sheets from his briefcase. To give him something to do, he read through them. The drifter in custody was charged with the barmaid's murder. He was awaiting his trial date. Police in Boston said he hadn't got a record. A harmless individual worked in a flower shop all his life.

They gave his real name. But it meant nothing till he was a free man again. He was Onion Head to the police.

Brady was pretty sure he didn't kill the barmaid; he didn't have it in him. He was irritated that the District Attorney went ahead with it. There were lots of unanswered questions.

Who took the barmaids wig? The drifter didn't have it.

The word whore was scrawled in lipstick on the toilet wall. Lab tests proved it was the barmaid's lipstick but it wasn't recovered at the scene either.

Was the killer a weirdo that collected victim's stuff?

Mrs Marie Duggan might have hated her sister. But she didn't use makeup or wear a wig.

So what old lady was in the bar on the night, did she open the door for the killer?

Maybe Dan Ryan provided the knowhow for that job. It was a task he was capable of carrying out. He had reason to do it, if the opportunity presented itself.

He wondered if the ex-nun knew the old caretaker in the past. The detective would keep a closer eye on Limpy Ryan. He appeared to be everywhere there was trouble, cripple or not he hadn't changed all that much. He might have had a hand in there somewhere. The cop was baffled by the hillbilly's disappearance. Duggan as always, denied any involvement.

It was a mystery to him too.

He would have to be released unless there was enough there to charge him. Even though the detective knew he was in the thick of it. There was still no evidence linking him to Lupe's arm. Who else had a motive for such an act? Without a body to match the hillbilly arm there wasn't much to go on. The corpse of the miner must be somewhere. But where do you look for a grave on a construction site?

Duggan had threatened to do Lupe in. That didn't mean much; it was just talk he said, a saying, like 'tearing someone a new asshole'. It never happens. His lawyer claimed that he was an innocent law abiding citizen. The kind of stuff lawyers were paid big money to say.

Detective Brady was being pressurized to press charges or release him. He would have to comply soon unless something solid emerged to go on. The creosote rope around Lupe's wrist must be significant. The detective saw that it had almost severed the hand. How could his arm have been so forcefully removed from his body?

The prostitute in the hotel investigation was also at a dead end. There were too many possibilities, anyone could have done it. Dulche the janitor wasn't saying anything significant about it. But he was still a person of interest to the police. The cases were going cold. Something might turn up out of the blue. The sooner it did the better.

He didn't notice her coming in the door, not until she was in front of him. With a big smile on her face, that didn't make things any better. Not when he had been worrying so much about her. "You're late, Ann; you nearly made our missing persons list."

"Well don't look so pleased about it then. I was shopping with my new friend Mrs Dillon. I got delayed, sorry to keep you waiting. Remember the old couple I told you about in the Celtic. Mrs Dillon, that's her name, she invited me shopping. She told me an interesting story, you need to hear it. But we must protect our source as rats don't survive long in the kitchen."

He maintained a respectful silence listening to her.

"Sister Marie O Connor the nun married Fr Thomas Duggan the priest for a specific reason. The whole thing was arranged to satisfy their immediate needs. Sex or falling in love had nothing to do with that. When the nun discovered her sister's child was taken into care by the CPS she arranged to get custody of the little boy. It was after all, her family blood. She was ideally placed to carry out the deception. Her position in the convent made everything possible. She found a willing accomplice in Fr Thomas. So they both left their respective orders to get married.

"Now, that was the first part of the plan; next they altered the adoption papers to reflect Mrs Duggan as the birth mother, not her sister Rosie. Then they registered the child as their own. The kid was subjected to a cloistered upbringing; he was dressed as a girl until he was twelve. It seems Mrs Duggan didn't like looking at the male parts so she covered them with a diaper, dressed the boy as a girl. She was a low grade teacher in the convent; she educated the child at home. Mrs Dillon ridiculed the child's treatment at the hands of the ex-nun. He couldn't help being all screwed up with the treatment he got."

"Why was the priest agreeing with this arrangement, Ann?"

"He had to get out of the religious way of life, Ben. It was beginning to stifle him. A place to live with consensual freedom suited him better. The opportunity to live his life the way he wanted. Or so he was led to believe by his co-conspirator, Sister Marie. Later on in the arrangement she demanded he change his ways. It wasn't as if she didn't know about his homosexual tendencies from the very beginning. He was truthful about that. She wanted him to place more thust in religion. God would stop him from being gay. In her mind the saviour would rid him of this urge. The priest was trapped, in more ways than one. This woman didn't tolerate any kind of sexual behaviour. She was hell bent on making sure nobody else got any either. Of course they never even slept in the same room. Thomas felt he was being used. She had roped him in as a surrogate father from the word go. He resigned himself to acceptance, fulfilling his sworn duty to raise young John. He had formed a friendship with his wife's sister Rosie back then. When she got out of jail it was him she turned to. He knew he must hide the fact that her son John was adopted by them. He took the necessary precautions to ensure Rosie never even suspected the betrayal. That was the easy part; she hated Duggan more than Onion Head."

"So the barmaid never knew John Duggan was her kid. She missed out on hearing that wonderful news."

"Correct, Ben, she never met him until after Vietnam when he started frequenting a bar she worked uptown. He was by then the terror of the neighbourhood. She knew of course he was her sister's son. But that meant nothing when she barred him from the bar."

"Ann, if John Duggan's real mother was Rosie O Connor, then his father would be Dan Ryan the sand hog caretaker known as Limpy. Shit, now it starts to feel worse. They hate each other without even suspecting they're related. I need to question Thomas now. Let's see what he's got to say about certain arrangements. He might disclose more if I can get him to open up about it. I wonder why he didn't tell the barmaid the full story. He takes that religious vow of silence to a new level. I hope that I can break that resolve when I'm speaking to him, I have questions that need answers."

"Yes, that's what I asked Mrs Dillon. How did the ex-priest keep the secret from the barmaid about her first son? She assured me Thomas is a very honourable man a real gentleman. Where can I find me a man with such character?"

The sergeant ignored the personal contribution. He saw it different.

"That's a load of shit, Ann, he's flawed too. Thomas signed up for God's army didn't he, but later deserted. I'm sure he made lots of promises along the way, he broke some too. It's all very interesting; Hell's Kitchen always had the code of silence. The priest just adopted a new code of his choice. There is nothing new about that shit. It still doesn't help us with Rosie O Connor's murder. What's the Dillon lady's opinion on that I wonder?"

"She said it was the Onion Head guy, Ben. They despised each other."

"We've John Duggan still in custody. He's saying nothing, his lawyer's on his elbow. There are three deaths starting with the prostitute. There is one name common to all of them, it's his. It couldn't happen, a murder in his place without him knowing about it. How did your contact know all this?"

"She was Mrs Duggan's only friend since grade school remained her confidante down the years. I'm like the daughter she never had; my newly adopted mother's worried about me."

"Yeah right, not many people grabbing that responsibility."

He laughed at her when she punched him. Then he got frustrated again.

"It's weird, Ann. Duggan's mother is strangled in his bar. He didn't know she was his mother. Then he threatened to take a guy's arm off. It happened like he said, still no body found. A young hooker's stabbed in a hotel he's somehow associated with. It would be easy to nail Onion Head based on evidence gathered in the Celtic bar alone. It's not that simple. Ann, we need to establish who tampered with the evidence. We need to know why Rosie's blonde wig, lipstick, earrings, went missing. They didn't walk."

"Okay, boss, I'm on it."

"We need to do it so we can get Onion Head off the hook before we all look bad."

Joe Flanagan was living rough, the clothes he wore the passport in his pocket. That's all he had left. A much worse off pilgrim than first arrived in America.

The passport proved he came from somewhere, one time. But bum on skid row is not much of a destination. Where you get to is who you are. Like vinegar the cheap wine tasted. Then it didn't taste at all. It stripped the lining off his stomach, drove him out of his mind. The place where you think you see everything, but register nothing. He begged next to the subway entrance with a coffee cup, gathering whatever change passing strangers saw fit to give him. It all counted towards his survival, fed his addiction. He got a few bottles every day. Keeping his brain numb, so caring didn't count any more, except for the struggle of getting more drink. He spent all his time looking out for it. A bottle, a can, even a swig, of anything would do.

Days passed by, unreal happenings, where everything was scary for him. His world became the spot on whatever street he was on. Sometimes depressed if he thought about Rita, but most times he was indifferent. In his mind he blamed her for going out to the Deli, never coming back, leaving him in such a state. His only consolation in the end was not caring where she was. Those times his thoughts about her were darkest. He imagined her going back to the hotel to work as a prostitute, to be with her friends. Bitterness replaced caring.

Regret got lost somewhere in the middle of everything. Rational thinking was not something he had power over. In this lost frame of mind he didn't know where he was at. Most people haven't had the misfortune of being there. They should be glad about that.

His mind played games, drink kept it going that way. There were days wandering any direction. Times when Zachary Cool Breeze seen change in everything around him.

Good things happened hanging with him. His presence defined his frame of mind. There were bad days. Trying to understand how it worked, learning to cope. Looking for a place to remember from before, a building, anything that said it was still there, where it was not so long ago. Sometimes he was sure of himself, but a mood change could finish up in a worse place, with a mind of its own to fret about. The paranoia always came back never missing a turn to get at him. It might be minutes that felt like a day. Or it could even be a day that passed like a minute. Emptiness didn't have a name for things. Trying to keep it simple was the struggle; hoping to be able to see.

On Bleaker Street passing a bar taking in a beer keg delivery. Two steel trap doors to the cellar opened up like jaws on the pavement. As if coming out of the sewers to devour him. He screamed with the terror of tunnel detail the alligator attacking him.

He ran as fast as he could for as long as he was able to escape it. That effort left him crumbled on the stoop of a derelict building. Lying across it with his hands spread out, like Jesus on the cross. There in some sort of reflective moment he could see the way he was.

His mind resembled the final hour of a beleaguered Alamo. His perception, like Davy Crockett was standing there in the centre of it, battling against hostile forces. After each conflict they departed. But not destroying him, they returned attacking him. That was the way he was, held under pressure of siege, all the time. Shivering withdrawal symptoms took him when alcohol effects wore off. Someone kicked his back lying on the sidewalk. A disgruntled pedestrian rid his own torment. He saw heavy steel toe boots walk on as if nothing happened. What deranged mind thought that action was necessary?

The pain of that kick the monster let fly would stay with him forever. Still felt to this day. In this empty space going around the streets like a zombie in brightness, darkness provided some kind of sanctuary. There were places to find. If he knew he was there, he'd realize where he was. That's how it carried on, blowing him away for a walk around journey.

If he couldn't recognise it when he saw it he'd sit looking at it till it went away again.

He'd hide till brightness found him wandering the beginning again. He might discover what it looked like in the light, if it was still there, where he saw it in the beginning. Or the journey might never end, but that was the good part of it. He didn't know where he was going, never even considered where it brought him.

There were stories to be heard from like-minded souls, someone murdered in Washington Square. A screwdriver stuck in this bum's heart for a can of beer. Left lying there on a bench before anyone knew he was dead. The flies figured it out first. Else nobody would know about it. A guy got his head kicked in for a cigarette, someone needed smoke that bad.

It sharpened the wits, when wits were there to be sharpened. The only thing that hadn't left him was a scent for trouble. He couldn't afford to lose it. How did that instinct survive the crash when the rest of him left for dead? He didn't have any say in the matter. It could take off when it wanted, like everything else he had. When he couldn't keep his wits about him for long, he hid in a box. Trouble would find him if he left it too soon. But when was that.

The café on Spring Street was his favourite place when he got hungry. The grub dumped out behind there was always good to eat. One day he came across another guy rooting in the dumpster behind the café. The man was bearded about his own age, frightened. He tried to shy away when he was approached. So he spoke to him without menace.

"Why not share, enough there for two, buddy."

It relaxed him to hear buddy. He kept repeating 'I'm from Nova Scotia' he had a bottle of vodka stashed nearby. They finished up on a construction site, sitting underneath a giant crane.

When the bottle was empty Nova Scotia took off without saying goodbye.

Joe crept under the platform of the crane to pass out. He awoke with a loud cranking sound banging in his ear. To his absolute horror the whole platform was moving. His arm lay on track of a cogged wheel turning the powerful machine. If he was drunk enough he'd have been cut in half. That sobered him, he got out without been seen by the driver. Even a bum has the right to a bit of luck.

Maybe he got his fair share of it then.

Chapter Twenty-two

Sally Baker strolled along Houston Street in New York's East Village. She wore a cream blouse over a loose skirt, brown boots, with a leather handbag tucked limply under her arm. A recently acquired engagement ring glittered on her finger. The street names, Suffolk, Norfolk, Essex made her think about her own country. The middle of August, England would be rich with country smells. That memory made her smile. New York had been good to her but she was going back home. In a few months she would be marrying her English fiancé, she could hardly wait for the day to arrive.

Today she was ticking off another promise, places left to visit. It was hot walking the streets, heading for the famous Katz's Deli. A kosher style place established in 1888, she wanted to see it for a long time. Checking out landmarks was an interesting way to pass time on lazy days off work. She had acquired the name of being boring, but that wasn't true, a happy reclusive maybe.

Her job in the Embassy was a conservative post, being dull wouldn't be disastrous working there. Apart from all that, this twenty-five-year old's country upbringing had instilled in her a great respect for the dignity of all fellow human beings. When she put the dark glasses on her head, the midday sun made her eyes blink. Then it happened.

Caught up in a sound of human chatter, she was left lying in a heap on the sidewalk. They ran down Avenue A, towards Tompkins Square Park. The youngest one of the bunch had grabbed her bag.

Joe Flanagan lay on the sidewalk watching the mugging take place.

They had him cornered one time, someone to practice violence on. When they noticed his injury they moved in on easy prey. Chasing him down a blind alley they knew they had him. He stood into a doorway to remove his clothes. Then, with them bundled under his arm he ran back whooping like an Indian. Taken by surprise they scattered before the naked maniac. The Indian woman's story was true; everyone on the street was scared of a mad person. Crazy gets right of way all the time.

But right now, they were running in his direction again.

He shoved himself along the pavement, frantically pushing on his ass to shorten the distance, for a trip. The little punk fell like he was shot, dropping the handbag for the man on the street to roll over it. When the thief got up he was alone. The gang wasn't there to protect him any more. Before taking off he threatened him with his knife.

"We kill you next time, bum."

Sally Baker was close enough to hear that, she saw the knife too.When he handed her the bag, she became concerned for his wellbeing.

"You're very courageous. Thank you so much."

"I'm glad to help you."

He could see her eyes dropping on his injured hand. Her kind nature wouldn't allow her to walk away from this situation. Maybe she couldn't forget the young thug's threat either.

He'd be lying there on the street for them to stab any time they wanted. She'd be back in her comfortable apartment cooking dinner.

"You're hurt aren't you?"

"I'm tired."

"Maybe a cup of coffee would help."

"It might."

They sized each other for signs, none of them were bad.

"Let's find a place near here, are you able to walk with me."

"They won't serve bums."

By the time they reached a cafe they knew each other's names. When they sat down at a table, she checked out a menu card. The owner didn't take much notice of the well-dressed lady. She was entitled to bring who she liked into his place.

"Yes here we are, flapjacks I love them, Joe, will you have some with me?"

"I will."

She ordered from the waiter before excusing herself heading for the ladies' room.The incident panicked her, her hands were still shaking. She had to freshen up.

Joe didn't know what flapjacks were, didn't care either. It was a long time since anybody called him by his first name. It sounded strange; her accent was similar to Rita's. Sometimes, the thoughts of never seeing her again filled him with dread. It all seemed impossible to resolve now. He began to feel insecure when he noticed some diners watching him. Were they trying to figure out how a dirty bum got into the place?

Paranoid, he was about to leave, when she arrived back to the table. He felt calm again when she sat down. He was soon stuffing his mouth with the dirty fingers of his good hand. The dry texture of the flapjacks sticking in his throat started him off on a coughing fit. He grimaced when his injured hand throbbed.

The longer Sally Baker studied him the more she felt his pain. The hopelessness of his situation overwhelmed her. "We are neighbours Joe."

"Do you live around here?"

"No I live on Second Avenue, midtown."

"You said we were neighbours."

"I'm sorry that was misleading of me. I was referring to the land of your birth; Ireland is a neighbour of England."

"I should never have left home, "he said simply.

When he looked at her face, the comforting brown eyes calmed him. It was a long way from the black terrifying eyeballs of the Indian woman in Howard Street.

He felt her kindness, he liked talking to her. She could see he was studying her that gave her a chance to observe him. It intrigued her to wonder where he came from, why he had fallen on bad times. Such a pity that he couldn't find himself again. How could it be that a young person was so lost? She needed to know more about this sad looking homeless young man. The chance of this unusual meeting, the resulting circumstances would provide powerful motivation for her to do what she could to help him. These were the kind of stories she was brought up on. Her family history was full of tragedy for many of her extended family connections. All those desperate situations people endured trying to make their way through life. Now she had a chance to do something helpful in her own way. She'd commit her energy to helping him out as best she could.

"The village near our farm in England is a carefree place. This part of New York, reminds me of it in some strange way. Maybe I feel closer to home down here because it doesn't feel cramped, like those high buildings towering over midtown where I live."

"You're from a farm?"

For the first time, she saw him smile.

"My father has a few fields in Ireland he calls them a farm."

"Well we should have a lot to talk about then, kindred spirits, farming stock. Do you have any interest in horses by any chance, most Irish people do I think?"

"I love horses."

It was her turn to smile learning about this common interest.

Horses allow people from anywhere in the world to communicate. It's this regard horse people have for each other. Like kindred spirits. As if they're all veterans of the same battles.

She ordered a big pot of coffee next time round.

The coffee made him edgy again. He began to fret.

She was posh, he was dirty, his good hand had the shakes the other one throbbed painfully it couldn't shake any more. Liquor top up was all he could think about. He rubbed his shoulder, to ease the discomfort.

"You're in pain?"

"Whiskey would fix it." He blurted it out; it was always on his mind. She was his only hope for a bottle. Who cared about manners the desperate want for booze had a mind of its own?

"I saw a liquor store nearby I will get some there."

When he heard she was going for whiskey he was relieved. He wasn't going anywhere.

Sally had a few words with the owner of the cafe before she left.

In her cultured tone of voice she told him about the British TV documentary series they were researching. It was all about the plight of homeless people in New York. Just to make sure her colleague wasn't made to feel uncomfortable in her absence. The owner knew how it worked, the likely publicity as a result. How popular the show might become in Britain.

He could see loads of tourists calling to his place. She praised the cordial treatment that they received in his establishment. But the production company hadn't finalized a location for the cafe scenes just yet. That selection process required a little more time.

Joe sat staring ahead; Sally's refined way reminded him of the woman he loved. He couldn't get Rita out of his head. It felt weird, not thinking about her for so long. Maybe guilt about antics in Jenny Lei's bedroom was behind that. There wasn't any personal commitment in such frolicking. It was just sex. That was how men sometimes excused indiscretions. As if absence of love in the equation made everything more acceptable. No point blaming the peace pipe or the drink, that wasn't how it was either. The temptation for sexual gratification is a powerful desire. There must be a layer of deceit over the male psyche, especially for erasing faltering ways. They're not concealed by accident.

When Sally returned from the liquor store, they moved to occupy a more discrete corner of the cafe. The coat stand made it difficult for anyone to observe what they were getting up to.

Joe was quick to decline another order of flapjacks. The content of the whiskey bottle was his only desire now. This whole operation was carried out effectively, in secret. Putting a good 'drop' in the coffee cup was what it entailed. Even though the owner was pleased to have actors in his cafe, drinking liquor on unlicensed premises was against the law. They did a good job concealing the crime though. Who would ever think such an odd looking couple would be engaging in some private booze up. Anyway it didn't come to the attention of management.

Everything carried on in apparent normality.

She was soon telling him about her life growing up on the farm in England. Her stories centred on horses in particular, as she recounted memories of show jumping.

Her pony's name was Billy. A fourteen-year-old veteran you couldn't fall off if you tried. She was ten years old at the time.

Even though they made a good team, winning competitions eluded them. She was quick to blame herself for that. Billy's heart was set on following the hounds. A sport he enjoyed all his life until she got her hands on him. An ordinary looking specimen, he wasn't made for the glamour performance. Rugged toughness provided him with enduring stamina for cross country. She got the hunting bug from him at this young age. Billy would never shirk a fence no matter how great. The story continued on into familiar territory. Similar in content to all well told hunting yarns, no matter where you go. Only the obstacles got bigger with the tale, some of the walls grew dramatically as a result. Stories like this always took a more interesting turn in mythology. Then fantasy could better express merits of the chase.

She would be going back home in a while, leaving behind the choking fumes.

They talked about the rural upbringing that gave them cherished memories. The value of country principles they were reared with. Her strategy might have been more about letting him feel comfortable. So she could learn something about his family background.

After a while, she listened with interest to the circumstances that brought him to America.

A harrowing tale of a young couple raised in an environment far removed from the frantic pace of New York. She could understand the disappointment they experienced in Philadelphia. How the problem of their daughter's handicap caused upset in their lives. Any hope of a satisfactory outcome destroyed by addiction to alcohol. Excessive drinking was something she knew nothing about. If it was the reason his wife returned to Ireland without him it must be significant. There was no alcohol in her family life. Jews wouldn't be big drinkers as a general rule, she explained. She frowned when he told her about his hand injury on the street. Wasn't it uncanny it happened over a handbag? He didn't say anything about his short stay in the Indian woman's home. There were some things better left untold.

But the injury didn't look good, that concerned her.

This handbag coincidence would implicate the effect of unlikely event. One woman stabbed him when he recovered her handbag. Now she was going to make it right by rescuing him when he retrieved hers. That was it, she reasoned, the way it was meant to be.

"Joe, I really think that wound needs medical attention."

"No, I'm an illegal alien the hospital will make a report."

"I have a good friend a doctor, are you okay to leave with me?"

"Yes."

"Let's get a cab; I know a rest home too. You came to my rescue, now it is my turn."

Weak with pain, any proposal sounded good to him. She was taking charge of everything that was another reason he liked her.

When the yellow cab pulled up at the sidewalk she helped him into it. She whispered to him in the back of the cab, in a caring way. "You're going to be all right, Joe, I'm Nurse Baker on a special mission, rescuing lost souls, please let me be successful. This is definitely one state of affairs I would like to resolve."

She felt she could get him back with his wife, away from the dangerous streets where free spirits sometimes lose their way. This helpfulness was the proper way to proceed. She wanted to carry it out to its final conclusion no matter what happened.

The fifties apartment had been updated to Sally's particular taste. A touch of style marked her out as a special talent. She put a lot of thought into doing up her home the way she wanted it. The final result a place most welcoming with a little grandeur about it too.

"I was not expecting a house guest today. I will fix up the spare room for you now, "she explained as they entered the living room.

"The bathroom is down the corridor on the right; you will find everything you need in there a hot bath would be helpful right now. Please wash your injured hand as best you can before anyone examines it."

He took a scissors to his beard while the bath filled. Listening to a song on the radio in the living room, he heard the words.

Maybe the darkest night had passed him by. He would have to take his chance now; it might be the last one he'd ever get. He was desperate to grab any opportunity. Just because it's not supposed to happen doesn't mean it can't. When fate takes charge everything else falls in place by design. So we're told. At least that should be the way it happens. But it requires something else to help it along the way. Some form of honest commitment. By times he didn't seem to have much motivation left. But even bums on the street have some form of intelligence; you can't survive for long without it. Perhaps it's basic animal instinct all that's left when everything else is gone. It would be hard to imagine being without it.

But luck had a lot to do with it too.

Sally Baker was convinced she did the right thing. Her new roommate wasn't capable of making decisions. It would take time before the burden of responsibility could be put on him. His trauma she hoped would ease eventually. She made a telephone call while the bathroom door was closed, body lice was a particular concern for her. She shivered when she thought about them. Her friend Dr Janet agreed to have a look at him. There might be something in the closet he could wear; her boyfriend was of similar build. She rummaged through clothes he left behind on his return to England. He wouldn't mind at all parting with the outfit she selected. There was nothing in there her man really liked anyway. Else it wouldn't be left hanging there when he was going home for good. Men were easy for her to understand.

She didn't look to deep into them they were just people.

Doctor Janet Robinson was relaxing at home when she received the call. The story concerned her a lot. Sally may not have thought this one out with a clear head.

She referred to him as her knight in shining armour. Wasn't it just like her to do the Good Samaritan? What if he was some sort of a weirdo, now that was a frightening prospect. The dedicated doctor packed her bag with the few things she'd need. Dressings, antibiotics, scalpel the best treatment for lice she could lay her hands on. A more important thing was remembering to call her police friend working for the NYPD. She related the whole story to her. They arranged a strategy to call the apartment in half an hour just to check that everything was in order. She gave her Sally Baker's home address as well. If she didn't answer the phone, get someone over there immediately. They left it like that.

Joe looked like a new man, all decked out in clean jeans, shirt, boots, the beard was gone. A bit thin, rough round the edges but the best he looked for a long time.

When the doctor arrived, she gave him a thorough examination. Opened his wounded hand, cleaned it up, it gave him instant pain relief. She prescribed antibiotics. There were no lice on him, much to Sally's satisfaction. "Antibiotics, booze do not mix so there can be no alcohol consumed." The doctor issued this stern warning before leaving.

He heard her talking on the telephone in the hall.

Not long after that Sally poked her head around the corner saying goodnight heading for her room. It had been a most eventful day for everyone. He climbed into the comfort of a real bed with soft clean sheets. It felt like coming alive again. As he tried settling under the duvet uneasiness came over him when the shakes arrived.

He knew straight away what was required. The call for drink was taking him again. It would persist till it succeeded. Every boozer has an eye for where the whiskey's kept no matter where it's at. It was the first thing he looked for when he entered the apartment.

The well-stocked drinks cabinet was in a corner of the living room. He had already thought about plundering it. The thing is, a drinker sees no harm in stealing alcohol. They think they have a right to it no matter who owns it. Because nobody needs it as much as they do. The doctor's scary warning was absolutely no deterrent. Mixing whiskey with tablets might bring him up there quicker, he reasoned. She could have given him something for withdrawal symptoms, if she was that concerned about him. She chose not to. So it wasn't his fault if it took alcohol to ease his pain. There were other things bothering him too. The fact he was so far up in a skyscraper scared him. Under the ground was okay, but he could never handle heights. Looking down on the street far below terrified him. The whiskey was close; he'd never been any good at resisting temptation. Not even if he wanted to. He'd give her a chance to go asleep. It wouldn't be right to be caught out like that.

Sally Baker lived in the apartment for the duration of her five year contract with the Embassy. She needed to feel more at home in New York, so she organised her accommodation accordingly. The company provided finance for her refurbish; the plan was based on comfort with style. Creating a design from the Laura Ashley collection exquisitely draped patterned curtains, with a plain mustard tie back. They hung from oak poles against white walls. The lounge had pine flooring with a Persian rug in the centre. She'd placed a few special pieces of furniture around the living room. A chair like one in her bedroom at home in England, she picked it up in the village, an old pine writing desk provided a colonial touch beside the door. This piece caught the eye immediately, an extravagant purchase. But in Sally's opinion it gave everything else in the room a new dimension.

Have something catching to complement the space around it, was her take on it? Nobody ever contradicted her on that one. Maybe Martians would understand her if they ever arrived. They might know more about space. Potpourri perfumed the apartment with a fragrant aroma.

A young woman that despised the social habit of frequenting bars, she liked having friends around to dinner. With a preference for small intimate gatherings, loads of fun, drinks with good conversation, entertaining was more her style. She was a cheerful host, as if she never had to endure a bad day. Everyone loved being her invited guest, even those that once considered her boring. But she knew well what they called her. It sounded like fun. It amused her they would think of her in that way. She presumed that it had something to do with her accent. Her private school education might give the impression she was a snob. That was not true at all. But of course where she came from that common perception was never aired.

The story goes, someone tanked up on her booze one night, famously said to her, "You're not a boring old snob at all you're a lovely person."

She was quick to retort, "There are plenty of candidates for either title in New York. Both species are indigenous to the city, in varying degrees."

When she was away from her desk she was her own person. How could you ever get bored in her company? This natural charm with people made her the darling of those she befriended. The boring thing was a joke, some said; she started that rumour herself, just for fun.

She talked to Joe about his wife at every opportunity, discussing Rita as if she knew her personally. Their relationship would remain strictly platonic, observing his marital status helped maintain that arrangement. She told him all about her fiancé Richard, how much they suited each other, sharing so many interests. He was a farmer in England. After a while she broached the subject of her writing a letter home to his wife. It wasn't right to keep the poor girl wondering what was happening to her husband. When he agreed, she wrote down Rita's address in Ireland, putting the pad carefully in a drawer. "I will write to her immediately", she promised.

He was dependent on her now, a mother figure, although she was about his own age. His fragile state of mind needed the kind of nurturing Sally found easy to give. Since she had someone in her apartment to cook for, her dishes varied. She presented him with small quantities rich in flavour, full of vitamins. His appetite was not what it used to be. It had suffered the pain of abstinence, shrunk in size with his stomach. She lavished praise on her homemade chicken soup, with the same healing properties as penicillin. Raised on this old Jewish remedy when illness hit the family, her mother always resorted to it.

'Just try a little chicken soup'.

There were things he wanted to hide from her. Like the amount of whiskey he took from the drinks cabinet when she went to bed. Drinking it in his room; polishing the glass afterwards to avoid detection. She wasn't a drinker, never checked the whiskey, he presumed.

He topped the bottles up with water before putting them back in the cabinet.

Sally already knew what he was up to, she could smell the booze. She diligently replaced the whiskey from the duty free commissary at the Embassy. He started cooking in the kitchen, under her supervision, becoming the most domesticated drunk in Manhattan.

Sally arrived home every second evening with a fresh bunch of flowers for the table. The allure of femininity was everywhere. She changed into her house clothes to cook recipes from her mother's farmhouse kitchen. Good wholesome dishes to warm the hearts in working men. He started to gain a little weight, it suited him.

She introduced the new house rule of one whiskey per night. Enjoying a drink after dinner was a civilized way of handling it she insisted. He continued on with the pretence of agreeing to this rule. But when she was sleeping soundly the drinks cabinet was plundered in the early hours of the morning. He took a bottle of whiskey to his room.

She was aware of it but couldn't curtail the amount he consumed. He'd fake sleep when she left for work in the morning. He'd try faking sober when she returned in the evening that was a more difficult proposition. He excused his strange behaviour by blaming the medication if he dropped anything. But that wasn't very convincing. The shakes were never far away, topping up with alcohol kept them at bay, for a while. But they never failed to return to haunt him on their own.

Too much booze made it worse, he hallucinated.

It was a delicate manoeuvre, like a lot of other things, he was bad at balancing. When she went to bed he drank, when she was at work he drank more. It was like being in the boozer's heaven with a devil bartending. Top shelf Johnnie Walker Black Label, at his disposal was too much temptation for him. His drinking taste had not become sophisticated in such a short time. Or anything like that. He'd drink piss laced with pure alcohol in a heartbeat, if he had too. It depended what was on offer.

One evening, Sally arrived home from work to find him in a disturbed state of mind, sitting at the dining room table drinking. He was deep in conversation with someone he imagined he was with. The experience scared her when she sat down in front of him. "Joe, are you okay?"

"I was just telling Doyle here about this horrible man with the turban. He doesn't believe my story, Sally." A stupid grin all over his face as if he was enjoying it.

"Where is your visitor now, Joe?"

He looked around the table. "He must've left when you arrived; we've been drinking all day."

"Maybe there was nobody here, Joe, only you," she suggested gently.

"I gave him your Scotch; the glass is still there on the table."

"Joe, you have got to listen to me, there is no glass on the table."

When he looked around the table, he knew exactly what happened. "The bastard, I should've watched him."

He became agitated.

"Joe, what is the problem please tell me."

"He's stolen the whiskey glass I brought him to your place."

She'd heard enough, heading straight for the drinks cabinet. Taking every last bottle out of it she poured them one at a time down the sink in the kitchen. Making sure he seen her doing it, the message was no more alcohol. When she finished there wasn't a drop of booze left in the apartment except for the half bottle in front of him. She thought it better to leave that one where it was.

"Tomorrow we make a fresh start, no more alcohol in this house. I'm going to help you to beat this but you must help yourself as well."

She looked at him more caringly. "You do want to get back with Rita? You're always saying how much you love her, well isn't it time that you did something about it. Make some kind of start. This place was not intended to be a glorified boozing

240

parlour, with more whiskey in it than the one you left. This is supposed to be rehabilitation with pain, Joe."

"Yes, I apologise, Sally, my confidence is gone."

"Good that's all I need to know the drinking is finished."

She was serious; what could he do only agree to it. "Okay, Sally."

"Good, you remember we discussed about a little job, nothing too strenuous to get you back into the flow of things. You need to have some self-respect again, time to buck up now I want to meet the real Joe Flanagan."

"So do I, Sally."

She watched him trying to busy himself in the kitchen. He'd made some progress since he was rescued, if showering daily could be called that.

"My friend owns a restaurant; he needs a good guy to help out in the kitchen."

"I can't cook that well."

"Well no, it would be more of a tidying up thing, like a busboy."

"A busboy, I'm a sand hog." He got irritable with her. "I'm not a dish washer how fucked up do you think I am."

"Joe, please don't swear in my home. I'm not accustomed to it don't know how to handle it. It makes me embarrassed." She spoke in her softest voice; it emphasized the roughness of his language.

This was her first serious reprimand of something he said. That had a profound effect on him. He regretted causing her any hassle. It distressed this genteel girl hearing such vulgarity in her home. He wanted to straighten out, she deserved some cooperation. She might get fed up with him, kick him out on the street again, if he went too far.

"I didn't mean to upset you. I will change my ways, any kind of work's fine. Thank you, I appreciate it."

"It's somewhere to start, Joe, not a career decision or anything like that. You need a job to help you climb back on the horse, to get you back on your feet, you must have purpose again. Put New York in context, it's a place that doesn't befit a man like you, so use it to get back in the saddle, Joe, back home to Ireland."

It turned out that after a week scrubbing pots washing dishes, he knew how important it was to have a job. His pay-packet told him that. He couldn't have done it without Sally's nourishment the detox medication she got from her doctor.

To get rid of constantly longing for alcohol, it kept the shakes away as well; death to the evil spirits type of stuff.

The boss mentioned to the nice English girl from the Embassy that he was somewhat distant. When he heard about his past alcohol related problems, how he was in rehabilitation. He understood everything. He confided in his staff, many of them had one like him at home.

A drunk they couldn't handle. They were more inclined to be sympathetic. Anyway it broke the ice. Things changed after that. He started talking with his fellow workers more often. They became less wary of him. He didn't reveal his street adventure to anyone. He was what he seemed to be, a struggling Irish immigrant that fell off the wagon for a while. They could all relate to that.

The chef was a kindly African American man from the Deep South. He was full of meaningful sayings. One of his favourite was, 'give me a place to stand on, I will move the world.' He might say it several times a day, said it was Archimedes the Greek.

Joe never tired listening to his ramblings; there were bits of wisdom in everything the old chef said. Things, that if you thought about them they'd change your point of view. The message was the same no matter who you were, the chef told him.

Joe had some ramblings of his own country to tell him about. Saying Ireland was a place where old sayings never went to sleep.

He told the chef one he could never understand even though it was said to him often enough. 'When you can't do what you want, do what you can.' There were many ways to reach the same place, was his father's way of explaining it. Because he wasn't going anywhere, that didn't make a lot of sense to him. The old chef laughed, saying his father's thinking was too old for him when he was so young. 'He was bringing you on so fast boy.' He liked that kind of stuff but it took time to get the answers even if you knew all the questions.

'That time you need is a lifetime; don't waste it by not thinking about it.'

Joe liked the kindness of this gentle philosophical man. He always felt relaxed around him. He had some money for the first time in months. His duties were not complicated, washing dishes, scrubbing pots. The part he didn't like was sweeping the restaurant floor. It brought him into closer contact with the customers; he was a bit distant when they tried talking to him. More than anything else his undocumented status bothered him. That problem aside, it didn't take him long to get into the swing of things, keeping occupied was the best kind of therapy. It cut the time for thinking about drinking. Sally helped him every evening with kind words, heaping praise on him. She knew how much he needed reassurance.

"It's not the times you fall, Joe, but the times you rise that counts."

That horse analogy Sally figured might register quicker. Anything to motivate him was her thinking. Getting him to respond positively by doing things for himself was still work in progress. She could see he was thinking things out better. He was making some kind of headway. He knew what achieving an end was about now, falling off, getting back on again. While all the time struggling to keep it going. But Sally convinced him to accept his lot. Whatever situation he found himself in that's where he was at in that point in time. Work his way out of it to some better place. Each situation was another step to a different level. If he fell back it might be for the best, because each level presented a different consequence.

None of them was permanent. If the route changed along the way that didn't matter, the destination remained the same. The goal was there with enough determination to reach it.

On a trip to the supermarket he bought a few things Sally liked. He stopped short of replacing the whiskey. It was still a bit raw to arrive in with a bag of booze under his arm. He knew he couldn't do that. Instead he purchased a scented candle he was sure she'd like.

The flower shop on the corner got a hit as well. A big bunch of white lilies to replace those on the living room table. She wouldn't be inside the door before spotting them. Having a few dollars to pay his way made him feel responsible again. It was a wonderful feeling to have.

Sally kept the tablets stacked up joking about Nurse Baker all the time. Any reference to medication felt like progress in the making, a new departure. Like some sort of desperate take-off from the drunk tank. The direction would be straight ahead, level all the way. Anywhere but down, to the emptiness at the bottom again.

Back in Ireland Rita's heart pounded thanking the mailman. When she signed for the letter, she ran upstairs to her bedroom locking the door. These registered letters were usually bearers of bad news. A New York postmark, she didn't recognize the writing on the envelope. Maybe something bad happened to Joe. How could she know? She hadn't heard a word from him for a long time. She was stressed out trying to conceal the worry of it from her family. They were watching everything she did, making it obvious too.

Her hands were shaking opening it.

Dear Rita,

Please forgive me for being so familiar but I feel I know you a little. Your husband has told me a lot about you and I know that you are a good person. His hand injury prevented him from working and he fell on hard times as a result. I have taken it upon myself to contact you on his behalf. But first I would like to tell you a little about myself, as it must be a strange feeling for a wife to be getting a letter from someone who is helping her husband. I'm from Somerset in England and I have been working in the Embassy in New York for five years. Some months ago my English boyfriend proposed marriage to me and we became engaged. I will be returning to England in a few months to get married.

I will be giving up my apartment and my job here in New York then. Settling down on a farm back home has always been my goal and I cannot wait for the start of my new life, where I belong.

Rita, your husband's hand required stitches, thankfully we managed to get him to a doctor and have it taken care of. He is now on the mend and he has started a new job. I have given him a room in my apartment until such time as I leave for home. I am writing to ask if you could return to New York, Rita. From what he has told me about the time you were here with your little girl, things were pretty bad for all of you and more difficult for you in particular. This City can be a hostile environment in those circumstances. I do not know what the position is with your daughter right now but I understand that you are home with your own family. Maybe that situation could help to take some of the responsibility that you have given unselfishly to her. To put it bluntly, Rita, your man will not make it without you. He loves you very much and he needs you now. Even if you could come here for a while to access the situation he might be better off going back home with you. I somehow get the impression that he might have a better chance with the woman he loves in the place he likes to be, his own country. I would not be too optimistic for his chances without your understanding to guide him. Most men are

245

rudderless without women and most of them would never admit it. He is down low enough to realize this now and only you can decide what the next move is going to be. If you want to come here you are welcome to stay in my apartment with him for as long as I have it. Please don't think that I'm interfering in your personal life. I was unfortunate to be mugged on the street and your husband came to my assistance.

He was very brave to get involved; now it's my turn to rescue him. You can telephone me at any time or I can call you back if you contact me to save you money on phone calls. Anyway please contact me by letter if you wish so I can tell him how you are. I hope that you can make it, Rita, the situation needs saving and right now you are the only one that has any chance of doing that.

I'm enclosing my card with work contact details.

Yours truly,

Sally Baker

Rita read the letter a few times to take it all in. He was still okay. She thanked God with a little prayer.

Mary was medically accessed when she arrived back to Ireland. It was verified by the doctors that her daughter's quality of life, could only be adequately maintained in full time care. It was distressing for Rita to make the final arrangements. She wasn't in good shape when she returned from America. It had taken a heavy toll on her mentally. Her family was initially pleased to see her arriving home with Mary, without her husband. But they were very keen to find out exactly what happened in New York. They voiced their opinion privately on what caused the decline in her health. But she was not prepared to bad mouth her husband. No matter how she felt about things. Or reveal any kind of personal information about their private lives. She wouldn't be giving them ammunition to blast the spouse they disproved off. That far away world would be too difficult for them to comprehend anyway. How could they possibly visualize the bird shit hotel?

Painting bad pictures was never her way of coping with her problems. It slowed down the retaliation time. She'd handle it her own way. This direct approach always suited her best. 'Do it now', she had that one in her bedroom growing up. Right there on the end wall where she could see it lying down. She had it in her head ever since. Her family were not to blame for being concerned but she couldn't be held back either. In the meantime they might have enough troubles of their own to deal with. Everyone was trying to make a go of things. In spite of what was going on around them.

As time wore on family inquisitions wore off. Things became settled, they were glad to have her home, Mary was taken care of. They would always be there for her. They hoped the careless husband would soon be forgotten. Maybe she could move on with her life then. But Rita was always on the lookout for some contact from America. She was worried her family members might conceal any attempt by her husband to contact her. Letting the mailman know she was living at home again. She would appreciate him handing the mail over to her in person. An annoying habit she developed in America was how she explained it. Not wanting him to think they were feuding in the home.

"There was a registered letter from America today, her mother whispered. We'll hear all about it when she comes down, I'm sure."

Rita closed the door loudly behind her. She didn't want to embarrass them by walking in on any discussion about her. When the family heard her coming they tucked into lunch as if there was nothing untoward happening. But Rita knew the story well, she'd been in the middle of it in the past, freaking out their father. Poor man couldn't have a drink in comfort with them watching his every move. Attack was always the best form of defence with this crowd. She'd put a tiny hint of venom in it to discourage any debate on the matter.

"Why didn't someone call me?" she said, sitting down at the table to say her piece. "I'm going back to America; Joe has injured his hand at work. I have no intention of leaving him to fend for himself in New York."

That was it. No one said anything they just continued eating in silence.

Rita was back working her old job as a school teacher. Living at home allowed her to save most of her income. The desire to reunite with her husband was strong. She was not interested in seeing other potential suitors as someone suggested. As far as she was concerned she was still a married woman. What she needed was definitive proof her husband was sober. That he wanted to be with her. Sally Baker's reassurance that he needed her desperately was what she wanted to hear. The meetings she attended when she joined Al-Anon convinced her he was addicted to alcohol, it was an illness. That pointed her in the direction she must take. She'd honour her marriage vows, 'for better, for worse, for richer, for poorer, in sickness in health'.

He was sick, she was on her way. Rita's renowned burst of energy clicked into top gear. In the current frame of mind she was looking forward to the hassle of sorting it. There would be nothing holding her back this time.

It felt like a battle she lost before but that ending wouldn't be acceptable next time around. No way. It had to be open war with no excuse tolerated. Chin protruding forward determinedly she went about getting herself organized. There was nothing any of them could do about that. She was getting ready to go.

Chapter Twenty-three

By this time her husband was busy working in the diner. He was still kind of awkward about it moving around with a self-conscious stoop tilting his head at an angle to hide his face. It was a hassle going round collecting dishes to wash in the kitchen. The stress of it didn't improve his sullen mood. He couldn't smile. Occasionally one of the patrons tried speaking to him; but he hurried on by not inclined to talk. There was one customer with a different way of approaching him though. He wanted to know how this big Irish guy finished up as a busboy. Hearing the name again made Joe try restoring a little dignity. He relayed some of his sand hog history to the interested patron. The short story was heavily laden with descriptions of intense physical labour. So much so the man seemed mystified by it, if his reaction was anything to go by. He gave him his business card saying if he wanted construction work, to give him a call. The salary would be more than his present income; he was on the lookout for a working foreman. A guy with this sand hog experience could fit the bill, lead his workers by example. They could do with some kind of motivation.

It said on his card, Mr David Bergmann, Attorney at Law.

Sally announced she was expecting her sister with the boyfriend around to dinner. Joe was looking forward to meeting up with her. He could envisage another Sally, similar in every way. Both of them would want everything to work out good for the wayward Irishman that landed in their midst. But that wasn't the way they seen things at all. They were on a more determined mission. Their message was quite clear from the very beginning. 'Get rid of embarrassing Irish layabout immediately. Anything to secure that result, fair or foul was perfectly in order it would appear.

Nothing went right from the moment Sarah Baker with her equally boring boyfriend in tow entered the apartment. They had to bring their stupid French poodle, Lauren, along as well. He had a similar intellect to his owners. It turned out he had some role to play in the eviction process. Ensuring the whole thing blew up quicker than it did. It would appear.

It kicked off with bad vibes from the outset. Sarah refused to take Joe's outstretched hand of friendship, as did her boyfriend. The dog growled approvingly from behind the couch.

All of them disliked him from the beginning presenting a united front against the lodger. It might be hard to blame them under the circumstances. That must be said. But they could have accepted the situation in someone else's house by pretending.

Their preconceived ideas would not be influenced by any notion of domestic bliss. Sally just took it all in her stride. She wasn't put out by the chilled atmosphere around the dinner table. She even had the presence of mind to block all attempts at interrogating him, changing topics of conversation with the guile of a slippery politician. It was the height of bad manners to make her endure such rudeness in her home. But the two phonies posing as sophisticated people persisted with it. Joe tried answering the personal probes as best he could, without giving away any revealing information. It was a tough task keeping things under control.

They were relentless in their pursuit of a conviction story. But the Irish are brilliant at this unique style of saying everything, while telling nothing. Passed down from generation to generation, blarney it was called so only they could understand it. He concentrated on the good parts of his life.

Reference to Ireland made the situation worse; they were English people that had a natural aversion of the Irish, especially Irish sleeping with their sister. So he talked about his wife instead, to encourage some human understanding. Their eyes misted with disinterest. They didn't even try to hide it. This arrogance annoyed him so much he finally shouted in frustration. "We're not an item, we're just friends."

The sister became more wary of him than ever after that outburst. This display of Irish temper made his bad manner more obvious she claimed. It got a lot worse from then on with open season declared on Joe. Sarah was adamant that anything of a sexual nature would be totally unacceptable. She had no difficulty stating it as bluntly as that, to highlight the issue even more as if it was a forgone conclusion. She said, her future brother-in-law would be horrified at his bride to be, sleeping with anyone. He would want a virgin on his wedding night. Richard was a close friend of the family in England. There were far reaching consequences to be considered in this regard. She was stubbornly refusing to let it go.

Sally wasn't making her much the wiser with her evasive remarks, giggling sometimes, when the fun side of the situation came over her. It was enough to make her sister furious.

She could hardly contain herself, not that she wanted to. There must have been some telepathy there with the dog. Maybe it was the sound of Joe raising his voice that gave him irritable bowel syndrome. During the beautiful dinner that Sally prepared with such care Lauren did his business under the table. It was a motion of the smelly liquid variety.

It might have been aimed at Irish legs. But it missed; the smell didn't. Powerful enough to clear a bar full of drunken Irishmen on St Paddy's day. Sarah was so wrapped in her blunt hurtful attack she didn't seem to notice the stink. That might be some indication of what their place in Brooklyn smelled like.

The thoughts of spending the evening talking in riddles with people he didn't like called for an exit strategy. A snobby little bitch with a creep for a boyfriend was very bad company. But a poodle with the shits was way beyond the tolerance level. He might do it all over his pants next time. Maybe he could use the dog to escape.

Thoughts of his old cronies drinking their heads off in the Celtic bar spurred him on. At least there would be laughter. That place was only a long walk away. There was a plan taking shape. A runner would take some pressure off the hostess, he figured. She looked as if she needed a little relief from the carry on around her. A breakout was the only kind of action available to him. It was the kindest thing to do. Most definitely the choice that appealed to him most.

During all the fuss about the cleaning up job, Joe persuaded Sarah to let him take Lauren for a walk around the block to empty his bowels again. In case he'd have another accident. Sarah was delighted to get rid of him, more than any concern she had for the dog's welfare. Or indeed Sally's pristine home. She encouraged his departure with all haste, saying, 'Don't forget to bring Lauren.' She could see an opportunity to discuss her sister's wayward ways in private. Having already told Sally their parents would be furious about their daughter cohabiting with an Irish vagrant in New York. In his presence, with no kind thought for a sensitive nature. Maybe she was right the way she saw it, but you know feelings are feelings.

Hurt happens when the main agenda takes precedence over everything else. But educated people should have some compassion, if that's what they were supposed to be.

The boyfriend picked up the tempo, suggesting quietly to Sally that the Irish bloke might harm her in some way during the night. She replied with boisterous hilarity, "He's more likely to do something to me during the day, when he's drunk, I'd say."

In spite of her laughter saying that, it was obvious she'd reached the limit with both of them.

Sally's good natured dramatic response horrified them. Now that they had established exactly what was going on, it was paramount to get rid of the Irish bum. If her boyfriend cancelled wedding plans, that would be a fate worse than death.

When Joe Flanagan stepped into the Celtic with the French poodle at his heels, the well-oiled sand hogs nearly brought the house down. Not that he cared what they called him. He expected it. Especially from his old gang boss Duggan, who called him a fuk'en deserter? Anyway, he brought a bit of life back into them for a while. Seeing his buddies again made the long trek worth the effort. Of course the boozed up sand hogs bought him drinks.

That was to be expected. He told them he was manager in a restaurant on the east side. With a day off work, took time to call by, see how they were doing.

The dog belonged to the girlfriend of a friend.

They didn't know where he'd been for a long time, but appeared genuinely glad to see him in spite of everything. None of them took anything he said seriously. Joe knew that too. The banter was the only part of the show that was real. If he was missing for longer he might have told them he owned the restaurant. They were glad he was still crazy as ever, a breath of fresh air. It was more likely he'd a shit job exercising owners' pets for a few bucks. When Doyle tested the water, asking him to put up some money on the counter he was caught out quick enough. All he had was ten dollars. The manager's job mustn't pay too well, they reckoned. He told them he'd left his wallet back in the penthouse apartment. It could happen to anyone.

"I didn't expect to see all you guys here, I would have brought more money with me."

They laughed, Doyle welcomed him back anyway. They bought beers.

He couldn't care what they thought about him once the booze was flowing; just the same as it used to be. He was back to forgetting about reality time again. He sat holding court on a barstool with the poodle tied to the leg of it.

Yes it was all happening for him in America, the land of opportunity, he preached. Duggan kept digging at him though, getting hurtful. After a while it was time to go. He headed for the toilet before starting out on the trek through the park to Sally

Baker's apartment. On his return to the bar he saw that things had turned for the worst. The dog was gone. Lauren did a runner when he left him on his own. Someone said he panicked pulled his lead off the barstool then ran out the door.

Duggan took after him to see if he could catch him

"Which way," Flanagan shouted going after them.

Left, someone roared, with the laughter bellowing in his ears.

He searched everywhere for the dog he didn't like. The only thing worrying him was Sally Baker, how bad he was letting her down. He couldn't stomach returning empty handed to the wrath of the unforgiving bitch of a sister or the scorn of her slimy boyfriend. He had to accept they had achieved their purpose of getting rid of him, for now. They'd use losing the dog to further humiliate Sally. He didn't want to see her degraded any more on account of his mistake. He might do something he'd regret, especially to the boyfriend.

A smack on the jaw was something he was looking for. That action crossed his mind a few times already. But he didn't want them adding the fighting Irish tag to his CV. They'd be keen to oblige. It was best for everyone concerned staying away from trouble.

Midnight was ringing on the old clock in the Celtic as he walked in the door. He asked Murtha if he could use Onion Head's old nest down in the basement for a night.

He wouldn't be sleeping much on account of the dog. To hurt the one person that tried to get him back with Rita was a big mistake. See how booze worked to land you in trouble. He was getting the lost feeling again, taken by the forlorn damp cellar atmosphere.

The feeling that had occupied most of his New York stay was with him again. It hadn't taken off for long enough. But the good news was whiskey on tap upstairs, if he wanted it.

Did he what.

When Sarah Baker ceased bawling her eyes out for the dog she loved so much, her boyfriend announced it was time to head to Brooklyn. Sally spent a long time cleaning up the apartment after them. She hoped to hear the doorbell ring, find him outside with the poodle. But hoping was as best it got; when the night wore on she gave up. There was work next day; she went to bed with a heavy heart. She spent a long time lying awake trying to ease her troubled mind. The Irish girl would be arriving in a few days. It was all meant to be such a wonderful surprise for him. Now he was gone, hadn't she got herself into a real mess? What was she going to do about it now? More questions with no answers the same as always.

The day after Joe disappeared with her sister's dog Sally received a phone call from Rita in Ireland confirming her flight itinerary. She did not say her husband had vanished again. That bad news would hardly give the girl a pleasant flight. Hopefully the situation would be resolved before she arrived. The series of events were becoming more bizarre by the minute.

He had gone missing walking a dog; now his wife was arriving on a flight from Ireland. What were her options?

Sally wanted to believe that having Rita in the city would help her efforts. She planned to meet her at the airport with a welcoming smile on her face. Battle on from there what else could she do. This whole experience had gone way out of control. It was now a search rescue mission in every sense of the word. She had to confess that life was boring since her boyfriend left her alone in New York. This episode changed all that, giving her a new interest in life. In spite of everything going pear shaped she was confident of a positive end result. The excitement of it all far outweighed any other trivial stuff. He'd turn up eventually she was sure about that. In Sally's opinion it would be worth the effort, when the couple got back together again. What she hoped for was that the Irish girl arriving in Kennedy was made of stern stuff. She just had to be. A lot of it rested on that happening.

With some anxiety keeping her company she waited at the international arrival exit.

A placard over her head with 'Rita' printed on it in black, hoping the young woman could handle the unexpected. It sounded like she might have experienced some of that in the past. She hoped they liked each other. It would be difficult otherwise. Just to think, her sightseeing trip down lower Manhattan caused all this excitement? What would the outcome be for this couple if she hadn't made the trip to the Village that particular day? She didn't even want to imagine that. Sally, the so called boring English girl was thrilled to help out in time of need. Since her boyfriend asked her to marry him there was not much excitement in her life. All that changed when she met the homeless Irishman on the street.

To bring about a happy ending was important to her. Maybe her farewell song would be worth all the isolation she endured in the big city.

She was pleased being involved in this Irish love story in New York. If it wasn't such a heart stopping saga it wouldn't be any good at all.

Unaware his wife was landing at New York airport; Joe was helping Betty Ann clean up the Celtic. She was telling him about the fright she got earlier that morning. The spectacle she witnessed had totally consumed her.

None of her experiences over the years prepared her for that. Maybe if she had been a nurse she might have seen something like it before. She could be saying things had reached a critical level with his alcohol intake. She described the first sight that met her eyes. It started with a terrifying scream she heard coming up from the basement. She felt obliged to investigate; he was rolling around on coats, a demented looking face on him, squealing 'get them off me;

"Apparently," she said, staring right through him, there were dogs attacking you."

After a while she convinced him the dogs were gone. Helping him upstairs to the bar she watched him drinking a glass of whiskey in one gulp. It was obvious how much he needed care. But there was no help for him here, only alcohol to abuse, more of the same to numb the feverish brain. What was she expected to do, she knew about his predicament. Her way of listening instead of talking had proved resourceful in the past. She knew everything, but had no way of solving this problem. It was not part of her agenda. Betty Ann felt sorry for him. Of course she knew all about the missing poodle. She was aware of the unfortunate situation with his roommate as a result of it. She already knew the whereabouts of the dog. But her undercover position prevented her from divulging it. Giving him whiskey was something that bothered her, but it had to be. It was the only way she could keep him settled.

The job she had him doing might occupy him for a while; it was the best way of keeping her eye on him. But here was a problem she wasn't prepared to deal with.

Joe couldn't bring himself to contact Sally without finding the dog. Losing the poodle would prove to the arrogant sister she was right about him all along. He didn't want to dwell on that bitter consequence too much. But what was he going to do about it.

He wanted to drink.

Maybe if he hung around the last place the dog had been, he might smell his way back to him. But why would he do that? He was rough with the dog on the walk across the park to the Celtic earlier, tugging the head of him when he didn't want to go any further.

So this desperately hopeful dog logic might be a long shot, even if the poodle had a hound's nose for sniffing his way around. But he didn't possess any instinct resembling that gift. Or he wouldn't have delivered the mother of all shits under the dinner table. Especially if he got the first stink of it himself.

There were a few benefits to be had for him staying on in the Celtic though. The barmaid kept his glass topped up without any apparent reservation. Booze allowed him to function in some blotted out version of the present. He'd pass out in the basement when he had too many. The hallucinations would arrive like the horrors from hell to scare the shit out of him again. But he had finding the dog for an excuse, one that made it right to stay.

Rita had not overstayed her US visa issued to seek treatment for Mary in Philadelphia. Hence she had no problem with INS on re-entering the United States. Before they sat into the cab at the airport Sally told her the bad news. She was unable to keep it to herself any longer. The circumstances surrounding her husband's disappearance, how she needed help to locate him. On the journey into town their common concern bonded them. They were determined to find him together.

After Rita unpacked she freshened up in the apartment. They ate some sandwiches Sally made before going to the airport. Then she told her everything in more detail. There was no fluff over. She was a good listener, not once did she interrupt the story. Sally told it all from the beginning, how she first met her man on the street, up to the time he disappeared with her sister's dog. Not forgetting to praise his bravery by intervening with the bag snatcher. But she did not disclose how he got his hand injured on the street. Some things were best left alone. Rita would find out all she wanted to know when they got together again.

After hearing Sally's account of things she requested permission to call a police friend in Manhattan. Sally was impressed by the resourcefulness of the new arrival. It was an indication she was capable of taking responsibility for her husband's welfare. That was all the reassurance she needed. While she cleaned off the table she listened to Rita explain the situation to the police officer on the phone. It sounded like they had some previous contact. That could prove beneficial if things became more difficult.

The detective sounded sincere when he promised to get back to her. He couldn't disclose of course that he was already aware of her husband's whereabouts. The sergeant had been given an update by Detective Spellman regarding the new occupant in the basement at her place of work. He was also aware of the Irish guy's frame of mind. But there were some things he wasn't at liberty to talk about. Ongoing police investigations prohibited that.

John Duggan was released without charge. He disappeared immediately to some hideout. But the police knew all about the house in New Jersey, they were keeping a watchful eye on him there. His employer the tunnel company, wanted to distance themselves from this embarrassing murder investigation.

The miner's body was still missing in spite of the intensive search. It would be impossible to initiate a murder charge on the strength of a mutilated arm. Detective Brady's boss suggested the hillbilly guy might be gone back down south. That proved how wrapped up in the case he was. More inclined to joke about the TV nonsense of a one armed fugitive on the run, instead of a more positive slant on Brady's effort solving a murder. His way of pouring scorn on the failure to produce one shred of evidence that moved the case forward. He wanted the sergeant to feel the pressure of it. Just how did these guys get promotion was Brady's quiet opinion on the matter. The pressure was never going to get to him, however. He was well able to handle it.

Forensic evidence verified the arm was ripped from the body using extreme force. A terrible sight with half the shoulder attached to it. The rope used in the gruesome task had cut into the bone, almost severing the wrist. It wasn't possible to visualize Duggan's foot on the miner's chest pulling the arm violently with a rope. What mechanical device was used the cop wondered, why was it done like that at all. Could the guy not have been shot? It would be easier for everyone, especially the investigation team. There was generally a body to examine if it happened the old fashioned way. These feud related gang crimes always seemed to finish up the same way, cloaked in mystery. An arm ripped off, or a cudgel shoved down a victim's neck after death. Were these two murders connected by this weird association? Everyone knew what John Duggan got up to, but there was never sufficient evidence to nail him, some kind of slippery son of a bitch for sure. Detective Brady hoped Ann Spellman had discovered something to go on. Things were getting more than stretched.

They had arranged to meet up to compare notes. True to form Detective Spellman was on the attack as soon as she sat into his car.

"Flanagan's wife told you the story, the husband missing, right. I know that he will not surface without this dog, something to do with honour, he keeps saying. Now that you offered to help your fellow countryman, you'd better locate that bloody dog, Ben. Get him to hell away from the Celtic before we have another corpse to deal with there."

"What has a dog to do with this murder business, tell me about that, he asked?"

"If you get the dog, the guy can take it back where it belongs; he needs help, Ben, to be reunited with his wife. He has to get far away from that constant hangover nightmare he exists in. I don't know how the guy stays sane he's a strange man. But if we don't do something he's a dead man from alcohol poisoning. How would you feel then, Ben?"

"Okay, where do I get this damn dog?"

"He's in John Duggan's apartment. He stole the dog for his mother, to keep her company while she prayed."

"Right, Ann, I've spoken to her about her sister's murder. I can say it's a follow up visit. Jesus Christ it gets crazier by the minute, now I'm hauling a dog in, Oh' Man."

He drove around for a while discussing other matters, then let her out of the Plymouth some distance from where she lived. It was a location safe from the preying eyes of anyone recognizing the barmaid from the Celtic bar. Brady weighed up the likelihood of turning up at an old lady's apartment to confiscate her new pet. The possibility that it mightn't be a straight forward matter, he hoped there wouldn't be any tears. She could have bonded with the dog might resist giving it back. He didn't see the need for a search warrant as he had been there before on official business. It was unlikely the woman knew the dog was stolen. He decided this information was an unnecessary burden for an old lady to deal with. So he would have to play it by ear, much the same as the rest of it.

Mrs Duggan seemed relaxed when she admitted him to her apartment. Maybe it was because her son was out of town the pressure was off her. Or was it the black poodle running around behind her that calmed her. Could she be having a run of pleasantness in her life?

Unless Ben Brady's instincts were way off kilter she gave the impression she was pleased to see him again. She made the same fuss as before about having coffee. Insisting there would be no conversation until it was served.

"Is your son gone to work, Mrs Duggan?" he enquired casually in his interested off duty voice.

"No, he's doing a job on his house in Jersey. I wish he'd make arrangements to have his dog taken for a walk. It has my apartment ruined."

A good start, she had no ties to the dog. Or did she seem to have any knowledge that her son had been arrested. He was surprised by her relaxed way of talking with him.

"You want to know about John, is that why you're back here again Sergeant? I always knew that this day would arrive. I have wanted to confess to the authorities for almost thirty years now. Just to set the record straight, there was never any malice intended I can assure you. I must tell you whatever law I may have broken, it was with the child's interest in my heart. You must be sure of that part of it too. God would never blame me for taking care of my own. I'll start at the beginning so you can understand it all better.

"My father was a coarse abusive drunken man, Sergeant. He made our lives a living hell; he was the direct cause of my mother's early death, with his carry on. As you already know my sister Rose was a different type of person than me. She started getting into trouble from an early age, coming to the attention of the police on many occasions. I was left with no alternative, but to abandon my strongly held vocation to God to resolve an evil situation as best I could. I was the only one left in the family, you understand.

When my sister Rose's illegitimate child came into our care in the convent, I quickly bonded with it. I always wanted a little girl of my own. But that way of life wasn't destined for me. Father Thomas encouraged me to take action so it would appear the child was ours. It was also important to prevent any direct involvement from my sister. Not to mention her appalling lifestyle. Sergeant, there was no other way of doing it at that time. So if I must be held accountable then let God give me strength to endure it."

"It's been a long time now, Mrs Duggan, I am sure you are way beyond any statute of limitation. But if there is anything else you would like to add, feel free. I have all the time."

When she closed her eyes in a trance, the sergeant examined the dog's collar. Lauren was printed on a brass disc with an address in Brooklyn.

"You are a very understanding young man, Sergeant. I feel I can tell you everything. Father Thomas was unhappy with his life. He has his own demons. Actions that even God with his powerful gift of forgiveness could struggle with. We decided to set up home together to raise our child. There were problems, changes we had to accept, but we persisted. We made our vows before a witness in a private ceremony for legal reasons.

"The marriage was never consummated of course. We were both in agreement about that from the very beginning. My sister spent two years in jail; I barred her from coming near me after her release. Never saw her again except in the distance, until she started working in the Celtic. I clean the place every so often as my son John is the proprietor. But I never entered it when she was on duty. Yes, Rosie the barmaid was my sister. She took Thomas away from me in the end to satisfy her spiteful way. He would never have told her she was John's mother; he was too much of a coward for that. No character, you see. The devil called on her when she gave him her total allegiance, it was her choice. Then she got what she deserved in the end."

"You've got a key for the Celtic bar, ma'am."

"Of course I do, Sergeant, its hanging on a hook beside the door."

"Mrs Duggan, did you attack your sister?"

"No, Sergeant, I already told you. I wanted to, God forgive me for saying that."

"Who do you think did it, ma'am."

"The devil, I just said it, Sergeant. Satan took care of her like I always knew he would."

"Did your son John know who his real mother was?"

"Yes of course, he knows his real mother is me."

"Do you get along with him?"

"No I don't, he is out of control." She lowered her voice to confide in the cop, the shame of it. "He has street girls in his bedroom; I can't sleep with the noise, the goings on. He shouts at them. Vietnam destroyed him as a young man. It left him without any respect, not even for his mother any more."

The cop was amazed that even a degenerate like Duggan would entertain hookers in his mother's apartment. It was difficult to imagine it happening, but he was sure the ex-nun wouldn't lie. But there was something wrong about everything, the cop didn't know what.

The drifter Onion Head was beaten with a brush, bullied constantly by Rosie, wasn't that motive for murder? He didn't seem as if he could kill anyone. Would an elderly catholic nun murder her own sister if she disapproved of her actions, it could be a more likely possibility than the Onion Head probability. Mrs Duggan might condemn her sister's behaviour, wish for the worst to happen to her, then what. This was a pretty strong condemnation he just heard. Was she the old lady that was allegedly seen in the bar that night? The cop wondered about the sighting again.

Then there was a chance the drifter might be trying to frame her. However he wouldn't be capable of constructing such a plot. Take up too much of his drinking time. He doubted his imagination would stretch that far either.

In spite of Mrs Duggan's apparent willingness to cooperate, she hadn't disclosed anything he didn't uncover already. The bit about cooking the books to get her hands on Rosie's kid was new. That might be examined at a later date under some other investigation. Now it was time for the main event, taking the dog with him. When he asked her about the dog she said John brought it home. She knew it was a stray, according to the collar it belonged to someone in Brooklyn. The detective offered to return it to the rightful owner. She was delighted to get rid of it, since it was ruining her home. There was a leash John brought home hanging in his room. She headed down the corridor to get it with the detective close on her heels. On entering the room she pointed to the wax mannequins standing in opposite corners. All scantily dressed in colourful ladies' wear, life like creations of hookers staring back at him, in wigs, jewelry, heavy makeup.

"See, Sergeant, the street girls, he keeps them here all the time."

The sergeant's attention was focussed on a framed photograph hanging from the wall. It was John Duggan in drag. She was under the impression that mannequins dressed like prostitutes were weird. Her son dressed up looking like her was even weirder, for a grown man. Was that okay. One thing for sure, he was on to something in this location.

"Why is your son wearing your clothes Mrs Duggan?" he asked, pointing at the picture.

"Vietnam, Sergeant, that's what did it to him. As a mother I treat it as normal, it's no harm, he doesn't go out on the street like that. Just something he likes to do on his own."

In that instant it became obvious how unbalanced she was. That her son was similarly inclined didn't matter any more. He had only one thought going around in his head. The murdered barmaid's missing scorched wig was somewhere in this collection. He came looking for a dog to discover a murderer. That was the bit of luck taken care of. But the dog would have to wait; he didn't want to remove anything until he had a search warrant. So he made his excuses before taking off a lot quicker than he arrived.

Down at the car radio he called in ordering the warrant. He instructed his staff to do the same thing on the house in Jersey.

"Take Duggan in for questioning about the larceny of a black poodle."

Brady called Rita as promised about her husband's whereabouts, giving her the Celtic bar address. He suggested before noon was the best time to visit the place. He also confirmed that the dog was located. It would soon be returned to his rightful owner. It was all good.

It was mid-morning when Rita gave a cab driver the address on the West side. She was nervous. Although far removed from the naïve girl that last visited New York.

She had prepared herself for any situation. From information relayed by Sally she knew if he was staying in a bar it wasn't good. Maybe even worse than expected, she was ready for it.

She wouldn't be going home without him this time. As she paid the driver outside the Celtic her legs started to shake. At the best of times bars were difficult for her. At least the place was empty; the barmaid looked about her own age. That helped a lot.

"Hello, my name is Rita; I'm looking for my husband Joe. Do you know where I can find him, please?"

The girl said, "Oh my God," pointing to the end of the bar. "He's down in the basement; I'll get him for you?"

"I'd like to come with you, if I may."

"Sure, if you want, I'm Betty Ann."

Rita braced herself going down the concrete steps. The cold dark staircase reminded her of bad times in this city before.

The despair of that first visit to New York was all around her again. Thoughts of this reunion had kept her awake at night. Now she prayed she was ready. The barmaid pointed to the figure sitting on a pile of coats, leaning back against the wall in the corner. His eyes were wide open staring in front of him, but did he see anything.

"Sometimes he's awake but doesn't talk much," she whispered, hoping he'd be all right. Not shouting like he did when he was a bit frightening. A single light bulb threw eerie shadows around the basement walls.

He looked forlorn, straightening up to say something, as if expecting her. "Did you come back from the deli, Rita?"

Her voice shook a little. "I'm taking you home to Ireland, my love."

She held him close to her for a while, her lips trembling. "Joe, we must go now."

"Why?"

"Please come on, Joe. I'll tell you on the way, to a nice place, you can have a lovely bath, a shower if you want too, I'll cook something special for you as well."

She caringly ruffled his head with her fingers, seeing how dirty his hair was. Sounds of her voice made scary go away, his eyes softened. The desire to hold her reached his arms out like a child. Tears welling his eyes rolled slowly down.

That look on his ragged face in the shadows of this place was truly haunting.

"I don't want to be lost any more, Rita. I'm afraid of it now."

The first steps to recovery, finally admitting defeat, she wept silently hearing it.

The cab ride to the apartment stayed silent, holding his hand for the journey. Stroking it, whispering things he'd be happy to hear. She knew there would be a battle getting him back to health. He would have to change the way he thought about many things.

Exercise, enrolment in AA would be her priority, having read about alcohol recovery before leaving Ireland. She was mindful of the grip that the addiction could take. The harm it can do to the mind, there was bound to be some concern for his health. It was time to start again, work for their future lives together. The past was history. She was determined to ensure it stayed that way. His yearning to breed horses was something he talked about since she first met him. She would use this to further motivate him. Together they would make it back to Ireland to pursue the dream. In spite of all the recent trouble, she knew he had overcome adversity in the past. He had it in him to learn from a severe lesson like this one in New York. Getting him back together again was the next trick. The makings were there already. Rita was sure of that. Rock bottom had turned up as expected, with a few benefits.

Another week passed before he was well enough to return to his dishwashing job. The boss thought he had left his employment, so he hired someone else.

Joe was downcast leaving the restaurant when the lawyer Mr. Bergmann noticed him. He called out an invitation to join him at his table in his legal sounding voice. Having listened previously to stories about sand hogging, he knew the guy could work.

There was desperation in his life that this Irishman could help with. He was convinced about that. This physical work sand hogging sounded like heart breaking stuff. If he could handle that kind of abuse knocking buildings would feel like a holiday to him. This young worker could motivate his bunch of disorganised labourers.

Joe sat down at the table with him; he wasn't in any hurry back to an empty apartment. No matter how nice it was.

"It's a demolition outfit actually he explained after exchanging a few formalities. I need a working foreman to inspire the men by example. If you can do that you will be doing a good job, me a big favour. I will pay you a lot more than you were getting here in the cafe. I need to get my damn building knocked quicker than what's happening now. Then we could line up more buildings if things work out."

Joe liked the way he explained the job, he sounded like a straight shooter. So he agreed. Wouldn't he be crazy not to.

Mr Bergmann arranged to take him to the site, introduce him to his crew. Let him make his own way after that. There wasn't much to know about knocking buildings he explained. Anyone could do it. All Joe had to do now was tell Rita about it. There was a bit of luck coming their way at last.

On the way to the site next morning the lawyer explained more about the project. He was interested in buying old buildings to demolish, sell the sites on for development.

Joe was introduced to the apparently undocumented workforce as the new foreman. It didn't occur to him that the men were less than enthusiastic about his appointment.

When the lawyer left the site, he took a look around the job, nodding at some of the men. It was odd that none of them nodded back at him.

They were a strange looking bunch, communicating in a language he didn't understand. The building was five floors high completely gutted inside. The roof was gone, so were the floors leading up to it. All that remained was timber beams holding it together. It would take much longer to demolish the remainder of it, running across beams was not only dangerous it was also time consuming.

It was obvious that the better strategy would have been to remove the building floor by floor from the top down with a chute to contain the brick rubble.

As the job progressed Joe became aware that the size of the workforce varied. They all spoke a French dialect, from an island in the Caribbean. He was the only English speaker on the job. How do you direct or instruct if they don't understand orders. Especially that all of them, it seemed, chose to ignore him. With so many illegals on one site it would be a choice target for the INS, he'd get caught in the net too. It gave him a lot of reason for concern, the immigration authorities getting on to it, a raid, that would be the end of him.

An accident or an emergency on site could involve the authorities as well. A call from the 911 responders, the police, ultimately the INS would finish him. He could see that the buildings could be knocked in half time. But these guys couldn't do it. The current method was dangerous. A small amount of organization might help to improve everything. But he was too worried around the job to bother with it.

After only one week he couldn't take the risk any more. He explained his concerns to Mr Bergmann in a quiet patient manner, regarding the current situation on the site. The incorrect method used to demolish the multi-storeyed building was problematic for him. Working with a reckless crew that couldn't comprehend instructions, displaying sparse knowledge of safety procedure only added to his woes. He couldn't accept responsibility for a job when there was obviously so much wrong with it. It was unsafe for everyone working there.

For these reasons he must resign from the job.

The lawyer understood his concerns, appreciated his advice. He gave him another of his business cards in case he needed his professional services in future. They parted company without any feeling of bitterness coming between them. Joe thanked him for the opportunity to better himself. But he was very relieved to get away from that kind of work.

He was determined to go back tunnelling again. The sand hog crew knew what they were doing, the money was good. The responsibility for getting the job done would be someone else's headache. He didn't want the role of foreman that he tried for a short time. The old saying, 'The working class can kiss my ass, I have a foreman's job at last', came to mind.

Well he'd been up there for a while; he didn't want his ass kissed any more.

Rita was disappointed that he gave up his job. But when he explained the risks involved on that site she understood. Then she informed him, using some of her usual placid logic, 'He was lucky to get out of it.'

The kind of reasoning that makes you feel you got it right when you did it wrong. Rita was great at keeping the head level no matter what kind of turn around hindered progress. She was expert at finding the positive slant on the negative deal.

Her initial disappointment at him losing his job was soon forgotten. Other than work everything else was going along great for the two of them. She had been accompanying him to AA meetings in the church hall off Second Avenue; they headed to the YMCA three nights a week as well. He was on track to recovery but she still had some concerns. He was becoming a bit withdrawn.

She didn't want him hanging around all day in the apartment watching television. When he suggested going across to the Celtic bar on the west side to make contact with Tash Doyle she freaked.

Maybe that's what the silent brooding was all about, scheming for a return to his boozing buddies? He swore it was about getting reinstated as a sand hog. She relented only when he agreed she could accompany him. She insisted on waiting in a coffee shop nearby. Just to be sure. She warned him; if he didn't show in fifteen minutes she'd saunter into the place to drag him out. He believed her. Would he want the embarrassment of a showdown like that? With the sand hog crew looking on, they'd surely enjoy the spectacle. It would give them something to laugh about for weeks.

Before the appointed time elapsed he arrived back to the coffee shop, pleased to tell her he was working again. She blamed that job as much as the boozing buddies he met up with for all their woes. But she knew that he was far from an innocent victim either. However, it was time to start believing in him again. The corner stone of his recovery was a lot to do with trust; they both had a share in that.

Christmas was just around the corner. A Broadway show was top of the list of things to do with a horse drawn carriage ride in Central Park a certainty. In the meantime if it happened to snow that would be better again. It would be more romantic if snowflakes fell like invitations from the night sky. That was something to look forward to.

Rockefeller Centre with its giant Christmas tree twinkling hundreds of colours like shooting stars in the night. Watching skating, eating junk food was traditional for the season. Sally Baker told them everything. They were really looking forward to it. Soon things would return to normal like it always did after every dramatic interlude. Until another compelling series of events changed everything for a while again.

The most important thing was he had a job to go to. The days lounging around the apartment brooding were over. That was enough to put a smile on his face for Christmas.

Sometimes thinking about what he left behind him in Ireland upset him. He enjoyed his salesman's job he'd made a success of it. Some people are not meant to travel far from home; they were two of those. Even though their liking for New York was growing they longed for home. The place they knew best. Christmas reminded them how much they missed absent friends. But they went on about enjoying themselves on their own. Everything they planned to do they did. The snow arrived to make it a white Christmas too. It was like dating again.

He was alcohol free for almost a month, his attitude changed, more responsible by times. A positive outlook kept him thinking more rationally than before. Time to deliver what his partner in life wanted. It was less selfish than his account of things so far. Hers were more geared towards reaping benefit for both of them. He had been self-obsessed, consumed for such a long time. Rita was more about the collective; she quietly encouraged change to his thinking. He was really enjoying listening to her. She made better sense of everything.

When she got herself a waitressing job within walking distance of where they lived. She was overjoyed. This bit of independence empowered her more. Their shared sense of humour was beginning to sparkle again more often than before. It had been absent long enough.

Joe knew Rita wanted him back in her life but she had rules to secure this objective. Now it was up to him. Hadn't he admitted at his first AA meeting he was crazy? When he stood up to tell everyone he was an alcoholic. Saying it out loud explained things to him as well.

When the booze happens upon you it behaves normal in the beginning. The whole purpose of indulging it is about enjoyment. To help people relax for their social interactions. But the mind altering component is unpredictable. How it reacts with different people. It has the ability of making them do things they mightn't think of doing. It says things it should never utter. It gives orders without thinking of consequences. It also has the power to impose its own will. It can turn nasty during a bout of frivolity. Everything can change when drink takes charge. Caring is the first casualty of this indifference. As soon as booze takes over responsibility gets side lined. It never feels like a problem until it's too late. So nobody's wary of it in the beginning. What started off as a tonic for enjoyment finishes up as some excuse for disaster? The journey's end follows a predictable course.

Human intellect cannot cope on its own with this recurring desire for alcohol consumption. It requires some outside influence to assist with the problem. The demon is far too powerful a persuader to be ignored. There is hope if there's anything left to hope for. If you couldn't hope for a woman like Rita there wasn't any hope left for you at all. Recovery would have to be taken from rock bottom, they said. Right, he was there. Whatever they told him to do he'd do it, rock bottom was a bad place. He'd been there too long already. But now he was ready to start all over again. A lot of it had to do with positive thinking they said. If you think you can do it you're halfway there. But the primary condition for progress was remaining true to commitment. Without fear or favour, Rita's strength would guide him through it. He knew that for sure. He didn't care what anyone thought about him, having dumped any pride he had left on the streets of lower Manhattan. He wasn't going around holding his head down due to past mistakes either. He knew more about things now; he didn't want to go back there again. Rita was helping him build up his self-esteem. She talked to him continuously about these things, encouraging him to be positive when there was more reason for doubt.

Losing confidence when the brain is ripped apart with alcohol is what happens. This was his only chance to make it right. He wasn't able to do it for himself but he could do it for her. Hearing those stories on alcohol addiction helped him to understand how it worked. They were all the same. All of them finished up in similar misfortune as himself.

You don't have to be homeless on the street to have lost everything. That condition can materialise when it appears you're well off. It is capable of destroying a house full of kids with a few cars parked outside the door. It's the state of mind that captures its victim. Like a spider watching a fly struggling hopelessly in its web. Alcohol is the spider that never sets responsibility free, instead it manipulates it to destroy itself. A cannibal spider, if you like.

Now that he understood the problem he'd do something about it.

One guy at a meeting got up to say something like, "We're all mad, one way or another, getting it out in the open is a freaking release. That madness takes on a new lease of life when it picks up another drink."

Everyone understood that, they were all on the same path. The sting in the tail didn't change much. Getting all messed up was the end of it, not once did he hear any of them complain. If they were into blaming someone else they wouldn't be accusing themselves. They had similar stories to tell, if they hadn't picked up that first drink none of it could have happened. It wouldn't happen again, if they didn't pick up another one. Broken but never conquered a sincere bunch of kindly hurting people. Wasn't he really lucky to have found them?

Chapter Twenty-four

Detective Brady made progress with the homicide investigation. The victim's blonde hair piece, earrings, lipstick were bagged, recovered from the kinky miner's bedroom. That should have been enough to put serious questions to John Duggan. He claimed he knew nothing about the stuff. Maybe his mother picked them up in the bar doing her cleaning job. When she denied any knowledge of it he said she suffered memory loss. If they interrogated her she might admit to killing the barmaid, he laughed. It had nothing to do with him.

That was before his lawyer put a gag order on him.

Detective Spellman sat on the edge of his desk discussing the case with him.

She was looking at the picture of Duggan dressed up as his mother.

"Nothing in the statute defines how to dress, you're free to put on your wife's gear in the privacy of your own home, Sergeant. If that's what you want to do."

She was right. There wasn't enough available at this stage for the DA to charge him.

"I followed up with the priest. I had to rule him in or out. It appears that Thomas is a genuine enough sort of a guy, Ann. He admitted that they didn't know much about rearing a child in the beginning. Their religious lives hadn't prepared them for this family role. Moving in with Sister Marie was not such an easy undertaking for him. He let her take control of things so he could enjoy an easy life. To be fair, she did her best he claimed. But her approach from such strict religious beliefs was at the root of her problems. She spent her life living like a recluse, dressmaking whenever the mood took her. She couldn't buy any clothes to suit her transformation from the convent garb. To save money, she made clothes for herself. She used off-cuts to make things for the baby too. Her expertise was making girls' clothes. So it was easier to dress young John as a girl. It was not an uncommon practice in Irish families anyway. A former teacher in the convent, she educated him in the home, a solitary existence for a kid. She maintained the streets were too rough for such a gentle child. The Doyle kid down the block came around to play with him sometimes. That was as much contact he had with people growing up. It got more natural when he became older. In the midst of living with deceit, religion was strictly observed in a home full of contradictions. That's why he's so screwed up, I guess."

"Okay I get it, Ben; Duggan had a very disturbed childhood. That's why he's able to pull your arm out of your body."

He tried laughing it off; they knew the case was in real trouble without more verification.

The Sergeant had made a lot of ground. Now Ann felt she needed to contribute. Doyle had discussed some of Duggan's bizarre behaviour with her, when they slept together. She wanted to share the details with the sergeant. But she couldn't. She'd wait for a chance to fill it in. Some girls were very private about their love interests.

The sergeant continued analysing Duggan. "He lives a double life, Ann; it must be frustrating for him. He dressed up as his mother to murder the barmaid, his real mother. Why did he want to kill her, there must be something we're missing. Then he poses as a sand hog while living like a gangster. Heavy isn't it?"

"Ben, when he dresses up as his mother he wants to be his mother, right, so why not interrogate him when he's her, it might work talking things through with Mom. My drama teacher insisted we get into the head of people we're playing. I took drama lessons very seriously, Ben, I learned a lot about human behaviour. We should be talking to him as his mother, get into the zone with him that way, see what happens then. It's worth a shot, might be all we got."

"No, Ann, we can't do that. I'll get my ass handed to me if it doesn't work, indicted if it does."

"We've got to pick him up wearing her clothes, Ben, interview him when he's her."

"Right, so how do we know he's in costume? Do we pounce, when he's climbing into bed at his home?"

"I can monitor his every move in the Celtic. I can indicate where he goes from there. I'll keep my ears open around his friends. Put a tail on him every time I tip you off."

"He qualified with Special Forces training. He's still a very dangerous character even dressed as his mother."

"Look, Ben, we have to cut him loose anyway. Let him think he's off our radar screen for now. He's on extended leave from his tunnel employer. We can ask him to notify us if he leaves the city for Jersey. It's worth a try, a long shot but why not."

Brady wasn't comfortable with this situation. He figured she'd do it her own way anyhow.

He didn't want to know too many details. It would be easier for him if the shit hit the fan later. Things had already escalated upstairs with the big brass. The chief wanted to know why Brady's cases were still unresolved. Why was the miner's body still missing? He was bitching about Detective Spellman still playing barmaid in the joint where the previous barmaid was brutally killed. Another thing that bothered him was the suspect in all the murders, this Duggan guy, in the precinct like he worked there. The chief was under pressure himself. Shit flows downhill, he was dumping on Brady. That's how it worked.

"Right, don't tell me anything, Ann; I'll leave it to you. Just get the guy with the lady gear on him. Stay in touch okay. Do you need anyone else assigned to work with you, or should I not bother asking that question."

"Yeah, I need help. I'm asking for Officer Stella Smith's assistance."

Brady was surprised by that choice of partner; he had to comment on it.

"Okay you got it. A tall black lesbian undercover cop will be just the ticket to keep you from being noticed. My God, Ann, you never fail to amaze me, do a real good job of freaking me out at the same time. I hope you know how to handle all this shit. It's real crazy stuff."

The sergeant stopped short of calling off the mission. But it was a simple calculation for him to make. There wasn't any other way of proceeding. The aces were all in the bad guy's deck.

The following afternoon Detective Spellman showed up at the prescient in disguise for the afternoon shift. The complete makeover it seemed was a resounding success. There was no resemblance to the far out dancing barmaid Betty Ann either. When she walked into the detective unit's meeting room, none of her colleagues including Brady noticed her.

She was carrying NYPD photo ID having passed the desk sergeant they accepted that she must be undercover. She had to admit it was how she got her kicks, in her own crazy little world of make belief. With her disguise costumes left over from the acting wardrobe.

Wasn't everyone an actor inside? She was just lucky to have an opportunity of letting it out. She always intended making a name for herself in amateur dramatics, just a small name.

Maybe that's what it was all about. A makeup friend from the theatre gave her the butch looking hairdo. Her lesbian friend Stella was ready made for action.

Their undercover target was the Volcano on the lower east side. A place where the bizarre was cool the outrageous a fashion statement.

The undercover officers were anxious to get down there to mix with their own kind of people. Before they departed, Detective

Brady insisted on obtaining full details of the sting location from Ann. He intended to have additional back up on standby.

The first week Joe Flanagan went back to work in the tunnels was a difficult time. He had to endure a lot of the alligator man disparaging treatment again. Having a go at him seemed fair game, the thing to do. Some of it got nasty, even though the guys intended to be funny. Doyle turned out to be a real good boss. That helped him get through most days. Doyle understood the trauma his friend was going through. He was sensitive in his dealings with the Irish guy trying to make a comeback. Joe knew they all saw him as a loser. The unreal alligator incident from his past wasn't going away anytime soon. It was a real crowd puller. Or just another opportunity to pile more shit on the Irish guy's cart, leaving him lots to carry round with him. He needed to focus, get his head into important things. His strength would continue to build. Muscles that diminished, softened on the street were becoming firm again. He sweated profusely the toxins of alcohol from his body. He drank billycans of iced water all the time to flush him out.

Rita kept a supply of fruit on the table, fresh vegetables with meals too. Coffee like alcohol was on the banned list. Toxins out vitamins in was the slogan, he felt good in himself about the whole thing. It was coming together nicely. The weight of trouble was slowly lifting off them. Natural vitamins were the best way to energize the body, she told him.

He said if he was a horse, there'd be a shine on his skin. If he sometimes felt like a stallion, that was in order too. Loving feelings were all the rage on Third Avenue things were buzzing again with this tonic for banishing bad times. Physical labour was the power that drove him. He was becoming addicted to it now. Alcoholics tend to overdo some things during recovery. Maybe it's to compensate for dumping the compulsive drinking behaviour. The regular sessions in the gym at the Y had become a sort of social event. The couple established a routine after their workout, chatting in the juice bar for a while. Sometimes on the way home they took in a movie. Now that Sally Baker had returned to England, they had her apartment all to themselves. It was wonderful going back there, as if it was their home. They treasured the independence of it. Sally was a very special lady. They were indebted to her for arranging an affordable rent, to give them a start. What would have happened if she hadn't come along? The answer to that question wasn't good, so they stopped asking it.

Like one of those things you think back on, it still scares you even though you're past it.

He knew Sally saved his life, his marriage, his self-esteem, he was eternally grateful to her. It's only as things got better they talked about mistakes made. From all those experiences, lessons would be learned that could stand to them later on in life. They would gather strength from it to sustain them in future times of need. They knew how fortunate he was to meet up with her that day in the Village. He was nearly gone at the time. God bless her for believing in him. Her patience for getting him to believe in himself was the start of it. He owed her for all that too. They would never forget it to her. How could they.

The sand hog tunnel race was a thing of the past. The general foreman was making moves to cover his ass; alcohol in the hog hut was banned. It took a mutilated arm in a locker to bring that about. Limpy was more relaxed knowing Duggan was suspended.

But that cop Sergeant was still bothering him, wanting answers to questions of a personal nature. Whatever happened to him in his previous years was well buried now. It was something he kept to himself for a long time. Limpy wanted it to stay that way.

But the nosy cop was still digging.

The January rain fell in a torrential downpour, causing street flooding that added to the pressure on sewer congestion. Some of the guys made comments for Flanagan's ears about alligators moving around in the fresh rain water. Doyle tried putting a stop to the continuous barrage, doing his best to rubbish the alligator story as urban legend. He never saw one in all the years working down below. The ball breakers wouldn't let it go but kept on reminding him. That's the way it was, ringing in his ears. For his part Flanagan tried ignoring it, never retaliating with comments of his own.

It wasn't the retraction the guys were happy with; they kept the banter up anyway to draw him in. But those times alone with his thoughts, he never took a step forward without looking where he was putting his foot. Things Limpy ingrained in him about alligators were still there. He had no way of dumping those fears. Concealing them was as best he could do.

Those reminders made it more difficult to get past it.

'Hi'ya doin, alligator man!' they taunted. Some things never went away.

It doesn't get much worse than been scorned as a dick head. It made him more determined to carry on. He knew his place was with Rita, she had come back to get him. No matter what happened, he wouldn't let her down this time. How long could he stand without her, didn't he know the answer to that one already? Not long.

Now he was doing it for Rita because he knew he couldn't do it for himself. He wouldn't be able, call it the way it was. The alligator crap would never get to him again. They could call him what they liked. He wasn't listening to them.

Mario Capatani dropped into the hog hut for one of his impromptu meetings. There was usually a problem on the agenda when he called around.

A hush came over the place to let him be heard. He spoke in a calm voice; they listened, waiting to hear the punch line. There was always a fear the job might be closed down for some reason or another. The men dreaded it happening. The general foreman spoke quietly as they listened.

"There's a pipe blocked in the tunnel, men. It's highlighted here in red," he pointed to his drawing. "The rainfall has increased the normal amount of water down the sewers in this area. Under normal conditions the pipes would cater for this surplus. But see this pipe here, it's blocked in some way. Probably with a big deposit stuck in the bars of the grate. These bars are six inches apart, a kind of filter to break up congealed debris. Rubbish washed down from the street drains gathers items in a solid mass that cause a blockage. The water racing through breaks up this debris. It's not clearing the blockage this time. We haven't got any way of releasing it. The only hope is getting someone down there to remove it manually. I need a man to volunteer for this job. We will have a safety rope around the guy all the time. If he wants to come up, he'll pull on it three times, we can take him back out safely. No problem."

"That's if the alligator hasn't got him after the first pull," someone said, but nobody laughed.

"I'll do it, sir." It was the greenhorn from Ireland talking.

'What's the story, Flanagan, you drinking again?'

That was the loudest comment. They all knew the story, he'd freaked out before, in the horrors with whiskey.

"Doyle, get two men to back your man up, secure the rope be ready to pull him out. It needs to happen right now, while the rain is easing up."

Joe Flanagan examined the wall chart as if it meant anything to him. Maybe this was his chance. The idea to volunteer came to him when he saw no one went for it. Not a good reason for basing a supposedly life threatening decision on. But then, from his point of view it had a different meaning. Circumstances change perceptions. Not thinking rationally is another trait of the free

282

spirit. He was eager to grab it, it wasn't about money. He'd show them up. Maybe then they'd have respect for him when he made it out in one piece.

Fuck the be-grudgers he was sober. Ready for work, there was a chance to take. He was taking it. That's all.

He helped the guys load up the red van with everything required from the stock room.

When they arrived at the drop area, the general foreman was there already. They harnessed him up in a water resistant suit with a life jacket attached, to deploy if he fell in a deep hole. They had constructed a strong tripod pulley over the street manhole. The general foreman gave him another instruction. 'To call the shots as he saw them in real time', he emphasized. There was a light on his helmet to show him where he was going.

The final apparatus, a breathing mask to filter foul air, was strapped on his mouth. But he could still hear everything the General foreman was saying.

"This is an old hole left covered from the original construction years ago. There are no steps down the shaft; we are going to drop you on a sling. At the bottom you'll stand up in water, walk about thirty yards downstream to the grate, the problem area. Use the long pole with the hook on the end to pull at the debris caught between the bars. When it's released, the water will pass freely, the job's done. It's a simple task. The water will subside after the initial rush."

His final instructions were to hold the pole upright for the descent. As if he was stupid enough to hold it like a tight rope walker.

Mario was still shouting instructions. "Take it easy, guy, don't rush your way along the pipe, make sure your footing is good before applying your weight. Good luck guy we're depending on you."

His focus on being calm occupied Joe. The inner strength wouldn't be there if alcohol was on board. Without it messing with his brain, he was a different man. At the bottom he tugged once on the rope, letting them know he had arrived. When he got out of the sling to stand up, the slippery ground almost took his legs from under him. There was consoling words from his AA meetings to remember. 'This too shall pass.'

He made slow progress, holding on to the side wall steadying himself. The noise was like a waterfall coming from the darkness nearby. In the close confines the echoes magnified. No one told him about that part of it. Was there something happening, could the tunnel be filling up with a flow of sludge they knew nothing about? Would he drown? No, he couldn't. 'This too shall pass.'

The helmet light cast a narrow beam only to reveal more darkness. He strained his eyes to make out anything in front of him. The bars were there hanging like dark icicles from the roof, water spilling through them. He reached out for the top with his pole dislodging mud from under his feet, something bumped his legs.

Sweat poured off him like water when he shook. 'There's no such thing as alligators, please God let it pass.'

He held on to the pole tightly pulling it down, dragging it back. It moved easily when the flow got behind it.

Then the blockage rolled, an arm shot up in the air; the ghastly face of a human corpse looked back at him from the dirt. He froze in horror. It was the first time he'd seen the remains of a dead person. He tried turning, panicked, forgot how to move until the water level dropped, then he frantically scrambled away from it. Tugging anxiously on the rope three times, tearing at the mask, puking his guts up.

"There's a dead person down there," he whispered when he saw them.

As white as a ghost he was a scary sight. The fresh air soon brought him back to himself. A good fright never killed many people. But it was another one he'd never forget.

Within the hour he was sitting in the general foreman's office drinking water, talking to Sergeant Brady about it. The cop was taking him through his experience slowly.

Mario suggested filling his mug with whiskey to help him get over the shock, the sergeant chuckled at the panicked rebuke.

"No, thank you, sir, I don't drink alcohol any more."

With a gesture of kindness Sergeant Brady offered to drive him home to his wife. He gave him instructions not to discuss his findings with anyone. In case it hindered investigations at some later stage. The general foreman gave him the next day off work, with full pay, to help him get over his trauma. He praised his effort highly before he left.

That was the best part of it all.

Forensics later confirmed that there were three distinct bodies or parts thereof. One of them was later identified as Lupe. The two other bodies were wrapped together in some industrial plastic covering. They were weighed to keep from rising. One of these bodies was that of Rosie's second son Bobby. Body parts of some other unidentified person lay beside it.

The story took legs without any help from Joe Flanagan. The sand hogs had predicted Lupe was there. Limpy knew for a long time that one of the other bodies was his son. Rosie was always saying it to him, 'Duggan got rid of their boy'.

But he knew where he was at.

Lupe was dumped in his long confederate coat that mistake cost Duggan. The coat spread across the bars causing the blockage that led to the discovery. The torrential rain brought it all out in the open. It looked like alligator man earned some respect in the end. Even if it had a sting in the tail, their new name for the Irish guy had a more sinister ring to it. Body snatcher, they called him now. It was hard to win a round in the tunnels of New York.

Rita got slightly flustered seeing her much loved New York cop arriving with her husband.

She was pleased to have the nice apartment, a place to be proud of. They had made some progress from last time they talked in the bird shit hotel. Now the cop was sitting back with his coat off eating her home baked scones.

He was comparing them favourably with his grandmother's baking in Ireland. She knew this was the biggest honour any Irishman could give. To be compared to grandmother's cooking was a recipe for success, she was delighted with the compliment. But hearing of the corpse drama in the tunnel with her husband playing the leading role came as a shock. She couldn't hide it.

"This man of mine gets himself into some bad situations drunk or sober. What am I going to do, Ben; will I ever get him back to Ireland in one piece?"

The cop made no comment, but might be forgiven for wishing 'the sooner the better'.

While he was busy relaxing himself in Third Avenue, his partner Ann Spellman was downtown, checking out unfriendly territory. Her partner for the evening big Stella the cop looked just like any other dyke. They both remained aloof, discouraging anyone from speaking to them. It helped them to remain discreet, stay focused, while at the same time blending into their surroundings.

They weren't long in the Volcano when they spotted their man.

"That's him, Stella, that's Duggan right over there, the lady with the black bonnet, long dress. I know you're starting to blend in here, Stella, enjoying this atmosphere but get your ass outside to call it in. Tell them we need someone watching the street."

"You got it; don't let him out of your sight till I get back."

The two cops selected as back up were already in place, just awaiting confirmation. They knew what Duggan looked like. They were told to treat their suspect with the utmost respect, being that she was an 'elderly lady'. If she wondered why she was being taken in for questioning the cops were advised to inform the lady that it was related to her black poodle.

Detective Brady was then advised that the subject was spotted; the stake out was in place. He relayed orders, to get the girls out of the area without anyone drawing attention to them.

He made his way back to the precinct, waiting at his desk, coffee in hand, with some anticipation for Mrs. Duggan's arrival. He was looking forward to meeting her.

"It's nice to see you looking so well, Mrs Duggan," he greeted her when she was brought in.

"Oh thank you, sergeant."

"I see you've been out late celebrating."

"Yes, Sergeant, sorry if I'm a little tipsy, I like to celebrate with special friends," she replied, as a matter of fact. It was a good start.

The audience in the CCTV room consisted of the undercover girls. Having ditched the garb, they gave thumbs up to each other; the sergeant was doing his thing. It was going along fine, just like she said it would. Detective Brady was getting it on.

"Do you still live with your son in your lovely apartment on the West side?"

"Yes, but he spends time in his house in Jersey too."

"Right, I understand you don't approve of ladies in his room."

"He's a young man, Sergeant, it happens."

"You didn't like the barmaid in the Celtic bar, did you?"

"She's very young, I don't dislike her."

"I was referring to the barmaid that was murdered. Mrs Duggan, you murdered her, didn't you?"

"Go fuk yourself, Sergeant."

She started laughing at the police officer. "Guess ya thought ya could fuk with me, sergeant. Do you think I'm that drunk? Thing is, I might dress like a woman but I piss with a cock, standing up.

Listen, cop, my name is John Duggan, my mother's at home, where I should be, so can I go now."

"Not yet, Duggan, we still have things to discuss so we are going to hold you over. It will give you a chance to sober up."

"Please, Sergeant you don't want me photographed like this."

Brady told the police officer standing outside the door to put him in a holding cell.

He instructed the cop to have someone borrow a jump suit from the Department of Correction at Rikers Island for Mr Duggan before they booked him. It was important to ensure all protocol was correctly applied. He didn't want a smart lawyer springing him on some lapse in official formality. The charge would be possession of stolen property, in the form of a French poodle named Lauren. When Duggan heard there would be no pictures of him in ladies wear he got cocky again, turning his scathing cynicism on the police officer.

"Thank you, Sergeant, I appreciate your sympathetic Mick upbringing."

Detective Spellman, conscious that her previous employer was in lockup down the hall, approached Ben at his desk. She felt bad for him, after agreeing to try her conspiracy theory. If it worked it would have been amazing, it didn't, but Brady was blaming nobody.

"Right, Ann, let's see where we can go from here. We need to move fast, so get forensics to prioritize the bodies from the sewers. "The hillbilly's coat contained a plastic wallet in which he had an envelope with the Celtic bar address written on the back of it." He looked at her sharply for a pause. "The company man Sullivan's names on the front of it. I find that strange, Ann, seeing he told me he didn't know the guy. This piece of paper says he did. I will have another talk with him, see what he's hiding. Keep pumping your Mrs Dillon from that Celtic, maybe gain some more chatter from her. Did you notice that Duggan didn't want his mug shot taken or request his lawyer? I think he doesn't want his lawyer to see him dressed like that. So that gives us a little more time to hold him, we can also delay the jumpsuit delivery from Rikers. I understand Limpy Ryan believes we have found the body of Bobby O Connor. Ann, get your Mrs Dillon to expand on Bobby's alleged murder without confirming his body's found. Let her think she's talking about something that'll never come back to bite her."

"You got it, Sergeant, sir." She saluted him, remembering something. "Hey I'm done working that joint now, but I will visit Mrs Dillon at her home."

Thomas stood in his green doorman uniform under the canopy of the plush apartment building on Park Avenue. He had been informed about the discovery of the boy's body.

Time to bring a few secrets out into the open; it would be his intention to give the remains a proper burial. He owed Rosie that much. His contact with the young teenager developed through friendship with his mother; they bonded in the few years before his disappearance. The young man trusted him, confiding problems relating to his personal life. Bobby got a compassionate understanding from the ex-priest, he needed that. But such things were best kept in the family. Thomas's priestly experience provided sympathetic counselling.

Although he had no knowledge of the drug scene, homosexual inclinations was something he had to deal with himself. This shared sexual diversity put him in the position of a mentor to the young man. There were things relating to Bobby's lifestyle that concerned him at the time. The unusual friendship with his son John, he opposed most of all.

He looked at his watch; he had planned for a little time off to visit the police station. The detective sergeant seemed to be a fair minded man; he would request Bobby's remains released to him after all forensic tests were complete. It wasn't something he was looking forward to but it must be done. There were obligations to be upheld.

Jim Sullivan was feeling nostalgic on the Staten Island ferry. He remembered when his daughter was young, her excitement accompanying him on the trip. It was always a great experience for them when she was on board, so full of energy. That vitality still existed in her to this day. The dark water of the Hudson River held no fear for her. She even liked it. He stared into its blackness for a while; the current could take you miles out to sea he was told.

There were many things going through his troubled mind. Maybe all this reminiscence was a vain attempt to remove the problem that wasn't going anywhere. The real issue was the police wanted to question him. He was suspected of being involved in Lupe's murder. The sergeant had made an early morning visit to his home on Staten Island waving the envelope under his nose. It had the Celtic bar written on it in his handwriting. The cop wanted to know why he denied knowing the deceased miner. When Sullivan said he never said that, the cop called him a liar. He figured Sullivan knew more about the murder than he was letting on. The sergeant assured him the police were now investigating all his activities to do with the company. Sullivan was certain they'd discover his corrupt financial dealings with Duggan in a short time. There were too many loose ends. That would cause his family, especially his daughter, a lot of grief. It was completely immoral to have innocently involved her in his financial scam. The humiliation, the shame he'd bring on his family was too much to confront. Mumbling a prayer for forgiveness raising the gun, he jumped, pulling the trigger before hitting the water.

Rita was busy waitressing eight hour shifts in the diner on Third Avenue. She hadn't time to think about anything. Everything was moving along well for her. But she couldn't imagine what it must be like to find human remains at your place of work.

When she had time for thought, her husband was the first thing on her mind. She knew he was traumatized in spite of the brave front he put on. He was determined to report for work again the very next day, as if nothing happened. Staying busy, taking things one day at a time, the AA mantra for staying sober he explained. The past didn't matter to Rita any more, only what they could accomplish together in the future. Mistakes can be lessons learned; she hoped they both benefited from them. It might sound like second hand wisdom, passed down from someone before.

But it registered the pain of making their own. They'd never forget it. Like putting your hand in the fire, to see how it burns. There might be merit in painful memories though, lest the feeling ever be forgotten. Some important things were starting to register. There was progress made in spite of everything. She knew her man was making his way back from the dead, as it were. It was great to see him so determined, focused on making money for their future. Soon they would be getting out of New York.

The lessons would pay dividends in the end. When they were well away from it all, with time to look back wondering how it got so out of control. They hoped to be in a good place then, better disposed towards rescuing their marriage. It was terrifying looking back at what could have happened. The less stressful atmosphere of Ireland would soften the blow for both of them. One day they would really appreciate the good fortune of escaping it.

Things work out like that sometimes, she knew. But it still felt frightening, even to contemplate the experience. It was too soon, the trauma remained nearby. The bad feeling would take a long time to go away.

How she longed for the comforting reassurance of friends gathered around her again.

Relax to relish the scent of flowers in the garden.

Enjoy life's simplicity that never made such harsh demands. She recalled how little she appreciated home when she was there.

That respect would never again be taken for granted. Maybe that was the best lesson of all she learned on her travels. To appreciate more what you have, because someday you might find out it was enough; after you've lost it. Life could be about losing then finding, making then breaking, learning then fixing to build sound character. One that chooses the wisest option most of the time. That deals rationally with problems if there is such a thing. We can do better if we put more belief into it. But keeping positive energy on tap is a wonder to behold.

It's all wound up in the human dilemma. Now that's another day's work.

Chapter Twenty-five

Detective Brady was looking at the spot where Lupe's body was possibly dumped. Watching the steel lid being removed, he was sure the suspect could have carried out the task on his own. When all photographs more measurements were documented, they examined the surface around the top of the manhole. The marks of a rope, traces of fibre were clearly visible in the groove where the lid would fit. The blood spatter that was taken earlier from the sidewall wasn't evaluated yet, but the cop had already figured how it happened. The miner's arm was pulled off, assisted by his body weight using a motorized vehicle. The skid tracks on the ground were almost indistinct.

Where did Duggan get the vehicle, he didn't own an automobile. Did he borrow one from the job site, or did someone help him. Who knew where that vehicle was now? Brady's earlier conversation with Thomas had unravelled some issues that had puzzled him for a while. The picture was becoming much clearer to him now.

Detective Spellman called him as he was wrapping it up at the alleged crime scene. She had something to say that would interest him. It was time to meet up again.

She was bubbling over with it when she sat into his car a half hour later. "I had coffee with Mrs Dillon in her home this morning. She confirmed that Bobby O Connor was a young gay man who was murdered for taking a new lover. It was rumoured to have been Bobby's former jealous boyfriend that whacked both of them. Who is that jealous lover, Ben?"

"Ann, please don't ask me to think, we have both been up all night."

"John Duggan was that boyfriend, now what do you think of that, Sergeant. Duggan's boyfriend was his unknown brother doesn't that surprise you?"

"Nothing surprises me any more with this crowd. Bobby was his half-brother, Ann, let's be clear about that. Limpy Ryan is John Duggan's real father. The ex-priest was Bobby O Connor's dad; he told me all about it earlier."

"Okay, would you like to hear how a jealous barmaid seduced a gay priest to get even with her sister? Mrs Dillon said Rosie told her all about it once when she was drunk. Rosie intentionally walked into the room naked when Thomas the priest called for a visit. He enjoyed the experience, according to Rosie he kept calling back for more. She kept giving it up, sick revenge against her sister; he wasn't getting any at home. He knew what he was doing, who he was doing it to, just another man taking what he could get. There's nothing surprising about that part of it, is there."

"Ann, unfortunately your Mrs Dillon's testimony cannot be used in a court of law because her source is dead. So will she if found snitching in the kitchen. Let me fill you in as best I can on what I believe is the chain of events now.

"Screwing the husband was the barmaid's vengeance against the sister that disowned her. Rosie got pregnant, later confiding in Thomas who swore her to secrecy. The priest asked me if he could be allowed to claim the body of his son. He wants to bury what's left of his boy with his mother's ashes. There's nothing wrong with that if he's the boy's father. Rosie kept their secret safe all the years by telling Limpy Ryan he was the father. She was a shrewd business woman, milking them both for child support. She had an expensive drinking habit to maintain. Now let's recap, we can assume Duggan killed them in his office at the Celtic. We know that both dismembered bodies were wrapped in heavy duty plastic to avoid blood trace evidence at the crime scene. He then dumped them in his hidey hole with some help from his drinking buddies.

"Thomas the priest was Bobby's father from his affair with Rosie the barmaid. She was also John Duggan's mother. Limpy Ryan her long standing boyfriend was Duggan's dad. I'm heading over to interview Ryan at the sand hog hut. I will see you back at the office in an hour or so. Can you pick me up a sandwich on your way, put on a fresh pot of coffee? It's been a long night, Ann, it's not over yet."

"You've got it boss."

If Joe Flanagan expected to be treated like a hero when he arrived into work he was disappointed. The hog hut was quiet; everyone drinking coffee waiting for what could be the final pay slips. The work was stopped. Some of the guys were assisting with police investigations. The entire job was a crime scene; it could take weeks to uncover whatever was down there. That was bad news for Doyle's gang; it looked like he was out of a job again. Some of the men, the usual culprits, blamed him for the pending disaster. If alligator man hadn't jumped the gun finding bodies they would still have their jobs.

A hero for a day wasn't worth it when the money dried up. He no longer gave a shit what they thought of him. It was all about what he thought of himself that's what mattered now, more importantly how Rita rated what he was doing. If he was all right by her he was on the right track. He couldn't wait to get to hell out of the place away from the lot of them.

Limpy was the only one left behind on the job, looking after the hut. Naturally he was delighted the police were holding Duggan for all the murders. When he first uncovered the plastic covered corpses in Duggan's dumping ground he paid for that mistake. As a result his life was continuously under threat. He kept his mouth shut in case he too got whacked. The man responsible for his 'limping accident' was currently suspect number one. It was up to him to provide the police with enough details so Duggan would be locked up for good.

Limpy was confident their vendetta would be finally over. His long patient wait had been worth it, payback time had arrived. Just in time too by the sound of it.

Joe was still considering his situation. Things had turned bad on him again with the loss of his job. He needed a new initiative to get his financial goals going again. His options were limited. Would he ever accumulate enough funds to establish himself back in Ireland? That bother was a constant source of his annoyance. A good paying job, like the one he just lost was an essential ingredient to achieve that goal. His sobriety was greatly treasured now, without that his ambition could never be realized. This illegal status was a hindrance, limiting his options. The possibility of being exploited as an undocumented employee was another deterrent. He had to keep on trying. Desperate times called for desperate measures. When he realized he wasn't the only miner out of work he started putting a new plan together.

Like all ideas imagined through the haze of desperation, the more he thought about it the more it made sense. He contacted Doyle to discuss the merits of the scheme with him.

Tash would be an essential cog in the grand project if it was ever going to fly. He desperately needed him now, because without his input it would be impossible to pull off. Doyle was well liked, trusted by the sand hogs. The scheme must be tempting to draw him in. But he had no doubt Doyle would know a winner when it was presented to him properly.

Before he met up with Tash, he called Mr Bergmann with a business proposition that would benefit all concerned. It might provide answers to some of the lawyer's more difficult questions. The lawyer was pleased to receive his call; he agreed to meet up in his office.

His demolition enterprise needed overhauling; he readily agreed to that, it could benefit from professional restructuring. If the young Irishman had any ideas, they might be worth hearing.

Bergmann's own knowledge of construction was purely speculative so he listened quietly, to take in the general outline of the idea. Flanagan with Rita's help had drawn up a plan to increase efficiency, enhance the profit margin. The first job would be a trial run, to see if there was money to be made. They might take it to the next level after that. The lawyer envisaged what they were capable of. If the unemployed sand hogs could be drawn into the project that would be well over half the battle. Flanagan knew Doyle would put a good crew together. They trusted him. Mr Bergmann trusted Flanagan to pull it off, he listened to him, understanding his hunger for success. It was similar stuff to where the lawyer was coming from; a potent mix of possibilities that clicked to make the whole thing work. Everyone must play their part.

It was a foregone conclusion the sand hogs would demolish buildings in half the time than any other crew currently available to the lawyer. This proposition was clearly enticing for the shrewd business eagle. He would reserve his final opinion until he could examine an outline plan of estimated costs. Flanagan promised more specific details were forthcoming.

It would depend on total square footage, number of storeys, location permit restrictions. They agreed that his team would need to complete one demolishing job to access more accurate figures for future contracts. Once this was known he would be able to present a formula that they could all profit from. The lawyer would commit when he was sure. But he was clever enough to agree it sounded an improvement on the present situation. That was a green light for the project; it encouraged the team to work diligently on costs. Like Bergman might have wished for.

Rita possessed a hidden talent for figures. With information sourced by her husband she put together a broad business plan. When structuring this proposal there would be clear emphasis on future profit sharing. A priority, if the project was ever going to materialise.

The young sober Irishman knew that limiting his time in America, depended on greater financial incentive. That was an important part of the deal. Mr Bergmann was optimistic that this venture would result in him flipping derelict buildings into vacant sites faster with more profit. He wanted to show his sand hogs the next building on his list for demolition. He gave Flanagan keys to the property so the men could evaluate the job. It would only be possible to discuss the estimated price then. Instead of being labourers The Doyle / Flanagan enterprise were sub-contractors in their own right.

"Now we're in charge of our own destiny," Joe claimed, justifying the position to Tash.

When Flanagan shook hands with the lawyer the deal was sealed. It signified a bit of honest endeavour from the outset. Mr Bergmann appreciated the sincerity of that commitment. Success would be greatly enhanced when everyone on the workforce knew more about the process of demolition. The lawyer's original gang lacked motivation.

He was forced to spend too much time supervising the job. Now he would have some relief on his work schedule. The result was less demanding on his personal involvement at the site.

There was something about Jewish people that Joe Flanagan respected. He never knew any in Ireland. But Sally Baker's attitude, her kind manner made a lasting impression on him. From their many discussions he understood that Jews shared common ground with the Irish. The wandering tribes of Israel subject to persecution since the beginning of time. The Irish, burdened with this siege mentality for eight hundred years had resentment imposed on them.

Kindred spirits maybe, the plague of famine haunting the Irish, the horror of Nazi holocaust rooted deep in Jewish psyche.

History had left them both with a powerful legacy to survive against the odds. Now this Irish Jewish venture had the combined means, a common motivation to prosper.

The love of money might well be the root of all evil. But you couldn't get very far without it. When things get better family life prospers as a result. You can't allow for everything that happens on the way. Sometimes good intention gets waylaid when honest endeavour falls foul of greed. It's a common recurrence one that has plagued the hearts of honest men.

Greed, the worst kind of parasite always presents itself as a decent person in the beginning.

As Detective Brady pulled in on the Manhattan site he observed Limpy Ryan going into the hog hut. He was curious how a guy with a bad limp, occasionally, could become mobile so readily. It looked as if he was in some way exaggerating his disability, when it suited him. He knew that he drove his old pickup truck around as if he was able bodied. It was parked right there, in front of the detective's idle gaze.

He could see the two other detectives waiting with a search warrant. Forensics had already confirmed his suspicion, that blood from the manhole matched the dead miner. It was possible that Duggan might have had the services of an accomplice. The Pontiac pickup looked as battered as the caretaker. Walking around the back, Brady looked it over; he noticed a piece of rope dangling from the hitch bar. With a low whistle he signalled to the detectives with his finger imitating a camera shot.

Then he went in for a chat with the owner. "We need to take your vehicle downtown for a forensic examination; we have a warrant to search the hut."

"Are you saying he used my truck to dispose of Lupe, Sergeant?"

"Who is he?"

"Vietnam Duggan murdered everyone down there. More bodies will turn up."

"My men will look over the hut they have a warrant, can I have the keys to your truck, sir?"

While he fumbled for keys the sergeant signalled his men to proceed. They collected the evidence using proper police procedure, putting the end of the rope in a plastic bag.

There was visible blood evidence on the tailgate of the truck. They may have found the vehicle that was used to transport the body. Nobody could have used it, unless the caretaker gave permission. He always kept a close eye on it, parked under the window of his kitchen.

Handcuffs out, Limpy was on his way downtown, in a marked police cruiser. He had something to say about John Duggan's activities too. Brady's brain was getting a boost from the progress made so far. Could it be that these two men were partners in crime?

Now there's a twist, he mused. Was all the bickering between them some sort of an elaborate cover up? What were they hiding? The questions mounted up. According to reports they hated each other's guts.

It didn't make sense, but the sergeant knew a few things were starting to crack. They were closing in, some hunches were paying off.

Brady called ahead to Ann Spellman; he informed her that Mr Ryan was on his way downtown for questioning. He instructed her to have John Duggan cuffed to a seat in reception wearing his Department of Correction jumpsuit. The pretence being he would be booked then released on Sergeant Brady's return to the precinct. He also gave instructions that Ryan on his arrival be cuffed on the opposite side of the room. With special provision made that they didn't have any opportunity of speaking to each other, even if they were so inclined. As luck would have it

Thomas also arrived in reception to see Detective Brady about claiming Bobby's remains. He was not surprised to see his boy John in reception, a smile appeared on the old priest's lips when he saw Ryan cuffed as well.

When Detective Brady entered the station he stopped to speak with him. He advised him that before anyone took possession of Bobby O Connor's remains it must be established who had the right to do so. Right now there were two men claiming to be the father of the young man. He asked the ex-priest if he would have any objection to discussing this problem in the presence of the other claimant. His son John must also be included in the discussion. Brady wanted it quick without waiting for paternity tests. It was in everybody's interest that the remains could be laid to rest as soon as possible.

Limpy Ryan's animosity was well known, stories of his jealous behaviour as a young man still talked about. Fights he fought in bars over women recalled in hush tones by older men remembering the times. Getting him irritated about past deeds might loosen him up a bit. Thomas being so naïve that he couldn't see any harm in telling it as it was. The paperwork was in order too, something he'd collaborated with Rosie a long time ago.

She was anxious to create some distance between these boys. Thomas never revealed the secret of John's true identity to her. He was too incriminated in the deceit, genuinely afraid of Marie's wrath. The danger of Rosie finding out was a constant concern. Thomas's closet was full of skeletons.

With permission secured from all interested parties Brady sat down at the table with the three of them. The two suspects were still in handcuffs as a precautionary measure. They seemed subdued in spirit, hardly surprising with such colourful history between them.

Limpy didn't even look in Vietnam Duggan's direction. The sergeant started off by telling them they were brought together at the request of Thomas. He advised all present that his own involvement was strictly as a mediator. Bobby O Connor's remains made this meeting necessary; it was also an urgent matter. A sensitive issue needed to be resolved quickly so a proper burial could take place. They all had an interest in Bobby's story, one way or another. They must take a positive approach to find a solution together.

Thomas's participation was an unknown quantity to either of the two suspects in cuffs.

"You are all advised of the purpose of this meeting so I start with you Fr Thomas Duggan. Do you, sir, have a biological son?"

"Yes I do."

"Is he sitting here present in this company?"

"No, sir, he is not."

"Where is your natural born son right now?"

"He's dead."

"Thank you, sir."

The sergeant noticed John Duggan's immediate reaction to those opening exchanges.

"My next question is for Dan Ryan. You had a relationship with the deceased Rosie O Connor. She bore you a son."

"Yes, that is common knowledge, two sons, one was adopted."

"What happened to your other son?"

Limpy thinking this meeting was some sort of a set up to expose Vietnam Duggan was anxious to help, nodding towards him. "My son Bobby O Connor was murdered by that guy right there."

"Please stick to answering my questions, Mr Ryan, this is not a murder enquiry, we're all mindful of what we are trying to establish at this time."

Then he focused on Vietnam Duggan saying it slowly, distinctly. "Rosie the barmaid was your mother?"

Duggan thought it was a wind up. "You're all smoking some kind 'a weird shit," he said.

Brady followed up quickly with the rest of it. "Dan Ryan here is your natural father?"

"You're pissing me off big time now."

The cop ignored his remark, turning to the ex-priest again. "What was your son's name, sir?"

"His name was Bobby O Connor, Sergeant."

"Is everything accurate, correct that was verbally established here this morning, subject of course to withstanding legal scrutiny? Should somebody wish to take that route?"

"Yes, Sergeant it is."

Ben Brady told them they should all get legal advice if they wished. Otherwise, the remains would be handed over to Thomas Duggan as soon as possible.

He advised them the meeting was now concluded, he was back on official police business. Then he informed the men in cuffs they would talk again after they were officially booked. Two police officers escorted them out of the room. Brady felt he had enough on Dan Ryan to prove he was involved in Lupe's murder. The next thing would be getting him to implicate Duggan. He was confident that a few hours in the hot seat would bring the results he desired.

Dan Ryan now realized that the revelations made him a victim of pure deceit. He blamed Rosie that broke his heart many times during his life. But he was going down on the evidence uncovered in the Pontiac. Limpy knew the police had enough on him since he neglected to clean his truck. Vietnam Duggan was always the smart bastard, a master at taking full advantage of everyone around him. The caretaker wanted to take this mysterious unwanted 'son-of-a-whores-bitch down with him'. No matter what it took to get that job done.

The next day Brady explained to Detective Spellman how everything was eventually resolved. She was sitting on his desk, taking it all in as usual, keeping up to date with the play.

He took his time explaining it, letting her know how much energy interrogating the two weirdoes took out of him. Like running a marathon, while having your brain surgically removed at the same time, he complained. It sounded like he went through a terrible ordeal.

She wasn't about to let him have all the credit for himself though. "I've been having nightmares about this case, Ben. It got too close to me."

"I know that, I'm going to recommend you for promotion, you did a great job."

"Thanks, pleasure doing business with you."

Acknowledging his effort could wait awhile. There would be a proper time to sing her praise of the team effort, how wonderful the sergeant's input was to the whole case. Right now she wanted to hear all the gory details for herself.

"A lot of things worked out like we figured but there were some surprises. Limpy Ryan finished off the miner when he was drunk. It was made easy for him when he passed out beside his truck. He loaded the unconscious body into the end of it. Then he tied a rope around his wrist. He dumped Lupe into John Duggan's dumping spot. He used the truck to pull his arm off then he hung it up in Lupe's locker. The idea came into his head when he heard Duggan make the threat to rip Lupe's arm off. It all made crazy sense to the caretaker with murder on his mind.

When Limpy Ryan was boss of the maintenance gang he accidentally discovered Duggan's dumping ground. When he wanted someone disposed of he gave orders to Red Mitchell. The other maniac Butcher carried them out.

Limpy tried to blackmail Duggan initially, but nearly got whacked himself. The butcher started on his ankle but Duggan called a halt to it. The reprieve came with a warning that the caretaker chose not to ignore."

"Ben, did the name Tash Doyle feature negatively in your investigation?"

The sergeant loved this charade, as if she had no personal interest but she blushed asking the question. She was trying it on. He smirked, like a nasty schoolteacher discovering his star pupil was vulnerable after all. So he decided to let her know how well protected she was on her undercover assignment.

"No, Doyle is in the clear, so far. The only thing we have on him is making a momentous pass at a pretty police officer. Come on, Ann, do you think I would let my undercover wander off downtown without back up. You strutting your stuff in that joint on the lower east side. What's the name, Old Havana, wasn't that it, Ann. Nice bit of salsa dancing to warm you up. I expect you finally pressed charges later on in the night."

She blushed again.

"Anyway, let me continue. Limpy Ryan was discouraged from revealing the dumping ground. Even though he knew that it was the last resting place of his assumed son after Bobby went missing. He wanted to call 911 but knew that Duggan would finish him regardless. He always intimidated Ryan in the sand hog hut as a reminder about snitching. We picked up the other two members of the gang last night to see what they had to say, got the rest of the story. The bit of luck we hoped for finally came from the Butcher the dumbest member of the gang. Isn't that always the way it happens, when you think about it. They don't seem to realise what they are saying most of the time. It's like they're proud of what they do, bragging about things they should keep their mouths shut about.

The janitor Dulche from the whorehouse hotel heard about the gang getting busted. He suspected everyone was singing. So he came in this morning to tell us about the prostitute in the yellow dress. He had no problem picking out Red Mitchell from a mug shot lay out, trying to pretend that he didn't know the guy well. It seems Red Mitchell had some sort of fascination for the young hooker, a weird love stalker thing. When she rejected his romantic advances he stuck a knife in her. There's a lesson in there for all pretty women. Be sure you're not dating a weirdo, Ann."

Knowing this was his payback for all the ball breaking she put him through. What comes around goes around, next time she'd get the drop on him? No harm giving her a little ruffling, for all the other shit she laid on him. Any time she got the chance.

"Once Mitchell knows he's fingered for the girl he'll have his lawyer plead down the charges in exchange for a full confession. Although he's scared of Duggan he never liked him. While Duggan's fascination with Bobby O Connor was harder to define. That means nobody ever saw them in bed together, they kept it private in the office at the Celtic bar. The rest of the gang suspected there was something strange going on between them. But I doubt if any of them knew what it was all about, except for Doyle maybe. He might have it figured all right. The macho Duggan wasn't coming out of the closet. Anyone that implied otherwise would finish up going down the manhole, with or without the plastic shroud. He was terrified his tough guy image would suffer if word got out about his sexual preferences. After some time Bobby took on a new lover. The big mistake he made was bringing him to the Celtic bar for drinks. That was too much for the old queen Duggan to accept. The floor in the office was covered in plastic sheets for a paint job starting next day according to Mitchell who witnessed the execution. Duggan shot the boyfriend in the head, butcher shot Bobby. They were dismembered on the floor, the body parts rolled up in plastic, duct taped dropped into the sewer. Nice clean job."

When Duggan was confronted with all this information he reluctantly admitted killing the barmaid. He claimed he never liked Rosie O Connor going back to the time she barred him from a bar on Ninth Avenue. That wasn't enough to get her murdered. He gave her a job in his place because his father asked him to. But when Thomas left the family home to move in with Rosie things changed.

His mother never stopped going on about the barmaid, he figured if Rosie was out of the picture his father might move back into the family home again, keeping the religious nut of a mother from doing his head in. He wore his mother's clothes the night of the murder as disguise. She sometimes cleaned the bar early in the morning; nobody was going to notice an old woman going to work like she always did.

He claimed it felt like it was his mother taking her revenge. When he was dressed like her, it was her carrying out the killing. He blamed his mother for brainwashing him into it with the bible reading. That's how he tried to excuse his actions in some way. It wasn't him doing it. He spent a lot of time on the night of the murder setting up the drifter Onion Head's fingerprints on the shillelagh. He needed to leave the body on the premises to implicate this innocent man. Duggan showed no remorse for killing Rosie his real mother. Limpy Ryan never showed an ounce of compassion for Duggan when he discovered he was his own son. It's kind of what these types have in common; they're all disconnected from reality, in some way or another. Our job is to track them down when they break the law.

Put them in prison when we catch them. So that's it, Detective Spellman. Fancy a drink?"

Chapter Twenty-six

The Doyle/ Flanagan gang did a great job demolishing their first building in six weeks. David Bergmann never dreamed such a result was possible. It might have taken his outfit six months at least.

He jokingly referred to his super hogs. They were now in a secure position for negotiating a satisfactory financial pay out. This result would pull in some new investors.

The lawyer would make more profit than he ever expected. He was prepared to pay top dollar plus bonus for early completion. The arrangement was based on costs, a basic rate per man hour with a 'variable sweetener' attached. They estimated each job in advance, prepared by Rita who excelled in her role submitting their requirements to BERGMANNS. He undertook the cost of every associated outlay. These included supply of all tools, materials, any rental or leasing equipment required, dumpsters, chutes, permits, haulage. Now that he knew what this reliable crew was capable of doing, he could expand his business. His increasing investor pool allowed him move on more buildings. It was a case of purchasing dilapidated buildings in potential development areas. Once the building was demolished the value of the site increased. Then it was quickly sold on to interested developers. Certain parts of the city were earmarked for restoration projects. Many of the eyesores, abandoned, or run down sites had to be demolished clearing the way for high rise apartments. There were also sites available for commercial entities. Bergmann could see expansion into the construction industry as a move for his budding demolition company. The signs were there.

Joe Flanagan was pleased with his partner's ability to get the most from the gang. Doyle was enthusiastic about his new position, always maintaining respect from the hillbilly. He had no difficulty getting them to buy into the project.

The bonus was shared between all of them that guaranteed their complete loyalty. So it was a seven man gang now. Wispy Steel knew his men would make a lot of money, it might prove difficult getting them back tunnelling again once the work resumed. No one would be complaining about that. In the meantime he'd throw his lot in with Doyle. As long as Duggan was off the scene the gang had no problem working with the guy.

For his part Tash was content to try a new occupation. He made sure that everyone on the job had a say in what was happening, a clear indication of his respect for them. He allocated men who were good on heights in certain positions; he had others doing a job they preferred. Anyone with an idea to improve the job at hand was listened to. Everyone had the chance to make a contribution. They all had a share in its success together.

When workers were happy in their surroundings the chances of accidents were greatly reduced. Wispy Steel's idea of having two dumpsters always delivered together prevented time lost if they were late collecting. There was never a bad word spoken between the men. It made all the difference, happy well paid workers made more progress.

The lawyer bought them an old truck too. It would facilitate moving around multiple sites in the City eventually. But there was one rule strictly imposed by Flanagan, saying that it was part of the Bergmann principle. No alcohol allowed on the job at any time, for any reason. All of them accepted this condition, because it helped to ensure their safety.

A secretary was provided at Mr Bergmann's office to take orders from Rita. She could show up on the job any time with her hard hat on, if something required immediate attention. She had gained a thorough knowledge of what the entire job entailed. It was normal for her to give her opinion at all levels of company procedure, including site meetings. Her wizardly recollection was regarded as an asset.

This included everything from providing permits, organizing chutes, road closures too if necessary. They were now a force to be reckoned with as they say; delays were kept to an absolute minimum. Their bonuses depended on this efficient system producing a satisfactory result, every time. Nobody wanted to lose any money. Standards started off high the way it must continue.

The person in charge of this administration portfolio, Rita, was delighted to spend hours of her time doing secretarial work for them. She was getting well paid for her efforts. With a good understanding of what was required from the start, she proved to be an indispensable part of the whole operation. Mr Bergmann was so impressed he suggested a fulltime position. But she wanted to stay in her waitressing job because she liked meeting people. She'd soon be on her way home to Ireland for good anyway, she explained, thanking him for his kindness.

Rita organized her work roster to have weekends off. She preferred cooking evening meals at home. One would imagine working in a restaurant would dampen the cooking inclination. She explained how it was her way of relaxing, she was always 'A happier girl in the kitchen'. Her husband insisted they went out every week to give her a break. There was lunch in their favourite restaurant on Second Avenue on Sundays. They got into a habit of watching television at home in the evenings.

With lots of energy left for the regular work out at the Y a few times a week. They still made sure to catch a good movie every so often. He always attended the AA meetings on Sunday mornings to stay connected with his programme of recovery. He needed to maintain his strength of character to keep away from the temptation of alcohol, in spite of all the bad things that happened to him while under the influence of it. It wouldn't go away. The desire to indulge it was an ongoing battle he endured every day. But it wasn't going to happen.

Ben Brady took them out for dinner one Saturday evening. The cop announced that he knew the best steak restaurant in Manhattan. There was a great seafood menu available in the place too. The ladies liked their fish, so everything was covered. Conversation took off in many different directions during the course of the meal.

When Ben mentioned the budding romance of a colleague with Joe's workmate Doyle, the ladies picked up on it, wanting more details.

The unlikely attraction of a police officer to a rogue philanderer sprung the trap; they couldn't get enough of it. Soon they were taking matters in their own hands, plotting a happy course of events for the unwary couple. Something about falling in love brings the matchmaking skill out in them all. Joe vouched for the character of his work colleague Doyle. He didn't know anything about the romantic involvement with a police officer. But he assured them of Doyle's total discretion with affairs of the heart. Not a man to discuss love affairs with workmates either, unlike the rest of them. He related how he tried talking with him in the back of a cab once, about his love interest at the time. A tall beautiful girl from the west coast called Jessica, making sure not to mention she was a pole dancer. Saying Doyle was so secretive about her, so loyal; he didn't even answer his question.

The ladies were taken with that rarest of manly attributes, keeping their mouths shut, they liked Doyle already. While Ben came in with his own recommendation, insisting the guy was on the periphery of everything, but involved in nothing criminal, an all right guy.

Detective Spellman could do with some help, if it wasn't made too obvious. She was a fiercely independent lady that liked doing things her own way. The girls could reason it out for themselves, he suggested. The general consensus around the table was the 'periphery of anything' wasn't quite the same as being involved in something.

As he was not a criminal that was enough to give love a shove in the right direction.

So it was decided that the Spellman girl, with so much bad luck in relationships with men, must get a little help. The two ladies would be the best judge of that situation; they were working on it already. If only they could see its development unfolding at close quarters. That's how a dinner party in the Flanagan apartment was scheduled. There it was assumed, in the confines of a small gathering, distractions from the main event would be negligible. They'd see it all happening for themselves. Indeed they would take time to voice similar anxious struggles with romantic inclinations implying how love remained work in progress for all couples. The guys soon shut up about it, when they realized how close they were to stepping in it. The women were lethal, always looking. For the unskilled operator, playing with female fire was more intense than the fire of hell. They both agreed that's what girls did best. Turn up the heat whenever the thought struck them. They were like flint to a gas fire.

Before parting company at the end of that wonderful evening Ben invited Joe down to the precinct to show him the detective unit in action. He'd give him a call some weekend when things were suitable. Joe grew up watching the lollipop detective Theo Kojak from the Manhattan South precinct; so he was looking forward to it. It would be another experience to add to his ever growing West Side story in Manhattan. He hadn't many good ones to talk about. There was a feeling that time left in New York was drawing to a close.

While nobody mentioned it, the Flanagans had lived through a good many life experiences in a short time. The next part of the roundabout was all about getting off it.

Tash Doyle's drinking buddies were all locked up so he had no reason to frequent the Celtic bar any more. Loneliness was beginning to take hold of the love warrior's bones. It was a new experience for him, this solitary way of life. Heartache was something new to him too.

He missed her for sure, you never know till it's gone, then it's too late. She left the Celtic job without telling anyone where she was going. Or saying goodbye to him, then he was shocked to discover she was a cop. Not that it had any bearing on it. His mind was preoccupied with good memories of her. He was too proud to let anyone know about it.

The longing for her was getting him down he was only half the man he used to be. The problem was he hadn't a clue how to go about contacting her again. It wasn't like he could walk into a precinct to report her missing, or demand to see her either. She had cut him out of her life so there wasn't much to hope for on account of that.

Doyle just couldn't get over it.

Mr Bergmann was showing his super hogs a new job site. It was a small building on Second Avenue up in the high seventies, crisply explaining the problem. It was funny how he lapsed into his lawyer manner, when he thought the occasion warranted it.

The guys were getting used to his ways by now, they enjoyed him. He liked being in charge of their company, took a lot of time explaining the way his business must function.

It was a good indication too how happy he was with their progress. They'd see opportunities for themselves, BERGMANN always encouraged that. A workforce with plenty of ambition was positive for him. 'A crew with the view to improve fits the grove,' he claimed.

He pointed out the building with pride, like they were all in it together. "This building is on our books also, but we have a sitting tenant on the third floor, an elderly lady, we can't knock the place until she moves out. She's not prepared to move yet; it might take a while to reach a resolution. We must consider her needs, cater for her demands."

"All other apartments in the building are empty, is that it?" Doyle asked.

"Yes, the florist on the ground floor moved to a new location a week ago. I know all about this case, I represented the previous owners. She's in there for the long haul I'd say. It's still good value for money a long term investment. We can afford to sit on it for a while. I just thought I'd mention it as I'm showing you the building at the end of the block here. That's going to be the next one on your list for demolition."

That evening Doyle confided in Flanagan that he was considering moving over to live on the east side. That apartment building the lawyer showed them earlier gave him the idea. There would be a business opportunity there for his old buddy Onion Head too.

The Celtic with Duggan behind bars was in the process of closing down; the drifter from Boston would lose his accommodation. His time on Riker Island as a murder suspect sobered him up. The inoffensive guy wouldn't last a week on the street. Doyle wanted to help him get a place of his own to live in.

"So here's the plan, Joe. I set Onion Head up, working in that vacant flower store we saw today that was his line of work in Boston, a flower shop man I intend making some money from this kindness venture as well, do you want in?"

Tash could smell the dollars along with the roses. Cheap rent was guaranteed while they waited for the lady to vacate her third floor apartment. In the meantime he would reopen the florist on the ground floor, use the apartment over the store for himself. Another one for Onion Head, he could take his pick, they'd bring the truck around to collect furniture from dumpsters. Nice stuff from apartment buildings on Park Avenue. A new home on the east side, he was going into the flower business. A nice touch he reckoned. Catering for the potential suitors of girls right up his alley, he laughed. With all his experience thrown in as a definite bonus.

"Do you want a slice of the action, Joe?"

He sincerely wished Doyle all the luck he needed, declining a partnership in the venture. If he was staying on in New York it would be a totally different matter. They wanted to go back home to Ireland where they belonged. This illegal alien status was getting to them again particularly when things were going so well. It was a recurring problem to worry about on top of everything else. They were continuously looking over their shoulder waiting for the hand of emigration to tap on it. The thoughts of getting caught by the INS concerned them every day. These negative thoughts of being lawbreakers interfered too much with their lives. They couldn't make any plans for the future in America that was the pity. The American dream was not an option for them to pursue. Reality dawned quicker in the reckoning of a sober mind. Whatever dollars they had gathered would have to be enough to keep them going at home for as long as it lasted. They were lucky to have anything at all. It was time to accept the end of the New York visit had arrived. But Joe was quietly having nagging doubts about going back to Ireland so soon.

He could see there was a secure future in this company. The generous business proposition Mr Bergmann offered him was totally unexpected. It was also much appreciated. Rita would have a job too. The lawyer would apply for citizenship if they wished.

He wanted them both to stay on in America.

Chapter Twenty-seven

Sometime after the dinner party outing Ben Brady called Joe one Saturday morning. He wanted to take him for a visit to the detective unit in the precinct. He already knew he had the same curiosity of most film buffs about a New York police station. Theo Kojak did that to a lot of people, he'd done it to him. So he wanted to show the guy around.

His wife told him about Rita's anxiety, the need to get away from the city before things went south. Joe's arrangement to make this trip downtown with the detective suited Rita's plans perfectly. She wanted a day on her own, browsing the stores with plenty of time left to spend in the beauty parlour. America was becoming a much better experience for her when things were going so well. She was kept busy with less time to think of the bad stuff. She knew her way around town now, felt comfortable doing things alone. Today was going to be hers, that facial she promised herself, a special treat from her husband.

When Ben Brady picked him up at the apartment door, he laughed at the cheap throwaway camera in his hand. "Gonna shoot a movie, Joe?"

"It was Rita's idea, Ben, taking pictures, she knows I'm no good at it but here goes anyway. I like cops but hasten to add, I've a preference for the prettier ones, know what I mean."

They laughed.

Nothing surprised him about the hustle bustle in the police station. He wasn't going to tell anyone he'd been in the back of a police cruiser before. That might spoil everything.

The television programs did a good job portraying activity inside reception. Watching cops, suspects, the booking process in general. It was great to be in the middle of the real thing, as a guest.

Sergeant Brady introduced him to a few of the guys; he didn't miss out on talking to some of the girls either. Then there was Celtic barmaid Betty Ann the undercover cop to meet. In the naive way you can assume to be part of the action he wanted to see her in her proper job. They had things to talk about he imagined. But when he tried conversing with Detective Ann Spellman, she was very remote. As if she didn't know him that well. He had to accept the strange performance. Those memories from the Celtic seemed erased forever. She wasn't in that zone any more apparently.

He became uneasy wondering if she thought he was a loser, choosing to ignore him because of that. Detective Brady knew all about him too, was there a difference? Did he care what any of them thought about him? Yes he did. When you're trying to get out of the gutter you have to care. Or else you could be left lying in it. New York being that kind of place where everything could turn fair or foul in a flash.

He needed to leave it all behind him now. Like some precious time stolen he'd never again squander the likes of it.

Remembering lessons learned; the lines would describe his situation forever. It was simple enough. Wherever you're at, that's who you are. Don't ever lose track of it. You'll lose the run of yourself if you do.

With Detective Brady on the phone for so long, everybody else was ignoring him. Joe started reading wanted posters. Disbelief registered with him as he surveyed the dark menacing face looking down at him from the rogues' gallery. He owed her some thanks.

This woman had sheltered him when he needed it. He enjoyed her whiskey; the pork fry she cooked up for him was delicious.

The time he shared her peace pipe, the comical dance moves she tried teaching him on the Barre. All came back to him in a rush; it was still that fresh. The magical moves in the sack were there too. He wished they weren't such a good memory any more. But this picture on the notice board told another story. That person left him scarred for life on the back of his hand.

The woman he knew in Howard Street had a different name. Not Jenny Lei Wovoka, from Canada.

In the unmarked police car on the way home he couldn't get her out of his head. He was finding it difficult to accept that she was a criminal in spite of all he knew about her. Maybe she was just a small criminal, prostitute or something like that. He desperately wanted to know what the Indian woman was wanted for. She was this far out dancer that could stick a knife in you at any time, a creepy sort of person. So you never know.

"Ben, about those pictures on the wall I know someone on it."

"Who do you know, Joe?"

"The Indian woman with the hat, her real name's Jenny Lei Wovoka."

"Did you know her on the street?"

"Yeah I was in her home in Howard Street fixing my hand."

He told him a refined edition of the Indian woman encounter, short on detail. Nor did he mention the peace pipe. Smoking dope would hardly be the sergeant's favourite topic. So he wouldn't be associating himself with anything like that. It was bad enough been a loser boozer.

The sergeant looked at him sharply; his pale face caught the side of his eye.

"I told Rita the story, Ben." He left it like that.

The police officer knew all about the Indian woman. "She stabbed several homeless guys; a suspect in two homicides. One was with a screwdriver through a bum on some park bench, coldblooded stuff. We have her listed as a homeless hooker, was that her situation when you encountered her?"

"No, Ben, she lives in a loft in Howard Street."

"A loft apartment is it."

"Yeah, second floor loft, but you can't tell anything from the entrance, no name no number no nothing. Just an old warehouse space converted. It's nice; she's a dancer I think."

"She's a prostitute, Joe. Right we got to go back, you'll come down there to show me where it is right."

"Okay, Ben."

"Just finger the entrance, I'll drop you straight back to Rita. We take it from, there, Okay?"

He did a hundred eighty turn with the undercover cop car, switching on his light. Let the sirens blast.

"She has reds blues hidden in the grill, strobe headlights, flashing red blues in the rear. You can hear the loud siren, Joe, so hang on let me give you something to tell them all back home in Ireland."

"Go for it, Sergeant this will be my first time to run red lights breaking the speed limit. Thanks for the treat," he roared above the noise.

"Take it on, Kojak, take it I tell ya."

Detective Ann Spellman located the florist on Second Avenue easy enough. She had been brought up to speed by Brady with information he received from Flanagan.

Doyle would be finishing work on Friday at five p.m. She waited at a location just down the street from the flower shop.

She was impressed to learn that Doyle was helping a wrongly accused man from the Celtic to get a new start in life. His compassion for an old drifter touched her professionally as well as her feminine side. Now it seemed that she had the whole thing timed to perfection. There he was coming up the street carrying his yellow hard hat with his boots coated in dust. That confident swagger she always liked was hard to miss. But she would be presenting herself in a professional manner. She was standing casually by her unmarked car holding a bunch of flowers with a distant expression, looking off into the skyscrapers to see where the pigeons were. But she watched her target approaching her at the very same time. There was a real actor touch about the whole performance. It would be hard to miss.

"Hello, Betty Ann, the flowers are for me I hope."

She ignored that presumption. "You can drop the Betty," she replied dryly, my name's Ann."

"Well I was very fond of Betty Ann; she just dropped me, ran without warning. Like a heart thief in the night."

"I'm sure you have been dumped before, Doyle, you're cheeky enough for dumping. It might just have been your time."

"But so cruel with such a crash, my head's still hurting about it."

"You'll get over it. You're a big boy."

As soon as she said 'big boy' she knew it was wrong. Too late though.

"Am I?" gazing longingly at her with that old Tash of his grey with dust.

'The bastard' He'd do me on the police car if he got his chance.'

"Doyle, here is my card; I am Detective Ann Spellman. You will see on the back I have written my home number. If you want me to take a look at your sore head you can give me a call."

She got into her car to start up the motor, rolling down the window for a final word.

Doyle looked in at her from the kerb. He had something to say. "If I contact you will you read me my Miranda rights?"

"Doyle, you have the right to remain silent, but I hope you don't." She drove off smiling.

Ben Brady briefed Ann Spellman on their execution of a search warrant resulting in the arrest detention of the Indian lady. He included a small detail for her ears only.

"She was at the address given to me by Flanagan. He noticed her mug shot when he was down here. They're going back to

Ireland soon so he will remain my confidential informant to avoid him being called to testify at trial. She had human body parts, male, in her freezer. He had the luck of the Irish saving his ass from being on the menu. But, Ann, I will not mention this gruesome detail to him, or his wife. No more nightmares for them. As they say back in the old country, 'What they don't know won't trouble them.'

She's talking, admits keeping the key to the freezer grave around her neck. It appears at this stage she recruited young homeless men to look for her fictitious father. Some were rewarded with whatever they wanted as well as becoming a readymade audience for her theatre shows. When she got bored they went into the icy grave. The perfect crime, I suppose, nobody misses a bum down the Bowery. She disposed of the bodies gradually by feeding her 'guests' what she called pork stir fry, sliced up human ass if you want to call it by its proper name."

"Holy shit, you mean, come on, Ben, you're joking of course."

"She admits it, Ann, she's proud of her pork stir fry idea as well."

"Oh-my-God, are you going to tell him about that?"

"Absolutely not!"

"I hope he's Kosher, Ben. Dinner at Flanagan's apartment next week better not serve pork on the menu, does Donna know yet?"

"No, she won't know till they have left New York. I heard you've hooked up with your salsa man again for the party. You're on your own this time, Ann, absolutely no back up allowed. I wish you luck. He's a good man, appears dependable; we are all rooting for you."

"Thank you, Sergeant, I really appreciate your opinion."

A few weeks before leaving New York, Rita reminded Joe he had no passport. She was determined to be back in Ireland for Christmas. He was required to appear in person with the necessary paperwork, photos as well, at the Consular General of Ireland in

New York, to apply for a new one. His first call was to his old associate, the lawyer David Bergmann. He assured him there was no problem. Mislaying passports was a common happening with visitors to America. But he was disappointed that Joe hadn't taken up his offer to join the new company.

It would present an opportunity to make a better life for himself. The lawyer told him serious investors had come on board that favoured a company expansion programme. There would be multiple sites around the city to supervise.

That job was his to take. His wife would be required to join the company also-if she wished. She was there at the start of it. The lawyer declined to present him with a bill either, for old time sake. The demolition job was going so well, making him loads of money.

Joe was finding it hard to let go of everything he worked so hard for when it came down to it. That deal Bergmann offered him was hard to pass up. If Rita suggested staying on he'd do it in a heartbeat. But he would never trouble her by bringing it up. She would think she was robbing him of a great opportunity. Maybe she'd want to stay when she shouldn't.

But a private conversation he had with Ben Brady at the dinner party helped make up his mind for good. So he'd remain quiet about it for a while.

The trial was still pending for Jenny Lei Wovoka on the homicide charges, when he learned how close he came to being in the freezer. The decision to escape with his skin was a powerful incentive to bid farewell to the bright city lights for good. There was something about being alive that made all other considerations totally irrelevant.

He took the day off work to dress up for a photograph. When Joe informed the Irish Consulate his passport was stolen they were prepared to issue a temporary one to get him back home. It would be restricted, could only be used once for a direct flight to Ireland.

It would be stamped accordingly. In Dublin he would have to apply for a valid passport in the normal way with his birth certificate. The Consulate in New York stapled his picture on to a restricted passport before handing it to him.

Rita was pleased to see him take the familiar book with the Irish harp from his pocket. "Look at the stamp they put on it, Rita, look." He handed it to her. "Read it out to me."

"Cancelled in New York," she read.

"That's right, Rita, but it could easily have been 'life' cancelled in New York."

He put his arms around his girl looking into her eyes. The love was there between them again like it was in the beginning.

"Thank you for coming back to get me, I was nearly gone, down there where nobody cares. Lucky once in my life, when I met you, but once was enough. I want to make you feel lucky for meeting up with me, for a change. I mean that, Rita, I'm changing my ways."

They kissed like it used to be before alcohol put such a bad taste on their mouths.

"Okay let's go home. But there's something I want to know. How do I make it up to you, what can I do. I want something to work at."

"The only thing I want you to do for me is something for yourself, never drink again, Joe, that would make me very happy, the best thing you could ever do for me."

"Okay, but I want you to say something else, especially for you."

She didn't think for very long. "There is one other thing I'd like, fill my life full of flowers that would be nice."

"You want me to buy flowers for you every day of my life?"

"No, nothing as dramatic as that, but when you build our new home plant flowers all around it, everywhere. So no matter where I look, loveliness will always be looking back at me. That's sure to keep me happy, seeing them there; I have a lot to forget."

It was so little to ask, her that gave so much.

"Okay I'll do it, put all my heart into it too. I promise you that. But you'll have to teach me all about flowers. Could there be enough time for Onion Head to educate me about them."

"No, I don't think so," her eyes rolling up to some flower garden in the sky.

She knew about all the moves now. That was the last hint he'd drop about staying on in New York. He couldn't put pressure on her any more. She'd done enough. Mr Bergmann's grand plan would have to remain one of those what if dreams. The day would come in Ireland though when the going got tough again. It was bound to happen the pressure on; would the lawyers proposition come into the reckoning then.

'We should have stayed in America, Rita; it's a great country to better yourself.

"Yes, Joe, if you have manners."

About those flowers, when we finally got home to Ireland?

Progress was slow; a lot of withering hope came our way before bloom's day arrived. That must be where 'life's no bed of roses' comes from.

It would be perfect if everything fell into place after our New York experience. The dreams we shared could become reality. The real world doesn't do perfection. That's just a place to aim our best hopes at, if we're so inclined. Staying focused is a key element for accomplishing goals, there are distractions along the way. They should be flagged obstacles that toughen us for dealing with failure. Pitfalls sour us; we look for someone to blame our misfortune. Trying to save face presents more dilemmas. Something in our upbringing programs guilt into our psyche, it's not enough to blame it all on religion. Those bad childhood experiences let negativity form in the mind. Future personal trauma compounds these issues. It's impossible to evolve without

324

some form of negative experience making an impression on us. This conditioning shapes our basic character; we're left to manage it for the rest of our lives. Trying to negotiate obstacles along the way, we struggle with mistakes.

Consequences test the fibre of character. The resourcefulness people display in demanding situations is what sets them apart. You can sense a capable person in a few minutes. You could bet on them in a while. It's a more difficult proposition to realize the dud. Pretence is so thick skinned.

When we got home from America we built a modest house in Ireland. Stables for horses too, with lots of room for flowers, we called it Bo-Ness like we planned. I got a job with the builder. My manual work sand hogging left me well prepared to toil on our own home. A wage coming in every week, till I found something else, was not to be sniffed at either.

We soon reconnected with the wonderful energy of Irish people, how they cope with adversity. You have to be of variable disposition to handle four seasons in one day.

Everyday struggle feels the same no matter where you go. There is always some kind of problem to deal with. The belief in things improving keeps most people going. After a while New York was just a memory. We tried to keep it that way. It was something we didn't want to talk about. Things move on quickly when you're young.

I found myself working in a hotel in Dublin. The role of bartender might be a big step for a wayward soul that lived on the dark side in New York. But I handled it well enough for a while. I met this bloodstock agent in the hotel that put me on to a horse. A young stallion, the breeding was good. The price was right. I made my first purchase. Remembering the bad times drifting the Bowery I named the horse Zachary Cool Breeze. The dream was to make the loser in New York a winner in Ireland. Make the guy in New Orleans proud of the two of us. The kid with the ghetto blaster on the stoop might hear about it too. As things turned out, the horse brought me on a great adventure. Albeit a different route than the glory trail he was bred for. But that's a story for another day. Like so many injury prone athletes the career was short. He was a resilient performer in his own right though. His call to greatness came from a different direction entirely. It was destined to bring out the very best of him.

Zachary Cool Breeze was a potent lover. If I could put it this way, when he couldn't do what he was bred for, he performed the task he was destined for.

The fact is Zachary Cool Breeze line produced two horses of international recognition from a progeny of three off springs out of three different mares is a remarkable statistic.

The one that didn't make it to the very top wasn't bad either. This horse competed in show jumping to Grand Prix level. That should be enough to qualify Zachary Cool Breeze a success of notable sort.

From the streets of the Bowery, he made some contribution to the story all right. Is that not a classic example of how the saying works?

'When you can't do what you want, do what you can.'

When you think about it you can't get away from it.

Keep it in mind anyway, in case you're stuck.

Then you'll try anything.

When I started breeding horses I tried to learn all I could about them. It was in my blood through my father's side of the family. Like everything else the struggle in the horse world is challenging. You'd wonder at people spending their lives doing it. For this belief in the impossible dream deserves a winning smile for a long time before it happens. Everyone's way of achieving goals is different but the purpose remains the same. To experience the satisfaction of getting it right against all the odds.

Winning the Dublin horse show was a highlight for me. Champion for a year is a wonderful endorsement of hard work. A generous helping of ragged belief is an essential requirement too. I think it helps to presume you're mad till you discover evidence to the contrary.

Maybe that little hint of craziness is the proper ingredient to master the struggle. I call the whole contradiction The Human Dilemma. We're all mad, those that think they're not, are just better at hiding it. Wouldn't it be more progressive to let the madness out? Then we'd all know what we're dealing with. That proposition will be brought under closer scrutiny another day; when it's raining? Lest anyone think the truth has fear.

There will be no shelter; nowhere to hide nowhere to run, just like it always was.